LONE
WOLF IN
JERUSALEM

LONE WOLF IN JERUSALEM

EHUD DISKIN

GREENLEAF
BOOK GROUP PRESS

During the 1940s, after fleeing war-torn Germany and Nazi concentration camps, Jewish immigrants sought to return to their homeland—the Land of Israel. Blocked by the British occupational forces, the Jews were forced into a struggle for freedom. These historical facts, and the events that followed, are described in this book and incorporated into the author's fictional plot. Although many characters, organizations and events portrayed in the novel are based on actual historical counterparts, many specific dialogues, thoughts, actions, and circumstances have been imagined by the author.

Published by Greenleaf Book Group Press
Austin, Texas
www.gbgpress.com

Distributed by Greenleaf Book Group

For ordering information or special discounts for bulk purchases, please contact Greenleaf Book Group at PO Box 91869, Austin, TX 78709, 512.891.6100.

Design and composition by Greenleaf Book Group
Cover design by Hagar Etzion Diskin and Greenleaf Book Group

Cataloging-in-Publication data is available.

Print ISBN: 978-1-62634-516-4

eBook ISBN: 978-1-62634-517-1

Part of the Tree Neutral® program, which offsets the number of trees consumed in the production and printing of this book by taking proactive steps, such as planting trees in direct proportion to the number of trees used: www.treeneutral.com

Tree Neutral

Printed in the United States of America on acid-free paper

18 19 20 21 22 23   10 9 8 7 6 5 4 3 2 1

First Edition

I wish to thank Rami Tal, Geoff Smith, Carrie Cantor, Steven Cohen, and Travis Marshall for their assistance in translating and editing the book.

Special thanks to Tess Mallory, who offered her excellent diagnosis and completed the final editing of the book, and my wife, Miri, whose dedication to the book, along with her ideas and insights, was invaluable.

JERUSALEM'S MAP AS IT RELATES TO THIS STORY

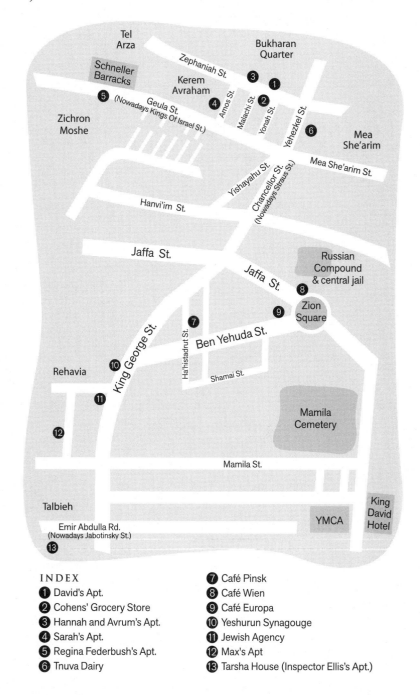

1

"KILL THE ONE WHO COMES TO KILL YOU"

(FROM THE TALMUD, TRACTATE SANHEDRIN, 3RD–5TH CENTURY)

Sergeant John Perry wrapped Sarah tightly in his arms once more, pressing his body to hers. The last thing he wanted this early in the morning was to relinquish the warmth of her embrace and step into the wintry darkness of Jerusalem. Had he known someone was lurking downstairs, waiting anxiously to snuff out his life, he surely would have stayed in bed.

He reluctantly shrugged off the blanket and fumbled through the dark room for his clothes. After dressing, he put on his coat and then paused to touch the cold Webley .38 revolver heavy in his pocket, loaded and ready.

"John? You're leaving already?" Sarah whispered in a voice hoarse with sleep.

"I have to report to my post within the hour," he replied. "I'll see you again next Tuesday night."

It was February 1946 in the Land of Israel, or Mandatory Palestine as it was called at the time. The League of Nations had granted Britain control over the historic Jewish homeland in the wake of the First World War. But Jerusalem was hardly a safe place for the British soldiers and police stationed in the ancient city, as their regime was frequently attacked by Jewish underground organizations. The darkness of night brought even more danger, especially in the quiet corners of the city.

I WAITED DOWNSTAIRS IN THE exposed stairwell, wincing from the sting of the icy wind blowing in from the street, reminding myself that life isn't always fair. While Perry was feeling the soft curves of a woman against his body in the apartment above, I stood shivering and alone. But soon he would lie eternally cold, I thought, taking grim comfort in the fact. My plan to send Perry to the gates of Hell did nothing to warm my own body, but it did warm my soul.

Killing has never been my first choice, and I only resorted to it when I didn't see any other choice. Perry was one of those cases. An agent in the CID, the intelligence unit for the British Mandate, he identified Jewish underground activists for arrest or assassination by the British army. He was in his late twenties, in excellent physical condition, talented, with a sharp mind—a real thorn in the side of the Jewish underground. It was essential to get rid of this guy for good. The rule of survival says, "Kill the one who comes to kill you."

I planned to strangle him. I'd have preferred to use a gun, as I often had against the German soldiers I once fought as a partisan. But shooting him would wake the neighbors, not to mention leave unmistakable evidence that he'd been assassinated. By strangling him, there would be an outside chance that a British investigator would rule his death a robbery gone wrong.

I heard Perry shut the door on the floor above and then

his heavy footfalls on the stairs. I hid in the dark alcove at the entrance to the stairwell, having already knocked out the overhead light to conceal myself. When Perry passed me, I leaped at him from behind, gripping his neck between my two forearms and pulling him back at the same time. He resisted, kicking his legs wildly as he tried to keep his feet on the ground.

I tightened my grip on his neck, using all my strength to drag him backward. Finally, the gasping stopped, and his body fell limp. I let go, and Perry slumped to the floor. Kneeling beside him, I checked his pulse—he was gone.

I quickly rifled through his pockets and was pleased to find his Webley, which I would add to my growing collection of weapons that I accumulated in the last five months, since I came to the Land of Israel. To create the illusion of a botched robbery, I slipped the money from his wallet into my pocket.

I didn't want to leave any traces around the building, so after checking to make sure the coast was clear, I hoisted Perry's body onto my shoulders and carried him to a nearby street, where I dumped him in one of the courtyards. With dawn about to break, I hurried back to my place on Zephaniah Street, not far away.

My apartment was a single room at the back of a one-story building. I silently opened the gate to the yard and followed the path to my private entrance in the rear. Before heading inside, I stopped in the backyard, which was enclosed by a fence of large stones. This part of the yard was visible only from my room. Crouching behind an apricot tree, I removed a large, loose stone from the fence to retrieve the locked metal box I kept in the hollow behind it. I placed the Webley inside. My arsenal of weapons and ammunition had become quite impressive.

Back in my apartment, I undressed and headed straight for the bathroom. A hot shower would have been welcome, but that required lighting a fire under the boiler and waiting for the water to heat. Instead, I stepped straight under the flow from the showerhead. It was a true Jerusalem winter, and the water was ice cold, but I had grown used to bathing outdoors in the Belarusian winters as a partisan and wasn't going to let a little icy water trouble me. All I wanted was to wash away the last traces of that lowlife Brit as quickly as possible.

Afterward, I lay in bed but couldn't fall asleep. My mind wandered back across the past five years, since the Nazis had invaded my home in Belarus in Eastern Europe. I tried to recall the faces of my mother, my father, my older brother and sister, all dead and gone, like most of the hundred thousand Jews who had lived in our now-destroyed community in Minsk.

As I stared at the ceiling, I tried to remember how I'd been back then—a sentimental seventeen-year-old boy who couldn't bear the sight of a chicken being slaughtered. How could acts of war come so easily to me now? But necessity can drive men to do unfathomable things. As I witnessed the unspeakable evils the Nazis had unleashed on my people, on my family, it had hardened my spirit. In the face of such devastation against the entire Jewish race, how could I not commit myself to doing everything in my power to create a safe and secure home for the Jewish people and for myself?

Of course, the British were not the Nazis, but they had taken control of our ancestral homeland and enacted policies to explicitly limit Jewish immigration. Their navy was blocking Israeli shores, stopping boats full of Jewish immigrants, most of whom were concentration camp survivors; then they were sending those survivors right back to camps in Cyprus or, even worse, in Germany.

We had no choice but to fight the British for a homeland where we could live free, and I knew I must use the skills I acquired fighting the Nazis in the forests of Belarus to accomplish that. I wouldn't stop until an independent state for the Jewish people in our ancient homeland became ours again.

At that moment, I couldn't shake the feeling that safety was an illusion. There I was, lying in my cozy bed, seemingly safe and secure, but at any moment something could intrude on this blissful state or even bring my brief but eventful life to an abrupt end. Once these thoughts crept in, they dragged me back to when the blood of the Jews of Belarus ran like rivers, when I struggled desperately to preserve my life and the lives of my comrades—and to kill as many Germans as possible.

I was the youngest in the Gabinsky family when life as I had known it was forever changed. In 1941, my brother and sister had already left home, married, and started their own lives by the time the war began. Only I remained at home with my parents. My father managed a flour mill in Minsk, and we were relatively well off. He was a tall, dark, well-built man, and my mother, a devoted housewife, was a pretty blond. They made a good-looking couple.

My mother would always tell me, "David, my dear son, you got your big brown eyes from your father and your blond hair from me."

Father wasn't religious, but he respected the Jewish religion and made sure I received a traditional education, which included private lessons in Hebrew. I adored my teacher, Rabbi Leib Briskov, who not only taught me Hebrew but also instilled in me Jewish values and wise teachings about life. Because the Communist authorities in Belarus had imposed a ban on Jewish studies, our lessons were conducted in secret.

On June 22, 1941, Nazi Germany violated the nonaggression treaty it had signed with Russia two years earlier. The German military advanced eastward, intending to occupy Russia and topple the Communist regime. Four days later, while we were eating dinner, we heard the blasts of the artillery shells coming ever closer and then the sound of small-arms fire.

"The Germans are approaching," my father said. "And quickly. It's only taken them four days to reach Minsk."

We felt no loyalty to the Russian regime—the Communists, like the czars before them, were not particularly fond of Jews, nor were our gentile neighbors—but the Germans were something completely different. We had heard terrifying stories about their hatred for Jews. Rumors from Poland told of them executing our people just for fun.

I was seventeen at the time. But instead of studying and hanging out with friends, I was destined to fight for the survival of my family and the Jews of Minsk. Thanks to my strength and size, I had taught my anti-Semitic schoolmates to fear me, but I knew I'd be helpless against a German soldier with a gun.

My father was right; the Germans had reached Minsk.

They soon appointed a Judenrat, a Jewish council, whose members, my father included, were tasked with compiling a registry of the entire Jewish population in the city and its suburbs. Through the Judenrat, the Germans made us wear yellow stars on our clothes, and within five days, all the Jews living in Minsk were forced into a newly formed ghetto, a warren of thirty-four streets ringed with barbed-wire fences and watchtowers. The size of the ghetto was about one square mile. The Judenrat, instructed by the Germans, assigned Jewish families to apartment buildings within that area, and it was extremely crowded. Often two to three families had to live in the same room.

One minute, I was lying in a warm bed, and the next, I found myself evicted from my home and forced to live in what amounted to a prison. My family and I were under constant threat of death or torture.

The Germans issued a warning that any Jew attempting to leave the ghetto without a permit from the military commander would be shot on sight. Gentiles were forbidden from entering the ghetto, but that didn't stop them from raiding our homes, robbing and killing indiscriminately. German soldiers and police officers—mostly Ukrainians, Lithuanians, and Latvians who hated the Russians and welcomed the arrival of the Nazis—would kick in our ghetto doors and take whatever they fancied. Anyone who dared resist was summarily shot.

These events had occurred five years earlier, but I lived with them every day.

SINCE ARRIVING IN THE LAND of Israel five months ago, my reality had changed. There was a new enemy that we, the Jews, needed to get rid of: the British forces occupying our homeland. Sergeant Perry was not the first scumbag I had eliminated here; there were others. This was my mission, my quest—to help my people establish a Jewish state. My arrival in our ancient homeland was the most meaningful event in my life, and that memory was never far from my thoughts, especially in the days that followed.

2

"WITH HEARTS ABLAZE AND ARMS OUTSTRETCHED— HOMEWARD"

(FROM "HOMEWARD," A SONG BY
AHARON ASHMAN, 1945)

The engines stopped abruptly, and the boat shuddered strongly before it came to a complete halt. Some of us fell down on the deck. A few seconds later, Uri, the Mossad officer who had organized the trip and joined us in Bari, Italy, appeared on the deck. He signaled us to be silent and instructed those who were smoking to put out their cigarettes immediately.

"We're about five nautical miles from the shore, and we have detected a British destroyer very near us," he whispered in Yiddish, the language spoken by most of us. "They are looking for Jewish illegal immigrants who are trying to enter the Land of Israel. If they detect us, we'll be stopped, arrested, and expelled to a displaced persons camp in Cyprus or, even worse, in Germany.

"There is a chance," Uri went on, "that due to tonight's darkness, and with a little bit of luck, we will not be detected, but for that we must be completely unheard and unseen. So please—no movement and no talking until we give you a signal that the alarm is over."

I looked at the people around me; they seemed fearful, and despair set in rapidly. Nelka, my Polish travel mate, sat nearby, huddled with a bunch of women.

She began to weep quietly, and I could only guess what she, who had barely survived Auschwitz after losing her husband and young children there, must be feeling now. After Uri spoke, most of the people around me immediately lay down on the benches. I did not. I stood on the deck, staring at the high waves.

Anxiety flooded over me. What would happen if we got caught? Should I jump overboard and try to swim to the shore? Although I was physically fit, I had no experience in swimming such a great distance in open sea and in pitch darkness. No, that would be suicide, and after all I had gone through, I was not going to risk my life unnecessarily.

And at that very moment, it dawned on me, almost like a prophecy. I now had a duty, a responsibility, toward my lost family members, toward my beloved Leah, toward all my brothers-in-arms—and, yes, toward the Jewish people as a whole—to fight for the most important, the most moral cause in the world: a homeland for the Jewish people. A homeland that would ensure that Jews in generations to come would never experience the terrible fate my loved ones and friends had endured.

I had been saved from their fate, but that survival put a burden on my shoulders, which I must now carry proudly. I would make use of the skills which I acquired in the forests of Belarus and use them to help restore the ancient homeland of my people.

I had no idea how long I stood there contemplating, completely disassociated from everybody else. All I knew was that suddenly I heard the soft murmur of the boat's engines and felt the jolt of the engines coming to life as the boat started to sail again, first very slowly, then gradually picking up speed. I continued to stand on the deck, motionless, until the Mossad officer approached me, smiling broadly.

"David," he said, touching my shoulder gently. "I signaled to you that the alarm was over, but you continued to stand there. In any event, the danger passed, and we will soon arrive." His eyebrows pressed together in concern. "You seemed so withdrawn from everyone around you . . ."

"Doesn't really matter much, Uri," I answered. "It's good to hear that we're no longer in danger." He was a nice man, but I did not want to share my thoughts and feelings with anyone else at that time.

When we approached the shores of the Land of Israel, Uri told us that the captain would try to land us on Caesarea Beach. We were warned there was a chance the British would be waiting on the shore to arrest us and place us in internment camps. It was a tense night for all.

We disembarked around midnight, with no sign of the British. Instead, members of the Haganah, the largest Israeli underground in Israel, were waiting for us. As soon as I stepped ashore, I dropped to my knees and kissed the ground.

"Mother and Father," I whispered, "I'm home. It tears me apart that you aren't here with me, but you will always be in my heart."

The Haganah escorted us to Sdot Yam, a nearby kibbutz, where we were welcomed with tea and sandwiches. Then we slept in a large hall filled with mattresses and blankets on the floor. We were all worn out but also very excited. It took me a long time to finally fall asleep.

In the morning, I approached one of the kibbutz members and asked him how to get to Jerusalem. I had decided to live in the ancient city my father had always spoken of with great longing.

"A driver comes here every day from Tel Aviv to bring us newspapers and various supplies," the man said. "If you have money, you can pay him for a ride to Tel Aviv. From there you can get a bus or taxi to Jerusalem."

I went to the kibbutz secretary and exchanged some Swiss Francs for local currency. I had no financial concerns. After the war, my group of partisans had robbed a Belarusian criminal named Nikolai, who had collaborated with the Nazis and amassed a huge fortune by stealing from Jews. We found him with diamonds, precious jewelry, gold coins, and cash—primarily Swiss Francs and US dollars. My share of the spoils went into an old but sturdy knapsack that I carried with me wherever I went.

The driver was happy to give me and Nelka a ride. He dropped us at a taxi station in Tel Aviv.

The taxi driver who drove us to Jerusalem suggested the Amdursky Hotel on Ben Yehuda Street, mentioning that it was located very centrally. I got rooms for Nelka and myself, and the hotel's reception desk connected us with a realtor. After a two-day search, the realtor found a place for Nelka in the Geula neighborhood and an apartment for me in Kerem Avraham. The streets there were named for the Twelve Prophets and, while not affluent, seemed quiet and discreet. The apartment was small and dingy, but it suited my needs, and I immediately decided to rent it.

The gray Jerusalem sky sat well with the gloomy mood of Kerem Avraham, a neighborhood of dreary one- and two-story stone homes with cypress and pine trees growing in many of the courtyards. Most of the neighborhood's residents were natives or had immigrated to the Land of Israel in the 1930s, though there were also some new arrivals from Central and Eastern Europe who had survived the Holocaust.

Most of the people struggled and worked hard to make ends meet. There were also teenagers and children who added a touch of joy to the neighborhood. For the most part, I tried to keep to myself, but some of the children captured my heart, and I'd occasionally join them for a game of soccer.

I often reflected on how fortunate these children were. They didn't have to worry about murderous anti-Semitic neighbors raised from birth to hate Jews. True, the Arabs were far from friendly, and the British antagonized the Jews, but it was nothing like what the Jews of Europe had suffered at the hands of the Nazis.

I was still not fluent in Hebrew, although the rabbi in Minsk had done the best he could with me. I had put a great deal of effort in to improving my accent, and my relationships with the neighborhood children came in handy to this end.

I kept myself in good physical shape and exercised every morning. I'd start with a two-mile run, followed by weightlifting and calisthenics in my room. Three times a week I went to the YMCA, the only sports club in Jerusalem, where there was a pool, gymnasium, soccer field, and tennis courts. I swam in the pool and trained in the arts of boxing and judo.

Although I despised the British, I knew I had to learn English. The British Empire had been showing signs of weakness, but the United States had assumed its position as the world's strongest power. As a result, English had become an important language to master, and I enrolled in an intensive English course at the YMCA.

I did most of my shopping at the Cohens' grocery store, right across the street from my house. A so-called pure Sephardic Jew, Mr. Cohen enjoyed boasting that his family had lived in Jerusalem for six generations. His wife, on the other hand, was a *yekke,* a Jew of German descent. They were religious and childless.

Mr. Cohen looked like a long and somber cucumber. His small eyes were hidden behind black-framed glasses, and I never once saw even the hint of a smile on his face. Mrs. Cohen was a short, plump woman with round, chubby cheeks, and her hair was always covered by some colorful headscarf. She perpetually had a fearful and suspicious look in her eyes, and whenever I tried to speak with her, I got the sense that there was something she didn't like about me.

ONE MORNING, SHORTLY AFTER I arrived in Israel, I was shopping at Cohens' when I saw a woman who captured my attention. I'm not sure what happened to me when I first laid eyes on her, but I suspect it was love at first sight. I marveled at her big green eyes, which expressed warmth and softness, along with a touch of sadness. And when my eyes wandered over her flowing blond hair and shapely body, I wanted desperately to take her in my arms and stay there for all eternity. I plucked up the courage and spoke to her.

"Do you live around here?" I asked.

"Yes, not too far from here," she responded in a soft and pleasant voice.

I picked up on her Belarusian accent right away.

"I'm from Belarus, from Minsk," I said in Belarusian.

"I'm from Novogrudok," she replied in the same language.

Mr. Cohen, characteristically impatient and surly, angrily stared at us through his glasses. "If you want to speak in your strange language," he scolded us, "I'd rather you did it outside the store."

That wasn't the only incident of its kind. Many of the Jews living in Israel felt that all Jews should be required to speak Hebrew, which until recently had been the language of the Bible and prayer only but had become an everyday language within just a few years.

Under different circumstances, I might have snapped at his rudeness, but he had given me the opportunity to invite the young woman outside. We stepped into the courtyard in front of the store, and I introduced myself. "I'm David Gabinsky."

"In Belarus, they called me Rosa, but here I'm Shoshana," she said.

The light outside offered me a clearer view of her—a shapely beauty of average height but with something fragile about her.

I asked her a few more polite questions, then, "Can I buy you a coffee?"

She gave me a shy smile. "Yes, thank you. How about Café Europa, in Zion Square? It's near my job."

I agreed, and we made plans to meet again in half an hour outside Cohens' and walk together to the café.

I returned to my apartment and changed my clothes. Shoshana arrived at the store a few minutes after I did, looking even more beautiful with a streak of red lipstick accentuating the sensuality of her mouth. A brisk twenty-minute walk took us to Zion Square in the center of the city, the heart of the Jerusalem Triangle, tucked between Jaffa, Ben Yehuda, and King George streets.

When we got to the café, one of the waitresses ran to Shoshana and embraced her. "Good to see you," she said in Hebrew, with a slight Hungarian accent.

Shoshana turned to me. "David, meet my good friend Eva. She's my roommate."

Eva was slim and of average height, with large breasts, curly red hair, and chestnut-brown eyes. She seated us at a table by the window and went back to work. I was surprised to notice that many of the diners were British soldiers and officers and that the menu was in English and German but not in Hebrew. I ordered coffee and apple strudel for the two of us.

As we began to talk, Shoshana told me that her entire family had perished in the Holocaust. She kept her eyes on the table, her hands knit together in front of her. A lock of blond hair fell across her face as she spoke. She was saved thanks to a family in the countryside that had given her a place to hide. Following the war, she had made her way to Israel with forged papers. After she talked for a while, she asked to hear my story. I didn't want to reveal too much about myself, but I knew I had to tell her something.

"I fled Minsk and joined up with the partisans," I said. "After the war, I managed to get here."

She must have thought I wasn't much of a talker, but she didn't press for more.

"Do you work?" she asked.

"Not at the moment. I have some savings, and I'm living off that for now. And you?"

"I work as a waitress at Café Pinsk. They're looking for a waiter, if you're interested."

"Maybe," I said. "What's it like?"

"The owner is a Jew from Pinsk. He lost his wife about a year ago, and they didn't have children. He was smarter than our families and came to Israel in the early 1930s. Perhaps you can walk me there? I'll introduce you to Max. If you want the job, I believe you can get it."

I wasn't thrilled by the idea of working as a waiter, but the job would keep me close to Shoshana. "Great, let's go," I said.

Pinsk sat on HaHistadrut Street, a small side road leading

off Ben Yehuda. The outer wall was decorated with a mural of the Jerusalem skyline. When I stopped to examine it, Shoshana simply said, "I painted that." I told her it was beautiful.

The restaurant wasn't very big, but it boasted a long bar with a beautiful wooden counter. Fixed to the wall was a mirror that stretched the entire length of the bar. Dark wooden chairs and tables added a touch of elegance to the restaurant. Glass chandeliers hung from the ceiling, and the walls were adorned with several landscape paintings.

"Max isn't an easy man, and he expects absolute obedience," Shoshana said to me. "There's no point in arguing with him, even if you're right."

She sat me down at one of the tables and brought me a glass of beer before calling Max over and introducing me to him. He looked as though he was in his fifties, a short man with white hair, a wrinkled face, and piercing blue eyes that reflected concern and uneasiness.

"Where are you from?" he asked me.

"I'm from Minsk," I replied in Belarusian.

"We're living in Israel," he snapped. "If you want to work for me, that's the last time I hear you speaking any language other than Hebrew or English."

I switched to Hebrew, saying, "I don't have any experience as a waiter, but I'm willing to learn the trade."

"I'll hire you on a trial basis. You start tomorrow. And remember—Hebrew only to the Jewish customers. And speak English to the British. Do you know that language?"

"Yes," I replied. "I took an English class."

"Okay, then. Be polite to our British customers. Some people are rude to them. I'm not one of those people. I have no interest in politics. All that concerns me is satisfying my customers—especially the British. They drink a lot more than my Jewish customers. That's good for you too, because they're more generous when it comes to tipping the waiters. See you tomorrow."

I drank my beer and watched Shoshana waiting on tables. Then I noticed a British officer who was having a drink at the bar. His long-flushed face displayed a look of angry superiority. Had it not been for his uniform, he could've been one of the German officers who had persecuted us in the ghetto. My thoughts wandered again to the ghetto and my escape.

Thousands of Jews, mostly the elderly and children who were unable to work, were murdered in Minsk in August 1941. Those who remained were forced to work at factories, workshops, and construction companies that served the German war effort. With just one public faucet in the entire ghetto, we were severely short of water. Conditions were atrocious and unsanitary. Electricity was forbidden, so we had to make do with kerosene lamps and candles.

Hardest of all was the shortage of food. We weren't allowed to prepare food in our homes, and all our meals came from the few public kitchens that operated in the ghetto. Those who didn't work received a daily portion of watered-down soup, five ounces of bread, a third of an ounce of margarine, and a few grains of salt. Because my father was a member of the Judenrat, our family received slightly larger portions, but we were among the very few who did. The poor nutrition took its toll, weakening the ghetto's residents and accelerating the outbreak of disease. We had no medication, and dozens died every day from scurvy, dysentery, typhus, and starvation.

In November 1941, seven transports carrying Jews from cities in Germany, Austria, and Czechoslovakia arrived in Minsk, and these Jews were all forced into the ghetto. On November 7, we had the first aktzia in Minsk, a systematic roundup and deportation of Jews to forced-labor camps or mass extermination. In the early hours of the morning, the Nazis surrounded several streets in the ghetto, loading all the residents into vehicles and taking them outside the city. The soldiers ordered the Jews to dig trenches and then shot them. Their bodies were unceremoniously dumped into the trenches and covered with a layer of dirt.

The second aktzia took place on November 20. The Jews were again led out of the city; this time, they were forced to walk into the valley of death. I hid on the roof of our house and watched that terrible march, organized by the auxiliary police forces, mostly Ukrainians and Latvians. My heart broke when I saw my friend Yehuda and his family walking to their execution.

Some twenty thousand Jews were murdered in the two operations, and my family knew we were living on borrowed time. At the end of February 1942, the Germans announced a third aktzia and ordered the Judenrat to provide five thousand Jews for "relocation." We all knew what that meant.

"My son, you are young and strong, and you have a chance of surviving if you escape this place," my father said to me on the day we learned of the third aktzia. "I must stay here—I am duty-bound to assist the ghetto's remaining Jews, including your brother and sister and their families."

I didn't feel good about abandoning my parents, but my father kept insisting that I leave. When the Jewish resistance operating in the ghetto instructed all those who could escape to do so, I decided to join the partisans. My father pulled some strings to get me food, warm clothing, and wire cutters.

He also managed to get a gun—a Soviet-made TT pistol—and a magazine with a half-dozen cartridges. He drew me a map and told me to make my way to the Koidanov Forest, where I would join up with a group of partisans under the leadership of Shalom Zurin.

The night before the third aktzia began, my mother readied my knapsack, filling it with anything and everything she could get her hands on to keep me going for two full days. When it came time to leave, the three of us held hands and wept. My father looked at me with large, sad eyes. "Be safe, my son. I hope you make it—and perhaps we will see each other again someday."

I gave my tearful mother one last tight embrace and left the house. I was nearly overcome with sadness, knowing it was probably the last time I would see them. With tears in my eyes, I crept down the darkened street and then crawled under the fence at the midpoint between two watchtowers, cutting through the barbed wire in my path with the cutters my father had given me.

It was March 1, 1942—two days before the Purim holiday. The night was cold and damp. As I hurried through the streets outside the ghetto, I stroked the pistol in my coat pocket. I had never fired a gun before, but I doubted that would be true for much longer.

3

"AND ALL AROUND US HORROR AND THE SHADOW OF DEATH"

(FROM "UNKNOWN SOLDIERS," A POEM BY
AVRAHAM STERN, 1932)

I was lost in my memories, sitting at the table in Café Pinsk, when Shoshana tapped me on the shoulder.

"I'm off at eleven," she said. "Do you want to wait for me and walk home together?"

Of course I waited for her, and when her shift ended, we headed back to Kerem Avraham. As we walked up Chancellor Street, we noticed a young man posting leaflets. Shoshana and I glanced at one another, both aware he was likely from one of the Jewish underground organizations.

All at once, two British policemen rounded the corner and started beating him with their clubs. I felt anger rise inside me, and I moved to help him, but Shoshana grabbed my arm.

"Don't," she said. "You'll only get yourself arrested too."

Before I could argue, she added, "If you want to fight the British, there are better ways to do it."

A British military vehicle arrived on the scene. Soldiers jumped out, handcuffed the young man, and threw him inside. My blood boiled as we walked away. I remembered what we had gone through in Minsk. The British authorities weren't killing people indiscriminately, but the Jews here still didn't have the freedom they deserved. The experience left me frustrated—as I'm not the type to stand by and do nothing—but I realized Shoshana was right.

"What did you mean back there, about better ways to fight the British?" I asked as we continued walking.

"Let's discuss it later," she replied, "in private. Perhaps tomorrow?"

I nodded, unwilling to press her, and walked her home.

"Let us meet tomorrow outside of the Cohens' store before work," she suggested.

"I'll be there," I said and leaned in to kiss her.

She turned her head, and I could only peck her on the cheek.

The next day at noon, we met at the Cohens' store and walked to Café Pinsk. After our arrival, I began waiting tables. The customers kept me running back and forth for hours as I catered to their petty demands. "The chicken you've served me isn't hot enough!" one British officer scolded me loudly. "Why didn't you bring it to the table the moment it came out of the oven?"

It took every ounce of strength I had not to throw the plate of chicken at his head and deliver a few punches to his rosy face. But I summoned the will to promise that it wouldn't happen again. Shoshana flashed me a quick smile when I apologized. Had she known just how much I wanted to break every bone in that arrogant Brit's body, she might not have been so happy.

The entire evening, Max paced around the restaurant like a cranky military commander, constantly checking whether Shoshana and I were attending the tables and asking customers if they needed anything. Occasionally, he'd head into the kitchen to pester the chef and examine the dishes. I thanked God when the shift came to a close. Feeling mentally and physically drained, I walked through the streets of Jerusalem with Shoshana, then exchanged yet another brief, cold kiss with her at her door.

On the second day, the job was a little easier. I knew what to expect and made fewer mistakes. Max offered no praise, but at least he didn't hassle me as much. It was a Friday night, and the restaurant was packed with British soldiers and policemen who ate and drank heavily. They talked loudly of girls and parties but also about their work. I heard one soldier mouthing off about the Jewish underground organizations. "They should all be hanged, every last one of them," he said.

One particularly self-important British police officer spent the whole evening bragging to his companions about all the activists he'd caught. I was shocked to see Max strike up a conversation with him.

"These underground movements are nothing but trouble," I heard Max say as I lingered at the next table. "If you need any help, you let me know. But please keep this between us."

"Thanks, Max," the officer replied, his accent thick and foreign to me. "Palestine would be a lot ruddy quieter if there were more people like you. I look forward to your help."

I felt stunned. How could a Jew offer help to occupiers engaged in acts of oppression against his own people?

On the walk home after our shift, I stopped and turned to Shoshana. "Although I like being around you very much, I can't work for someone who betrays his people."

"You mean Max?" she asked. "What are you talking about?"

I told her about the conversation between Max and the officer, and her face turned serious. "I've only known you for a few days . . . I thought I'd size you up a little longer before talking about this," she said, "but I guess I'll have to take a chance." What she said next astonished me.

"Max is part of the Jewish underground. He gathers intel for the resistance. That British officer Max was talking to plays a vital role in the war against the underground, and Max is trying to establish ties to gather information."

I nodded but remained silent.

"You can join us if you want," Shoshana said, her gaze searching mine. "I'm a member too. I use my free time to design the same kinds of leaflets that the young man posted before he was arrested. I've often wished that I could do more, maybe even be involved physically in some of the operations."

I frowned. "That could be dangerous."

"No one has asked me to do more than print and hand out leaflets," she said with a shrug, "so don't worry. But if you believe in an independent Jewish state, you should help us."

She probably expected me to agree on the spot, but that would mean telling her my original plans to fight the British. I wasn't ready to do that. Instead, I told Shoshana that I needed to think it over and I'd let her know soon. We made plans to walk to work together the next day, and then I headed home.

I thought about Shoshana's proposal as I lay in bed. I knew the British weren't the same as the Nazis, but by keeping the Jewish immigrants from returning to their homeland, they had made themselves our enemies. I thought long into the night. I was determined to help my people; I just had to find the right way to do it.

My mind drifted, pushing me toward sleep, but nighttime was a different kind of enemy, and as usual, unwanted memories of my time as a partisan fighter and my struggle against the Germans surfaced.

After I escaped the ghetto, I did my best to follow my father's instructions. I tried to avoid the farmhouses. Most of the Belarusian peasants hated Jews, and now that they could kill us without being punished by the authorities, I certainly couldn't knock on their doors and ask, "Excuse me, do you by any chance not hate Jews?"

I tried to move quickly, but after several hours, my depleted body was exhausted. I passed through a field dotted with haystacks and crawled inside one to rest, immediately falling asleep and only waking from the early morning sunlight. I wasn't sure what to do. If I pressed ahead during the day, I could be spotted by German soldiers or farmers who would alert the Germans. I decided to stay and soon fell back to sleep.

Sometime later, the sound of loud voices startled me awake. Two villagers were standing nearby, talking to one another, but eventually they moved on without noticing me.

I stayed hidden until nightfall and then began to travel again. Wanting to find the partisans as quickly as possible, I hurried all night and kept going during the day, always under cover. By the next evening, I was nearing the spot where I expected to find the Jewish partisans. The sun had yet to set, and I thought it would be a good time to show myself. I approached the supposed rendezvous area with my arms raised.

Soon a bearded man confronted me with a rifle. "Who are you?" he barked at me nervously.

I didn't know who he was, but he appeared to be a Jew, and I had no choice but to risk identifying myself. "I'm a Jew," I said in Yiddish. "I escaped from the ghetto. My father told me to look for Shalom Zurin. Can you take me to him?"

He chuckled. "You won't be the one who decides where to go."

With his rifle still aimed at me, he told me to remove my knapsack and empty it onto the ground. Left with no choice, I did as he ordered. He looked through my things and told me to return them to the knapsack. "Come with me," he said.

We soon reached a group of armed men roasting a deer in a clearing. Among them I was pleased to see my former neighbor Zusha, an average-sized man in his forties with gray eyes. He recognized me too. "Lower your rifle," he ordered the partisan who had escorted me there. "This young man has suffered enough already. Leave him with me."

I raised my eyebrows and nodded at Zusha to thank him. "My father told me to find Shalom Zurin," I said.

"I don't know where Zurin is. It's best if you join us," Zusha responded. "But there's a problem. You don't have a weapon, so you won't be much help."

I reached into my coat pocket and pulled out the pistol my father had given me. Zusha's eyes widened with surprise.

"Do you know how to use it?" he asked.

"Only in theory," I replied.

"Don't worry, we'll teach you to shoot. It's important for you to be prepared as soon as possible, because we're going to attack a German patrol in two days. We'll need every able-bodied person and every weapon that can be fired."

I was exhausted from my long walk, but the notion that I would soon be killing Germans filled me with excitement. After dinner, I was given two blankets. I slept on the cold ground, but it was the first time since the Germans' occupation of Minsk that I fell asleep with my mind at ease, ready for the start of a new day.

Zusha turned out to be one of the group's most experienced fighters, and he took me under his wing, teaching me to shoot with both a pistol and a rifle. He also taught me hand-to-hand combat and how to use a knife. When he told me that I was a quick learner,

pride welled up in my chest. The next morning, only the third morning after I'd arrived at the partisan's camp, we would make our
attack on the German patrol.

There were ten soldiers in the patrol. Our plan was to ambush
them at dawn, with some of the resistance fighters positioning themselves ahead as a blocking force and others hiding among the trees
lining the road, opening fire on the Germans from the flank. Because
I was armed only with a short-range weapon and lacked experience,
I was instructed to hang back and keep watch from a lookout point in
a tree where I could spot any Germans trying to flee.

The initial attack from the forward group of partisan fighters left
five Germans dead. The others tried to run into the forest, where
three more were shot and killed. One soldier was shot in the leg.
He could barely walk as he struggled to get away and was quickly
chased down and shot dead. Only a single soldier managed to slip
through our net. From my vantage point, I could see him retreating
at first and then advancing cautiously, clearly intent on attacking the
partisans who had just killed his comrades in arms.

I quietly lowered myself from the tree and drew my pistol as I
maneuvered through the underbrush. I ducked behind a tree, then
jumped out from behind him as he crept past.

When he whirled around, I put two bullets into his surprised face.

It was my first kill, and my hands trembled as I approached the
body. Without thinking, I fired a third shot into his head. I told myself
it was to make sure he was dead, but I later admitted the truth to
myself: I took pleasure in putting another round into that Nazi.
Those bastards had taken everything from me—my loving parents,
my siblings, the rabbi who had tutored me, the friends I'd had before
the Germans forced us into the ghetto. I was eager to take revenge
on those who were persecuting us and seeking our annihilation,
and I quickly adopted the partisan mindset that the more Germans
we killed, the better.

I knelt down and took his rifle—a Mauser K98—and his ammunition as the other partisans ran up behind me. "You did well," one said. "We could have paid a heavy price if he'd gotten away."

"Now that you have a rifle too," Zusha said, clapping me on the back, "I expect you to kill more than one German per mission."

The operation to take out the German patrol earned me not only the Mauser K98 rifle but also the admiration of my new partisan brothers. Moreover, I won Zusha's close confidence, and he became both a friend and a father figure to me. Zusha continued to train and guide me until one day he simply said, "I've taught you all I know. You're a skilled fighter and know your weapons. Now you must put it into practice."

We would spend hours in the evening talking, usually about our families. He told me that the Germans had murdered his wife and daughter but that his son, a year older than me, had escaped. He didn't know what happened to him.

"I want you to promise me," he said, "that if I am killed and you survive, you'll try to find my son, Izak, and tell him that I died fighting the accursed Nazis."

"You have my word," I said, "and I want you to promise me the same. I don't know what happened to my family. I hope they survived somehow."

Our group numbered fifteen members when I arrived, and we gradually grew to twenty-eight fighters. We were constantly looking for ways to strike at the Germans, and for that we needed information. One of our best informants was a man named Pavel, a portly Belarusian farmer with a round face, thick black mustache, and bushy eyebrows above a pair of nervous blue eyes.

He wasn't much of a farmer, because he spent most of his time drinking homemade vodka. When our assaults on the Germans left us with valuable spoils like watches or cash, we'd trade them to Pavel for useful information. He had told our group about the

German patrol that we'd attacked and successfully eliminated, so when he told us about a new patrol, we immediately got to work on a plan.

We decided to follow a similar tactic as before: a blocking force on the path ahead of the patrol, with a second force attacking from the flank. The ambush would take place where the path was bordered on one side by a river and by a forest on the other. Based on Pavel's information, we would outnumber the Germans three to one—and have the element of surprise in our favor. We felt confident, maybe too confident.

When the day came, the vanguard and assault forces took their positions just before dawn. Having learned our lesson from the previous operation, we also stationed ten men a short distance behind the ambush site in case any of the German soldiers managed to escape the initial assault. Just as before, I was part of the rearguard, only this time I had nine partisans by my side.

From our hiding spots in the forest, we watched the Germans approach, holding our fire as we waited for them to enter the trap. But when the patrol got about a hundred and fifty yards from us, a terrible surprise began to unfold.

The Germans halted and took up positions across the wide path and along the side bordered by the forest, opening fire with machine guns and rifles. A moment later, artillery shells began erupting in the forest. As we clung to the earth and wondered what to do, we heard the shouts of German soldiers running through the woods to attack us from behind.

The men in my rearguard force were the only ones who survived, and we were lucky to slip away with our lives. When we returned to our hideout in the woods, we were frightened and confused, but as we replayed the events, the answer was obvious: Pavel had betrayed us.

I felt stunned when I learned my good friend Zusha had been killed, and my heart ached with the loss. How could Pavel have done such a thing to us? Sitting silently together, those of us who had survived knew, without even discussing it, what must be done.

We waited until nightfall, and then two partisan brothers and I made a beeline for Pavel's farm. We cautiously approached the farmhouse and peered through the window to see Pavel sitting at the table, feasting on a sumptuous dinner served by his wife. The table was laden with juicy sausages, roasted meat, and two bottles of Sekt, an expensive German sparkling wine, presumably his reward for selling us out.

One of my comrades guarded the window while the other man and I kicked in the front door. Pavel began babbling, his mouth full of food. I slapped him across the face and demanded to know why he had sold us out to the Germans.

"If you don't start talking, I'll shoot you in the kneecap," I hissed.

He choked, and bits of sausage sprayed from his greasy lips. "What do you mean?" he sputtered. "You're my friends. I would never betray you."

I fired a shot into his foot, and he screamed in pain.

"Pavel," I said, "If you don't tell me the truth, the next bullet will be in your knee, and I won't stop until I get the truth from you."

Tears rolled down his cheeks as he realized his fate. "I had no choice. After the ambush on the last patrol, the Germans realized someone was passing information to the partisans. They guessed it was me and said that if I didn't cooperate, they'd send me and my wife to a concentration camp."

I fired a bullet into his forehead, and he slumped to the floor. His wife started screaming that we were dirty Jews and that she'd make sure the Germans killed us. I didn't like the thought of killing a woman, but we couldn't take a chance on her reporting us before we got far away from here. Making up my mind, I grabbed the woman and stuffed a napkin from the table into her mouth, stopping her screams. I tore the sashes from the apron she wore and used them to bind her wrists and feet.

"Keep quiet," I warned as I pushed her down beside her dead husband. "Or I'll rethink the merits of being merciful." Her eyes were wide with fear, and she obeyed.

Although the smell of the food made our empty stomachs growl, we had lost our appetites. Instead, we packed the food and took it to share with our partisan comrades. As we made our way out of the traitor's house, all I could think about were the deaths of Zusha and my other partisan brothers. I promised myself I would avenge them further, fighting the Germans with everything I had inside of me.

After Pavel, I learned never to place my fate in anyone's hands but my own. Once I arrived in Israel, I resolved to take on the British alone, in complete secrecy, using the instincts and experience I had accumulated fighting the Germans.

The memories began to fade as I lay in my apartment, so far away from my childhood home in Belarus. My eyelids grew heavy, and at last, I found a blessed oblivion.

I MET SHOSHANA OUTSIDE COHENS' the following day, and we started to walk to work.

"I've been thinking about our conversation," I said to her. "Ideologically, I support what you and Max are doing, but my spirit needs a break. It's only been a few months since the Germans were defeated, and my time as a partisan has left me exhausted from fighting. But I do have experience with guerrilla warfare and sabotage, so maybe I can help you plan operations against the British."

Shoshana thought for a moment. "I understand. I'll tell Max what you said."

When we arrived at the restaurant, Shoshana called Max into the kitchen for a private talk. Max didn't say a word to me when they emerged, but an hour or so later, he walked by as I was clearing a table and uttered a single word.

"Wimp."

Two weeks on the job had been enough to make me feel like an accomplished waiter. The customers, for the most part, were happy, and criticism from Max was rare. The bartender had even taught me how to prepare drinks. But I was growing weary of working six days a week. Now that I had made the decision to fight against the British oppression of the Jewish people, I needed time to learn more about the country, the various underground organizations, and the British Mandate authorities. I told Max I wanted to switch to a five-day work-week. He looked at me with disdain and called me a wimp again. I took that as a yes.

I soon got into the habit of reading the *Yedioth Ahronoth* evening newspaper, both to improve my Hebrew and to get a clearer picture of what was happening in the country. At the same time, I began visiting the editorial office of the English daily, the *Palestine Post*. The office was on HaSolel Street, near Ben Yehuda Street, not far from Max's restaurant. Every time I had a break at work, I'd go in to read the previous day's paper, improving my English and keeping pace with events in Israel and around the world.

I also began to strike up conversations with some of my neighbors about the immigration struggle, the underground organizations, and the British authorities. Some of them were reluctant to say much, fearing perhaps that I would report

them to the British. But others spoke willingly. What I heard
from them made me decide to visit the library at Hebrew Uni-
versity on Mount Scopus, to dig up information on the various
underground groups.

My reading taught me that the Haganah, the largest of the
underground organizations, had been established in 1920 to protect the Jewish community from Arab hostilities—most notably
through their elite strike force, the Palmach, led by Yitzchak
Sadeh. In 1939, the British published the White Paper, which
rejected the idea of a Jewish state and the partitioning of Palestine. The White Paper limited Jewish immigration to seventy-
five thousand for five years and ruled that the Arab majority
would determine any further immigration. Restrictions were
also imposed on the rights of Jews to purchase land.

During World War II, the Jewish community fiercely
opposed the restrictions the British forced on them. David
Ben-Gurion, leader of the Haganah under the authority of
the Jewish Agency, didn't initially support the illegal immigration organized by groups outside of the Jewish Agency, but
he changed his mind in the wake of the pogroms against the
Jews of Germany and Austria. It was clear that the Jews under
the reign of Nazi Germany faced an existential threat, yet the
Mandate authorities refused to lift the severe limits on Jewish
immigration to Israel.

Most Jewish residents of Israel identified with the Haganah and supported Ben-Gurion's policies, though they
seemed too restrained to me. I continued to read about the
other organizations that had adopted a far more aggressive
approach than Ben-Gurion's.

The Irgun, an offshoot of the Haganah, was established in
1931 by Jews unhappy with the Haganah's policy of restraint.

Their organization was formed following the Hebron massacres by the Arabs in 1929, which left sixty-seven Jews dead. They demanded a more aggressive response to Arab terror.

Opposing the ban imposed by the British, the Irgun managed to bring about thirty refugee boats carrying close to twenty thousand Jews to Israel. With the outbreak of World War II, the Irgun decided to suspend its struggle against the British, viewing the war against Germany as the Jewish people's—including the community in Israel's—primary concern.

In 1943, Menachem Begin arrived in Israel and took charge of the Irgun. In 1944, with the war coming to an end, Begin officially declared an end to cooperation with the British, stating that they had betrayed the Jewish people. From that point on, Irgun activists launched a series of attacks against the Mandate authorities. These actions were condemned by the Jewish Agency and the Haganah, but the Irgun nevertheless won the support of a relatively large number of Jews who had grown increasingly critical of their leadership's moderate positions.

A third and smaller underground organization, the Lehi, arose in 1940, established by a group of Irgun breakaways under the leadership of Avraham Stern. Unlike the Irgun, the Lehi wanted to continue the struggle against the British, despite the war against the Germans. In February 1942, the British authorities discovered Stern's hideout, and he was shot and killed after he surrendered. He was replaced by a trio of activists: Natan Yellin-Mor, Israel Eldad, and Yitzhak Shamir.

The Lehi viewed the Mandate itself as an illegal occupation, and some of the group's attacks were against British civilian targets. Militant Lehi members attacked British soldiers in the streets, planted explosives under British vehicles, and carried out an assassination attempt against the British high

commissioner of Palestine, Sir Harold MacMichael. Sir Harold
and his wife survived, but the Lehi managed to kill Thomas
James Wilkin, a high-ranking British police detective who was
among those responsible for Stern's murder.

The ties between the various underground organizations
started to improve near the end of World War II, when it
became apparent that the British had no intention of abolish-
ing the White Paper, nor did they plan to lift the immigration
restrictions and allow the hundreds of thousands of Holocaust
survivors, crammed into displacement camps throughout
Europe, to make their way to Israel. More and more members of the Haganah and the Jewish institutions in the country
began calling for an all-out struggle against the British.

The British, of course, did not sit idly by. In my research,
I learned that they deployed networks of spies and informants
within the Jewish community. The information they collected
helped them thwart underground operations and arrest many
Irgun and Lehi members.

The knowledge I accumulated through my studies only
strengthened my resolve not to join any particular organization
and, instead, to act alone. I recalled the line from the Amidah
prayer, which every Jew—even nonobservant ones—should
know by heart, according to my rabbi: "For the apostates let
there be no hope."

As partisans, we hadn't been able to fight the Nazi occupiers with large military forces, heavy weapons, and airplanes,
but we had managed to undermine their morale and fighting
spirit through relatively simple measures. I wondered how we
could do the same in Israel. The British prime minister and
foreign secretary intended to hold firm, but if they witnessed
future attacks upon their brothers-in-arms, surely rank-and-file

British soldiers and the families of the victims would question their country's presence in this foreign land.

As a partisan, I had viewed every German soldier as my enemy, but I did not feel that way about the British in Israel. Not every Englishman was necessarily my enemy. The British officers, soldiers, and policemen acting to prevent the establishment of a Jewish state by physically attacking the underground organizations and the immigrants—those men I deemed my enemies.

I soon learned who the most valuable targets were—the British soldiers with the red berets. They were in charge of internal security, and they fought violently against the Jewish underground, enforcing curfews and arresting civilians.

But I still had to find a place to start.

"All beginnings are tough," as the saying goes, and at that early stage in the game, I wasn't sure how to begin.

4

"THEREFORE NEVER SAY THE ROAD NOW ENDS FOR YOU"

(FROM "SONG OF THE PARTISANS" BY HIRSH GLICK, 1943)

Almost every night, I'd walk Shoshana home after our shifts at Café Pinsk. Much to my disappointment, our relationship did not move beyond a reluctant goodnight kiss. I once tried to turn the kiss into something more intimate, but Shoshana took a step back, smiled nervously, and went inside. Twice I invited her back to my apartment, but she turned me down both times. I was deeply attracted to this beautiful woman, and her reluctance to take our relationship to a physical level left me confused and downhearted.

Two months passed. After many restless nights alone in my bed, it occurred to me that feeling sorry for myself was useless. I felt a magnetic connection with Shoshana, and I had realized that I had serious feelings for her. I wanted her to be with me always. Apparently, she was not ready, or she didn't feel the same way that I did. A thought suddenly dawned on me.

Perhaps Shoshana didn't know how much I cared for her. After all, I had never confessed my feelings for her. Maybe it was time to take the next step.

On a breezy Friday morning, I set out on a brisk walk toward Tel Arza, an untouched meadow northwest of my neighborhood. I hoped I might find a bunch of wildflowers and thought about how happy it always made my mother when my father brought her a bouquet of flowers.

I felt a surge of longing to bring flowers to Shoshana. Unfortunately, when I reached the meadow, there were none—it was the wrong season. As I was walking home through the narrow streets of Kerem Avraham, feeling dejected, I noticed a woman sweeping the walkway to her house. The walkway lay between two rows of beautiful rose bushes in a meticulously tended garden.

"Good morning to you," I said. "And what beautiful flowers you have!"

"Yes," said the woman. "They're about the only flowers blooming now."

"It's funny you should say that. I went looking for wildflowers this morning and couldn't find any. Would you be willing to sell me some of yours?"

The woman leaned against her broom and looked at me with growing interest. "And why would a young man like you be so eager to find flowers today?"

Her smile made me a little shy, but I figured the truth could only help. "I am in love with a beautiful young woman named Shoshana, and I want to do something nice for her."

The woman nodded, her eyes growing misty as she gazed into the distance. "I haven't heard a sweeter thing in a long time," she said, glancing back at me. "You are a nice young man." And with that, she pulled a pair of clippers from the pocket of her apron and started cutting some long-stemmed roses from the bushes.

When she was done, she went inside her apartment and came back out with the roses arranged in a bouquet and wrapped in newspapers. I tried to pay her, but she refused. I couldn't thank her enough.

I rushed to Shoshana's apartment, even though it was several hours before we were due at work. She seemed surprised to see me standing on her doorstep that early. When I handed her the bouquet, she appeared baffled, but after a moment, she smiled.

"They're so beautiful, David. Thank you." She leaned her face into the flowers and took a deep breath. "Ah. Let me put them in a vase." She stepped back into her apartment, barely opening the door.

When she came back out, she kissed me on the cheek and said she never got any flowers.

"Shoshana—" I began.

"I haven't had any breakfast," she interrupted. "Would you like to go to Café Europa?

"That sounds good," I said, and she squeezed my hand.

Shoshana's friend Eva welcomed us warmly when we walked into the café. She sat us at a sunny table by the window, and after she left with our order, I took Shoshana's hand.

"I'm very attracted to you, Shoshana," I said, unable to look her in the eye. "And even more than that, I admire and respect you. These last two months have been wonderful, and I think that I am falling in love with you. Sometimes I think maybe you feel something too, but I'm not sure."

She didn't say anything. But I was now committed to this little speech and soldiered on. "I confess, I'm puzzled. Every night when I walk you home, you don't allow me to get closer to you than a friendly goodnight kiss." I forced myself to meet her gaze. Her eyes looked troubled, and I spoke quickly. "I'd love to know how you feel about us. About me." I whispered the last two words.

A look of pain darted across Shoshana's beautiful face, surprising me. "David," she said, pulling her hand away from mine, "it's not you—on the contrary, I think I'm falling in love with you too—but . . ." She dropped her gaze to the table.

"But what?" I asked.

She shook her head. "I just can't bring myself to get physically close to a man." Her eyes met mine again, and this time they were filled with anguish—the kind I had seen many times after the Nazis took over. "Terrible things happened to me during the war," she whispered, "things I can't and don't want to talk about. There were many times I thought I should have just killed myself." She looked away from me. Her words shocked me, especially the last ones, and I reached for her hand. She shrank away from my touch.

"Shoshana . . ." I began and then fell silent. I had no idea what to say. After a moment, she filled in the awkward silence.

"You're a good man, David," she said, "and I wish I could act like any other young woman would with a man she loves." Tears streamed down her cheeks.

"Do you want to tell me what happened?"

She closed her eyes and shook her head, then covered her face with both hands. I felt paralyzed, wanting to help her, having no idea what to do. I wanted to hold her, to take away her pain, but her reaction to my simply taking her hand made me hesitate. Finally, she took a deep breath and wiped away her tears. Her hand trembled as she picked up her cup of coffee. The dark liquid sloshed over the sides, and she set it back down.

We sat like that for quite some time, neither of us speaking.

After a time, I glanced up from my coffee to find Shoshana staring at me. Her green eyes were no longer sparkling, or even tearful, but dull, as if every ounce of life had been drained from her soul.

"It's time to go to work," she said, rising from the table. I paid the bill, and we walked together to Café Pinsk without exchanging another word.

We each stumbled through our shift. I wanted to talk to her but still had no idea what to say. So I avoided her, even as I longed to help her.

"Is something wrong?" Max asked Shoshana. She shook her head and kept working.

For my part, I mixed up two separate orders and got chewed out. When the night was finally over, she told me it wasn't necessary that I walk her home, but I insisted. Halfway there, Shoshana suddenly stopped and turned to me, her eyes finally meeting mine.

"David," she said, "I'd like to come over to your place tonight."

I was taken by surprise and, for a second, felt hopeful, but then my joy faded. She had just told me, only hours before, what the war had done to her, how she couldn't be physical with a man. We both knew what it meant for a woman to come to a man's apartment. And we both knew that she wasn't ready for such a huge step.

I knew she wanted only to satisfy me and perhaps was afraid she would lose me if she didn't. I shook my head. "It's late. Come over another time."

"Don't worry," she said. "I know what I am doing."

When we got to my apartment, Shoshana undressed without saying a word and slipped under the covers of my bed. I removed my clothes and joined her, holding her close and caressing her softly. She didn't resist but didn't respond in kind either. She just lay there silently, her eyes shut.

"Shoshana . . ." I said, confused, uncertain.

"Make love to me, David," she whispered.

And so I did. But when I touched her, she barely moved and didn't make a sound. Afterward, I brushed the hair from her face and could feel that her cheeks were wet with tears.

"Time will heal everything," I whispered, failing to convince even myself. She rose from the bed to dress. I got up too.

"Why are you getting up?" she asked.

"To walk you home," I said.

"I'd rather go alone. I'll see you tomorrow." When she closed the door behind her, I wondered if I had just made the biggest mistake of my life.

SHOSHANA AND I CONTINUED OUR regular walks together to and from Café Pinsk, but I didn't invite her to my apartment again. A week later, she suggested that we meet at Café Europa on our day off. After we sat down and ordered coffee, she said what I had been dreading to hear.

She kept her gaze on the table top as she spoke. "David . . . that night I spent at your apartment was very difficult for me. I had thought maybe it wouldn't be because, well, because I love you." She fell silent and I waited. After a moment, she sighed and looked up at me.

"I love you too, and if I did anything wrong—"

"I'm so sorry," she interrupted. "I do love you, David, but I can't make love to you again. The things that happened to me during the war—" She broke off for a moment and then began again, speaking quickly. "I'm just not capable of having a physical relationship. I know you have desires and needs, but

I can't satisfy them, and so I'd like us to be good friends only and nothing more." She lifted one shoulder in a shrug. "You should find a normal relationship with another woman."

"Things change," I said. "Give it time."

"I know you mean well," she whispered. "And I know you would try, but eventually . . ." She shook her head. "You deserve more. I won't do this to you or to myself."

I stared at the houses behind her for a long moment, watching the lights from their windows glowing. My first thought was to protest, to convince her that she was wrong, that we could work through this. But what would it be like to be with Shoshana but unable to touch her? It would be torturous. And she would sense how I felt—I knew she would—and she would offer herself to me again. And I would accept. And then regret.

No. She was right. We couldn't do this.

I nodded. "All right, if that's what you want, then that's what we'll do."

We didn't have work that night. Shoshana insisted on walking home alone. Feeling at loose ends, I decided to go see my friend Nelka, who had arrived in the Land of Israel on the same boat with me. She was in her forties and kind. I had met her in Krakow during the chaotic aftermath of the war.

We had developed a true friendship since arriving in Jerusalem, and I occasionally visited her home on Geula Street. Like most people in the city, neither of us had telephones, so I had to walk to her apartment in hopes of finding her at home. I was lost in thought when I arrived on Geula Street. There I noticed several British soldiers with red berets walking to and from the Schneller Barracks, the headquarters for the British forces in Jerusalem.

Still unhappy over my situation with Shoshana, I turned

my thoughts to my plan of helping the Jewish people reclaim the Land of Israel. As I watched and listened to the soldiers, with their loud laughter and their haughty attitudes, all at once I realized how I could kick off my personal vendetta against the British authorities and, at the same time, obtain a gun for future operations.

All I needed to do was find a secluded place for an ambush, hide there at a time when only a few people were on the street, and attack a lone soldier as he walked past. My goal would be to take his gun in order to continue to build my own small arsenal for the future. I frowned.

I knew that I was heading into murky waters. Though they were persecuting us now, the British had fought the Nazis and helped to liberate the Jews of Europe. In an attempt to assuage a sudden surge of guilt, I promised myself that I would only attack soldiers with red berets, knowing that they were on the front lines in the fight against the Jewish underground.

Satisfied with my plan, I reached Nelka's apartment and knocked on the door. Several loud raps failed to elicit a response, so I reached into my pocket for the small pen and notebook I often carried and left her a note: *I came to see you. I've started working as a waiter at Café Pinsk, so if you're in the area, come say hello. I'd love to see you.*

On the way back to my apartment, I took a quick look at the courtyards and entranceways along Geula Street, looking for the best location to put my plan into action. I found a courtyard that seemed suitable and decided that midnight or even later would be the right time frame to act.

The following night, I moved swiftly and silently to my chosen courtyard, carrying a length of rope in my pocket. Unfortunately, most of the red beret soldiers I saw were in groups, and the few who were alone weren't armed. I had no luck on the second night either. But on the third, as I waited, I suddenly knew I was onto something.

A solitary British soldier, his red beret cocked to the side and a revolver holstered against his hip, stumbled toward me, presumably on his way back to base after a few drinks. As he passed the courtyard where I was hiding, I leaped out from my hiding place and jumped him, slamming the side of my right hand against his neck below his ear.

When we were partisans, Zusha had taught me that by striking the side of the neck at a certain point, you could immediately disable your opponent. Zusha was right. I dragged the unconscious Brit into the courtyard and dropped his heavy body to the dirt. After seizing his revolver and cartridges, I removed the money from his wallet to make the attack look like a robbery.

I returned home at a leisurely pace so as not to arouse suspicion. When I got to my apartment, I examined the revolver. It was an Enfield No. 2—a British-made .38 caliber. I had used a German-made Walther P38 during most of my time as a partisan. I preferred the P38, but if necessary, a British bullet fired into the head of a British soldier would do the job just as well.

I hid the revolver and ammunition in a concealed nook I had made above the curtain cornice in my room. The same nook held the box of jewelry, gold, and cash that I had taken from that Belarusian bastard, Nikolai.

THE DAYS PASSED, AND I missed Shoshana terribly. At first, we continued to walk to work together, but then we began to avoid each other, making up excuses. I even began thinking I should find another job.

One morning, when I was in the Cohens' store, I noticed

a woman loading a mountain of groceries onto the counter. Her dark hair tumbled over her shoulders, and her eyes were large and brown. I watched as she examined products on the shelves. Her blouse and skirt did little to hide her fair skin and curvy figure.

After paying, she packed all her goods into the two floral shopping baskets she had brought with her. She tossed me a casual smile, and I smiled back. I thought of Shoshana—I still loved her—and then pushed the thought away. She had told me to find someone else. I had no reason not to pursue this attractive woman.

"Would you like some help with those, ma'am?" I asked. "I can see they are very heavy."

"Sure. Why not?" she said, flashing me a look of playful curiosity and, again, a smile. "Thank you."

Clearly aware of my intentions, Mrs. Cohen peered at me through her glasses with a look of disapproval on her round face. I ignored her and picked up the baskets.

"I'm Hannah," the woman said to me as we left the store.

"David," I responded.

It turned out that she lived just a few buildings away from me on Zephaniah Street. I followed her up the stairs to her second-floor apartment and placed the baskets on the floor by the door.

"Thank you very much," Hannah said. "Would you like to come in for coffee?"

"Gladly," I said. I picked up the baskets again and carried them into the kitchen. As I sat at the table, she started making coffee. I learned that she was twenty-eight years old and had lived in Jerusalem for several years.

When she asked about me, I just said that I was originally from Belarus. She wanted to know how I had spent the war, but I deflected her questions as best I could. A few minutes later, I finished my coffee and stood up to leave.

"You're a nice person," she said and leaned in toward me. It started out as a farewell kiss, but then she pressed against me, holding me tight, and we soon found ourselves in bed together.

Hannah proved to be a good lover—mature, experienced, and sensual. Later, as I started to get dressed, she lay watching me from the bed.

"David," she said, "my husband is always on duty on Mondays and Wednesdays, and I'd love for you to spend the mornings with me. If there's ever a problem, I'll hang a colorful handkerchief on the balcony facing the street."

"Husband?" I stopped buttoning my shirt and looked down at her, a little stunned by her words. I shook my head. "Funny, you didn't mention him before."

"Well," said Hannah, "the thing is that I married him when I was quite young. He is much older than I am—sixteen years—but it has been a good arrangement for the both of us. He was a friend of my sister and her husband. I lived with them after my parents died. After a while I began to feel as though I was becoming a burden. I had no way to support myself, no skills." She looked away and shrugged.

"Did they force you to marry?" I asked.

"Oh no," she said quickly. "They were quite kind to me. But Avrum would stop by frequently, and he and I became good friends. He always said that he didn't want to marry, nor have children, but when I turned twenty, he offered to marry me. He and my brother-in-law are very close, and I think he wanted to help all of us. He promised to take excellent care of me. We like each other, he is a good man, but that's pretty much the relationship we have." She gave me a smile. "And he doesn't . . . satisfy me. Not like you do."

I hesitated. Shoshana had said we would be friends, but so far, she had seemed to avoid me. Was there any reason to think she would change her mind and give me another chance? And what if she found out about Hannah? I had never had an affair with a married woman—but losing Shoshana had soured something inside of me, and right then, I just didn't care.

"All right, I'll come back soon," I said. "By the way, what does your husband do?"

"I'll tell you the next time," she replied.

AFTER ANOTHER WEEK OR SO, my friendship with Shoshana suddenly began to get better. She stopped avoiding me, and we began to walk together again to Café Pinsk in the afternoons. Along the way, we had conversations about politics and local affairs, and then we would walk back to our apartments at night. I no longer tried to kiss her, and she seemed relieved.

One day, on our way to the restaurant, Shoshana asked me if I'd like to join her at the Edison Theater to see Alfred Hitchcock's *Spellbound*. I was excited. It would be the first movie I had seen in Israel. I also hoped that her invitation meant she wanted to try moving our relationship forward again. Unfortunately, the man operating the subtitles reel, which was separate from the film itself, seemed less than fluent in English. Sometimes the translation lagged behind the film, and at other times it raced ahead.

The audience's resulting catcalls got a little annoying, but the film was captivating, even if we didn't understand all the words. Even better than the film itself, Shoshana willingly reached over to clutch my hand during the suspenseful moments. It thrilled me, and I wondered if the night would end with more physical contact between us. Alas, when we left the theatre, she held her hands together firmly in front of her. It was obvious that all she wanted from me was my friendship.

THE FOLLOWING MORNING, I WENT to Hannah's apartment. Seeing no handkerchief on the balcony, I bounded up the stairs, two at a time, and knocked lightly on the door. Hannah opened it wearing a robe, which she hadn't bothered to close, and I saw that she wasn't wearing any underwear. I wrapped one arm around her waist and slipped the robe off her shoulders, regretting the fact that I still had to remove my own clothing before we would be naked in bed together.

Sex with Hannah was, again, wild and passionate. We devoured one another.

During one of our breaks, she surprised me with a question. "Do you have a steady girlfriend?"

I thought for a few seconds before answering. "I used to, but now our relationship is platonic, unfortunately."

"Why?" Hannah asked.

"It's a long story. I'll tell you another time."

Hannah just stared at me thoughtfully, but she didn't press for an answer.

I remained silent for a few minutes and then turned on my side to face her, reaching out to stroke her hair. "You still haven't told me what your husband does," I said.

She hesitated slightly. "I'll tell you, but you have to promise to keep it to yourself."

"I'll do my best," I said.

She ran her fingers lightly across my chest. "My husband is an undercover officer in the British police."

My smile disappeared. I was stunned. "Is your husband a Jew?"

"Of course," she said with a shrug. "My husband's service and the fact that we're Jews don't contradict one another. Yes, the Irgun and the Lehi fanatics think differently, but we believe that British rule is good for the Jews. If they leave, God forbid, the Arabs will slaughter us. There are many Jews who think the same."

The look of astonishment on my face must have intensified, because Hannah continued, "Don't get me wrong—my husband and I are good Jews, but we're opposed to fighting the British."

To my thinking, one could hardly be a "good" Jew and also be opposed to those who were fighting for freedom and independence for the Jewish people. But I decided that nothing good would come from a political argument with Hannah. Moreover, it occurred to me that I could use our relationship to glean information that might help me in my struggle against the British. I recalled Max and the British officer and decided to play the same game.

"I feel the same way," I said. "I'm just surprised—I thought I was the only one."

"That's wonderful to hear," she said. "You're good in bed, and we think alike! I'd like to keep you around."

I raised both brows. "I'm not all talk. If you or your husband ever need any help, I'd be happy to do what I can."

Hannah thought for a moment, put on her robe, took me by the hand, and led me into a small office. She opened the door of a cheaply made wooden cabinet, pushed her husband's clothes to one side, and removed the plywood panel at the back. I was shocked to see a small weapons cache in the wall—two Lee Enfield rifles, one with a telescopic sight; two Sten 9mm submachine guns; and a .38-caliber Webley pistol.

"Just so you can see that we're serious," she said. "Avrum's a gun fanatic. He's a skilled sniper and goes to the firing range at least once a week to practice his technique. It's a shame his technique in the bedroom isn't nearly as good—but never mind. That's what I now have you for." She slid her arms around my neck, and I smiled.

"I have an idea," she said. "Maybe I should find a way for you to meet my husband. Then if he finds us together, it won't be suspicious—so long as we aren't naked in bed at the time . . ." she added with a grin.

"Sounds like a good idea," I said. "How would we arrange that?"

She kissed my neck and then flung her head back. "I know—the sole of one of my shoes is worn out. I'll ask my husband to drop it off at the cobbler up the road one of these days, and I'll let you know when I do. You'll take a pair of shoes there to be repaired and find an excuse to strike up a friendly conversation with him."

I agreed with her plan and then led her into the shower. We enjoyed the hot water together before I dressed and returned to my apartment.

Shoshana had already left her apartment, so I walked alone to the restaurant, my mind awash with thoughts. Hearing about Hannah's husband—a fellow Jew—working with the British brought me back to my purpose in Jerusalem. I had been too distracted—contemplating my failed relationship with Shoshana, going to the movies, fooling around in bed with a married woman—now I needed to focus, to bring the fight to the British soldiers and police.

As I walked to work, the thought of fighting the British brought back memories of a revenge operation I had put in motion after my friend Zusha was killed in action, along with most of our partisan group.

After our disastrous battle with the Germans that day in May 1942, our group numbered just ten resistance fighters. I was the youngest. I was surprised when the others came to me a day or two later and asked me to be their commander. I tried to refuse, but they insisted that I was a capable fighter who kept a cool head, even in the heat of battle.

Reluctantly, I agreed and immediately began planning our next operation. The Germans always maintained a high level of alert when in the field; because of that, I thought it would be a good idea to attack them in the places they felt most secure. Having learned a hard lesson from Pavel's betrayal, I decided to seek out our own information rather than get it from the locals. To that end, I sent a young partisan named Alec to keep track of the Germans' activities so we could plan an offensive against them.

Alec was twenty-six years old. Although his facial features were delicate, he was strong, fast, and daring. What was most useful to us was his blondish hair, fair skin, and green eyes, which made him look Aryan. He carried an ID, forged with his photo, that had been taken from a villager the partisans killed for collaborating with the Nazis. Even better, Alec was fluent in German.

He began his surveillance near Minsk, and a few days later, his observations paid off. He discovered that a squad of six German soldiers patrolled the forest near the ghetto every night. This was where the Jews of the ghetto frequently tried to escape by breaking through the fence. The German soldiers would lie in ambush and pick them off as they broke through the barrier.

Our enemies were armed with MP 40 submachine guns that fired upward of five hundred rounds per minute and came with a large magazine holding thirty-two rounds. A coveted weapon, its only drawback was that it had a relatively short range, but we planned to use it primarily for nighttime operations and close-quarter combat in wooded areas.

Alec believed the best time to attack the German ambush force was an hour before dawn. "The six soldiers are on duty in rotation, with two soldiers awake for an hour and a half at a time while the other four sleep," he explained. "An hour before dawn, the pair on duty will be tired and not fully alert."

His reasoning made sense, and I instructed my men to prepare for the assault. The moon that night was only partially full, and the streets of Minsk were dark and empty. When the hour came, we had already taken our position in absolute silence some forty feet behind the German force, ready to open fire.

The two on-duty German soldiers were chatting cheerfully. They quieted when a figure emerged from under the fence, then a second and then two more. As they crept down the street, I heard muffled German voices and then saw the German soldiers raise their machine guns.

At that second, I yelled, "Now!" We opened fire, shooting the first two Germans and then killing the other four as they scrambled for their weapons. When the smoke cleared, we approached the soldiers carefully and found one alive, writhing in his blood.

"Leave him to me," Alec hissed. The German's face was contorted with pain, his eyes pleading for mercy. "Thank you very much, you filthy German pig," Alec said in perfect German. "Thank you for giving me the pleasure of killing you." He put a bullet through the man's head.

I turned away and suddenly saw four dark figures pressed against a building halfway down the street—three young men and a young woman. No doubt they were Jews trying to escape from the ghetto. I summoned them to approach, and when they did, I recognized two as a brother and sister who had lived near my family's home. The brother, Misha, was a year older than me, while his sister, Leah, was my age.

We stripped the soldiers' bodies of their weapons, ammunition, and other equipment. We took their uniforms as well so we could carry out future operations disguised as German troops. A brisk two-and-a-half-hour walk saw us out of the area and back to a pre-arranged rendezvous in a ditch a few miles outside of the city. Fearing that the Germans would send out patrols to hunt us down after discovering the deaths of their comrades, we decided to remain in the ditch until nightfall. Our plan was to reach a more remote and less dangerous hideout before daybreak.

While we waited, I sat with Leah and Misha. I wanted to hear about the lives of the Jews in the ghetto since my escape and hopefully learn of my family's fate. With tears in his eyes, Misha told me that the killing of Jews hadn't ceased after I had escaped.

"Our parents were on the way home after a day of forced labor outside the ghetto," he told me, "when a German soldier shot them for no reason. Things like that happen all the time. When they get bored, the Germans smash their way into our apartments, abuse and torture the residents, and finally shoot everyone. They're being helped by squads of Belarusian policemen who have gladly seized the chance to abuse and murder Jews."

"What about my family? Do you know anything about them?"

"Your parents were still alive yesterday," Leah said. "We don't know anything about your brother or sister."

I was pleased to hear my parents were still alive but knew all too well that they could be murdered at any moment.

"Friends, I'm pleased you've escaped," I said to them and to the other two in their party. "Your only chance of survival is to remain with us, but for that, you need to be fighters like us. And of course, we will help you become a part of our group."

After the sun went down, we made our way to our regular hideout and bathed in a nearby stream, with Leah moving a little away from the rest of us. The clothes on the backs of our four new recruits were worn out and filthy, so we gave them clean ones. We didn't have any women's clothing, so Leah had to dress in menswear. She was relatively short, and the clothes were baggy on her slender frame. She wore her blond hair tied up with a strip of cloth.

I felt drawn to her—to her delicate features and to the mature, yet earnest, look in her blue eyes. I knew it wasn't a good idea to get involved with her, knew she could distract me from the dangers that lurked all around us. Moreover, she was the only girl in the group. Despite my tender years, it wasn't hard to realize that a relationship between us could cause envy and undermine the close ties among the group, weakening us as a fighting force.

All of that was clear to me—but our decisions aren't always guided by rational considerations. There was also biology, a man's primal and powerful sexual instinct, coupled with the knowledge that we were living on borrowed time, that every day could be our last on earth, and that the things we put off until tomorrow might never come around again. And I had seen how she looked at me when she thought I wasn't looking.

Leah's expressions of admiration and gratitude soon turned to affection and, shortly thereafter, to love and adoration. Everyone in the group, including Misha, noticed. One day I was conducting one of my weapons-training sessions with the four new partisans. I had just given them a demonstration on the proper way to hold and fire a rifle and was moving from one to the other to correct their stances and grips when I got to Leah.

As I stood behind her, she leaned back and pressed herself against me. I found myself blushing and embarrassed. It was clear she had something other than fighting on her mind.

A day later, she approached me and said she wanted to talk to me in private. We headed off into the thicket. After we were out of sight of the group, Leah embraced me. "I love you, David, and I can't stop thinking about you. I hope you have feelings for me too."

I held her close as she kissed me on the lips. Nature took hold, and we soon found ourselves naked, with Leah lying on her back atop our clothes and me on top of her. After making love, I said to her, "You know this must stay between us."

Leah beamed with joy. "I'll do exactly as you tell me, and I love you very much." She paused, and we gazed into one another's eyes for a long moment. "I haven't felt this happy in such a long time," she finally said. "I'm so glad I had the courage to escape from the ghetto; otherwise, I would never have met you."

I took Leah in my arms and held her tightly against me. I had not felt this good in what seemed like forever.

5

"OUR STEPS BEAT OUT THE MESSAGE: WE ARE HERE!"

(FROM "SONG OF THE PARTISANS" BY
HIRSH GLICK, 1943)

It did me no good to wallow in the past, and as I neared the restaurant, I pushed away the memory of how Leah had felt in my arms and forced my attention back to the present. The Germans had been defeated, and we Jews who had survived that brutal genocide needed a fresh start here in our ancestral homeland. Yet a new enemy stood in our way. I reminded myself that it was my duty as a Jew to rise up against the British.

Had I not allowed my emotions to get the better of me, I would have already started a new operation. But I knew I was not really ready. Experience had taught me that time and planning were key to a successful operation. Not for the first time, I wished I had Alec by my side to watch my back.

Hannah's idea for me to befriend her husband could open new avenues, and I needed to patiently explore them. The "chance" encounter with her husband had been arranged for Tuesday morning, when Avrum was free. Hannah told me to go to the cobbler at ten o'clock and wait there for her husband to arrive with a pair of her shoes. The cobbler, a man named Gershon, had a store at the western end of Zephaniah Street, at the top of the incline, where the road starts making its way down into the Tel Arza neighborhood.

I arrived at the planned time and went into the shop. Gershon was hammering away at the heel of a shoe, his eyes fixed on his work and several nails clenched between his lips. He plucked them out, one by one, before driving them into the heel of the shoe. He didn't respond to my greeting, only stopping to look up at me after he had hammered in the last of the nails he held between his lips.

"What do you want?" he snapped.

"There's a problem with the sole of my shoe." I removed my right shoe and handed it to him.

Gershon examined it briefly. "Your shoe is just fine," he said.

"No," I replied, "this sole is slightly more worn than the sole of the other shoe so that when I stand in them, my foot twists a little and it hurts my ankle." Before Gershon could say anything, I added, "I'm not in a rush. I'll wait for you to finish what you're doing."

"Heaven help me—as if I have nothing else to do. Can't you see I'm busy?" Gershon grumbled, perhaps hoping I'd give up and walk away. I pretended not to hear. After a few minutes, he finished hammering and growled at me from under his mustache. "Okay, give me the shoe. Let's see what I can do with it."

I took a seat on the bench near the door. As he was frowning down at my shoe, a short man with a slight paunch, thinning hair, and a rather forgettable face walked in. I found it hard to believe that such a man could be married to an attractive woman like Hannah, but he was carrying a pair of women's shoes and addressed the proprietor the moment he stepped into the store.

"Gershon," he said, "you have to do me a favor. My wife, Hannah, you know her—she thinks the entire world was created to do her bidding—she got up on the wrong side of the bed this morning and insists she has to wear these shoes tonight. She said I shouldn't bother coming home before they've been repaired."

Gershon gave him the same irritable look I'd received. "You can wait here. It'll take me a few minutes to repair this one's shoe, and then I'll take care of your wife's."

Avrum sat down next to me and sighed. "At least you're here to repair your own shoes. It seems like all I do is run errands for my wife. You married?"

"No," I replied.

"Lucky you," Avrum said and then laughed. "I'm joking. Marriage has its advantages. It's not all doom and gloom."

I smiled politely.

"I haven't seen you around before. Are you new to the neighborhood?" he asked.

"Not really. I've been living here for a few months now."

He held out his hand. "I'm Avraham," he said. "But everyone calls me Avrum."

"David," I said, shaking his hand briefly.

"I hope you don't think I'm trying to pry, but can I ask you why you chose this neighborhood? It's very quiet—not exactly the place for a young man like you."

He certainly was prying, but snooping was his profession, after all.

"I was constantly on the run during the war," I said. "I'd fall asleep at night never knowing if I'd see the next morning. Now I just want to live my life in peace and quiet, and this is a quiet place. Plus, it's close to British headquarters, and I figure they'll keep the peace here."

"Interesting," he said. "Aren't you bothered by the fact that we're under British rule?"

"Bothered? They were our allies in the war. They defeated the Nazis. I think we're lucky to have someone here to maintain peace and security and help with the development of this country. I realize others might not see it that way, but I'm not ashamed of my opinion."

Gershon continued to work on my shoe and didn't appear at all interested in our conversation. Avrum, on the other hand, was looking at me with a pleased expression on his face.

"I like you," he said.

"Thanks," I responded.

"You are so right," Avrum went on. "Good on you for your independent views and having the courage to express them. Too many think we should fight the British, without realizing that the Arabs are the true enemy. I'm a longtime Jerusalemite, and I've seen the antics of Haj Amin al-Husseini since I was a young man in the 1920s. You've heard of him, haven't you?"

I shook my head.

Avrum rubbed his hands together, obviously pleased to have a captive audience. "Haj Mohammed Amin al-Husseini was a Palestinian Arab nationalist and Muslim religious leader in Mandatory Palestine," he said. "He was fiercely against the establishment of a national home for the Jews. The Hebron massacre, which put an end to the four-hundred-year-old Jewish community in that city—"

"Yes, I've heard—"

But Avrum ran right over me, his face turning red as he spoke. "—was a result of his relentless and unbridled incitement. In 1933, when the Nazis took over, al-Husseini rushed to let the German consul in Jerusalem know that he couldn't wait to join the bastards in knocking Jewish skulls. Years later, he asked Germany and Italy to recognize the right of the Arab countries to 'solve' the 'problem' of Jews in Israel—and in the Arab states—in the same way the two fascists were solving their own Jewish problem in Europe. He met with both dictators in '41. Hitler assured him that once the Germans occupied the Middle East, all the Jews in the region would be exterminated." Avrum paused, his eyes bright as he watched for my reaction.

"Unbelievable," I muttered. He nodded in satisfaction and continued.

"In 1942, al-Husseini helped establish a special SS force attached to Rommel's army in Africa; its job was to organize the extermination of all five hundred thousand Jews in Israel. The son-of-a-bitch planned to establish a concentration camp north of Jerusalem, near Jenin, for this purpose."

"What a despicable man," I said. "It makes no sense to me that we'd be fighting the British when the Arabs are obviously the true threat."

"Listen, I need more smart men like you around," he said. "Come visit me at my house, and we'll chat over coffee. What do you say?"

I pretended to hesitate for a moment, then nodded my head. "Sure," I said.

He gave me his address. "When can you come?"

"I'm usually free in the mornings."

"Okay," Avrum said. "I'm pretty busy tomorrow, but I'll tell my boss that I'm coming in the afternoon. Come see us at ten o'clock."

"I will. Thank you for the invitation."

Avrum's smile widened. "What a coincidence. We both came here to repair shoes, and we found some common ground."

I nodded, knowing as well as Gershon did that neither Avrum nor I had shoes that needed fixing. With a grunt, the cobbler announced that he had completed the repairs, and I paid him and took my leave.

The following morning, I went to Avrum's house. I knocked on the door, and Hannah's husband opened it, extending his hand to greet me.

"Hannah, come meet David," he called out to his wife. He clapped me on the back and ushered me inside. "I need to apologize for moaning about you sending me off to the cobbler," he said to her, "because I just happened to meet this very pleasant and smart young man there."

Hannah smiled and shook my hand. "Nice to meet you."

"Hannah, can you make us coffee, bring a cake, and join us?" Avrum asked.

"Coffee and cake coming up, but I have many errands to run and won't be able to join you," she replied. When she turned to go to the kitchen, she flashed me a smile and a wink behind Avrum's back.

After Hannah served the coffee and cake, Avrum asked me where I was from.

"I'm from Minsk, Belarus."

"I know where Minsk is," he said. "Most Jews there were murdered."

"Yes," I said. "We suffered horribly."

"Have you thought about what I said yesterday?"

"Yes, I hadn't given the Arabs much thought, to tell you the truth. But you're right; they hate us as much as the Germans did."

Avrum appeared satisfied with my response. "The Haganah once had a clear picture of the situation and was able to focus solely on the fight against the Arabs and on protecting the Jews. I don't like this turn they've made against the British."

As I nodded, Hannah walked into the room, and Avrum

turned to her. "David is a great guy—smart—and I'm going to think of a way to help him with . . . a project." He looked back at me and winked. "I'm always working, but if you need anything, contact Hannah, and she'll pass on your request. I suggest you come to see us next Tuesday for breakfast, and we'll talk some more."

"Thank you, Avrum," I said. "I'm pleased to have met you—and you too, Hannah. I'll see you then."

On my way to Café Pinsk, I thought about what Avrum had said about the Arabs. We clearly faced great dangers from men like al-Husseini. On the other hand, I thought about the Arabs I had met while training at the YMCA gym. They hadn't come across as Jew-haters. My boxing coach, Yousef Bustani, often told me that he admired the Jewish people.

In the meantime, I was still formulating a plan of action against the British. The principle was a simple one—to strike at them in locations where they felt secure, like the Schneller Barracks, which was crawling with red berets. The idea had been sparked when Hannah had shown me Avrum's rifle, the one with the telescopic sights.

Perhaps I could steal it, find a hiding spot somewhere overlooking the Schneller Barracks, and shoot as many red berets as I could in a short time. Then I'd slip away and return the weapon to Avrum's cabinet.

It would be a complex and dangerous operation, but doable, I thought. I was not going to seek out and kill British soldiers just because they were British. I just wanted to convey a strong message by wounding them. It would be a serious blow to the pride of the British. Someone shooting into their headquarters would show them that they were not safe anywhere. Hopefully, such an attack would help convince the powers in Britain that they should withdraw from Israel.

After a thorough inspection of Geula Street, I found a building that offered unrestricted access to the roof. Like most buildings in Jerusalem, this stairwell had no door and opened directly to the street. The roof of the building offered a clear line of sight to the grounds behind the wall that surrounded the barracks. I memorized the names of the tenants on the shared mailbox so I'd be able to offer an explanation if any of them were to pass me on the stairs and question my presence.

A week went by, and I showed up for my breakfast date with Hannah and Avrum. He steered the conversation toward his favorite subject—the shortsightedness of the Jews fighting the British.

"I think I have an idea on how to revive the cooperation between the Haganah and the British," he told me over breakfast.

"That sounds exciting," I said. "How can I help?"

He pursed his lips and rhythmically nodded his head, presumably composing his thoughts. "I'll think about it and let you know. I'm leaving in three days on a two-day tour of the Haifa region. Let's arrange to meet here again in a week's time."

I realized that this was my moment. With Avrum out of the picture, my only problem was finding a way to smuggle the rifle out of the house—and back in again—without Hannah noticing. Fortunately, it was mid-November, and the weather had turned cold. Three fabric straps sewn to the inside of my long winter coat would allow me to securely tie the rifle in place and keep the weapon concealed.

I RETURNED TO AVRUM'S APARTMENT on the day I planned to attack the barracks. Hannah was waiting for me, dressed only in a robe, and immediately led me to her bed.

After a stormy two-hour session of lovemaking, I pretended to doze off, and Hannah soon fell asleep herself.

Sliding carefully out of the bed, I dressed and went to the room where Avrum hid his guns. I dismantled the plywood partition and removed the rifle, slipping a box of cartridges and cleaning tools into my pocket. After replacing the partition and tying the rifle to the inside of my coat, I put it on and returned to the bedroom.

Gently shaking Hannah awake, I whispered, "I have something urgent to do at work. It'll take me about two hours, and then I'll come back to you."

"Come back as soon as possible," she said in a sleepy voice.

It wasn't easy to walk normally with the rifle inside the coat, but I did my best not to attract any attention. I arrived at the building and climbed the stairs to the roof. I removed my coat, loaded the rifle, lay on the roof, and fixed my sights on the inner courtyard of the Schneller Barracks. I wanted to hit multiple targets, so I would watch and wait until I saw at least three red berets together.

After a few minutes, I spotted three men wearing red berets, standing together and talking. I trained the rifle's sights on one of them, but just at that moment, I heard the door slide open on the balcony directly below the roof. Peering over the edge, I saw a woman step out to hang washing on the clotheslines strung across the balcony. Based on the names of the tenants and the locations of their respective apartments that I had memorized, I assumed the woman was Mrs. Regina Federbusch.

By the time she had finished hanging up her laundry and gone back inside, the three red berets had disappeared from view. I waited patiently for a while longer until another group, this time four soldiers, moved into my line of sight. Three of them were wearing red berets; one had green.

Fixing the sight's crosshairs on one of the red berets, I squeezed the trigger, aiming at his leg. I struck him in his right leg, and he dropped to the ground. Before the others could react, I fired at a second man, striking him just below his knee. As the third soldier ran for his life, I shot him in the back, in the shoulder.

I lowered the rifle and watched as the remaining soldier, the only one wearing a green beret, scurried for cover. Then I had a great idea. Why not stop the big famous clock at the top of the tower, in the center of the barracks? I shot three bullets into the clock but could not verify that I had succeeded. If I had, it would be quite a blow against these Brits—a far cry from London's Big Ben but still meaningful for them here in Jerusalem.

I collected the empty shells, stuffed them into my coat pocket, and retied the rifle to the inside of the coat. I hurried down the stairs and out of the building, turning onto Geula Street. Nothing was happening around the entrance to the Schneller Barracks. I forced myself to walk at a moderate pace and turned onto Amos Street, heading for Hannah and Avrum's apartment.

When I reached the entrance of the building and stepped inside, I stopped for a moment to slow my breathing before I entered Hannah's apartment. When I walked in, Hannah called to me from the kitchen. She came into the living room, wearing only her robe, and smiled when she saw me.

"Great, you came back early. Take off your coat, and I'll make you a cup of hot chocolate."

"That sounds good," I said. "I just need to wash my hands." In the bathroom, I took off my coat and quickly cleaned the rifle with the kit I had in my pocket. I folded the coat lengthwise, wrapped it around the weapon, and then, making sure she had gone back into the kitchen, hurried back into the living room and slipped it under the sofa.

A steaming mug of hot chocolate was waiting for me when I went into the kitchen, and I sipped on it happily. Afterward, she took my hand and led me to the bedroom.

"I can't spend the night," I told her. "I have to be at work early tomorrow morning."

"Then let's make good use of the time we have," she said. She pushed me onto the bed and then straddled me with her eager thighs.

An hour or so later, she fell asleep, draped over my chest. I slowly eased myself out from under her supple body and slid out of bed. I dressed and then went into the living room, removed the rifle from under the sofa, and replaced it in the gun cabinet. I kept the spent shells in my pocket, planning to dump them in an out-of-the-way place the following day.

That night, after I went to bed, I couldn't sleep. I kept seeing the soldiers I had shot, falling to the ground. I closed my eyes, and older memories, the usual memories I battled, returned to haunt me.

It was August 1942, a few months after Leah had come into my life. By this time, I had fallen for her hard and begun focusing less on our operations against the Germans and more on our efforts to survive. We knew that the Germans, despite their impressive series of victories during the first two years of the war, had run into difficulties, particularly on the Russian front.

Word had come that the United States had entered the war, and though we had no idea when or if they would ever land their armies in Europe, for the first time we had hope that we might see the end of this hideous conflagration and that we could hold on until the day our people were liberated from Nazi occupation.

Our main objective was to obtain food and other essential items, and we did so by force. One day, we stormed a village and raided the homes, holding the villagers at gunpoint while we ransacked their kitchens and took their food. On the way back to our hideout, we spotted a group of fifteen people—men, women, teenagers, and two small children—who were following one of the paths through the forest.

We approached them with caution and soon discovered they were Jews who had fled the Minsk ghetto a few days earlier. I recognized the oldest member of the group—Andrei, a farmer who used to sell wheat to my father's mill. We took them to our hideout in the woods, and after they had eaten, I questioned them about the situation in the ghetto. Unfortunately, the sense of foreboding I had carried in my heart for a very long time proved prophetic.

"In April and May," Andrei began, "the Germans started conducting nightly raids on the ghetto, targeting a single building or group of buildings and murdering all the occupants."

He estimated that they had been murdering upward of five hundred Jews every night. Then in late July, the Germans had forced thousands of Jews to assemble in Jubiliej Square, the central meeting place of the ghetto.

"We feared that they were planning to kill all the remaining Jews," Andrei said. "Moshe Yaffe, the head of the Judenrat, was instructed by the Germans to reassure the crowd, but as he started to speak, he saw the gas trucks approaching. When he saw those trucks, he shouted, 'Jews, the godforsaken murderers have deceived us. Run!' And the Nazis shot him on the spot."

"Gas trucks? What do you mean?" I asked.

"They're trucks with airtight compartments inside; they pump exhaust fumes into them while the engine is running. The Jews are forced into the compartments and locked inside while the trucks drive. Everyone inside dies an agonizing death from poisoning and suffocation. At the end of the journey, there are mass graves, where the Germans open the compartments and dump the bodies."

After a long silence, I asked Andrei the question that had been on my mind for so long. "Do you know what happened to my family?"

He looked down at his hands. "I don't have good news for you, David. Your father was shot to death in the square, and your mother was killed trying to protect him."

"And my brother and sister? Their families?"

"I don't know. I saw your brother in the square. Unless he escaped, they would have, well . . ."

My throat tightened, and tears blurred my vision. Although I had thought often in recent months about the possibility of never seeing my parents again, the confirmation of their cruel deaths was too much to bear.

Alec glanced over at me and then back at Andrei. "And how did you manage to escape?"

"My family and I were at the far end of the square," he said. "When we heard Moshe cry out, we fled. We hid in the ghetto for a few days and then escaped into the forest with the rest of the group you found."

"How many are left in the ghetto?" Alec asked.

"I'd say no more than ten thousand," Andrei responded. "Perhaps an equal number have managed to escape like we did."

I closed my eyes. If we also considered the additional Jews transferred from Germany, Austria, and Czechoslovakia to Minsk, the ghetto had housed about one hundred thousand Jews in the first few months. If Andrei's figures were correct, the Germans and their collaborators had murdered eighty thousand of our people in just a year and a half.

After composing myself, I turned to Andrei. "It may be too late for my family, but if ten thousand Jews are still living in the ghetto, we have to save as many as possible. And if we manage to kill a bunch of Germans in the process, all the better. Do you think there's a way?"

Andrei paused for a moment before answering. "There are two young men in our group who have been in and out of the ghetto before. They know all the breaches in the fence, and they're experts when it comes to avoiding the German and Ukrainian patrols. They didn't know exactly where you were, but they led us here. We can ask them to return to the ghetto and make contact with the Jewish underground."

"Is there still an active resistance movement in the ghetto?" I asked. I had assumed that they had all been hunted down and killed by now.

"Yes," Andrei replied. "After the third aktzia, the underground intensified its activities and helped Jews escape into the forests to join up with the partisans." He gestured toward two young men nearby. "Michail and Iser are part of the underground."

I thought about what Andrei had just told me. "If the boys were captured, the Germans would torture them until they divulged our location."

"There's always that danger, of course," he said. "But I don't see any other way if we want to help the Jews in the ghetto."

I called Michail and Iser over, and Andrei and I briefed them. I gave each boy a pistol and ammunition and a brief lesson in how to use their weapons, along with instructions on how to secretly mark their trail to find their way back to us. Because our ability to absorb new people was limited, I made them promise to bring back no more than ten escapees, preferably of fighting age.

The next day, we equipped them with clothes and food. I gave them a final shooting lesson, and they headed out. In the hours that followed, I instructed my group to pack up all our equipment and move deeper into the forest. Then I set up a lookout point not far from the previous hideout. I thought that in the worst-case scenario, if the boys were caught and forced to give away our hiding place, we had better not be there when they showed up. At the same time, we needed to be nearby to greet the boys if they came back with escapees from the ghetto.

Two days later, word came from the lookout that German soldiers were spotted advancing toward our previous hideout, their rifles drawn and ready for an assault. Much to their disappointment, they found no one, and they retreated empty-handed. I consulted with my people, and we came to the tentative conclusion that it was not the boys that had informed on us. The boys needed at least two days to reach the ghetto, and unless they had been caught along the way, there would not have been time for the Germans to organize their attack. A Belarusian farmer, we decided, had likely betrayed our location.

A week passed, and Michail and Iser had yet to return. I wanted to move to the other edge of the forest entirely, but I eventually agreed to Andrei's request that we wait another two days. And indeed, the following day, our lookout spotted the boys approaching the old hideout. Instead of a group of ten Jews, however, Michail and Iser had brought thirty people with them.

When our lookout returned to our new hideout with the new group of arrivals, I greeted the group with mixed emotions. I was pleased that Michail and Iser had returned safely and managed to rescue so many Jews who would have otherwise been killed. On the other hand, I was concerned that we couldn't support that many people and that our large numbers would put us in even greater danger, especially now that we had children and elderly people among us.

I longed for my father, who'd always known the right thing to do, but he was dead. I had only myself to rely on now. I knew all too well that even if we defeated the Germans in the end, it would still take many months, maybe even years, for us to be free from danger. I decided to completely alter our modus operandi.

I divided the fifty-nine people into two groups, one of fighters and one of children and the elderly. Thirty-two individuals comprised our fighting group—the ten original partisans and another twenty-two people who had joined since, including seven women. We equipped the new fighters with weapons and put them through intensive training.

With winter approaching, we found a new hideout for the non-combatants—a deserted warehouse in a town that had burned to the ground during the German's advance. The rest of us split into small groups and carried out numerous raids to secure food, clothing, and other essential items. In order to lessen the danger to ourselves, we raided only isolated hamlets. And to make it harder for the Nazis to anticipate our strikes, we took great care to make the pattern of our attacks as random as possible.

In the midst of all of this, my relationship with Leah intensified. I felt as though I had found my soul mate. Despite her youth, she proved capable and wise, acting as both mother and sister to everyone around her. She devoted herself to playing with the children and caring for the elderly. With her help, we became one large family.

Her brother, Misha, also fit in well, and he reassured me that he was happy about my budding relationship with his sister. From time to time, Leah and I would find a secluded spot to be alone, but other couples soon formed, and we no longer needed to keep our trysts a secret.

We knew that any day could be our last, but we were both optimists by nature and believed we would survive the war. I told Leah of my plans to immigrate to Israel after the war and live in Jerusalem, a place my father had spoken of with such longing.

"Would you join me?" I asked.

"Of course I would," she said. "We'll raise a family there—have at least two children. Promise me?"

"I promise, my love," I said as I kissed her.

A few days later, I was teaching a weapons lesson when Leah showed up and winked at me from the sidelines. When the lesson was over, she and I went for a walk in the forest. It was a sunny day, and a light breeze was blowing through the treetops. In her back-pack, she had a blanket, which we spread out on the ground. We made love and then both dozed off.

Suddenly, I heard a faint noise. I opened my eyes and saw two Belarusian farmers standing twenty feet from us with rifles at their sides. I rolled over and reached for my submachine gun as they opened fire. Bullets sang through the air around us, and my vision narrowed and darkened as I pulled the trigger, my heart pound-ing; when the magazine in my gun was empty, there was no one left standing.

I dropped the gun and turned to Leah to find her lying motion-less on the ground, a large blood stain spreading across her chest. Her eyes were open, and she was alive but couldn't speak. There was a look of helplessness in her blue eyes as she gazed up at me, and then there was nothing.

I fell to the earth, with my face against hers, and wept as I never had before.

6

"Though the storm is ever mounting"

(from "Song of the Palmach" by
Zerubavel Gilad, 1942)

When I arrived at Hannah and Avrum's home a week later, Hannah opened the door and surprised me with a fleeting kiss on my lips. "Avrum's gone to the pharmacy to get me some sleeping pills," she said with a seductive smile. "I'd sleep like a baby if you were taking care of me every night."

Alarmed, I suddenly realized that Hannah obviously wanted a very different kind of relationship than I ever wanted to have with her. And in that moment, I knew how much I wanted to be with Shoshana.

Ignoring Hannah's remark, I quickly changed the subject.

"Listen, I'd like to bring my friend Shoshana along the next time we all get together. I know Avrum doesn't suspect anything yet, but it might be a good idea if he sees I have a girlfriend." By putting things this way, I hoped Hannah would remember our arrangement and agree with my suggestion. I didn't want to hurt her feelings.

She pouted a bit but then nodded. "Yes, that's smart," she agreed.

"Just keep in mind that Shoshana isn't too fond of the British, so we should probably stay away from political issues when she's around."

Avrum returned home a few minutes later. "Why isn't breakfast on the table by now?" he joked. "Let's hurry up and get our young friend fed before he goes to eat somewhere else."

When Hannah disappeared into the kitchen, Avrum took me to the room where his arms cache was hidden. He closed the door behind us and invited me to take a seat across from him at his desk.

"David," he said, "it's time for us to speak frankly, but you have to give me your word that what I'm about to tell you will stay between us."

"Of course," I said.

He nodded. "All right. Well, what you don't know is that I serve as a plainclothes policeman for the British police. And that has to remain a secret, of course, because if it gets out, my life will be at risk. Resistance groups like the Irgun and Lehi have killed undercover policemen in the past."

As I searched for something to say, Avrum continued. "You're new to the country, so you probably aren't familiar with the story of Aryeh Polonsky, the Jewish policeman who was shot and killed by the Irgun shortly before the outbreak of the war. Polonsky was a liaison between the Jewish Agency and British law enforcement. He also provided the Jewish Agency and the Haganah valuable intelligence. He would even forge transit papers that allowed Haganah members to pass through British checkpoints unhindered. But none of that mattered. He was murdered because the Irgun thought he'd turned some of their fighters over to the British."

"That's awful," I said.

"Polonsky wasn't the only one. In Tel Aviv last year, the Lehi assassinated Ze'ev Falsch, a Jewish detective for the British police. And in Ramat Gan, two months later, they murdered Haim Gotowitz, a Jewish policeman who was working as an undercover Haganah agent. When I first started working for the British, I told them unequivocally that I was a Zionist and that I wouldn't be party to any action taken against the Jews for political reasons. They heard me loud and clear, and I deal mainly with property crime, such as theft, robbery, or embezzlement—and believe me, I don't make any distinction between Jews, Arabs, and the British.

"I'm a staunch supporter of the Zionist ideal, of Ben-Gurion and the Haganah, but I'm opposed to violent confrontation with the British. We need to persuade them to leave in a peaceful and cordial manner. They may be gentlemen, but they're also powerful and determined. Picking a fight with them won't do us any good."

Gentlemen? I was careful to keep my expression one of interest, not astonishment. *But how could Avrum consider the British to be gentlemen when they attacked and beat Jews on a regular basis?*

Avrum paused for a moment, perhaps waiting for a response from me. When he didn't get one, he went on. "I understand you read the papers, so you must know that the Haganah, Lehi, and Irgun recently joined together against the British, creating the so-called Jewish Resistance Movement, which carried out a series of operations a short while ago. The Irgun and Lehi mounted an assault on the train station in Lod, while the Haganah sabotaged the rail network in several locations. Not even in my worst dreams did I envisage the Haganah playing a part in the Irgun and Lehi's criminal actions."

He paused, raising one brow in my direction. "You must have heard about that homicidal maniac who fired on the Schneller Barracks with a sniper rifle, injuring three soldiers— one of them severely." Avrum's face twisted as he recounted the attacks I had carried out with his rifle. "The British have reason to believe the Lehi were behind the operation," he continued, shaking his head. "Indiscriminate murders of that kind are totally counterproductive to our ultimate goal—the establishment of a national homeland for the Jewish people."

It was obvious Avrum felt passionately about his cause. That didn't mean he was right. After a few seconds, his features relaxed, and he smiled, inclining his head. "I need a drink of water. Would you like one too?"

"Yes, thank you."

He stood and walked out of the room, leaving me there to think about how I would respond to all he had told me.

When he returned, I took the glass of water he offered, took a long drink, and then spoke. "I completely agree with you about all of this. Cooperating with the British is the only chance we have of establishing a national home for our people here. What can I do?"

Avrum bobbed his head, as he always did when he was thinking. "The foreman at the Tnuva dairy south of our Zephaniah Street, in the Bukharan neighborhood, is a man by the name of Yaakov Dover, and he's also a high-ranking Haganah official. Stop by and ask to speak with him. Tell him the truth—that you survived the horrors in Europe and that you're a Zionist Jew who believes in cooperation between the Jews and the British. Tell him that you want to help, and he will find something worthwhile for you to do."

"All right, I'll do that," I said.

"I'd like to develop ties with the Haganah myself, but it's

impossible. I find myself in fear of the Jews, who may know or suspect that I'm an undercover British policeman, and in fear of the British, who, under the current circumstances, are suspicious of all Jews." He was practically wringing his hands, and I frowned.

"That sounds like an untenable position, my friend."

"Yes!" he agreed. "And the army and the police are full of Jew-haters. At the Schneller Barracks, for example, there's a sergeant by the name of John Perry who despises us. And he excels at capturing members of the Jewish underground. What's strange, though, is that he keeps a Jewish lover. She even lives in the neighborhood."

It occurred to me that getting rid of a man like Perry would be a significant act to help the Jewish underground. "What a hypocrite," I said. "And the girl too. Do you happen to know her?"

"No," Avrum said, "but Hannah might. Let's go eat, and we can ask her."

We left Avrum's study and sat down to a sumptuous breakfast—omelets with fresh cheese and chopped scallions and a salad of cucumber, tomato, and onion. We finished off the meal with strong Turkish coffee and apple strudel. In addition to her virtues between the sheets, it seemed Hannah was an excellent cook.

As I ate with gusto, Avrum turned to his wife. "Look, Hannah, at how much he's enjoying your food! Perhaps we should invite him for breakfast again next week?"

"I'm willing." Hannah smiled. "Just be careful not to get between him and his plate; you might lose a finger."

I smiled and put down my fork. "Would it be okay for me to bring my girlfriend along? She has better table manners than I do."

"Of course," Avrum responded.

"Thanks," I said, "but I should warn you—we shouldn't talk about politics around her. She's not a fan of the British because of the hardship they impose on the Jews here in Israel. Once I complimented their bravery during the war, and she didn't talk to me for two weeks!"

We shook hands and parted ways. Back in my apartment, I spent the rest of the morning mulling over everything Avrum and I had talked about. I realized he wasn't a traitor but rather a wholehearted Zionist who was naïve.

My conclusion, from all that I had read and heard, was that the British had reneged on their commitments to the Jewish people. They were never going to allow us to establish a national home. They were never going to allow unrestricted immigration for the Jewish survivors living in misery in the refugee camps throughout Europe. The only way to achieve these goals was through force.

When I was a partisan, our motto had been "What can't be achieved by force can be achieved by more force." We had to make life here impossible for the British.

I LEFT MY APARTMENT AND made my way to Shoshana's house. I loved our walks together to and from the restaurant. Not being able to express my love for her was so difficult, but at least I could still spend time with her and still appreciate her gentle nature, her kindness, and her wisdom.

As we walked to work together, I told her I had met a nice couple in my neighborhood, how we had become friends, and that I had been to their home for breakfast. When I said they had invited us both to breakfast next week, she readily agreed.

The moment we arrived at Café Pinsk, I could tell by the look on Max's face that something was wrong. He greeted me with a larger-than-usual dose of nasty remarks. At one point, he called Shoshana into his office and closed the door. They were in there for at least fifteen minutes, and when they stepped out again, Max gave me another scolding.

As I washed dishes in the kitchen sink with an angry clatter, Shoshana pulled me aside. "I just asked Max to invite you to join us, but he called you a coward and a wimp."

"Sometimes I really think he does not like me," I said.

She gave me a rueful smile and then frowned slightly. "Do you remember Inspector Greene, the British police officer that Max was talking to?"

"Was that his name?"

"Max and Greene have grown a lot closer lately," Shoshana continued, ignoring my sulky mood. "Max discovered that the inspector plays a key role in the capture and arrest of underground members, and Max has won his trust by occasionally providing him with minor bits of information about the underground. A few days ago, Greene called Max to his office and told him that he is planning to arrest several dozen underground members. The inspector asked him to provide some intelligence for the operation. Max not only wants to stop the operation, he also wants to send a warning to the underground, but he's worried it could expose him."

I'm sure he is, I thought. *For all of Max's contempt toward me, he was fighting for the same end goal that I was—a Jewish homeland. I knew Shoshana wanted me to help him, and I wasn't opposed to the idea; however, right now I needed to keep a low profile.*

"Perhaps you could do something to prove yourself to him," she said. "He doesn't understand what you've been through."

Shoshana waited for my response, and when none came, she sighed. She picked up one of the dishes I had just washed and began to dry it with a dishtowel as she spoke. "I told Max that you commanded a group of partisans during the war and surely have a better understanding of such things than he or I do. But he said he was thankful to have more serious people as consultants." She rolled her eyes and looked over at me. "I hate that he keeps calling you a coward, insulting you, when I know how brave you are."

I folded my arms over my chest and leaned against the sink behind me. "Max's problem is complex. Give me a day or two, and I'll try to come up with an idea that you can pass on to him. He certainly won't listen to anything I have to say."

I didn't need a day, certainly not two. I already had a solution in mind. Since I first started working at Café Pinsk, I had kept a watchful eye on the British soldiers and police officers who visited the restaurant regularly. Greene typically came in on Wednesdays around seven o'clock, always got drunk on whiskey and beer, and then left at around ten.

As much as I preferred to avoid committing outright murder, sometimes there was really no other choice. If I wanted to save Max and stop Greene's plan to arrest underground members, it looked like the good inspector was going to have to die.

ON THE FOLLOWING DAY, A Wednesday, I made my way to Shoshana's home at noon. I told her that I wasn't feeling well and that Max should find someone to cover for me.

"Do you need any medication?" she asked. "Would you like me to bring you anything when I get home from work tonight?"

"I don't need anything right now," I said, touched by the offer. "But I'd be very happy if you were to come by on your way home to check up on me."

"Gladly," Shoshana responded, flashing me a look that made my heart beat faster. I was ever hopeful.

I went back to my apartment and spent the day resting and reading. I also found time to pull my Enfield revolver from its hiding place, clean it, and load it. At around nine o'clock, I left my apartment with the pistol in my jacket pocket. I knew the British had set up a checkpoint at the top of Chancellor Street a few days earlier, so I bypassed it by heading along Yishayahu Street instead. Then I slipped into the dark stairwell almost exactly opposite Café Pinsk and waited, my eyes fixed on the door of the restaurant.

In all the time I had been working at the restaurant, Greene had never missed a single Wednesday, and I was hoping he wouldn't break his habit. Indeed, just minutes after ten o'clock, he stepped out into the cold, buttoned his coat, and turned toward Ben Yehuda Street. I decided it would be best to approach him from the front rather than the rear—if he noticed someone coming up behind him, he could get suspicious.

I hurried to Shamai Street, which ran parallel to Ben Yehuda, then turned into an alley that connected the two streets and made my way back. I cocked the revolver and put it in my coat pocket, then headed up Ben Yehuda from the lower end of the street. All at once I saw my target. Greene was walking down the hill, coming toward me.

The street was deserted. As I walked, I held the upturned collar of my jacket with both hands, giving the impression I was shielding my neck from the cold air. I swayed a little to make the Brit think I was drunk.

Greene approached, his gaze upon me, his right hand in the pocket of his coat, probably wrapped around the butt of a loaded weapon. He must have suspected something, because he moved slightly to the side and out of arm's reach, presumably to give himself some room if a fight broke out. Such precautions might have saved his life had I been less experienced.

As I passed him, I swiftly pulled the revolver from my pocket and shot him in the temple. He was dead before he hit the ground.

"The wimp has solved your problem, Max," I muttered.

A quick search through Greene's pockets revealed two .38-caliber Webley revolvers and several spare cartridges, which I grabbed before returning to my apartment. There, I cleaned the weapon I had used to kill Greene and put it and the two new revolvers into my hiding place behind the curtain cornice.

I took a shower, and then to make my eyes red and weary, I rubbed them a lot. An hour or so later, there was a knock on the door. When I opened it, Shoshana was standing there with a concerned look on her face.

"Have I woken you up?" she asked as she entered. "Your eyes are red." She peered at me closely. "I hope you haven't come down with anything serious. I've brought you some soup for dinner."

"Thank you for the soup," I said. "I think I'm getting better, and I'm sure I'll be fine in the morning."

"Would you like me to spend the night and take care of you?" she asked, leaning to the side to look around the place. "I could sleep on your couch."

I smiled outwardly but felt a sharp twinge inside at the reminder of our lack of intimacy. "You don't have to do that. Just the sight of you makes me feel better. Go home, and I'll walk you to work tomorrow."

She surprised me with a kiss on the cheek. "Good night, then. Please get better."

The next day I was, indeed, "better." As Shoshana and I

walked to the restaurant, we encountered three British check-points. Shoshana and I both had the necessary papers and weren't detained. When we got to the restaurant, Max looked at me scornfully, as usual.

"I had a problem that Shoshana said I should consult with you about," he said. "I didn't because you're a wimp. Thankfully, something happened last night that solved my problem without any need for your help. Carry on having a good time while your Jewish brothers, who so desperately need help, continue to suffer."

"I'm pleased to hear that your problem has been solved," I said. "But if you ever need my advice or help in the future, don't hesitate to ask."

Max snorted and walked away.

Later that night, while walking home with Shoshana, I saw British soldiers patrolling the streets in pairs, more alert and vigilant than ever. A sudden thought struck me. If an experienced policeman came to my apartment to conduct a search, he wouldn't have much trouble finding my weapons cache.

When I woke the following morning, I went out to the backyard and inspected the stone wall that encircled the yard. In a section of the wall behind the apricot tree, I managed to dislodge a large rock and discovered that there was a hollow space behind the front and the back stones of the fence. All I had to do was place my weapons in the hollow space and chisel the rock down slightly. It would make a perfect hiding place. I decided to visit the Bukharan Market, where I was sure I could find a box for my pistols, and also check out the Tnuva dairy that Avrum had mentioned.

I arrived at a three-story building topped by the dairy's water tower. I opened the door to the ground floor, which served as a warehouse, and asked one of the workers to call

Yaakov Dover. The man walked over to the opening of a large pipe fixed to the wall and shouted into it.

"Yaakov, you have a visitor!"

A strange method of communication, I thought, but apparently an efficient one. A few minutes later, a tall man with curly black hair and a bushy mustache came down the steps and asked how he could help me.

"My name is David Gabinsky. I live in Zephaniah Street and work as a waiter at Café Pinsk. I'm a new immigrant from Belarus who wants to take part in the struggle for Jewish independence," I said. "I was told that you could help me in this regard."

I expected him to ask who had suggested that I approach him. Instead, he gave me an appraising look and then spoke. "Your Hebrew is good for a newcomer, but I'm Bukharan, so we can speak Russian if you prefer."

"Interesting," I said, still speaking in Hebrew. "I was planning on going to the Bukharan Market after this."

"Have you visited the Bukharan Quarter before?" he asked.

"No, this will be my first time."

"Pity," he said. "If I wasn't so busy right now, I'd give you a tour." He told me how wealthy Jews from Bukhara, including his own grandfather, had established the quarter as a wealthy neighborhood outside the walls of the Old City some fifty years before.

"At the time, it was Jerusalem's most luxurious neighborhood," he explained with a broad wave of his hand, "with spacious stone mansions and large courtyards and pretty public gardens, but most of the residents were forced out by the Turks during World War I. The Turks confiscated homes and turned them into warehouses and stables."

"That's terrible," I said.

He nodded. "Some of the homeowners returned to Jerusalem after the war, but they were no longer the wealthy individuals they once were—the Bolsheviks took care of that. It's not the same now, with all the mansions subdivided into apartments, but the architecture is still beautiful if you know how to look for it."

"Interesting," I said sincerely. I was always eager to learn more about Jerusalem.

"If you have the time, check out the Yehudayoff-Hefetz building on Ezra Street. They call it the Palace, and it deserves its name—Italian Renaissance with beautiful arched windows. Some say it was built for the Messiah, whenever he gets here."

"I'll do that," I said. "Thanks."

"I have to get back to work," Yaakov said, glancing at his watch, "but come back tomorrow, and we'll talk some more."

So I was being evaluated. Yaakov was a smart man. "Yes," I said. "I'll be here at ten."

I made my way to the Bukharan Quarter, asked for directions to the Palace, and spent a few minutes admiring the impressive structure. From there, I went to the market. The entrance was packed with vegetable, fruit, poultry, and fish stalls, but I figured I'd find what I was looking for deeper inside.

And indeed, at a used-goods store, I came across a metal box with a latch on the side. I haggled over the price and eventually purchased the box, along with a lock and a large iron hammer. I took everything back to my apartment, satisfied, so far, with my plan to hide my weapons.

The next morning, after waiting for my landlords to go to work and their children to leave for school, I removed the rock in the stone wall. For the next hour, I hammered at the rock until I had broken off enough to make a place for the metal box behind it. Inside my apartment, I retrieved the weapons, jewelry, and money from my hiding place above the curtain and placed them in the box. Back outside, I fitted the box in the wall and then wedged the rock back into place, leaving my stash completely concealed. I swept up the shards of rock, mixing them with the trash in the bin.

I made my way back to the Tnuva dairy, where Yaakov Dover was waiting for me at the entrance to the building. We crossed the road together and sat down on a ledge.

"Level with me, David," Yaakov said. "What brings you to me?"

"I want to protect the Jewish community against the Arabs," I responded. "I commanded a group of partisans in Belarus, and I have combat experience." I knew that, unlike the Irgun and Lehi, the Haganah viewed the Arabs as the principal enemy.

Yaakov thought for a moment, then nodded. "We're meeting this Saturday at eleven in the morning. I suggest you join us. You'll get to know us, and we'll get to know you."

"Gladly," I said.

"We're meeting at the Glicksteins' house on Zephaniah Street. I don't remember the number, but it's the building next to the hairdresser, on the corner of Malachi. They live on the second floor. If you have trouble finding the place, the neighbors will help you."

I left, aware that Yaakov, no doubt, either would have me checked out before the meeting or already had. Resistance fighters knew better than to trust every random man claiming to be a patriot. Time would tell what he thought about me.

TWO DAYS LATER, SHOSHANA AND I walked to Hannah and Avrum's place for our breakfast date.

"You didn't tell us your girlfriend was so pretty," Hannah said when she opened the door.

"Thank you," Shoshana said, blushing. "You're lovely too."

"I have something in my study that I must show David," Avrum said after shaking Shoshana's hand. "Excuse us. It'll only take a minute."

We went into his study, and he closed the door. "Did you meet with Yaakov from the Haganah?" he asked.

"Yes," I said. "We arranged to meet again. You know, if you were to give me information about the British to pass on to Yaakov, it could help me win their trust. Nothing top secret, of course."

"Let me think about it. Can you meet me at eight o'clock tomorrow morning at the cobbler's?"

Hannah and Shoshana were having a lively chat when we joined them at the table. The conversation among the four of us flowed nicely, and before we parted, Avrum invited us for breakfast again the following Tuesday.

"I had a good time at your friends'," Shoshana said on the walk to work, "but we don't spend enough time alone. How about we go on a picnic this Saturday, just the two of us? I know of a wonderful spot in the Tel Arza Grove."

I was thrilled with the idea. I had been thinking for some time that I should express my love for her again. Perhaps enough time had passed for her to consider us having a close relationship instead of just a friendship.

"I'd love to go on a picnic," I said, "but I'm busy this Saturday. Let's make it for the following one."

"Perfect," Shoshana said. I briefly took her hand and squeezed it, and she squeezed mine back.

The next morning, I met up with Avrum outside the cobbler's shop.

"I gave your idea some thought," Avrum said, "and I've decided to give it a chance. You can tell Yaakov that this coming Monday evening, the British have plans to arrest members of the Haganah, as well as supporters of the Irgun. So far as I can tell, they don't have any precise intelligence, but in light of the recent murder of Inspector Greene, they want to make a show of force."

"Excellent," I said. "I'll tell Yaakov."

Avrum's expression turned serious. "David, I want you to remember something. I'm a Jewish patriot, and I don't want Jews to be arrested—unless we're talking about maniacs like the one who shot those soldiers at the Schneller Barracks. If they had a chance of apprehending that criminal, I'd be happy to play a part in it."

"I understand," I said, keeping a straight face.

He shook my hand and headed off to work.

An hour later, I went to visit Hannah. I was beginning to feel bad for Avrum. He was my friend now—a nice person, really—and here I was, having an affair with his wife. Had I known Avrum before I met Hannah, I don't think I would have had an affair with her. Hell, if I had known she was married, I probably would have run in the opposite direction.

But now . . . now I felt that my time with Hannah was essential to my mental—and physical—well-being. We had become friends and had fun together. Most of all, being with her helped me not think about Shoshana so much. She helped keep me going.

Moreover, I realized from things she had said what Hannah's relationship with Avrum was really like. I felt that it was just happenstance that I was there with her. It could have been any other man. I wasn't really a disturbance in their marital life.

After an enjoyable hour in her bed, we dressed and went to the kitchen for some coffee.

"Your girlfriend is a charming young woman," Hannah said. "We've arranged to get together—just the two of us—in a couple days, and I'm hoping we can become friends."

I didn't respond, no longer sure that my idea of introducing Shoshana to Hannah and Avrum was such a good one. It seemed strange that Shoshana hadn't mentioned anything to me about her upcoming date with Hannah. After talking for a few more minutes, I said goodbye and then walked to Shoshana's apartment to pick her up and go to work.

At Café Pinsk, I waited until Shoshana was busy taking a customer's order before approaching Max to ask if I could speak with him in private. He led me into the kitchen and instructed the chef to go to the shop to restock the English pepper. Once the chef had left, he gestured for me to start talking.

"Yesterday," I said, "I was walking down Geula Street when I had to piss so bad that I couldn't wait until I got home, so I ducked into a courtyard. Two British officers passed by, and I overheard them saying they were going to launch a raid on the underground on Monday night."

"Is that all?" Max asked. "Did they say exactly who they were targeting?"

"That's all I heard."

Max's face darkened like a thundercloud. "You're infuriating! You tell me you were a partisan commander, but I find that very hard to believe. You listen to an important conversation between two British officers yet carry on pissing away in peace without even bothering to try to get more information! It's a shame, but I guess that's all you're capable of. I'll warn whoever needs to be warned, and I really hope you properly understood what you heard."

ON SATURDAY MORNING, I WENT to the Haganah meeting at the Glicksteins'. It was a small, modest one-bedroom apartment, with simple wood furniture and some photos of family members on the wall. The owners had arranged about twenty folding chairs in a circle in the living room. A jug of water and some glasses had been placed on a small table in the corner of the room.

Yaakov was already there, along with about twenty others. He introduced me as a partisan during the war, which sparked much curiosity among the others. I fended off their questions, not wanting to seem like I was boasting. More than that, I worried that one of them was a British informant. I told them that I worked as a waiter at Café Pinsk, which was very popular among British soldiers and policemen, and had overheard a conversation between two British officers about the operation planned for Monday night.

"Thanks, David," Yaakov said. "We'll relay your information to the appropriate parties. And now let's talk about how you can help us and how we can help you."

"Look," I said, "I went through some very difficult times as a partisan. I stared death in the face every day, and I still struggle to understand how I survived the war, not to mention the hardships of immigrating to Israel. For the moment, at least, I'd like to take it easy. I'd be happy to serve in an advisory capacity, if you think that would be helpful. And if I hear anything else, I'll pass it on, of course."

If Yaakov had expected more, he managed to hide his disappointment. He shook my hand and thanked me. I started to leave and then turned back.

"I thought of something else. The British officers who come to the restaurant are always trying to get me to talk. If you give me a piece of harmless information to pass on to them, I could use it to gain their trust."

"I'll try to come up with something," Yaakov said. "Come here again next Saturday."

"I can't make it next Saturday."

"In two weeks, then. We meet here every Saturday."

"I'll be here," I said. We shook hands again, and I bid farewell to the group.

I seemed to be making progress, but at the same time, I wondered if I was spreading myself too thin. Perhaps, I thought, I'd be wasting my time with the Haganah. I admired David Ben-Gurion, who had proven to be a leader of rare quality, a man of both vision and action, but I didn't like his obsessive persecution of the Irgun and Lehi. We were all Jews, and even if some of us had different opinions, they weren't the enemy, and we should not be fighting among ourselves.

On the other hand, the Haganah had recently allied with the Irgun and Lehi in the fight against the British, and I viewed the agreement as atonement for the mistakes of the past, at least to a certain extent.

The Irgun was the organization that I sympathized with most, since it had always seen the true picture. The Irgun was the military wing of the Revisionist Movement. I knew all about it because when I was a youngster, my father had been one of its supporters. In the 1930s, Ze'ev Jabotinsky, the leader of the movement, had been one of the first to recognize the terrible threat that Nazism posed to the world in general and the Jews in particular.

He'd urged as many Jews as possible to leave Europe, even if it meant violating the laws of the British Mandate that restricted immigration to Israel. With the outbreak of World

War II, the Irgun had suspended its struggle against the British and fought alongside them in the war against the Germans.

But in 1944, the new commander of the Irgun, Menachem Begin, had realized that the British were not going to fulfill their commitment to establish a Jewish national home in Israel, and he'd called for an uprising against the British authorities. At the same time, he'd forbade reprisals against the Haganah, even though the organization had turned in several Irgun members to the British.

"There will be no civil war," he'd said. "Our soldiers will not raise their arms against Jewish opponents." I admired Begin for his bravery and ingenuity; the British had placed a hefty price on his head and made concerted efforts to capture or kill him, to no avail.

The Lehi, a much smaller organization than the other two, had shown itself to be a determined and capable resistance movement, and its members were willing to sacrifice themselves without hesitation for the sake of the Zionist cause. I was troubled during the war when Lehi members had held talks with the Nazi regime, seeking permission for European Jews to immigrate to Israel in return for the Lehi's help in the fight against the British.

I knew that the Haganah viewed the Arabs as our people's primary threat. Yes, the Arabs hated us, as they had shown in the past. But right now, the Arabs weren't our immediate enemy—the British were. For the time being, we needed to invest our efforts and resources into driving out the British.

As I thought about the different Jewish resistance organizations, I realized that I was doing a kind of balancing act. I was trying to gain information from each group in order to ultimately aid my own mission—to help establish a Jewish state.

When I was a child, my rabbi had taught me to always be

honest and fair. There was a special verse from Deuteronomy he often quoted that advised a man to "keep your leaps," which means "be honest and don't lie." I had been raised to follow these edicts, but when it came to saving the Jewish nation, or family and friends, sometimes I had to keep the rule "The end justifies the means."

I decided that if it came down to it, I would join the Irgun. But in the meantime, I'd be helping them, even if they didn't know it.

7

"THE EARLY MORNING SUN WILL BRIGHTEN OUR DAY"

(FROM "SONG OF THE PARTISANS" BY
HIRSH GLICK, 1943)

I eagerly awaited the picnic with Shoshana. When Saturday came, the weather was mild and sunny, despite the season, and we met near her apartment. Shoshana came outside with two knapsacks for us to carry and two folded blankets.

We made our way up Zephaniah Street and then down toward Tel Arza, turning onto a dirt track at the end of the street and following its winding course down into a valley. Trees and wildflowers, unlike anything I knew from Belarus, lined the path. The only flowers that I recognized were the pink cyclamens nudging up between the rocks.

When we reached the bottom of the valley, we found a secluded spot to spread out the blankets and sat down. Shoshana pulled a bottle from one of the knapsacks—Stock 84 Italian brandy from the Carmel Mizrahi distillery—and told me that Max had donated it to our picnic.

"Max sees himself as a father figure to me," she said with a shy smile. "That's one of the reasons—maybe the main reason—why he's so hard on you. He sees there's something between us." She poured two fingers of brandy into a pair of tumblers, and we raised them for a toast. "To our lives," she said, and I repeated her.

Our first drink was followed by a second. After pouring our third, Shoshana lay down on the blanket. Her loose blond hair made a glowing halo around her face as she looked up at the sky.

"David, I'm so happy to be with you. I felt so dead inside before I met you. I was like a machine, going about my days, feeling nothing. My heart was burned to ash, but somehow you lit the fire inside it again, and now I feel like I have a reason to live."

She paused for just a moment, and when she continued, her voice was soft yet determined. "I want you to know I haven't resigned myself to the way things are between us. I talked with Hannah about how I wish I could be more physical with you, and she promised to refer me to a good psychologist. After all you've been through, you deserve a loving woman in all senses of the word, and I want to be that woman."

The beautiful day, the brandy, and her words made my head spin. Staring into her green eyes, I opened my heart and told her how I felt.

"You're an extraordinary woman, Shoshana, both beautiful and intelligent. I'm lucky to have met you, and I love you very much. I feel as if you are truly made for me."

She smiled as I gently stroked the back of her hand.

"We've never spoken about your past," I said. "I know that you were born in Novogrudok. I would love to hear more about you . . . about your life . . ."

She squeezed my hand as I trailed off. "It's hard for me to talk about, but I'll try. I grew up in a loving family with a younger sister. From a young age, I loved to draw. I would make birthday cards for my friends and family and decorate our storybooks so they looked more interesting. My mother always encouraged me—she kept everything I drew and said that they would be valuable when I became a famous artist one day." She laughed, but her smile quickly faded. "That never happened, of course. The Russians came, then the Germans. They put us to work in a factory that made blankets for the German army. Terrible things started happening to the other Jews, as you know."

"Yes," I said softly. "I well know."

She closed her eyes and fell silent for a long time. A single tear ran down the side of her face. I waited, afraid to speak lest she stop telling her story. All at once, she sat up, linking her arms around her knees, her dress flowing around her ankles.

"We were living in an apartment with several other families," she finally said. "I was sitting at the table playing Trust, Don't Trust with a girl named Riva. She wasn't a pretty girl, but she had beautiful black hair and a beautiful smile. Then all at once, the door slammed open with a *bang*! The sound was so loud I thought something had exploded!" Her fingers tightened around the cloth of her dress, and I could see them trembling as she turned and looked at me.

"You don't have to tell me," I said, alarmed by the terrified look in her eyes.

"It was the police," she went on, as if I hadn't spoken, our gazes locked. "They raped the women, tortured the men, and finally shot and killed everyone, or thought they did." She lowered her eyes then, and her voice became a whisper. "They raped my mother and killed her in front of me."

"Shoshana . . ." I said, "I'm so sorry." My words offered poor comfort, but I didn't know what else to do. She began to speak again, this time her words monotone, emotionless.

"They shot in my direction. They missed me, but I fell to

the floor right beside Riva's body. I pretended to be dead. They left as suddenly as they'd come. A small resistance movement in the city helped smuggle me out of the ghetto to a family in the country. They gave me shelter. I pretended to be a Christian, and that's how I remained alive until the Russian army arrived."

She stared up at the sky. I took a long drink of the brandy. I had seen my own terrors in war, but the thought of gentle Shoshana being put through such madness—I shook my head and took another drink.

"I know that you crave physical contact with me," she finally said after several moments of silence, "and I am trying to get there. Until then, is there any other way I can show my love for you?"

"After all I've been through in life so far, all I want is you by my side," I said. "Our love gives purpose to my life."

She leaned over and rested her head against my shoulder. I stroked her beautiful golden hair. "I love you, David," she whispered.

I held her nestled against me for several long, wonderful moments, both of us satisfied to just be quiet, thoughtful together. Eventually we began to talk again, shifting the conversation to less troubling matters—funny stories from our childhoods, our favorite movies and books, places that we would like to see. Then Shoshana pulled away from me slightly and looked into my eyes.

"Have you noticed how Hannah looks at you?" she asked. "She definitely wants you for more than a breakfast guest."

She said this with a teasing smile, and though I had the presence of mind to laugh, I was shocked. I knew women sometimes noticed things that men would never give a second thought to, but this was a reminder that I needed to be careful. I didn't want to lie, so I played dumb.

"Really? Are you sure that's what you saw?"

"Of course. You should be careful. Her husband might notice those looks too, and then there'll be trouble."

"Thanks for warning me," I said, making a mental note to discuss the matter with Hannah as soon as possible.

Shoshana opened the other knapsack and started pulling out the lunch that she had packed—a small Hungarian salami, crackers, yellow cheese from the Tnuva dairy, a little container filled with Arabic cracked olives, a cucumber, and a tomato. For dessert, we ate two hefty slices of a home-baked cake.

We drank the rest of the brandy and then made our way back to Kerem Avraham. We parted outside her apartment, where the usual kiss on the cheek and hug she gave me felt warmer than usual.

On Monday, I went to Hannah's apartment. For the first time since our affair had begun, I had a difficult time enjoying our lovemaking. Whether I wanted to admit it or not, Shoshana was very much on my mind. After we'd spent an hour in bed, we got dressed and had coffee in the kitchen. I asked her to tell me more about the therapy she had recommended to Shoshana.

"I like Shoshana, and I want to help her," she said. "I know a woman, an immigrant from Germany, who studied psychology there. Her professor was a student of Sigmund Freud himself," she added. "I hope she'll be able to help your girlfriend."

"By the way," I said, "Shoshana noticed the way you look at me. She doesn't suspect anything, but we need to be more careful—both of us."

She gave me a tentative smile. "I admit, it's hard for me to hide. This started as a flirtation, something purely physical, but it has developed into feelings beyond my control."

She seemed to be expecting similar sentiments from me,

but I didn't say a word. I changed the subject and asked her how Avrum had secured his job with the British police.

"I don't know," she said, though I had a feeling she did.

I decided to try a different approach. I asked her if Avrum ever socialized with the British. "Absolutely not," she said firmly. "I don't think the British are interested in hanging out with Jews. They call us 'natives'—Jews and Arabs alike. The only relationships they have are with Jewish women, like my friend Sarah. She's seeing a sergeant in the British CID named Perry."

I was intrigued, but I didn't want to appear too inquisitive. Hannah, however, seemed just as eager to talk as I was to listen.

"We used to be really good friends," she continued, "but our friendship has gone cold since she started seeing Perry. He spoils her, and she's become such a snob, as if she's a queen or something. As a CID detective, he earns good money and doesn't have any expenses here, not to mention he gets a nice bonus every time he brings in underground members. And he spends almost all of it on her. Besides going out for groceries, all she does is lie around at home and wait for him."

"At least she's happy, I suppose."

"Well, he's tall and muscular, with blond hair and blue eyes. He has these big ears that she doesn't like very much, but she says he's an animal in bed."

"Is that how you girls are, gossiping about your men?" I asked. "I hope you haven't said anything about me."

"Oh no," she said. "I don't say anything about you because I want you all to myself!"

Hannah gave me an especially passionate kiss before I left, and as I walked home, her words echoed in my mind. She wanted me all to herself. And she'd said our "flirtation" had developed into feelings beyond her control. Obviously, our arrangement wasn't as casual to Hannah as it was to me.

I returned with Shoshana the following day for breakfast at Hannah and Avrum's. While there, it occurred to me that I was spending too much time with this couple—with one of them especially. Remembering Shoshana was working hard to get over her emotional problems regarding physical intimacy, combined with Hannah's sudden possessiveness the day before, was making me rethink the situation. I decided to limit my visits with Hannah to once a week and the breakfasts to once a month. Rather than say anything, I'd simply gradually extend the time between each meeting.

Avrum once again dragged me off to his office the moment we entered the apartment. "Did you arrange to meet again with Yaakov Dover?" he asked.

"Yes, this Saturday," I replied. "Tell me, did the operation to arrest members of the Haganah and Irgun go ahead last night as planned?"

"Yes, but the results were poor. The British had a list of people they wanted to arrest, but almost none of them were home. They think someone on the inside may have tipped off the underground, but so far as I know, they don't have a suspect in mind," Avrum said with a wink. "I assume it'll be easier for you to work toward improving ties between the Haganah and the British now."

"I'll see what I can do," I said.

As we were standing by the front door after the meal, Avrum said that he looked forward to seeing us next week.

"Unfortunately, I won't be able to make it," I replied. "I'm up to my neck with things to do. But I can come the week after." Avrum looked disappointed but said nothing.

When I arrived at Café Pinsk that afternoon, Max greeted me warmly, perhaps for the first time since I'd started working for him, and dragged me into the kitchen. The poor chef, again, was sent to the store.

"Thanks to the information you gave us, several of our friends in the resistance escaped arrest," he said. "You have my gratitude, and a senior member of our organization wants to thank you personally. He'll come to the restaurant after closing time, and I hope you agree to wait for him."

I asked Shoshana if she would be okay walking home alone, and she just laughed. "Before I met you, I walked home alone every night. I'm sure I can manage." She seemed pleased by Max's change in attitude toward me, even if it came at the expense of my company.

Our guest showed up around midnight. He was a broad-shouldered man of average height, dressed all in khaki. He had brown eyes and brown hair, graying at the temples, and a warm expression on his face. As he shook my hand, however, he fixed me with a piercing stare, as if he were trying to size me up.

"This is David," Max said, "the young man who warned me about the raid."

The man said a few words of thanks for the information I had provided. Max, uncharacteristically, didn't utter a word but simply nodded as the man spoke. It seemed clear he was someone important, and Max was like a shy kid around him.

"I hear you were a partisan in Belarus," the man said. "Please tell me more about it."

I offered him a brief history of my life and the operations my group and I had carried out against the Germans.

"I'd be very happy to have you join us," he said when I finished my story. "You seem to be an intelligent young man, in good physical shape, brave and experienced. I understand that you sympathize with our struggle against the British, and you could be of much help to us."

From the corner of my eye, I could see the anticipation on Max's face. I hated to disappoint him again, but I still preferred to work alone.

"I appreciate the offer, and I'm flattered, but I can't accept at this time. I just arrived here a few months ago, exhausted from the war, from all the horrors I'd experienced, from the loss of my entire family. I still need time to rest and recover."

Max's face turned as red as a tomato, but the man just smiled and extended his hand. "I hope you have a change of heart." He nodded to Max and stepped out into the street.

"I thought meeting such a man would change your mind, but you're hopeless," Max said.

I ignored his comment, said goodbye, and left. It was already past midnight by the time I made my way up Chancellor Street, where I spotted a young man and woman posting flyers on a wall. I was about thirty feet away from them when two British policemen emerged from the darkness and began brutally beating them with their clubs. This time Shoshana wasn't by my side to stop me.

As I approached the scene of the beating, wobbling a little with feigned drunkenness, one of the policemen turned to me and hissed in English, "Get out of here," adding a curse and raising his club to indicate the direction I should follow.

"*Prosti*," I said, and as I stumbled past, I whirled and kicked him in the groin. He doubled over with a vomitous gurgle. I grabbed his club and slammed it against his head; he fell to the ground unconscious.

The second policeman stumbled to his feet with panic in his eyes. He swung first, and I blocked his club with mine. As we strained against each other, I kicked him in the groin as well. He doubled over just like his friend, and I swung at the back of his head, sending him to the ground.

I ran over to the young man and woman who had been attacked. They were both wobbly but able to stand.

"Go!" I yelled, interrupting their frantic words of thanks. "A military vehicle could be here any minute."

The policemen lay motionless on the ground. I didn't bother to check whether they were alive or dead. I wiped the fingerprints from the club I had used and tossed it over the wall by the sidewalk, crossed the road, and continued on my way up Chancellor Street at a regular pace. No military vehicles yet. I made my way home, taking the side streets when I could.

When I reached my apartment, I felt satisfied with my actions. I knew that one such incident wouldn't be enough to deter the British from their violent assaults on people posting leaflets, but I hoped that they would think twice about it from now on.

I showered and got into bed, but I couldn't fall asleep. I thought about Shoshana and everything she had told me. Those thoughts carried me back to Leah, who was gone from my life but not from my heart.

I loved Shoshana, but our relationship had yet to reach—if it ever would—the same level of openness and warmth that Leah and I had shared. Our constant fight for survival during the war had united the two of us in a way that was physical, emotional, and spiritual. We had been willing to sacrifice ourselves for one another without the slightest hesitation.

In those intense days, when we were fighting against the Germans, Leah and I had both longed for those moments when we could get away from the group, find a private spot, lie down on a blanket, and make love. How would I ever find that kind of passion, that intensity, again? The crucible of war was a terrible thing in every way, but it had forged a love that bonded me to Leah for eternity.

After she was killed, I struggled to regain my focus on our mission. I blamed myself for her death, for irresponsibly falling asleep in the forest. Why had she died, while I survived? The thought continued to haunt me.

Misha, who had loved and admired me, became cold and distant after Leah's death. He didn't say it, but I knew he blamed me. I couldn't console myself with the empty words that people always say—that she'd had a good life or that at least her death had come quickly, and she hadn't suffered.

I no longer cared whether or not the Germans killed me, because everyone who mattered to me was gone. I had no one left to love. Only my sense of responsibility to my fellow partisans and the families we had taken under our wing gave me the strength to go on. I had to look after them, and I was determined to do so.

More refugees from the ghetto joined us in the second half of 1943, and they filled us in on events from the front lines. The Germans were in retreat. In early 1943, the Russians scored a significant victory, both from a military perspective and for morale, when the battle for Stalingrad ended with the German forces' surrender. In July, British and US forces landed in Sicily and kicked off the Allies' campaign in Italy, and there were rumors that the Americans and British would soon land forces in France and launch an assault on Germany itself.

We expected the Germans, concerned now with their own survival, to focus on their battles against the Allied forces rather than their murderous vendetta against Jews. We were very wrong. The Germans' hatred for Jews was so intense that they actually stepped up their extermination efforts. Their desire to "purify" Europe of Jews seemed even stronger than their desire to win the war.

As for the Minsk ghetto, the refugees told us it was no more. It had come under the command of Adolf Ruebe, who had murdered the last five thousand Jews of the original hundred thousand once crowded into its confines. Although almost all of these last survivors had worked in factories that produced supplies for the German war effort, Ruebe had three thousand of them killed in August and September. On October 21, 1943, German soldiers rounded up the last of Minsk's Jews and marched them to the train station for transportation to the death camps in Poland.

After hearing of these atrocities, we desperately wanted revenge. We carried out sabotage operations against the Germans' telephone and power lines, but that wasn't enough to satisfy us. It became our sacred duty to kill as many Germans as possible.

Following their defeat at Stalingrad and the advancement of Russian forces, the Germans retreated to the west, where they suffered heavy losses. We received reports that the Russians had reclaimed Ukraine. The Germans were no longer self-assured. They moved only in large groups, fearing surprise attacks by partisans.

The villagers in the area where we fought were well aware of the situation by now and began showing us more respect. The Russian partisans adopted a more sympathetic attitude toward the fleeing Jews, and large areas fell under partisan control.

Our group now numbered sixty-eight people, including thirty-four fighters. We needed to carry out a major assault as soon as possible in order to play a real part in defeating the Germans. Alec, who had proved himself to be an excellent lookout and scout, left on a reconnaissance mission for a few days and returned with information.

He had found a small supply base adjacent to a factory where the Germans were using Belarusians as forced labor. About three dozen German soldiers manned the base, along with a handful of administration personnel who oversaw the laborers. A small observation tower stood over the camp, always manned by one soldier, with another stationed at the gate.

A nighttime assault would be too risky, Alec believed, because security at night was tighter, and the guards were more alert. During the day, the Germans seemed less concerned about an attack. The best time to launch an assault was in the evening at sunset.

In light of his report, I decided we needed to surprise the Germans and kill as many of them as we could before they had time to respond. After much thought, I came up with a plan: We would disguise ourselves as German soldiers escorting a group of new laborers to the base. We'd hide grenades and other weapons under the ragged clothing, ready to be used at a moment's notice.

Alec, dressed in the uniform of a German officer, led the way. When we reached the gate, the guard snapped to attention and saluted Alec, who crisply snapped a flat hand to his helmet in return. "I've brought some more scum to work," he said in perfect German.

The German at the gate scowled. "No one informed me of this. And some of these look like Jews. We've been ordered to kill Jews, not work them. Have you not heard this?"

Alec shrugged. "As far as I'm concerned, you can kill them all right now. But my orders are to bring them here." He pulled a bottle of schnapps from his pocket. "For your morale. Have a sip, and take the bottle to your commander."

Alec approached him with the bottle, and when the guard reached out to take it, Alec smashed the bottle over his head and plunged the broken end into his throat. Quickly, we entered the base.

Alec ran into the commander's building and shot and killed him while the rest of us stormed the soldiers' living quarters, gunning them down with our MP40s. We took them all out before a single German had a chance to fire his weapon.

"What's going on down there?" the guard in the observation tower called out. "Report!"

Alec approached the tower and waved at the man. "Some of the pigs who work here were making trouble—they didn't like the food!" he shouted. "Do you feel like coming down and helping me drag out their carcasses?"

"Certainly," the guard called back. He made his way down from the tower, frowned at Alec, and said, "I don't recognize you. Are you new here?"

"Let's get acquainted," Alec said and fired point-blank into the man's stomach. The guard stumbled backward, hit the wall, and slid to the floor. "I'm the Jew who is sending you to Hell."

We heard shots coming from the administration building, and seconds later, one of my men rushed up to tell me that everyone inside had been eliminated. We headed to the laborers' quarters, filled with Belarusians.

"You are free, my friends!" Alec shouted. "Tell them, David!" I explained how they could join up with other groups of partisans, and then we gave them food and supplies for their journey. They thanked us tearfully before streaming out the gate and into the forest.

The base provided fine spoils for us as well. We loaded food, clothing, blankets, and tools onto three carts and filled several knapsacks with supplies. After removing what we wanted, we torched the base. As we headed down the road, from time to time we turned around to watch the fire consuming the base and the bodies of the Germans.

I OPENED MY EYES. SUNLIGHT poured in through my window, and I realized I had fallen asleep in my clothes, once more trapped by my memories through the night. It was Saturday and almost time for my meeting with the Haganah members at the Glickstein family's home.

I showered quickly and changed my clothing before heading out. I went without much enthusiasm, but I had to fulfill my promise to attend. The meeting, like the previous one, was friendly and pleasant. There were many members in attendance, and they were all cordial and friendly to me. Yaakov immediately kicked things off by expressing his heartfelt gratitude for the information I had shared about the British manhunt, noting that several of the Haganah had avoided arrest thanks to me.

"So tell me again why you do not want to join the Haganah?" he asked. The gazes of some of the men sharpened as they waited for my answer.

I repeated my explanation of my weariness after the war, my need to recuperate. "Besides," I added, "my long hours at the restaurant would prevent me from attending the meetings more than once a month, and I want to spend some of my free time with my girlfriend too."

"Bring her along," someone said.

"Not a chance." I shook my head. "My girlfriend's views are more extreme than yours. From an ideological perspective, I'm somewhere in between. I greatly admire your activities, but I believe that the Haganah should do more to drive out the British. We should look for ways to cooperate with the other underground organizations. We're all Jews, right? And we're all working toward the same goal of unrestricted Jewish immigration and the establishment of a Jewish national home in Israel."

The room fell silent for a few seconds, and then an elderly man with glasses stood up and introduced himself as Moshe Fingerhof. "Maybe because you're new to this land," he said, "you don't know the other underground groups like we do. The Lehi and Irgun murder the British indiscriminately and without any moral compunction. There's no difference between them and the Arabs who have killed hundreds of Jews. The only way to deal with the British and the Arabs is through diplomacy, not physical violence."

I clenched my hands into fists and fought to contain the sudden anger that swept over me. "Sir," I began, carefully measuring my every word, "your opinions must stem from the fact that you were here in Israel during this awful war. You didn't witness even an iota of the horrors I experienced. You didn't see thousands of Jews led into the forest, forced to strip naked, and executed. You didn't see your loved ones murdered before your eyes until you were left alone in this world. If you had, you would understand how unforgivable it is that the British are breaking all their promises to the Zionist movement. They are preventing the refugees who survived the horrors of this war from immigrating to Israel."

My voice had grown hoarse from intensity, but I went on, growing more fervent.

"Comparing the Lehi and Irgun fighters to Arab rioters and murderers is absurd. I may be new to this land, but I know that the Arabs don't want any Jews in Israel—"

"Sir—" the old man tried to interrupt.

"And they have attacked us indiscriminately with the purpose of wiping us out! Had the Germans won the war and occupied the Land of Israel, they would have killed you and everyone you know. Don't forget, sir, while the Arab murderers have killed and have plotted to kill innocent Jewish civilians, the activities of the Irgun and Lehi have been directed only against British soldiers, policemen, and government officials responsible for implementing the policies of the British government and the so-called White Paper, which didn't allow Jews to flee to Israel even while the Nazis slaughtered us."

I found I was really getting irritated and took a moment to collect myself before speaking again. When I did, my voice was calm again. "I'm not saying that we should join the Irgun or Lehi, but if there are those who are willing to sacrifice themselves, we should support them. Pacifism may be a nice idea, but it's impractical and dangerous in real life. The Jewish community in this country didn't suffer during the war, but they must take action on behalf of their people who did."

I stopped talking, and a heavy silence fell over the room. I could tell that my blunt words had dampened the mood, but I did not regret saying them.

"It's natural to have disagreements among us," Yaakov said in an effort to ease the tension, "and it's good for everyone to speak their mind. The most important thing for us to remember is that we are all Zionists supporting the establishment of a national home for the Jewish people in this land."

With this, the meeting adjourned. I left, not knowing if my words had had any effect on the men of the Haganah or not.

THE FOLLOWING DAY, WHEN I met Shoshana to walk her to work, she kissed me on my lips and offered me her hand. "I've had a few sessions with Brigita, the psychologist Hannah referred me to," she said. "I feel like she's really helping me. She said she'd like to meet you too. Would you mind?"

"Not at all," I said, raising my brows in surprise. This was the first I'd heard of Shoshana beginning her therapy.

"Great. I was hoping you'd say that, so I made an appointment for you next Tuesday morning at nine." She produced a note with the name of the psychologist, Brigita Shlaufer, and her address, at the edge of the Tel Arza neighborhood.

On the day of the appointment, I walked to the psychologist's building, climbed the stairs to the second floor, and knocked on the door. A diminutive woman in her sixties opened it. Her short hair was white and curly, her face was wrinkled, and her nose was broad and pudgy. The most prominent features of her face were her piercing blue-gray eyes. When she looked at me, I could feel her gaze peering deep into my mind and soul.

"Good morning, David," she said in a German accent. "I was hoping that you'd come." We sat down in her living room, her gaze still fixed on me. She offered me tea, which I politely refused, and then after a couple of moments of silence, she spoke.

"I'm very taken with Shoshana, and I'm trying to help her come to terms with her trauma. You're very special to her, so it's important for us to discuss her problems and try to help her together. Does that sound good to you?"

"Certainly," I replied. "That's what I'm here for."

"I must point out," Brigita said, "that our session is a deviation from accepted practice. In principle, a psychologist doesn't work with two halves of a couple at the same time. But in this case, I see my role not as a professional psychologist but as a friend with psychological knowledge. I'm going to be frank with you. Shoshana has asked me to share intimate details you are unaware of at this time."

I nodded, and Brigita went on, her voice growing more serious. "I know that Shoshana has told you that she witnessed the rape of her mother and other women before they were murdered, but you may not realize that Shoshana was also raped by those policemen. She also suffered terrible and prolonged sexual abuse at the hands of one of the sons of the family that adopted her after she fled the Nazis. She hasn't been able to tell you about these things, and she asked me to do it."

My throat tightened, and I could not prevent the horrible images her words brought to my mind. I sat quietly, dumbfounded. I realized Brigita was waiting on a response from me. I cleared my throat and nodded for her to continue.

"Trauma of this kind can reoccur when an individual feels trapped, helpless, and incapable of protecting herself. It's a side effect of a defense mechanism, a hypervigilance against future dangers. This is exactly what has happened to Shoshana. Her self-preservation mechanism is constantly switched on, as if the threat could resurface at any given moment, and those past experiences are never far from her mind. Shoshana has lost all faith in the world; her fundamental sense of security has been crushed, and this has given rise to feelings of alienation and disconnection. She lives in constant fear of the return of the horrors she experienced."

At that moment, I just wanted to hold Shoshana in my arms and comfort her. I felt sick at how selfish I had been. "Is there any way I can help her?" I asked.

"Yes, certainly," Brigita said. "The most important thing is to allow her to feel safe with you and to give her your full support at all times. Never try to pressure her physically. Let her initiate any physical contact between you. She has to be the one to discover the healthy and enjoyable aspects of an intimate relationship, in a safe and protected environment, with someone who cares about her and loves her. She loves you very much, you know."

"I understand," I said, "and I will follow your advice."

"Excellent," Brigita said. "I will continue to treat Shoshana, and together we will try, very carefully, to reconstruct the traumatic events, with the aim of helping her let go of the negative feelings that have built up inside of her."

"I'm impressed with you and your approach," I said. "And I am grateful for the help you are giving Shoshana."

Brigita gave me a long appraising look before speaking again. "David," she finally said, "I know that you have gone through tough times as well, and I can see that you are keeping it bottled up inside you. Shoshana told me that you were a partisan fighter and that now you want to take a break from everything. But the look in your eyes doesn't say the same. I'm guessing that you've learned to hide your emotions well."

I shrugged and smiled at her. "I've been a fighter for a very long time. Now all I want is to live without strife." Well, in a sense it was true. I didn't want strife between myself and Shoshana. Between me and the British—that was another thing entirely.

Brigita returned my smile. "You'd be a good poker player, though not if you were at the table with Brigita Shlaufer. If one day you feel that you'd like to speak openly to me about yourself, I'd be happy to oblige. Of course, it would remain between us."

I thought about it for a moment. It was true that my past still disturbed me. That was evident from the intensity of my dreams and my frequent inability to sleep because of the memories running through my mind.

I had recently begun to feel somewhat fatigued, and my mission required me to have my wits about me. Perhaps Brigita could help me learn how to "turn off" the feelings these memories provoked.

"I wouldn't be averse to meeting with you," I finally said.

"In two weeks? At the same time, here at my apartment?" she asked.

"Yes, thank you," I said. "And thank you for your work with Shoshana."

After leaving Brigita's home, I felt a slight lifting from my shoulders of a burden I hadn't known was there. As I walked down the street, however, two British officers passed by me; one scowled in my direction and muttered something to the other. The two laughed, and the weight of my responsibility to my people seemed to suddenly double.

8

"INTO BATTLE GO, THE FLAME ALIGHT"

(FROM "FEBRUARY 1946," A POEM BY
MICHAEL ESHBAL, 1946)

The year had come to an end, and 1946 was looming. Few of Jerusalem's Jews recognized New Year's Eve—or Sylvester's Day, as it was called locally—but Shoshana and I decided to celebrate the way we had in Belarus, where the New Year was welcomed with banquets and dances. We spent a romantic evening at Café Wien on Jaffa Street, not far from Café Pinsk.

Sitting at a small table, lit by a candle in the center, I felt myself sinking into Shoshana's large green eyes as I gently caressed her hand. She placed her watch on the table.

"We have to kiss at exactly midnight," she said, blushing slightly.

When midnight came, Shoshana kissed me on the lips. Desire welled up inside me as her tongue slipped into my mouth, but I remembered Brigita Shlaufer's insistence that I let Shoshana take the lead. Her kiss was long and passionate, and when she finally broke away, she gazed tenderly into my eyes and said, "I love you very much."

I longed for her to take me to her bed, but when we stopped in front of her apartment, she gave me another long kiss and said, "I had a wonderful evening. Thank you."

Despite the elegant dinner and Shoshana's company, after I went to bed that night, I couldn't sleep. Shoshana's kiss had been wonderful, but it was difficult not to want more. Shoshana was the woman I loved, the woman meant for me. I pushed the desire from my mind and turned my thoughts to other matters.

As I lay staring at the ceiling, missing Shoshana, my thoughts drifted to more existential things. Was I truly at the helm of my life and steering its course? Or had I become some kind of machine following a predetermined path? Perhaps Brigita could help me see more clearly. And with that on my mind, I drifted off to sleep.

TUESDAY CAME, AND WITH IT, breakfast with Avrum and Hannah. As usual, Avrum left the women in the kitchen and ushered me into his study.

"David," he said, "I'm so discouraged. The British are becoming increasingly hateful toward the Jews. Sergeant Perry is no longer content with simply tracking down and arresting underground members. His hatred for Jews is starting to consume him. He's saying things like 'It's a shame Hitler didn't wipe out all the Jews before the war ended.' And making sick remarks like 'All of them should be put into concentration camps, except the young women, whom we should keep for ourselves.' And it's not just him. It was wrong to believe cooperation between the Haganah and the British could work. Let's call it off."

I was happy to learn of this change in attitude, but I thought to agree too readily might seem suspicious. Instead of voicing my satisfaction, I hedged a bit.

"Avrum," I said, "while I agree with what you're saying, you're putting me in a very difficult position. I've put a lot of effort into developing a relationship with Yaakov and the Haganah."

He nodded. "You're right. I've thought about that too, and I'll try to make up for my mistake by getting you some information Yaakov can use that has nothing to do with getting along with the British."

"Great," I said. "If you hear anything that's urgent, come find me at Café Pinsk."

We went back to the kitchen and ate breakfast, and when Hannah went to the sink with the dishes, she turned to me and mouthed the word "tomorrow." I nodded my head slightly.

When I returned the next morning, Hannah opened the door with tears in her eyes. "I think about being with you all week long," she said. "Let's go back to twice a week—please? And I want us to go away together, somewhere out of the city. I can arrange an alibi with a friend."

"Hannah," I said after a short pause, "you have to remember that you're a married woman and that I have a girlfriend I care about deeply. We must keep things as they are."

"I thought I could do this at first," she responded, her words broken by sobs, "but I've fallen in love with you."

"We have two options, Hannah. We either keep things as they are or break it off completely."

Her sobs intensified. "I can't even imagine not seeing you anymore. Our relationship is the most important thing in my life."

I reassured her that I cared about her too and wanted to continue seeing her, and we went to bed. But it felt different. It wasn't fun anymore; it had become a liability. I lay there pondering how to get out of this mess without hurting Hannah too badly.

As I began my shift at Café Pinsk that evening, Avrum walked in and asked to talk to me in private. "He's a friend who needs a favor," I said to Max, who waved me off like he was shooing away a mosquito. Avrum and I stepped outside.

"My boss told me that Sergeant Perry is planning a major operation aimed at all the underground organizations, including the Haganah," Avrum said. "And Perry will be leading these raids himself. He may not be a high-ranking officer, but he's been incredibly successful. He must have informants feeding him intelligence."

"This is huge," I said. "I'll pass it on immediately. You know anything else about him?"

"He looks like something out of a Goebbels poster with his blond hair and blue eyes. Except for his ears. It looks like he's got a couple of mug handles stuck to the sides of his head."

My mind was made up. Sergeant Perry would be my next target. I'd tell Avrum that I'd passed on the information to Yaakov Dover, and Avrum would think the Haganah was responsible for the assassination. And even if he were to suspect me, he wouldn't dare say a word, since he had provided the information.

I SHOWED UP FOR MY appointment with Brigita Shlaufer as scheduled. She greeted me with a friendly smile and offered me a cup of tea. As we sipped our drinks, she asked about my life in the ghetto and with the partisans and about my relationship with my parents.

I felt somewhat reluctant to talk openly, but I managed to share a little. After a short while, she tapped the pencil she held on the notebook in her lap and leaned forward slightly.

"Your life until now has not been easy. I think outwardly you wanted to play a part in the war effort against the Germans, and the deep driving force was your desire for revenge."

I thought her conclusion rang true, even though I had left out the explicit acts of vengeance I had participated in against the Germans and their collaborators.

She paused for a moment and then asked me, "With the situation in this land today, do you feel driven to fight the British, to kill their soldiers and policemen?"

"All I want to do right now is rest for a while," I said.

She didn't say a word but fixed me with a look that clearly suggested she didn't believe me.

When I stood up to leave, I offered to pay her for the time she was devoting to Shoshana and me. She said she was simply trying to help and didn't want any payment, but Hannah had told me she was a single woman who didn't earn much money. I pulled a five-hundred-mil banknote from my pocket. "I'd feel better if I paid you," I said. She hesitated briefly before taking the money, and we scheduled another appointment for the following week.

As I walked home, I thought back on the events I had yet to tell her about.

In March 1944, with the Germans retreating westward, the Russian army was advancing and had reached the borders of Romania. By the end of June, our group of partisans could hear the thunder of Russian artillery. Focused on killing as many German soldiers as possible, by any means necessary, we didn't tackle them head-on but rather picked off straggling units as they retreated. We ended up killing close to a hundred German soldiers in this way.

The Russians liberated Minsk on July 3, 1944. We hastened to the ghetto, but all we found were ruins, along with thirteen survivors sheltered by a man named Pinchas Dubin in underground hideouts.

We had lost four men and two women in our battles with the Germans, and our group now numbered twenty-eight fighters. Almost all our loved ones had perished. We decided unanimously that we would turn our sights on the collaborators in a campaign of revenge against the Belarusians, Lithuanians, and others who had helped the Nazis massacre our people.

Our first target was a Lithuanian auxiliary battalion that had killed more than thirty thousand Jews around Minsk, but they had already fled. Instead, we moved on to the Belarusian police force that had helped the Germans patrol the ghetto. Based on the names we uncovered, we tracked down and killed thirty policemen. We also assassinated Belarusian villagers who had murdered Jews or turned them in to the Germans.

It was during this time that we learned about the Belarusian warlord Nikolai Petrov. Feared by many, he was known as Nikolai the Butcher. During the war, his mercenaries had stolen vast amounts of Jewish property, but he hadn't been afraid to get his own hands dirty, joining raids and personally killing entire Jewish families.

Our group of partisans had grown weary in recent days. When Alec and I brought up the subject of Nikolai Petrov, the men agreed to do it, but several said this would be their last mission. Others joined in, and all at once, I realized that I, too, was ready for my own personal war to be over.

Alec didn't say much during the discussion that followed. He remained silent when we decided that this monster would be the target of our final operation. He didn't protest and agreed that if successful, we would divide the spoils among all of us evenly and go our separate ways, in an effort to finally begin our lives again.

Alec made a deal with Nikolai's brother-in-law to sell them a large stockpile of weapons and ammunition that we had taken from the German army. The arrangement was to bring the arms to Nikolai's estate and make a deal. Nikolai lived in a luxurious house with expensive furniture, and even in this time of famine, we were told he had a private chef.

With a well-placed bribe, we acquired vital information about the layout of his property and the positions of the armed security guards who protected it. When it was time to meet, Alec and three other partisans made their way to the gate with bags containing the promised armaments. The rest of our group waited nearby. When the four partisans reached the gate, they struck up a conversation with the guard and two individuals who had arrived to usher them in.

While they were talking, Alec and his men drew knives and killed the three men with barely a struggle. They signaled to us, and we joined them, slipping through the gate. Our partisans went methodically to the positions of each guard, picking them off one by one. Alec and I headed for Nikolai's residential wing, killing two guards along the way.

We burst into Nikolai's dining room, where he was having dinner. I took out the head of his security detail with a burst from my machine gun and then turned to Nikolai.

"I know where your vault is," I said. "If you don't open it, I promise you a slow and torturous death."

Nikolai was a bastard, but he wasn't a fool. He looked at me and Alec. "Come with me," he said. Alec and I walked right behind him, with my gun stuck in his back. He led us to an adjacent room, moved a cabinet aside, and opened the vault door.

I knew that Nikolai had robbed and murdered extensively, yet I was stunned to see the vast contents of his vault: jewelry, diamonds, banknotes—primarily US dollars and Swiss francs—and gold coins. As we stared at the pile of loot, Nikolai made his move—he grabbed the barrel of the machine gun I held and tried to wrestle it from my hands. Alec instantly shot him dead.

Our crew had managed to take out all the guards, but we'd lost two men during the assault. The survivors assembled in the dining room, and I divided up the treasure. Alec was guarding the hallway, so I took his share for him.

When we left the estate, I turned to my men, knowing what I was about to say wouldn't be easy. "My brothers," I began, "our mission is complete, and it's time to go our own ways. I plan to leave this cursed land and go live in Jerusalem to help our brothers and sisters there build an independent Jewish state. It's been an honor and a privilege to serve alongside all of you. I hope we meet again under happier circumstances."

We buried our two dead and prayed for their souls. A quick embrace brought the years we had fought together to an end, and our group began to disperse.

Alec came over to me and put his hand on my shoulder. "I want to immigrate to Israel too, but I have unfinished business here. If I make it, I will look for you."

I understood what he meant—he hadn't finished exacting his revenge. I wished him luck, and we embraced. "I hope to see you in Israel," I said.

He walked a few steps and then stopped, looked back over one shoulder, and saluted me. Something tightened in my chest. Pushing away the sentimental reaction, I nevertheless smiled and returned his salute, and then I quickly turned away to face my next task.

I walked over to Misha, Leah's brother. He sat against the wall, brooding, stroking the barrel of his rifle. He had no doubt overheard my conversation with Alec.

"Do you want to join me?" I asked.

Misha remained silent and then finally began to speak, still staring down at his gun. "David, before we part ways, there is something that has troubled me for a long time that I must get off of my chest." He paused, and then his blue eyes flashed up at me. "I'm angry that you didn't protect Leah."

I met his gaze without flinching. Of course, I had suspected he felt this way, but it was hard to hear it spoken aloud, since I blamed myself for Leah's death. His next words seemed to echo my thoughts and surprised me.

"I don't blame you for her death," he went on, "but you were there, and you survived. Leah was the only family I had left. While we were fighting the Nazis, I could push it all down, but now I want you to know that I don't ever want to see you again."

I nodded, unable to speak for a moment. "I wish you luck" was all that I could manage to say. I had never told anyone exactly what happened when Leah was killed, and to do so at that moment would have sounded like an excuse and probably made matters worse. He didn't respond, simply stood and walked away.

With the fighting over, the Russians occupied Minsk, and the Communist regime of the Soviet Union regained control over the region. They bulldozed all signs of Jewish life in the city, including the synagogues and rabbinical seminaries. I wanted to get out of there, and the sooner the better, but before I could make my way to Israel through Western Europe, I had to wait until the Germans were completely defeated. Leaving the war behind would mean leaving everything I had ever known behind as well, but I had a new goal, and I was eager to start working toward it.

Getting to Israel was not easy. I planned to make my way through Poland to Germany's displaced persons camps. I had heard that the Jewish community in Israel was trying to bring Jews from these camps to their ancestral homeland, despite the objections of the British.

I reached Lublin, Poland, in August 1944, just weeks after the

Russians had invaded. All I carried was a knapsack filled with my share of the spoils from Nikolai's vault, a commando knife, and the Russian pistol my father had given me on the day we'd said goodbye. It was the only tangible memento I had from him.

I was in much better physical and mental condition than most of the Jews I encountered on the way to Poland. Those poor Jews, survivors of death camps, most of whom had lost their entire families, were stricken with hunger and illness, and their spirits were shattered. Society—the Germans' perversion of it, at least—had completely broken down, and brigands were everywhere. But they left me alone, perhaps preferring easier targets. Once in the city, I used some of my newfound wealth to rent an apartment with three young Jewish men.

In January 1945, the Russian army reached Krakow. My three roommates and I left Lublin and made our way to that city, where we rented another apartment together. One day, I noticed a woman wrapped in a shabby blue coat, standing on the street and crying. She looked about forty years old and was short and thin, with brown hair that was starting to gray.

"Can I help you?" I asked her in Russian.

She sobbed louder. "No one will help me," she said in broken Russian. "I'm a Jew."

"I'm a Jew too. My name is David," I said in Yiddish. Her eyes widened. An able-bodied, well-nourished, and well-dressed Jew was not a common sight.

"I'm Nelka," she said. "I returned here just a few days ago, after spending several months at the Auschwitz death camp. When the Germans fled, they took with them any Jews still alive, with the intention of killing them elsewhere. I'm one of the very few who managed to escape. My husband and two children were murdered in the gas chambers." Her face contorted for a moment, and I looked away. Her story was one I had heard many times before. She regained her composure and went on, her voice trembling.

"We had a beautiful apartment here in Krakow before the war. When I went to the apartment yesterday, a young Polish couple was living there. I told them that the apartment used to be mine and asked if I could spend a few nights there, as I was homeless." Her lower lip began to quiver. "The woman yelled at me, 'Beat it, dirty Jew!' Her husband said it was a shame the Germans didn't kill us all; then he said he was going to get an ax to kill me himself."

I asked her to point out the apartment to me.

"What for?" she asked.

"Maybe I can do something to help you," I said.

She hesitated for a moment and said, "You look like a strong young man. Perhaps they'll have more respect for you than for a weeping Jewish woman."

She showed me her building and pointed out her apartment, which faced the street. I convinced her to come with me to my apartment to get warm. There I introduced her to my roommates and told her to wait for my return.

I walked back to the building Nelka had shown me and knocked on the door of her apartment. "Do you understand Russian?" I asked the man who answered.

"Yes," he said, "but I have no use for Russians. I suggest you get out of here before I beat you bloody."

"This apartment belongs to Jews who lived here before the war," I began, and as he picked up an ax from behind the door, I kicked him in the knee. He crumpled to the floor.

Before he could get up, I drew my pistol and fired at him twice. He fell dead on the floor. His wife came running from the kitchen with a big knife, shouting hysterically, "I'll kill you, filthy Jew!" I shot her too.

I stared down at the two, feeling little, except perhaps a sense of justice for Nelka and others like her. After a moment, I roused and went through the man's pockets. I found a set of keys and left the apartment, locking the door behind me.

As I walked down the stairs, I thought about what I would do with the two dead bodies. I headed around the back of the building and, surveying the backyard, decided I could bury them there. I planned to come back that night with a shovel.

When I returned to my apartment, Nelka ran to me as soon as I walked in the door. "Where have you been?" she asked, her eyes wide with fright.

"I had a long talk with the couple who chased you away," I said. "I told them you have connections with the police and that they'll be showing up there tomorrow to force them out. It seemed to scare them, so I offered to pay for their move if they left willingly. They agreed and asked for two days to get packed. You can stay with us until then."

Nelka's face lit up, and she hugged me. "It's a miracle, and you are a real angel! I hope I can repay you one day. After all I've been through, I didn't think I'd ever meet someone like you."

That night, I returned to Nelka's apartment with a shovel to bury the bodies, but when I approached the building, I spotted a Russian-made ZIS truck parked on the street and changed my mind. During my three years as a partisan, I had taught myself to drive using stolen German vehicles and had become an expert at hot-wiring them.

I opened the truck's door and leaned under the steering wheel to cut and strip the wires. In a matter of moments, I got the vehicle running. I moved the truck to the front of the building and went up to Nelka's apartment. I wrapped each of the corpses in a rug, tied them with rope, and loaded them into the truck. I also grabbed four large bricks from the courtyard.

From there, I drove to the Vistula River. It was late at night, and the riverbank was deserted. I stuffed two heavy bricks into each roll of carpet and threw the bodies into the river. Then I drove back to Nelka's neighborhood, parked the truck a few blocks from her apartment, let myself back into her place, and cleaned up the bloodstains. I got home just in time to go to bed for an hour.

When I got up in the morning, Nelka served me a breakfast of bread and margarine. She was giddy with anticipation. After she'd spent another day with us, I offered to escort her back to her old home.

When she stepped inside, there were tears in her eyes. After checking every room, she landed in the kitchen. "Apparently, the couple living here weren't such bad people after all," she said. "Look how much food they left for me. Thank you so much for convincing them to leave." Then she added, "I have an idea. Why don't you and your friends move in with me? This is a much larger and more comfortable place than the one you're living in now, and you'd save on rent. I'll cook for you too."

"That would be wonderful," I said. "And if someone asks about the couple who used to live here, just say you paid them to move out."

This was the beginning of a quiet and peaceful period in my life. Nelka was a wonderful cook, somehow managing to make the powdered eggs and turnips that we subsisted on palatable. But I had no intention of staying in Poland or even in Europe. I wanted to leave this cursed continent as soon as I could and begin again in Jerusalem.

I MET BRIGITA FOR MY second session two weeks later, over another cup of tea. She asked me to tell her about my experiences following the Russians' recapture of Minsk, and I decided to answer her in detail. She listened without saying a word, but I could see the astonishment on her face.

"I'm troubled by all the killing," she said. "You grew up in a warm home, with loving parents, and all of a sudden you and your family were treated like animals, hunted and persecuted by the Germans. Survival in a world like that requires that you fight back. The barbarism of the Germans caused many to lose all semblance of humanity and morality."

I didn't respond, and she continued. "You perceived your vengeance as justice for your loved ones, and meting out that justice diminished the intensity of the anger and frustration you felt as a result of your helplessness. You proved to yourself and to the Germans that you could rain down pain and suffering on them just as they had done to the people you cherished. The question is, do you want to continue living this way? Vengeance can become an obsession, a way of life. Are you still fighting?"

"All I want to do these days is rest," I said.

I could tell from the look on her face that she wasn't convinced. After a few moments of thought, she said, "The British have no desire to kill us merely for being Jews. They want to keep control, and so they oppose a national home for the Jewish people and they arrest those who interfere with their regime. But this is nothing like what happened under the Nazis. You must have heard about that sniper who injured three British soldiers at the Schneller Barracks a few weeks ago. I'm not a pacifist, and I can understand the need to fight one's enemies, but we have to preserve our morality too.

"I adamantly oppose that sniper's actions, because it's clear to me that those three soldiers were injured only because they happened to be there, not because they did something that warranted the attacks upon them. On the other hand, this Officer Greene who was recently killed on the street had a reputation for cruelty against the underground. If you do join the underground and want to live with your conscience, my advice to you is to target only those who harm Jews and to kill only when it is an operational necessity."

Her powers of perception were unnerving. For a moment,

I imagined she could hear exactly what I was thinking and see what I had done in the past.

"Thank you for your advice," I said in as calm a voice as I could muster. "I'll do some thinking, and I'll be in touch with you again soon."

As I walked home, I thought about what she had said. Anyone who hadn't lived through the hell that my friends and I had endured would have a hard time understanding our feelings. But Brigita seemed unusually wise, and I decided to take her advice and be even more discriminating with my targets. Fortunately, Sergeant Perry fit her rules perfectly. But I had yet to locate him and was feeling frustrated. I mulled over my options.

It hardly ever snowed in Jerusalem, but on February 17, 1946, snow blanketed the city, covering the roads, trees, and rooftops in thick white sheets and forcing the schools to close, much to the delight of the children. I went to the Cohens' store that day, where I ran into a smartly dressed, auburn-haired woman. She didn't have a particularly pretty face, but her provocative figure was most distracting.

After the woman had finished packing her shopping bag, Mr. Cohen said in a fatherly tone, "Be careful not to slip on your way home, Sarah."

I smiled at her. "He must like you," I said. "Mr. Cohen has never shown the slightest bit of concern for my safety." She looked right through me and left the store.

"Hey, Don Juan!" Mrs. Cohen barked. "You flirt with every woman you meet in here, but I suggest you leave her alone. Her boyfriend is a big shot in the CID, and you may get more than you bargained for."

I took a second to realize what she was saying, but once

it clicked, I mumbled an excuse about leaving the heater on and raced out the door with my shopping basket still on the counter. When I got down the front steps, I saw Sarah strolling up Zephaniah Street.

I followed at a quick pace but kept some distance so she wouldn't notice me. She turned left onto Amos Street, and I watched her go into a building about one hundred yards from the corner. I crossed the street and then stopped, making a show of shuffling through my wallet while actually keeping an eye on her building. After a few minutes, I saw Sarah open the curtains of one of the windows on the second floor.

My heart filled with joy. I had just been given a gift from heaven. Finally, I had gotten a break. I could now start planning my next course of action.

9

"ON RED DAYS OF
RIOTS AND BLOOD"

(FROM "UNKNOWN SOLDIERS," A POEM BY
AVRAHAM STERN, 1932)

When I got to work the next day, I pulled Max aside.
"I'm really sorry, but I'm feeling sick. I'll work today since it's last minute, but I think I need to take the next few days off."

"Damn, a coward and lazy too," Max muttered. "Okay, then, go home early, but you can only have two days."

"Thank you," I said.

When I told Shoshana I wouldn't be at work for a couple days, she immediately grew concerned.

"I'll come take care of you when I get off work. I'll bring you some food."

"You know how much I enjoy your company, but I need some time to myself," I replied. "I'm just feeling run-down, because I'm not getting enough sleep—my nights are haunted by bad memories."

"I totally understand," Shoshana said, glancing away. "The same thing happens to me at least a few times a week."

I bent and kissed her on the forehead. "I'll talk to you later," I promised.

"Get some rest," she said with a smile, then moved to a table full of customers.

My plan over the next two days was to study Sergeant Perry's routine and scout out the area around Sarah's apartment and the neighboring buildings. The next morning, I went to Amos Street, looking for a place where I could keep watch without drawing any attention to myself.

It was a relatively warm winter day, and the sun was shining. On my third pass around the block, I noticed an elderly man soaking up the sun on the second-floor balcony of a building almost directly across from Sarah's apartment.

"Good for you, finding time to sit back and enjoy the warm sun," I called up to him.

"Find the time?" he said. "I'm a pensioner, so I have nothing but time."

"I'm a new immigrant who's trying to get to know Jerusalem."

"Instead of shouting to one another, why don't you come up and join me? We can have some tea and cookies and talk a little."

"Gladly," I said, and I climbed the stairs to the second floor. The man was waiting for me in his open doorway.

"Baruch," he said, holding out his hand.

"David," I responded, and we shook hands.

Baruch appeared to be in his late sixties. He was a tall yet stocky man, with a bald head and a wrinkled face. He ushered me into his kitchen, and I watched in silence as he stuffed leaves from a package of Wissotzky tea into a silver tea strainer and then retrieved a steaming kettle. He poured the boiling water into two glasses, dipping the tea strainer back and forth into both. Then he reached into a cupboard for a packet of Froumine cookies and arranged them on a plate.

"Let's sit on the balcony and enjoy our tea in the sun, before it disappears behind those clouds," he said.

I followed him to the balcony and glanced over at Sarah's building. Baruch's apartment was at an angle from hers, but I could see it well enough. He kicked off the conversation by telling me that his wife had died a year earlier, and he was lonely. From time to time, I nodded or hummed in agreement, keeping an eye on Sarah's apartment all the while.

"You've got to have hobbies when you're alone," Baruch continued. "I collect stamps and play chess, checkers, cards, mostly rummy. Now and then, I get together with a couple of old friends, and we play. Do you like those kinds of games?"

Games had never interested me much, but I was certainly interested in sitting on Baruch's balcony. "I play checkers," I said.

"Great," Baruch exclaimed, jumping up from his chair. "Don't be upset if you lose. You should know that I'm an excellent player."

I realized there was little chance of Perry showing up in the morning—he was far more likely to come for an evening rendezvous. "I'm sorry, I hadn't expected to meet you," I said. "I actually have some errands to run. Could we have a game this evening, say around six o'clock?"

"Okay," Baruch responded, clearly disappointed.

When I returned that evening, he welcomed me warmly, and we sat down right away to play checkers. I couldn't win a single game. Not that I cared much, but his constant gloating got on my nerves. I was starting to think it would be better to let Perry live than continue playing checkers with this elderly man.

"Baruch, how about we give the checkers a break and you teach me rummy?" I said. "I've always wanted to learn."

"Gladly," Baruch said. "But you should know that I'm going to beat you at that every time too."

Baruch began teaching me the game, though I only half listened while keeping one eye on Sarah's apartment. Just before nine o'clock, I saw a tall, well-built man approaching her building. A closer look revealed his unusually large ears—just the thing that Avrum and Hannah had told me to look out for. "Who's that man?" I asked Baruch, pointing at the figure. "He looks familiar, but I can't place him."

"I hope, for your sake, that you're confusing him with someone else you know," Baruch said. "He has a lover in that building. He visits her twice a week, always on Tuesdays and Thursdays, always at this time, and he leaves in the early hours of the morning. It's disgusting, the immorality of that generation."

I was tired, and rummy was as boring as I'd feared. I barely managed to finish the first game before yawning and telling Baruch that I had a long and busy day ahead of me. I promised to come see him again the following Thursday.

The best time to assassinate Perry would be when he was leaving Sarah's apartment, when there would be fewer people on the street than in the evening. To allow myself sufficient time to prepare, I decided to carry out my mission in the early hours of the following Friday morning, but I would need to do some reconnaissance tonight. If what Baruch had said was correct, Perry would still be sleepy after waking up from a night of lovemaking.

Despite my impatience, I wanted to get a little sleep, so I got into bed as soon as I returned to my apartment. I awoke at four in the morning and walked to Amos Street, where I sat down on a low stone wall about two buildings away from Sarah's building. I took out a pack of Matossian cigarettes and lit one. I hated the taste but needed an excuse for lingering outside.

The street remained deserted, and for the first half hour, only a single car went by; it was a British army jeep, and without warning, I found myself lost again in the past, this time in memories of my journey to Israel.

That winter in Krakow was hard, but it gave us time to begin recovering from the trauma of the war. Nelka's eyes lost some of their fear, and the beauty began to return to her face as we fattened up on the black-market food I bought with Nikolai's cash. Nevertheless, I would sometimes hear her sobbing at night as she mourned her husband and children and all the others who had been lost.

In late April 1945, the Russians occupied Berlin, Hitler committed suicide, and Germany surrendered unconditionally. One day, after breakfast, I was sitting alone with Nelka.

"I plan to leave this place," I told her. "I intend to make my way to southern Italy, where I hope to find a ship to Israel. My friends have plans to leave Krakow too. What do you want to do?"

"David, you are a special person," Nelka said. "You are tough but, at the same time, caring and kind. I have nothing keeping me here in Poland. My entire family was murdered, and I don't like the Communist regime. I've never been a Zionist, but after experiencing the terrible anti-Semitism here, I think I want to go to Israel too. I want to live where I don't have to hide the fact that I'm Jewish. If you would consider letting me accompany you, I'd be very happy."

So Nelka sold her apartment, and I bribed our way across the border from Poland to Germany. It gave me a grim satisfaction to see the devastation left by the Allies' air raids on the German cities. Watching the German families rummage through the rubble of their homes made me feel that justice had been done, at least in a small way. When any hint of compassion arose within me—usually when I saw children—I imagined they were the children and families of the soldiers who had persecuted and killed my family and friends; then any sympathy I might have felt ebbed away.

We made our way to Italy on trains and buses, occasionally

hitching rides on American military vehicles, and then we headed south to the large port city of Napoli. On the Sabbath, I went to the synagogue in the city. The handful of Jews in attendance welcomed me warmly, and I talked with them after the service. Although they spoke very little Hebrew and none of them knew Russian, they had no trouble understanding what I sought. Several suggested I try my luck in the city of Bari, where there were several Jewish refugee camps.

Nelka and I followed their advice, and as soon as we reached Bari, we learned that there was a ship in port bound for Israel. We made our way straight to the port and met a man running around and barking orders to the people on the dock. I addressed him in Hebrew and asked if I could make the trip with them.

"Who are you?" he asked suspiciously.

"I'm a Jew from Minsk, Belarus," I said. "I was a partisan. I am a Zionist, and I want to immigrate to Israel."

He checked to see if I spoke Yiddish and asked me a few more questions. Once he was convinced I wasn't a British agent, he said, "The voyage has been arranged by the Mossad LeAliyah Bet, the organization that smuggles Jews into Israel. They're getting clandestine help from Jewish soldiers in the British army, like me. You'll have to speak to the Mossad—they decide who gets on the ship. This one carries only seventy or eighty people, and there are more than two hundred trying to get on board. But maybe you'll get lucky."

"Thanks for your help," I said and handed him two packs of cigarettes as appreciation. "Any advice on how I can improve my chances?"

The man looked at me and smiled. "The Mossad is made up of people from all sorts of political movements in Israel. When you talk to them, you'll soon learn that everything is a matter of party affiliation. Go look for a man named Shmerl, and tell him you used to be a member of the Gordonia movement in Minsk. That may assure you a place on the ship."

I did as he suggested and, sure enough, got berths for myself and Nelka, who I presented as my aunt. At three in the morning on August 27, 1945, we set sail from the port of Bari.

Originally christened *Nettuno*, the ship was purchased by the Mossad and renamed *Natan*. It was a wooden cargo ship, less than one hundred feet long, with an Italian crew. There were seventy-three Jewish refugees on board. The commander was a gentleman from the Mossad named Uri. The voyage took a week. Thanks to the soldiers who'd taken supplies from the British army's warehouses, we had enough food, but the ship was overcrowded, and the journey was uncomfortable. We landed on the Caesarea beach, and from there, we arrived in Jerusalem.

Upon arriving in Israel, I knew that the second part of my life as a fighter was just beginning. I had a new mission, a new goal—and my decision to help reestablish the homeland of the Jewish people gave me a renewed purpose in life.

THE MEMORIES OF MY JOURNEY to Israel faded as I waited to strike at one of the new enemies of my people.

The sun was about to come up when I saw Perry emerge from the building's stairwell. I looked at my watch—4:55 a.m. Perfect. The time of day when every self-respecting resident of Jerusalem was sound asleep, which meant no witnesses.

Perry turned and headed toward Geula Street, in the opposite direction from where I sat. I considered following him, but as a British policeman, he had the right to stop and question me or even shoot me if I tried to flee. I had seen and learned enough.

Once Perry turned the corner, I cautiously went into Sarah's building to have a quick look around the stairwell. Inside,

I found an alcove where I could conceal myself as I waited for him to come down the stairs. There was a light fixture overhead, and I made a mental note to take out the light when I settled in to wait for him.

Exhausted from my lack of sleep and feeling somehow edgy and unsettled, I went to see Hannah. Later, as we lay in bed, she mentioned that I had made quite an impression on Brigita Shlaufer. Concerned, I asked what she had said.

"Nothing much," Hannah replied. "Just that she enjoys her talks with you."

After leaving Hannah's apartment, I went to Café Pinsk and told Max I was feeling better. Max responded with a growl, but Shoshana smiled at me happily. We had another week of walking together to work, holding hands, talking about anything and everything. I treasured those moments with her; they were the closest I had felt to being at peace since before the war.

On the following Wednesday, I made one final inspection of Amos Street and spotted Perry leaving Sarah's building at 5:05 a.m. On Thursday afternoon, I stopped by the pharmacy to buy sleeping pills, and later that evening, I went to visit Baruch.

He brought out his deck of cards and asked me whether I'd like to play in the living room or on the balcony. I pretended to think for a moment before choosing the balcony. We began to play rummy.

I saw Sergeant Perry's tall figure enter the building across the street at exactly nine o'clock. I waited for about half an hour and then asked Baruch to make me another cup of tea. Baruch poured another for himself too and brought the tea out to the balcony.

When he went back in to get some cookies, I dropped a sleeping tablet into his cup to make sure he wouldn't have any trouble sleeping that night. I said farewell to Baruch a little later, promising to return again the following week, if only to keep up appearances. He bid me farewell with a deep yawn.

I went back to my apartment to sleep for a few hours before being awakened by the alarm at four. I dressed, washed my face, and made my way to Amos Street. I stepped into the stairwell of Sarah's building, hid in the alcove, and used a piece of cloth from my pocket to unscrew the scorching light bulb above me.

About half an hour later, I heard voices from the floor above, followed by the sound of a door closing and a lock turning. Perry descended at a quick pace, and when he reached the bottom and strode past me, I launched myself at him from behind, using the rear sentry takedown technique I had mastered as a partisan. Less than two minutes after emerging from Sarah's apartment, Perry had become a mere statistic, who would no longer trouble the underground.

After dumping his body, I went back to my apartment and slept for a few hours. I woke again at noon, feeling relaxed, and soon left to meet up with Shoshana for our walk to the restaurant.

Over the following days, the British increased their military presence in Jerusalem. I was stopped and questioned several times by British soldiers who eyed me suspiciously, but all my papers were in order.

On Monday, three days after I had killed Perry, I went to see Hannah. But we didn't head straight to bed this time. Instead, we sat in the kitchen drinking coffee. Hannah asked me if I had heard about the assassination.

"I heard something about the murder of a British policeman," I said, "but I didn't think anything of it."

"Surely, you must remember him," Hannah said, clearly surprised. "I told you my friend Sarah had a boyfriend. He was the man murdered!"

"Oh, really. How is she doing?"

"She's upset but not for the reason you'd hope. She wants Avrum to introduce her to another policeman. Now that John's dead, she'll have to go back to work, and that's the last thing she wants."

AFTER I LEFT, I STOPPED at a barber near Hannah's apartment for a haircut. The barber was busy, and I didn't really want to wait, but he told me to hang around for just a little longer.

"I'll be done with this gentleman in ten minutes," he said. "Sit here and read the papers in the meantime."

Resting on the table was a pile of newspapers and magazines, all at least a month old. With nothing else to do, I began browsing through the stack and came across a weekly magazine called *Close and Far*, a publication Holocaust survivors and refugees were using to locate relatives in Israel. It occurred to me that I should have known or imagined that something like this existed. I found a relatively recent issue and began flipping through the pages.

I felt a surge of sudden joy when I spotted a small advertisement that read: *Alec Rozonovsky from Minsk is looking for David Gabinsky from Minsk. If anyone knows of his whereabouts, please contact the Jewish Agency's Bureau for Missing Relatives in Jerusalem on King George Street, Room No. 5.*

I tore out the page, sprinted out of the barber shop, and hurried to the Jewish Agency building. The line outside Room 5 was long, and I waited impatiently for my turn. There were only two clerks in the room. Finally, I was able to approach one and introduce myself.

"Wait just a minute," she said and began looking through the files that were in the cabinet next to her. It took her about a minute to find the right one, and she jotted down Alec's address on a piece of paper. I was surprised to discover that Alec was living on Ezra Street in the Bukharan Quarter, just a few minutes' walk from my apartment. I hurried to the address on Ezra Street and knocked on Alec's door, but no one answered.

I left a note on the door: *Welcome to Israel! I saw your ad. You can find me at Café Pinsk on HaHistadrut Street. I work there as a waiter most days of the week, from 1 p.m. until 11 p.m. David G.*

Alec showed up at the restaurant that same evening, and we greeted one another with quiet exuberance. I had feared I would never see my friend again. We embraced one another, and then I introduced him to Shoshana.

"I'll pay for my friend's dinner," I told Max.

"Your friend can eat on the house," Max responded sternly, "but perhaps you should get to work instead of standing around chatting."

I winked at Alec. "You heard the boss. I'll be done in an hour. Sit here and enjoy your dinner."

After my shift was over, Alec joined me and Shoshana on our walk home. We told him bits and pieces of our lives since coming to Jerusalem, and I asked him what he'd been doing since we'd parted.

"Our raid on Nikolai drove me to hunt down others like him," Alec said. "I figured I'd be able to take revenge on those who plundered our people and also secure my financial future. I was joined by four former partisans, all of them Jews. We robbed and killed Nazi collaborators, and I even found a Jewish man who helped us transfer our spoils to a Swiss bank. You could say I'm a wealthy man. But as you know, I've never been interested in money for its own sake. So a couple months ago, I decided to come here. And although I don't need to work, I found a job at the Berman Bakery in Mea She'arim. I work the night shift there four days a week."

When we got to the corner of Ezekiel and Zephaniah streets, Shoshana and I said goodnight to Alec. "I'll come to visit you on Saturday morning," I said, "sometime around nine."

Shoshana didn't say anything as I walked her home, but I felt the need to explain my relationship with Alec. "Alec and I were brothers-in-arms and very close friends during the war. We were willing to do anything for one another."

She nodded. "I understand. War seems to create a bond of brotherhood between men."

When we reached her building, we hugged. "I don't want to say goodnight yet," she said. "I feel like I want to be with you. Take me home with you."

I silently took her hand in mine, and we walked to my apartment.

"Let's continue the hug we broke off," Shoshana said as we went inside and took off our coats. She wrapped her arms around me, bringing her lips to mine. I felt overcome with desire, but again I heard Brigita Shlaufer cautioning me to let Shoshana make the first move.

Shoshana pulled me down on the low settee in the small living area. She removed her sweater, helped me out of my own shirt, and then took off her bra. She wrapped her arms around me, and when she pressed her bare chest against mine, I was in ecstasy. I held her tightly, and after a few minutes of passionate kissing, she looked up at me lovingly.

"I love you, David, and I feel safe with you. I hope this has shown you, a little, how much I want to give myself to you."

She began to dress, and I realized this was the furthest we would go that night. She kissed me again and left the apartment.

Although I felt frustrated, as any man would, I was nevertheless encouraged by the progress in our relationship. Brigita's sessions were truly helping her find a way past her trauma.

OVER THE NEXT FEW WEEKS, I took some time off from my after-hours activities, but I still thought occasionally about new targets. The Irgun and Lehi were pressing ahead with their attacks on the British. On February 25, as part of a coordinated operation with the Haganah and Irgun, a group of Lehi fighters infiltrated a British airfield near the village of Kfar Sirkin and blew up eight aircraft. That same day, the Irgun launched an assault on Lod Airport, blowing up another eleven British planes.

These attacks made me feel proud of my Jewish counterparts, and I resolved to continue playing my part. I would track down and eliminate policemen and British soldiers who were ruthless, cruel, and trying to prevent the creation of a Jewish state.

On Saturday, I went to visit Alec. He was waiting for me with a bottle of vodka instead of the tea and cookies typically offered at the other homes I visited in Jerusalem. We filled our glasses and raised a toast to life.

I briefly told him about Krakow—and Nelka—and our journey to Israel. And then I said, "There's more. I trust you completely, but I must emphasize that this has to remain between us."

"Of course."

"Like you, I wasn't done fighting on behalf of the Jewish people. I considered joining one of the underground organizations, but their internal security is terrible. Instead, after I got here, I struck out on my own, and I've been assassinating the British soldiers and policemen who hunt down members of the resistance."

"You always were a fighter," Alec said in admiration. "Do you need any help?"

"Of course," I said. "But you must be careful. There are spies everywhere. I haven't told anyone about this, not even my girlfriend."

Alec nodded.

"We should visit together more often," I said. "And I think you should meet the people I spend time with." I told him about Hannah and Avrum. "If you're free this Tuesday, I'll ask Hannah and Avrum to invite you to breakfast."

"I'll try to take Monday night off; otherwise, I'll have to come straight from my shift."

"That's the other thing I wanted to discuss with you," I said. "Perhaps you should come work at Café Pinsk. Max has been looking for another waiter for a month now. The hours at the restaurant are easier, and it'll allow us to spend time together."

He agreed to think about working at Café Pinsk. I left his apartment, feeling happy that my old friend was in Jerusalem, ready to join me in this new fight for independence.

The following Monday morning, at Hannah's, I told her about my reunion with Alec.

"Bring him along for breakfast next time," she said. "I'll prepare an extra plate."

"Don't you think you should ask Avrum first?" I asked.

"I'll ask him. But I have no doubt that Avrum will be happy to have your friend join us." She laughed. "I think Avrum likes you as much as I do."

Alec showed up at my apartment the following morning, and we walked with Shoshana to Avrum and Hannah's place. As usual, Avrum gestured for me to join him in his study.

"David, I'm sick of working for the police. The place is rife with anti-Semitism, and if it weren't for my boss, I would have left already. My boss secretly supports the struggle for unrestricted Jewish immigration. He told me, in absolute confidence, that his grandmother was Jewish. And do you know what else he said?"

"He wants to help us?"

"I certainly couldn't ask him that, but he told me a lot. You know that CID officer who was murdered a few days ago? Apparently, now his superior officer is on the rampage. He's a particularly bigoted inspector by the name of Jeffries, and the CID has given him a special budget to create a unit of six senior investigators who will gather intelligence about the resistance. My boss was shocked that they'd give so much power to a man who has so much hate for Jews—especially after so many of us volunteered to serve in the British army during the war."

"Calm down," I said. "And don't even think about quitting the police. Use your position to get more information about this Inspector Jeffries. Any bit of information could be useful. I'll pass the information to Yaakov, and I'm sure they'll put it to good use.

"You're right," he said after a moment. "But make sure that Yaakov has no idea where the information is coming from."

With that, we returned to the kitchen. Shoshana, Hannah, and Alec were talking about a ship carrying illegal immigrants that had been waylaid by the British navy off the coast, not far from the city of Netanya.

"Sometimes the British seem just as bad as the Germans," Alec said.

To my surprise, Hannah, who usually refrained from political discussions and was in favor of good ties with the British, adamantly agreed. "Your friend is right, David. Preventing these poor refugees from coming here is practically the same as killing them."

I didn't want to upset Avrum, whose mental state regarding the British he had admired so much must have been precarious at that moment. Instead, I changed the subject by complimenting Hannah on the delicious omelet she had made.

After the meal, Shoshana, Alec, and I walked together to Café Pinsk. When we arrived, I told Max that Alec wanted to quit his job and be one of our waiters.

"I'm willing to take you on a trial basis," Max said with his usual unsmiling growl. "Your friend may be a coward, but he's improving as a waiter. I hope to see the same from you."

I had already told Alec about Max's moods, so he put on his most captivating smile. "Thank you for the opportunity. I will do my best, and I hope I won't disappoint you."

When our shift was over, Shoshana and I walked home together. When we reached Kerem Avraham, Shoshana took my hand and asked if she could come with me to my apartment.

I was afraid the night would once again end with me sleeping alone, but at the same time, the fact she was willing to try meant a great deal. I silently reminded myself of the advice Brigita had given me.

We walked to my apartment with our arms around one another, and once inside, Shoshana led me to the couch and we sank down on it together. She pressed herself against me and put her lips on mine. After a few minutes of passionate kissing and intimate touching, she undressed and started to undress me too. I stopped her and, picking her up in my arms, carried her to my bed, where, for the first time, we made beautiful love.

Afterward, as we lay wrapped in each other's arms, breathless and trembling, I whispered, "I love you," my lips against her neck.

She pressed her body against mine and kissed me again.

"Thank you for your patience," she said. "It felt wonderful with you, and I love you."

We lay together for a long time, dozing and waking, until she whispered that she had to go. I wanted to walk her home, but she told me to go back to sleep. I watched her dress, and then she blew me a kiss and closed the door softly behind her.

I didn't fall asleep right away, and when I did eventually drop off, I had a strange dream. I saw myself lying helpless on Hannah's bed, my body limp. Hannah lay next to me with an intense expression on her face, her brown eyes fixed on mine.

Brigita Shlaufer stood next to the bed. She said to Hannah in a stern voice, "This young man's body belongs to you—take him!" Hannah's expression changed to one of satisfaction, and she wrapped me in her arms.

I woke up with a start, and at that moment I knew Hannah and I could no longer be lovers. That chapter had ended, and a new one was beginning.

10

"MANNING THE BARRICADES, WE WILL MEET"

(FROM "MANNING THE BARRICADES," A POEM BY
MICHAEL ESHBAL, 1946)

The next morning, I went to visit Hannah with a sense of dread in my stomach. I was relieved when she offered me coffee and cookies instead of pulling me straight into the bedroom.

"It was so nice to meet your friend," she said as we sat at the table. "Not only is he handsome, but he's smart and sweet too. It's amazing he doesn't have a girlfriend."

After our coffee we had sex, but my heart wasn't in it.

"What's up with you?" Hannah asked. "There was a time when you couldn't wait to jump into bed with me, but now it's as if you've lost all interest."

I was grateful that she had initiated the conversation. "You're a wonderful woman, Hannah, but I have to tell you something. During all the time you and I have been seeing each other, my relationship with Shoshana has been purely platonic, but she and I have grown closer now. I love her, and

I can't keep seeing you like this. I hope I can keep you and Avrum as friends, but I understand if you don't feel the same."

"Oh, David, I understand," Hannah said with sadness in her voice. "But I've become so attached to you, and Avrum just can't satisfy me the way you do. Can't I see you a few more times before we break it off completely?"

I had no intention of ever getting back into her bed, but I didn't want a huge scene. "I'll come for breakfast next week," I promised, trying to change the subject. "And I'll bring Alec again." She brightened at that idea.

I hugged her briefly and left with a sense of relief. The next visit, I hoped, would net me new information from Avrum about Inspector Jeffries. And although I intended to use Avrum's information myself, I did want to renew contact with the Haganah.

The next morning, I went to the Tnuva plant and asked to see Yaakov. He came down to meet me, clearly surprised. "Where did you disappear to?" he asked.

"I'm sorry," I said. "I've been very busy."

"Well, I'm pleased to see you again. We're meeting on Saturday. Same place. You want to come?"

"Gladly. Can I bring a friend with me?"

"Certainly," Yaakov responded.

I thanked him and walked to Alec's apartment. He was home, and we decided to go for coffee at Café Europa. Our waitress was Shoshana's friend Eva, who was always smiling and full of life. Her chestnut-brown eyes framed by curly auburn hair sparkled with life, and her shapely figure drew the attention of several men in the restaurant, including the two of us. She clearly took a liking to Alec, fussing over him constantly.

When she left us alone for a moment, I said, "You've certainly managed to charm our waitress."

"Yes, I noticed," Alec responded. "But she's too sweet for my taste. I'd prefer a wildcat, like your friend Hannah."

I thought for a moment and then told him about my affair with Hannah. "As far as I'm concerned, our relationship is over," I said. "If you want to get involved with her, I don't mind. She even told me that she likes you."

"Hmmm," Alec said. "I'll think about it."

"I wanted to talk to you about one of the underground groups." I began telling him about my previous experience with the Haganah and invited him to the meeting.

"They want to bring Jews to Israel," he said, "so sure, I'll come along."

On Saturday, we met and walked to the Haganah meeting at the Glicksteins'. I introduced Alec to Yaakov and pointed out that they both lived in the Bukharan Quarter. Yaakov got excited and started telling Alec all about the wonders of the neighborhood. They agreed to meet so Yaakov could show him around.

Yaakov opened the meeting with a brief overview of the Haganah's latest activities, specifically their activities regarding immigration to Israel. In recent months, he said, the *Berl Katzenelson* and *Hannah Senesh* ships had made it through the British blockade. The *Enzo Sereni*, however, was spotted by British destroyers and escorted to the port in Haifa, where all 908 Jews on board were transferred to the Atlit internment camp near Haifa.

A discussion ensued once Yaakov finished with his report. I didn't speak, and neither did Alec. When the meeting was over and everyone but Yaakov and the hosts had left, I asked Yaakov if there was anything we could do to prevent the British from apprehending and detaining the Jews attempting to flee the morass of Europe.

Yaakov hesitated for a moment before responding. "Maybe,"

he said. "The issue is of paramount importance to us, and we're working to resolve it at the political level. The Jewish Agency is trying to get international support, mainly from the Americans. But the Haganah is also attacking British targets related to their blockade. Our strike forces, the Palmach, have been destroying the radar stations the British use to locate immigrant ships along the coastline.

"After one of these operations, the British laid siege to the settlement of Kibbutz Givat-Haim. When our people protested, British policemen opened fire on them, killing seven and wounding dozens. We won't be deterred, of course. If you and your friend really want to help, you can join one of our Palmach units. I can connect you with the right people."

"The assaults on the radar stations are good," I said, "but the British can rebuild such things quite easily. From my experience as a partisan, there is always someone among the enemy who acts as the driving force, who's indispensable within his own sphere."

Yaakov nodded. "Unlike the Irgun and Lehi, the Haganah usually doesn't target specific individuals, only military objectives. When we face a specific problem with a British individual, we may forward it to the Irgun. Recently, we chased out a man by the name of Raymond Cafferata, who led the British police in Haifa and the north region. He tortured and killed Irgun and Lehi members and many civilians. With our help, the Irgun nearly assassinated him a couple weeks ago. Cafferata returned to England shortly after the assassination attempt. We won't be seeing him again."

I praised the operation, all the while thinking that if Alec and I had carried out the attack, Cafferata would have gone back to England in a box.

Alec and Yaakov confirmed their plans to get together for a tour of the Bukharan Quarter, and we said goodbye. I took Alec to Amos Street and showed him the spot where I had killed Sergeant Perry. I also told him about the red berets I had injured in the Schneller Barracks and on the street.

Alec asked if I had considered Yaakov's suggestion of joining the Haganah. "I've thought about it," I said, "but there are people in the Haganah who collaborate with the British. More importantly, I think we can prove more helpful on our own."

We arranged to walk together to the restaurant the next day for Alec's first shift as a waiter. I went home and spent a few hours reading and napping, and it was already evening by the time I woke.

I missed Shoshana, so I went to visit her at the restaurant. Her face lit up when she saw me, and when her shift was over, I helped her clear the tables and wash the dishes. We walked home afterward wrapped in each other's arms, and again she suggested that she come back to my place.

When we got to my apartment, she quickly undressed and started unbuttoning my clothes. Making love to her was even better than before, and as she lay on her side next to me, with her legs resting on mine, she nuzzled my neck, pressed her lips to my cheek, and said in a soft voice, "It would be so wonderful to sleep together every night. I love you and want to be with you all the time. Why don't we move in together?"

I was taken aback. In Minsk, living together before marriage had been unheard of. Among the partisans, the attitude toward sex before marriage had been very liberal—with the shadow of death hanging over us every day, we'd taken whatever truth and happiness we could snatch from the moment. When I had first reached Israel, I had heard that couples in the kibbutzim tended to live together before getting married. But the people in the cities were more conservative.

"Are you sure?" I asked.

"I'm lonely, David. I don't have parents to object." And before I could respond, she added, "I'll cook for you and take care of you all the time. Eva will be disappointed to see me leave, but I can't stay with her forever."

I hugged her tightly. "I think it's a wonderful idea. I'll speak to my landlords, and hopefully they'll agree. If not, we'll find another apartment."

As we lay in bed, wrapped in each other's arms, Shoshana said, "I'm too excited to sleep. I can't wait to get up and start packing."

I thought about Brigita and her wise advice. "Are you still seeing Brigita?" I asked.

"Certainly. She's a big part of why I'm in your bed right now. Her counseling and her sexual guidance have been very helpful. I'm meeting with her tomorrow, actually."

"Would you ask if she can see me this coming Monday?"

"Sure." She kissed me and slipped off to sleep.

The following morning, we walked to Café Pinsk with Alec. Max and Shoshana gave him a basic lesson in waiting tables as I busied myself rubbing the spots off the silverware. I knew Max would scoff if I gave Alec any advice about being a good waiter.

ON MONDAY, I WENT TO see Brigita. She served tea and asked how things were going with Shoshana.

"That's precisely why I asked to meet with you," I said. "She's going to move in with me. We've grown very close in all respects. I feel wonderful with her, and I think she's enjoying the sexual side of our relationship. You have played a big part in it all, and I want to thank you for your help."

The expression on her face told me she wasn't surprised. "I'm very pleased to hear that. You must continue to be gentle with her, allow her to take the lead, and make her feel safe and secure." Then she looked me straight in the eyes. "And how is my friend the partisan? Is he playing a role in the national struggle yet?"

"I'm still looking for a path," I said.

Her smile was wry. "I'm sure you were a lot more decisive during your time as a partisan. What's happened to you, David? Have you changed? Or perhaps you simply don't want to share your secrets?"

"I have a question for you," I said, trying to move our conversation in a different direction. "You must have heard about the attempt on the life of a British officer by the name of Cafferata, the police commander in the north. The Irgun carried out the assassination attempt, claiming that Cafferata was responsible for the detention and torture of Irgun and Lehi members in the region. Do you think the Irgun did the right thing by trying to assassinate Cafferata?"

After pondering my question for a moment, Brigita said, "I'll answer you both as a psychologist and as a Jewish woman living in this country. If the plan to kill Cafferata was motivated purely by revenge, then I don't think I could justify it. But as I see it, it was motivated by the desire to prevent him or other British officers from hurting more of our people. And even though the assassination was unsuccessful, Cafferata and his cronies will certainly think twice about their methods. All told, I do justify the deed."

Before I could respond, and with her eyes still fixed firmly on mine, she added, "A British officer who arrested members of the underground was recently killed in our neighborhood. I have no objections to that. On the other hand, as I said before, I think whoever fired on the Schneller Barracks was very wrong to do it. What do you think?"

I answered honestly this time. "I think just like you.

Indiscriminate attacks on the British are wrong. Some of them deserve to be killed but not all."

SINCE MONDAY WAS HANNAH'S FREE day, I decided to stop by her apartment to say hello. Pleased to see me, she ushered me into a chair in the kitchen and served me a cup of coffee.

"You left me very hurt last time," she said. "I decided that, if this is how you feel, it's best if we break things off completely. You know, women talk. Shoshana already told me you're moving in together. I understand Brigita was a big help, and I'm glad I introduced Shoshana to her, even though it ended our relationship. From now on, Avrum and I will be your friends and nothing more."

I left, relieved that things could remain friendly between us, though I had to admit, Hannah had rather quickly changed her tune. Likely Alec had a lot to do with that. I was surprised Shoshana had confided in Hannah about moving in with me.

My thoughts shifted to my landlords. I had the feeling they were short on money. If I offered to increase the rent, I thought they would likely agree to let Shoshana move in with me. I resolved to speak to them that evening when they were back from work.

I had tried, successfully until then, to keep my distance from my landlords. With my activities against the British, it was too risky to have them stopping by for visits. I paid the rent once a month and otherwise kept to myself.

I knew a few things about them. They were both in their forties. The wife, Varda, was a short woman with brown hair and brown eyes who worked as a teacher. Her husband, Binyamin, was a small, bespectacled man, a clerical worker for the Mandate government. They had both been born in Israel.

When I'd moved in, Binyamin had tried to befriend me,

but Varda was quiet and withdrawn. They had two children, a girl named Elinor and a son named Eitan, with whom I played the occasional game of soccer. Every Friday evening, I could hear the blessings and songs they sang through the walls. I would lie on my bed, lonely for my family and the Shabbat dinners we used to share.

When I knocked on my landlords' door later, I asked them about Shoshana moving in with me. I told them she was her family's sole survivor of the death camps and that she worked as a server at a restaurant, just like me.

"Terrible things that war did to the Jews." Varda sighed. "All right, we certainly won't stand in your way, but I hope to see you getting married and standing under the chuppah one day soon."

At breakfast with Hannah and Avrum the next morning, this time I was the one to drag Avrum into his study.

"Please provide me with the intelligence you've collected about Inspector Jeffries, and I'll pass it to Yaakov," I said as soon as he closed the door. "I've spoken to him, and he said he personally supports operations to eliminate individuals such as Jeffries; however, the Haganah doesn't target specific individuals, only military objectives, so he will pass it on to the Irgun."

Avrum lowered his head. "Unfortunately," he said, "I wasn't able to come up with anything at all."

I stared at him, more than a little surprised. "Avrum, you claim you want to help to establish a Jewish homeland, but you're not doing anything about it, even though you're in a unique position to play an important role. You're the one who told me about Jeffries, yet you're doing nothing to stop him. What's going on?"

"I'll see what I can do," Avrum snapped. He stood up to leave the room, but I gestured for him to wait a moment.

"If you come up with anything at all," I said, "come find me at the restaurant and let me know. It's extremely important."

Avrum nodded and headed toward the kitchen. Over his shoulder, I could see Hannah talking to Alec with that familiar seductive expression on her face. I felt a sense of relief that Hannah had moved on so quickly.

A FEW DAYS LATER, SHOSHANA and I decided to have another picnic in Tel Arza. March was coming to an end, and the weather was pleasant. Like before, I carried the two knapsacks she had packed with food. We walked to the valley that ran through Tel Arza, climbed a little way up a hill, and spread our blankets alongside a large boulder.

There was no bottle of brandy from Max this time. Shoshana had told me on our way that he was angry with her for moving in with me. I was lying down, my hands linked over my chest as I gazed up at my beautiful girlfriend.

"In Max's opinion, with my looks and personality," she said, "I could easily find someone better than a good-for-nothing coward," she said and burst out laughing.

She lay down beside me and caressed my face. And at that moment, I realized I had to be more open and honest with her.

"Shoshana, if Max knew what I've done over the past few months, he'd be one of my biggest fans. I'm about to tell you my most guarded secrets. The only other person who knows about them is Alec, who is like a brother to me."

She gripped my hand as I continued. "When I declined your offer to join the resistance, I wasn't completely honest with you. The real reason I said no is because I'm concerned about informants. When I was a partisan, a Gentile named Pavel betrayed us, and it cost the lives of several men, including one who was like an older brother to me. I support the fight against the British, but I've chosen to operate alone and in secret.

"On Geula Street, a few months ago, I attacked a British soldier and stole his weapon. I was also the sniper who fired on the Schneller Barracks. Max thinks that the death of that officer from the restaurant was a miraculous coincidence, but I was the one who lay in wait for him that night he was at the restaurant. I also killed that sergeant on Amos Street."

While I was talking, she had sat up and was hugging her knees and staring out at the horizon.

"If you don't wish to see me hanging by the neck from a British rope, you must keep everything I've said to yourself," I concluded.

Shoshana looked stunned at my words. "Of course I will. I'm . . . well, I'm shocked, but it does explain a few things." She lowered her gaze and was quiet for a moment, then glanced up. "I admire you for what you're doing. I wish I could be part of the resistance in such a way. Are you planning more operations?"

"Alec is going to join me, and together we will strike the British in any way we can until they leave Israel. I won't tell you about our future operations, but I wanted you to know who I really am."

Shoshana smiled and then hugged me tightly. "The moment I laid eyes on you, I knew you were someone special. I knew it was worth overcoming everything I'd experienced just to be with you. Please be careful, since I need you forever."

Her words reminded me of Leah's, and I felt a pang in my heart. We may not have been under Nazi occupation any longer, but the dangers we faced were still real. I had failed the first love of my life. I was determined to stay vigilant and make sure nothing bad ever happened to Shoshana.

11

"Unknown soldiers are we, without uniform"

(from "Unknown Soldiers," a poem by Avraham Stern, 1932)

Alec suggested that I give myself a break from planning new ways to attack the British. "Shoshana is moving in with you. You need to focus on her for a while. Things are too hot right now. Go quiet until the British ease up a bit."

I knew he was right. As partisans, we knew we had to go to ground after a successful operation. At the same time, I had to continue gathering whatever information I could about Inspector Jeffries, even if I couldn't act on it right away. Not that I was willing to wait too long. Taking him out of the picture could save lives, and every day we waited put the underground at more risk.

Alec quickly got the hang of things at the restaurant, lightening everyone's load. Even Max seemed less stressed, though he never eased up on me.

"I don't think you're right for Shoshana," Max said to me one evening. "I can't change her mind, but I'm warning you . . .

if you hurt her, you'll have me to deal with, and it won't be pleasant for you at all."

I nodded as he stared at me, and then he let out a long-frustrated groan. "The commander who met with you a while back would like to see you again. I told him it was a waste of time, but he insisted that I ask."

"Why not? That's fine," I said, shrugging my shoulders.

"All right!" Max snapped. "They'll send a car to pick you up one of these evenings."

Two days later, just before closing time, a man walked in and immediately seized my attention. His hair was cropped short, and the pugnacious expression on his broad face made him look like a brawler. I sized him up and came to the conclusion that I'd be in real trouble if we ever got into a physical confrontation. Max pointed to me, and the man wordlessly gestured for me to follow him outside.

A black Ford Anglia was parked in front of the restaurant. The tough guy ushered me into the back seat, slid in next to me, and told the driver to go. As we rolled down Ben Yehuda Street, he took a black scarf from his pocket and blindfolded me.

After a short drive, we came to a stop. The man opened my car door and led me down a gravel path into a house. With the door closed behind us, he removed my blindfold. Standing in front of me was Max's old hero from the restaurant.

"How are you, David?" he asked, extending his hand. "I apologize for all the cloak-and-dagger stuff, but as a former partisan, you surely understand the importance of secrecy." He escorted me into a sitting room, where two men I gauged to be in their late thirties were sitting on the sofa. Hanging on the wall were three large photographs of British men in uniform.

"Regrettably, I'm unable to give you my name or the

names of my colleagues," the commander said to me. "I'm sure you understand. I'm usually very good at reading people, and you sparked my curiosity the last time we met. I did some digging, and I was very impressed by your fighting record as a partisan commander."

He paused, apparently waiting for a response that I would not give, and then he continued. "We've been fighting the British for several years, and we've gained valuable experience. Our people are brave, loyal, and patriotic, and we've carried out dozens of successful operations. But I've been thinking that someone like you could offer insights we haven't considered, that your perspective could improve our performance."

The commander turned to one of the men sitting on the sofa. "Brief David on the three men in the photos."

The man stood up and tapped the photograph on the right. "This is General Archibald James Halkett Cassels, Jim to his friends. In 1944, he led a brigade that was among the first British forces to land on the beaches at Normandy. He fought alongside his troops and was highly decorated for his excellence in the field. He was promoted after the war to the rank of general. He arrived here in March to take command of the Sixth Airborne Division, which is spearheading the Brits' fight against the Jewish resistance movement."

I looked at the picture of Cassels, a tall man with a large droopy nose and a smile on his face. He wore the same red beret as the soldiers I had wounded at the Schneller Barracks. It saddened me to know that this man, who had fought courageously against the enemies of the Jewish people, had joined the war against us.

The man pointed to the picture in the middle. "This is General Evelyn Hugh Barker, known simply as Barker. He's the commander in chief of the British forces in Israel and Transjordan.

He served in Israel between 1936 and 1938, returned to England, rose through the ranks to become general, and was named commander of the Forty-Ninth Infantry Division. His division also landed on the beaches in Normandy and excelled in battle. In December 1944, he was named commander of the Eighth Army, directly under Montgomery. On April 1, 1945, his soldiers reached the Bergen-Belsen death camp, where he got a firsthand view of the horrors perpetrated there by the Nazis. Nevertheless, Barker is a rabid Jew-hater and enemy number one of Israel. We know he's having an affair with a young Christian Arab woman who stages parties at her home in Jerusalem for members of the Arab elite and British officers."

I looked at the photograph. Unlike Jim Cassels, Barker, with his elongated face and cold eyes, didn't look like a particularly pleasant individual.

"The man in the third photograph is Inspector Malcolm Jeffries. He's the lowest ranked of the three, but he represents a major problem for us. An unidentified cell whose members aren't affiliated with one of the known underground organizations killed his deputy, one Sergeant John Perry, a threat in his own right. Jeffries's primary objective now is to apprehend the killers. To this end, he's assembled a team of six men who've been tasked with hunting down as many underground members as possible. The members of his team are professionals, hard men who served in an SAS commando unit under Colonel David Sterling. They wreaked havoc on the Germans both in North Africa and in Europe. Two of them are currently accompanying Jeffries as his bodyguards."

The man stopped talking and waited for a signal from his commander to continue. I gathered they were waiting for a response from me. I looked at the photograph of Jeffries, the man I already had in my sights. It was my first time seeing his face. He had red hair, small hostile green eyes, and the same patronizing expression Greene had worn in the restaurant, but this man looked even tougher and more determined.

"David," the commander said as I studied the photograph of Jeffries, "can you offer us any ideas on how to safely assassinate these men?"

Although my three years as a partisan had left me well versed in the art of killing Germans quickly and efficiently at a moment's notice, every situation was different. There were no hard and fast theoretical principles on assassinations.

"The most important thing," I said after a few moments of thought, "is to make sure that the people entrusted with the mission have the right skills for the job. If they plan to hit the targets up close, they must be in excellent physical condition and well trained in hand-to-hand combat and silent weapons, like knives and ropes. If they are to use a firearm, they must be talented long-range marksmen who've trained on and calibrated the exact weapon they'll carry into battle. And your choice of weapon should suit the environment in which you are operating. At night or in urban areas, it's best to use a weapon that's effective at close quarters. Selecting level-headed individuals for the job is the most important thing. People get killed when their comrades lose their heads."

I stopped for a moment, gathering my thoughts.

"Clearly, intelligence is vital," I said. "You have to collect as much information as possible about the target so you can choose the right time and place for the hit."

The men listened attentively as I told them about our operations against the German ambush force near Minsk and the German supply camp.

"I think you should create a small unit that specializes in targeted killings," I continued. "Unfortunately, some of those skills can only be learned in the field. It's an art—a mixture of bravery, pragmatism, creativity, and an instinct for the unexpected." I nodded at the photographs on the wall. "Let me ask you something. How would you rank these men in terms of importance?" "General Barker tops the list," the commander said. "Then Jeffries." He paused, staring at me to let me know that his next question would address the crux of this meeting. "David, would you join us on this mission? We'll provide any weapons and support you need."

"I've already told you where I stand," I said. "I identify with your objectives and admire your bravery, but I need a break from fighting."

He stared at me with a baffled look and then shrugged. "Think about my proposal," he said. "We'd greatly appreciate your advice as we move forward on this. Thank you, David."

We shook hands. My burly escort stepped forward with his blindfold.

"There's no need for that," the commander said. "From what we know about David—and we know quite a lot—he can be trusted."

We said goodbye, and I got into the car. I could see now that the house was in the Talpiot neighborhood in southern Jerusalem, although I doubted I could've found it again on my own. The driver, however, required no instructions from me and dropped me off outside my house on Zephaniah Street. They had clearly done their homework.

Shoshana hugged me warmly when I opened the door. She told me she was planning some changes to the apartment and had gone to see the landlords to get their approval. "Varda agreed to everything I asked for," she said. "She even invited us for dinner at their home this Friday. What a nice woman!"

I was surprised. Varda had always struck me as sullen and

standoffish, and she'd never offered me so much as a cup of tea, let alone invited me to Shabbat dinner. I was forced to admit to myself that Shoshana's social skills were much better than mine.

At the beginning of our shifts the following night, we asked Max for Friday off. "Alec is worth two of you," Max sneered at me. "We'll miss Shoshana, but we'll get by."

For Friday's dinner, Shoshana put on a beautiful white dress that I'd never seen before. I wore a white shirt and blue trousers that I kept for special occasions. Varda and Binyamin gave us a warm welcome and ushered us to the table.

Binyamin sat at the head, and I was shown to the seat at the opposite end. Varda sat next to Shoshana, and their children sat across from them. Binyamin poured the wine and recited the Kiddush prayer, something I hadn't experienced since my own family's Shabbat dinners at our home in Belarus.

The sounds of my landlords' family celebrating the Shabbat had made me feel lonely before, but as I sat with them at their table, I was gripped with a sorrow that caught me by surprise. I could picture the delicate features of my beautiful mother putting on her white lace headscarf and lighting the candles. I recalled my father saying the blessing over the wine and the challah before tearing off pieces of the bread to pass around a table covered with a similar white tablecloth.

There I was, having my first Shabbat meal in Jerusalem with my love, and my family wasn't there to share it—and never would be.

When I looked over at Shoshana, I could see that she shared my thoughts. Sorrow darkened her face, and tears clouded her lovely eyes.

Varda served a delicious meal, and the family's warmth lifted our spirits. Varda and Shoshana chatted as if they had known each other for years. Binyamin and I, on the other hand, hardly exchanged a word.

"We enjoyed your company very much," Varda said as we were leaving. "We'd be very happy for you to join us next Friday evening too."

"Thank you," Shoshana replied. "We enjoyed ourselves too, but we both have to work at the restaurant most Fridays. We'll try to arrange a Friday evening off every now and then, and we'll let you know if we can."

When we got home, we undressed in silence, then lay down on the bed, facing each other. "When Binyamin recited the Kiddush," Shoshana said, "it brought back memories of my father when he used to say the blessing over the wine. I miss my family so much, David. You and I, and thousands of others just like us, are trying to survive, to move on from our terrible past. Most people here can't understand what we went through. They've heard about it, and they sympathize, but they can't know the pain deep in our souls, the pain that surfaces with such intensity from time to time."

"Yes," I said. "I remembered my mother lighting the Shabbat candles and my father reciting the Kiddush over the wine too. Tonight it hit me that my entire family is gone forever. I remembered the dinner when we heard the thunder of the German artillery shells as Minsk was overrun. However—everything has changed for the better since I reached Israel. I hope that, now we're together, we will know only happiness."

She gently kissed my face, and I stroked her cheek. She turned on her side, and I hugged her close, her warmth giving me comfort. I felt that the two of us, having endured similar horrors, strengthened one another. We fell asleep like that, my arms wrapped around her.

Two days later, Shoshana and I were working our evening shift, with the restaurant packed to the brim, when four British policemen stormed through the door with their revolvers drawn. They ordered everyone to line up along the wall. Two policemen pointed their weapons at us while the other two went into the kitchen and dragged Max out in handcuffs.

"A friend of ours, Inspector Greene, left your restaurant and was murdered just a few minutes later," said their commanding officer, a florid man with the insignia of an inspector on his shoulder.

One look at the officer's face was enough for me to recognize him: Inspector Jeffries. His beady green eyes flashed with hatred. He cracked Max on the head with his club, pressed the barrel of his gun into his back, and pushed him outside. I had a hard time controlling my rage but knew the slightest move could result in a bullet to my head.

The rest of the crowd endured sloppy pat-downs, and once the policemen were satisfied that none of us were armed, they left the restaurant and drove away. Shoshana and I kept the restaurant running, but the cook could not hold the kitchen together, and the diners soon drifted away.

After a sleepless and frustrating night, I got up the next morning and went to Alec's to tell him what had happened. He struggled to control his murderous rage, making me glad he hadn't been there. The hatred in Jeffries's eyes had made it clear he would have welcomed an excuse to shoot any Jew who had riled him.

After leaving Alec's apartment, I made my way to the office of the *Palestine Post*. I remembered General Evelyn Hugh Barker from my meeting with the underground commander and his colleagues. They had said General Barker led the liberation of

Bergen-Belsen in April 1945. I decided that if Jeffries and his men were to return to the restaurant to take me in too, I could try to pass myself off as an ardent supporter of the British and an admirer of the general who liberated the concentration camp. After browsing through several old editions of the newspaper, I came across an article that described the liberation of Bergen-Belsen and mentioned General Barker's name. I found an image of Barker in a separate article. I tore out both articles and put them in my wallet.

Sure enough, Shoshana and I woke up the following morning to the sound of loud banging on the door to our apartment, followed by shouts from the police. I opened the door to see Jeffries and two other officers with their weapons drawn. A quick glance over their shoulders revealed three more policemen searching in the yard.

"Are you David?" one of the men asked in Hebrew.

"Yes," I replied.

"Do you understand English?"

"A little."

"Your boss," Jeffries said, his British accent thick, his voice dripping with suppressed rage, "has denied any involvement in Greene's murder, but he suggested that we question you. He suspects that you were involved."

"I don't know anything," I said in a low voice. "I'm not even sure I know who you're talking about."

Jeffries slapped me hard.

"Leave him alone," Shoshana shouted.

"Shut your mouth, bitch," he hissed, and my desire to kill him only intensified, though I made sure not to show it on my face.

"Get dressed, you bloody Jew," Jeffries ordered. "We have

interrogators at the CID who can get a mute to talk. We'll see what you have to say to them."

I started to dress, and before I put on my trousers, I placed my wallet and keys on the bed. Jeffries walked in, tapping the walls and furniture with his club as his men tore apart the room. He picked up my wallet and started rifling through it. "What are these newspaper clippings doing in your wallet?" he growled. "You planning another murder?"

"General Barker and his forces liberated my aunt and uncle from the Bergen-Belsen concentration camp," I said. "The general is one of the people I admire most in this world."

A look of hesitation appeared on Jeffries's face, so I kept talking. "The Nazis murdered seventy thousand Jews at Bergen-Belsen. If it weren't for General Barker, twice that many would have died there. While most of Europe conspired to kill my people, or at best turned a blind eye, he and his brave soldiers risked their lives to save the only family I have left."

Now Jeffries looked somewhat conflicted. He stared at me for a long moment, then went out into the yard and told his men to stop their search. "General Barker is a great man," he said when he came back inside, "and I know he appreciates your support. I won't bring you in, but if you'd like to come by willingly, perhaps I can arrange for you to meet him." Then he gave me a crude approximation of a friendly smile. "And perhaps we can find other ways for you to express your gratitude and sense of admiration toward Great Britain, hmm?"

"Gladly," I said.

"Then come to the gates of the Schneller Barracks tomorrow morning at ten. Give the guard your name, and tell him you have an appointment with Inspector Jeffries."

"Thank you, sir," I said.

Shoshana and I watched them drive away, and then we

both sighed in relief. She threw herself into my arms and held me tightly.

"Oh, David, if you hadn't had those articles in your wallet—" She drew back and frowned up at me, her tearful eyes turning curious. "Why did you have those articles in your wallet?"

I explained my preparation the day before, and she hugged me tightly again.

"I am in love with a genius," she said into my shirt. I kissed the top of her head and smiled.

I wasn't a genius, but the good fortune and foresight that had kept me alive for three years as a partisan was serving me well in Israel. If they had found my arms cache in the stone wall behind the building, I wouldn't have seen the sky again until they marched me to the gallows.

I REPORTED TO THE ENTRANCE of the Schneller Barracks at precisely 9:45 the following morning, despite Shoshana's protests that the meeting could be a trap. I stated my business to the guard at the gate, they searched me for weapons, and then I was escorted to a conference room in Jeffries's spacious chambers. I could see an office, a kitchenette, and a closed door, behind which, I assumed, were Jeffries's private quarters.

Hanging on the walls of the conference room were photographs of Perry and Greene. Two of Jeffries's goons stood at attention on either side of the large table, fixing me with unflinching stares in a show of force and security for their commander.

The great man himself walked in a half hour later. "Take a seat," he said, motioning to a chair near the two bodyguards. "Scotch?"

"Gladly," I said. I preferred vodka, but to each his own. Jeffries pulled a bottle of Grant's Scotch whiskey and two glasses from a cabinet and poured a generous glug into each. He didn't offer any to the bodyguards.

"Cheers," he said, and we both sipped on our drinks. "I'm trying to arrange a meeting for you with General Barker and hope he agrees to see you soon. But perhaps you could help us in the meantime. Do you see the two photographs on the wall?"

"Yes," I said.

"These men were murdered by terrorists in two separate incidents over the past few months—British policemen whose killers have yet to be caught," Jeffries continued. "What's your take on the matter?"

He fixed me with a piercing stare, and I looked him straight in the eyes as I responded. "It saddens me to hear of the murder of anyone, unless we're taking about Nazis. Your people fought bravely against the Germans, and I struggle to understand the motives of the Jewish underground. They underestimate the debt our people owe your nation."

Jeffries stopped me with a wave of his hand. "During his interrogation, Max Slucki described you as a good-for-nothing fool," he said, flipping through his notes. "He said that if it weren't for some waitress named Shoshana Bukstein—your girlfriend, I assume?—he would fire you and tell you to go to hell."

I knew that Jeffries was telling the truth this time. "Max is a grumpy man who doesn't let up for a second," I said. "If I had any other options, I'd quit my job at the restaurant in an instant. But I don't have a profession, and you don't have to know much to be a waiter. I hope you don't tell him I said so, but I got a little pleasure out of seeing you hit him with your club."

Jeffries gave me a thoughtful look.

"Nevertheless," I continued, "I should say that Max has always told me to treat our British customers well, and I've heard him say on more than one occasion that the British protect us and that if it wasn't for them, the Jewish community would be massacred by the Arabs. I can also tell you that Max and Officer Greene enjoyed a friendly relationship, and Max was sorry to hear of his death."

Jeffries chuckled. "You are far from a fool. Listen, as a waiter, you're in a position to gather useful information. If you hear anything that could be of value, come back here and ask to see me. I'll reward you generously."

With that, our conversation was over. I went back to my apartment, where I found Shoshana pacing the floor. I told her that I spoke in Max's favor and that Jeffries didn't suspect me of anything and that we had no cause to worry.

"I believe they'll leave me alone for now. And, hopefully, Max too."

"Thank you for speaking up for him," she said. "I wouldn't have blamed you if you hadn't, after the way he's treated you."

"Oh, Max is all right. If I were him, I wouldn't trust me either."

Shoshana giggled, and the sweet sound made me pick her up in my arms and carry her off to bed.

Max returned to the restaurant two days later. His face was bruised and swollen, and his usual arrogance was gone. He called Shoshana and me into his office and thanked us for running the restaurant while he was gone.

"My interrogation was brutal and humiliating," he said. "When it was over, the inspector told me that you had come forward to speak on my behalf. I greatly appreciate what you did to get me out of there. I have to admit, I may have misjudged you."

"The most important thing is that you're back," I said. "We'll beat those British bastards together, and we won't stop until our people have a national home in Israel."

Max said nothing, but there was a sincere look of gratitude in his eyes. Shoshana hugged him, and then she turned and embraced me too.

"I'm so happy that you are finally friends," she said with a smile.

12

"WE ARE SEEKING OUT THE FOE"

(FROM "SONG OF THE PALMACH" BY ZERUBAVEL GILAD, 1942)

Shoshana and I slowly settled into a routine. With her help, my unkempt bachelor pad started looking more and more like a warm family home. She started painting again, and our walls came alive with beautiful landscapes and portraits. She cooked breakfast each morning, and lunch and dinner on our days off, and regularly sent me out with precise, well-ordered shopping lists to keep our kitchen stocked.

One morning as I walked into the grocery store, Mrs. Cohen welcomed me with a cynical smile. "Good news, Don Juan. That young lady you were flirting with, Sarah, is available now. Rumor has it that someone took her boyfriend out of the picture. All you have to do now is simply approach her, and she'll fall into your lap like ripe fruit from a tree."

"Thank you for your concern, Mrs. Cohen," I replied politely, though with a touch of sarcasm in return. "I have a steady girlfriend, whom I actually met here at your store. If it seemed as though I was flirting with Sarah, you're mistaken. I was simply trying to be nice."

"This girlfriend you met here," she asked, "would that be Shoshana or Hannah?"

I was a little put out that she had such a long memory of my personal life, but I just bagged my items, paid, and said goodbye. On the way home, I thought about my plans for Jeffries, irritated it was taking so long to put them into action.

My attack on Sergeant Perry had matured much more quickly, as I had been able to obtain information about his habits and movements easily. I knew next to nothing about Jeffries's activities outside the Schneller Barracks, and it was becoming clear that Avrum either couldn't or wouldn't follow through on his promise to help. As usual, I had to rely on myself.

With that in mind, I stopped at the apartment to put away the groceries and then made my way to the Schneller Barracks. I told the guard at the gate that I needed to see Inspector Jeffries, and one of his bodyguards appeared a few minutes later to pat me down and escort me to his office.

Jeffries welcomed me warmly, poured some whiskey, and asked what I was doing there.

I described my chance meeting with Sarah at the grocery store. "The owner of the store, Mrs. Cohen, thinks I was flirting with her," I said. "And she told me Sarah had a British lover who was recently taken out of the picture. It occurred to me that he may have been one of the murder victims you showed me. Maybe you should question Mrs. Cohen? She might have information that could help solve at least one of these mysteries."

After feverishly recording everything I said, Jeffries stood up and thanked me. "I'll be in touch," he said.

"Before I go, I hope we can agree that these conversations should be completely confidential," I said. "If the Irgun or Lehi learns that I'm helping you, they'll kill me without hesitation. If you need to speak with me, send one of your men to the bar at Café Pinsk for a drink. When he gets the chance, he should say to me, 'Your service here has improved greatly,' and I'll come to you the next morning."

"Not too shabby for an ignorant waiter," Jeffries said. He offered me another shot of whiskey, which I declined. I then stood and offered my hand. He shook it with a leering smile.

During my shift at Café Pinsk that same evening, I spotted one of Jeffries's bodyguards, in civilian attire, sitting at the bar and having far more than one drink. After downing his fifth shot, he turned to me and said, "The bill, please. And by the way, your service here has improved greatly."

I nodded. "Thank you, sir." Things were progressing nicely.

"I don't know if you noticed," Shoshana said to me on our way home, "but there was a man at the bar who had his eye on you."

"There's no need to worry," I said. "He's one of Inspector Jeffries's men, and I've convinced Jeffries that I'm an informant."

I didn't know if her fears were eased, but she didn't mention it again. I reported to the gates of the Schneller Barracks the following morning and was soon ushered into Jeffries's office.

"David," he said, "I'm most grateful to you. You have given our investigation a significant boost. This Sarah you mentioned was indeed the lover of Sergeant Perry, my distinguished deputy, who was strangled by some monster." He tossed back his drink and scowled. "His murder was a great loss to both the army and the police. We questioned the girl's neighbors, and one of them, an elderly man who suffers from insomnia, told us he had seen Perry leaving early in the morning on several occasions."

That gave me a moment of alarm. If Baruch had mentioned

me—but no, why would he? Jeffries went on, his eyes narrow with hatred. "We're almost certain that he was murdered just moments after leaving her apartment. The same man also told us that she's taken a new British lover who comes once a week. We suspect that this Sarah Mizrahi may be a Jewish terrorist who's luring British soldiers and policemen for assassination. What do you think?"

"Is she in custody?" I asked.

"No," Jeffries replied. "I've yet to decide whether to arrest her or keep her under surveillance."

"Leave her be for now," I said. "I'll try to get some information from her myself. I'm Jewish, so she'll trust me."

"Excellent. Let me know what you find out."

"Of course, sir, but I have concerns about coming to the Schneller Barracks so often. If I'm spotted at the gate by a member of the underground, I could be targeted as a collaborator. Is there any other place we can meet?"

Jeffries's beady eyes narrowed. He frowned and looked me straight in the eyes. I knew I had made a mistake, possibly a fatal one, but I kept my eyes fixed on his.

"David," he said, "I have reason to believe that the Irgun is planning an attempt on my life, so I have to be careful. At this stage, this is the only viable arrangement."

"Yes, sir, I understand completely," I quickly agreed. "I hope you catch those rats soon."

On my way home from the barracks, I stopped at the Cohens' grocery store. It was around noon, and only Mrs. Cohen was inside.

"I have something to admit," I said. "I'm interested in Sarah after all. Shoshana is wonderful, but I'm not sure I'm ready to be tied down to one woman."

"I knew it! I wasn't wrong in recognizing you as a Don

Juan!" Mrs. Cohen said with a smug smile. "It will be interesting to see if you have any success with her too."

"Would you mind helping me? What if I buy something Sarah normally gets and take it to her, saying she forgot it at the store?"

Mrs. Cohen snorted. "So, you've been following her around?"

"Actually, I was hoping you might have her address." Although I knew Sarah's address, if Jeffries were to investigate, he needed to believe that I received it from Mrs. Cohen.

She gave me a shrewd look. "Sarah always gets a half pound of this yellow Tnuva cheese. If you pay me double, I'll throw in the address for free."

After buying the block of cheese, I made my way to Sarah's place. I was happy to see that Baruch wasn't on his balcony as I entered the building.

I knocked on her door, and Sarah opened it a minute later. "Who are you?" she asked, squinting. "I think I've seen you before."

I put on my most charming smile. "Yes," I said, "you've seen me at the Cohens' store. I live nearby. I was at the store and heard Mrs. Cohen say something about putting aside this cheese you'd bought but had forgotten to take with you."

"Ah, yes, from the grocery store . . . but I don't remember buying the cheese. But if Mrs. Cohen says so . . ." Sarah took the packet from my hand, hesitated for a moment, and then invited me inside.

"How did you know where I live?" she asked.

"Mrs. Cohen gave me your address," I said.

Sarah smiled and offered me a cup of coffee, gesturing for me to take a seat in her living room. After she brought the coffee, she sat down beside me, and we began to talk. She told me that she preferred British men to Jews.

"They know how to treat a woman, and they have more money too." With a sigh of longing, she told me about her previous boyfriend, John, and how generous he was.

"So why did you split up?" I asked.

"We didn't split up. He was murdered by some bastard from the underground, not far from here."

"I apologize if I'm about to be rude, but do you have a boyfriend now?"

She thought a moment before responding. "I'm seeing someone, but I'm not entirely happy with our relationship. He's a financial services officer in the British army who serves at the Schneller Barracks. But as he's married and has two children, almost all his salary goes to his family in England. I would much rather find another man like John."

She waited for my response, and when it didn't come, she added coyly, "You look like a man who knows a thing or two."

I had no interest in any kind of a relationship with her, but I didn't want to offend her. "I believe in true love," I said.

With that, she seemed to lose all interest. "When you grow up and become more practical, little boy, come see me again," she said impatiently. "Meanwhile, thanks for bringing the cheese."

When I stepped out onto the street, I spotted Baruch on his balcony and lowered my head. But he shouted after me to come visit him in his apartment. Left with no choice, I did.

"You were at Sarah's," he said.

I nodded. He had seen me walk out of Sarah's building, so there was no point in denying it. "I delivered something she had forgotten at the grocery store," I said.

"Did she tell you about her new boyfriend?" he asked with a crooked smile. "He's British too, but he comes to see her only once a week. I don't think he'd be much competition for you—he's really ugly."

"Baruch," I said, "don't get any ideas in that head of yours. I was simply doing her a favor. I have a girlfriend."

The last thing I needed was for Baruch to make some kind of connection between my visits to him and the death of John Perry.

After about thirty minutes of rummy and Baruch's meandering stories, I apologized and told him I had to go to work, which was true, but I needed to get out of there regardless. When I'd been following Sergeant Perry, I'd had no choice but to listen to Baruch's long, tedious stories and play cards with him for hours. I was thankful I would no longer have to suffer that boredom.

When our shift was over, Shoshana and I had a wondrous night together in bed. It was hard to believe that everything I had wanted for us had finally come together. Some days it seemed like a dream, but it was real. I felt so lucky that our relationship was in full bloom.

As I rested on my elbow and watched her sleep, I felt a sudden depression sweep over me. I was happy, but did I deserve to be? I lay down, and after tossing and turning for several hours, I decided to go see Brigita in the morning.

"SORRY FOR SHOWING UP UNANNOUNCED," I said when Brigita opened her door a few hours later. "I can come back another time if it's more convenient."

"It's fine," she said. "I'm free. Have a seat, and tell me what brings you here."

"I wanted to thank you for the wonderful work you are doing with Shoshana. Our relationship is getting better and better, and you've played a big part in that."

"I appreciate your gratitude," Brigita said with a smile, then raised one eyebrow. "But I don't think that's why you showed up without an appointment."

"I don't know exactly why I came," I said. "Perhaps I just needed to speak to someone whose opinions I value."

She looked at me for a few seconds. "Can I be brutally honest?" she asked, though in an uncharacteristically soft tone.

"Yes," I replied, sensing that it wasn't going to be easy for me to hear what she had to say.

"From what I can see," she began, "you are a young man who has endured extremely difficult experiences. You've built a wall around yourself, and you are very careful not to allow anyone into that enclosed space. You emerge from behind the wall from time to time to accomplish important goals you've set for yourself, including some that put you at risk. You focus on these tasks until they've been completed, and then you move on to your next objective." She paused, as if waiting for me to respond.

"I won't say you're wrong," I answered.

She nodded and leaned back in her chair. "I think you've filed away parts of your past—and your soul—that you never delve into at all. A young man like you, living in such a harsh world, without his family, without the embrace of his loving mother or father, without siblings—that's a hard life to lead. I've never heard you speak of anything personal. How does a young man like you cope with the huge personal losses you've suffered?"

Brigita's words stunned me, and for a moment, I felt the full brunt of the loss I had experienced. To my shock, I wanted to cry. I wanted to see my mother again, and my father. I wanted to see Leah. My throat tightened. I was a fighter. These feelings were unwanted. They made me feel weak, and yet Brigita's eyes were full of sympathy. I found myself wanting the comfort she offered.

Brigita reached out to place her hand on mine. We sat like that for a short while, and I knew then I had found a good friend, an intelligent woman, who knew me in a way very few did.

After pulling myself together, I said, "This wall I've built around myself ever since leaving my old world, at the age of seventeen, has always weighed on me. I didn't know anything else, because for years my daily reality set my pace. I needed to survive, to push away fear and sadness, to cast away my feelings of dread and use all my strength to cope with the murderous anti-Semitism in Europe. And now I must cope with the same here in Israel."

Brigita listened intently, and as I spoke, I was soothed by the empathy in her piercing eyes. I began to feel as though I wasn't alone, and it suddenly seemed easier to open up to her than to keep it all in.

"From a practical perspective," Brigita said, "you functioned exactly as you should have, but your soul has been damaged." She paused, giving me a gentle look. "That's what makes you ill at ease these days, causing you to look for a way to heal your wounded spirit. In Belarus, you didn't have time to think. Now that you're no longer fighting a true war, with your life in danger every moment from an enemy who ruthlessly destroyed your people, you don't always know what to do. Perhaps in your subconscious, you are trying to conflate the British with the Germans. It makes things simpler for you, but that way of thinking is toxic. You are a lone wolf, David, without counsel from anyone but yourself."

She gazed at me thoughtfully for a moment. "I think I can offer you some counseling, but only if you can talk honestly and openly about what exactly is troubling you."

I stared down at the floor, composing my thoughts. "I think it's much like you say," I began. "When I became the commander of a group of partisans, I did everything in my power to lead my people wisely and effectively. I learned not to hesitate for a second and to focus on a single objective—killing the enemy before he killed me."

"Not unusual in wartime," she interjected.

"Yes. I learned how to stay alive, but I wasn't afraid to die. The people close to me were more important than my own safety."

"It sounds like you were a good leader, David."

I raised one brow and shook my head. "Does it? I'm not so sure. When I was a partisan, I met a resistance fighter, a woman, Leah. I loved her. One day, Leah was killed, and I felt—I still feel—that it was my fault. I should have protected her." I paused, the memory like a knife in my heart. "I wished it had been me instead."

"That is a normal reaction," Brigita murmured.

"After I got to Israel, I thought I'd have the chance to grow, to nurture my spiritual side, to study and perhaps even to write, but the situation here won't allow me to live that way. I'm shocked by the injustice, by the fact that my Jewish brothers and sisters who survived the horrors and persecution of the Nazis in Europe are now being persecuted here by the British."

"And you feel you must do something about it," she stated.

I struggled for a moment to find the right words. "I've always seen the Jewish people as one big family," I finally said. "My Jewish patriotism is the most important aspect of my life, more important than myself and more important than my relationship even with Shoshana. My father and my rabbi imparted these values to me. Even before the war, I believed that I would dedicate my life to such matters in Israel. I've dreamed of coming here since I was a small child."

"It must be gratifying to have your dream come true at last," Brigita said.

I nodded. "Yes, but the war stunted my intellectual development. I changed from a young boy who devoted most of his time to studying and reading into a fighting machine. After surviving for three years in a world that was conspiring to kill me, I came here, only to find Jews treated cruelly at the hands of the British. My people sit in refugee camps with the gates of their homeland closed to them." I shook my head. "That thought won't allow me any rest or peace of mind. I feel personally obligated to fight against this injustice, and I feel that I need to forgo my own well-being until we secure a national home for the Jews."

Again, I considered telling Brigita about my assassination operations in Jerusalem, and once again, I decided against it. I didn't think she'd divulge the information intentionally, but I had already told her enough for her to piece together what I was talking about, and she didn't need to know the specifics.

"One of the underground organizations has asked for my help in assassinating British targets," I said. "I didn't say yes or no, but I told them I needed to rest after all I've been through. They accepted my response and said they understood, but they also said they would approach me again soon. What would be your opinion on my agreeing to a mission like that?"

Brigita fixed me with a stern look. "I understand your desire to help our people, but I wish you would consider your partner too. Shoshana needs to fully recover from the trauma she experienced—if something were to happen to you, that might be more than her still-fragile psyche could handle. And doesn't she deserve a future here as much as any other Jew? For your own good, my advice is to focus on building your new life. And if you don't take my advice, I suggest you at least stay away from anyone who asks you to kill indiscriminately."

She stood. "I have another appointment, but I'm so glad you came to see me," she said. She reached out, and we hugged instead of shaking hands.

"Thank you for your support and for caring," I said.

"You're a special young man," she said softly, "and I will

always be here for you. Take care of yourself, and step out from behind that wall. There are a lot of good things in this world too. See you soon."

I WENT BACK TO THE Schneller Barracks the following morning to meet with Jeffries. In spite of Brigita's advice, I couldn't help but plan his death. I imagined killing him in his office but knew it would never work. I would never be able to sneak a gun or knife in, and though I could try to kill him with my bare hands, his two bodyguards were always nearby. I couldn't take them on all at once without a weapon.

Jeffries seemed pleased to see me. "What do you have for me today?" he asked as he retrieved his bottle of whisky.

I told him about my encounter with Sarah. "I didn't get the impression that she's working for the underground organizations," I said. "She mainly seems concerned with getting financial support from her lovers. That's what Sergeant Perry did, and her current lover also supports her. He serves here in the barracks as a financial services officer. If you ask me, he's probably doing a little embezzling here and there to pay for the girl's affections." I had no idea if this was true, but the more I could create discord within the British ranks, the better.

"I'll put him under surveillance immediately," Jeffries said.

"Sarah tried to tempt me into supporting her too," I added. "But I turned her down."

Jeffries flashed a smile. "I've seen your girlfriend. She's a real beauty."

"Thank you," I said.

"By the way, I've been informed by General Barker's people that he's willing to meet with you. They will advise me of the time and place soon."

"Great," I said. "I'm looking forward to it."

Jeffries held his glass of whiskey up to the light, then set it down and looked at me.

"Listen, David, you aren't a typical Jew. Perhaps it's because you didn't grow up in Palestine. The Jews here have only two things on their minds—money and getting rid of us. Some say I favor the Arabs over the Jews, but that's not true. I fought against the Germans, and if it's true what they say, that the enemy of your enemy is your friend, then I am your friend."

"Thank you, sir," I said. "Anyone who killed Germans is a friend of mine."

"Anyway, I appreciate your help," Jeffries said. "How can I repay you?"

I wanted to ask him to put his gun in his mouth and pull the trigger. "I feel like I'm paying my debt to the British people," I said instead, "for fighting the Nazis and for managing affairs in Israel so efficiently and fairly. I don't want any reward, and if you think I can provide more help in the future, don't hesitate to contact me."

I spent the days that followed thinking of ways to kill Jeffries but failed to make any progress. I also focused on nurturing my relationship with Shoshana—a most enjoyable task indeed. Work at the restaurant was more pleasant now that Max had grown friendly toward me. One day, he pulled Shoshana aside and offered to celebrate our moving in together with a party at the restaurant, at his expense. It would be held on the following Sunday evening, typically a quiet night for the café.

On our way home, Shoshana and I thought about who we should invite. She suggested Avrum and Hannah, Brigita, Varda and Binyamin, and her friend Eva. I added Alec, of course; Nelka; my boxing coach, Yousef Bustani; and his sister Rayan. As a joke, I suggested adding Inspector Jeffries too. Shoshana didn't find it funny.

I went to Nelka's apartment to invite her to the party, and she greeted me with a warm hug. "I miss you and think about you often," she said. "You've done more for me than anyone else, especially when you persuaded that Polish couple to leave my apartment."

I thought that now that we were in Israel, there was no reason not to tell her the truth. The Polish authorities weren't going to come find me here, after all.

"Nelka," I said, "I didn't tell you the truth back then. When I knocked on their door, the husband attacked me with an ax and his wife approached me with a knife. I shot and killed them both, and later I tied bricks to the bodies and threw them into the Vistula River."

Nelka struggled to speak for a moment. She started sobbing, and then she hugged me. "You are so brave and truly a hero," she said. "I didn't know that you had put yourself at such risk for me. How can I ever repay you?"

"Don't even think about it," I said. "Is everything okay with you? How are you getting along? Do you need money?"

"I'm getting along just fine," she said. "I'm working from home as a beautician. I don't have any concerns."

I left her apartment feeling happy that my friend had found some peace and that I had played a small part in it.

SUNDAY EVENING ARRIVED, AND WITH it all the guests. Max and Alec served us, having prepared a festive table with plenty of wine and brandy. Nelka sat next to Brigita, and the two struck up a lively conversation. Nelka asked if it was okay to tell Brigita about her past in Poland, and I had no objections.

Nelka barely resembled the haunted, frail woman I had found on the streets of Krakow, and I noticed that Max was especially attentive to her, constantly refilling her wine and plate. When she complimented him on the wine, he fetched her a pen and paper, asking her to write down her address so he could personally deliver a bottle.

By the end of the evening, we were all a little drunk, and I couldn't stop smiling at Shoshana, who couldn't stop laughing. It was hard to believe that the two of us, so recently and so brutally persecuted, now found ourselves surrounded by friends who loved us and wanted to be with us. After hugging and kissing everyone goodnight, we walked home together and got into bed, where we held each other without words and felt truly happy.

A few days later, at the end of our work shift, Max called Shoshana and me over to sit down with him. He poured us some wine.

"David," he said, "I was very taken with your friend Nelka. I went to her apartment yesterday to give her two bottles of the wine she enjoyed so much at the party. I was pleased to learn that she likes me too, and I hope it's the start of something special."

"That's wonderful," I said. "Nelka is a very special woman."

Max waved my words away, seeming a little embarrassed. "But that's not what I wanted to talk to you about. Nelka told me about all you did for her, out of the goodness of your heart." He gave me a pointed look. "Everything you did."

I glanced over at Shoshana, who was frowning thoughtfully, as Max hurried on, his voice gruff but gentle. "I'd like to apologize for the way I treated you. I'm usually a good judge of character, but I was very wrong about you. I went this morning to the commander you met, and I told him what Nelka had said to me. We both think you could make a valuable fighter. He asked me to approach you again and implore you to join us."

"Thank you," I said. "And please thank the commander for the compliment on my behalf, but I still would rather not be active in any of the underground organizations at this stage."

"I understand. Take all the time you need," Max said, surprising me. He surprised me even more when he bid us goodnight with a warm embrace.

"What did Max mean when he said 'everything'?" Shoshana asked on the way home.

Briefly I told her the story of the Polish couple and how I had killed them in self-defense.

"Why didn't you tell me about it?"

"I didn't think it was important," I said. "As far as I'm concerned, it was simply one more terrible event in a long string of horrors. Unfortunately, I had to kill quite a few people to survive."

Shoshana stopped walking and fixed me with a long stare. "I want to know about everything you went through—everything—even if you repeat things I've already heard. If Max hadn't said anything, I wouldn't have known that you helped Nelka in such a noble way. There aren't many people who'd be willing to risk their lives to help a woman they'd never met before."

"I couldn't let such an injustice remain," I said with a shrug.

She wrapped her arms around me. "You are so wonderful to me too. You're helping me recover, and I want to reward you for everything you've done." She leaned back and looked up at me with a mischievous smile on her lips. "And I believe you're going to like your reward very much indeed."

13

"TO DIE OR CONQUER THE MOUNTAIN"

(FROM "THE SONG OF BETAR" BY ZE'EV JABOTINSKY, 1932)

On the surface, life was good for Alec. He had a steady job. He spent Monday and Wednesday mornings with Hannah. And he and I had renewed our friendship under more peaceful circumstances. It seemed to me that he was content, and I mentioned this to him over breakfast at Café Europa.

To my surprise, I learned that not all was to his liking. He was already growing bored with the purely physical relationship he had with Hannah. He was eager to find some way to recreate the action from our partisan days, this time fighting the Brits.

"What happened to you, David?" he asked me. "You used to be so daring and efficient. Why haven't you come up with a plan to assassinate this scum, Jeffries?"

"Surely you remember one of our most important rules as partisans?" I responded. "We need to stay objective and wait for the right moment. Especially when the target is so tempting."

But my explanation didn't satisfy him. I had to promise there would be a plan and that it would involve him.

I spoke to Max later and told him I wanted to arrange a meeting with the secretive commander I had met with before. That same evening, the tough guy who'd picked me up before showed up at the restaurant right before closing time. He was friendly this time, gesturing me to the car waiting outside, and we drove away with no mention of a blindfold. We soon pulled up outside the same house in Talpiot.

"Good to see you, David," the commander said when I walked inside.

"Good to see you too, sir," I responded, somewhat annoyed as I realized that I had yet to learn his name.

"Max told me how you helped that woman get her apartment back in Poland," he said. "I was impressed. Can you tell me more about what happened?"

I gave him a blow-by-blow account, and he listened attentively.

"Anti-Semitism is the mother's milk of the Poles," he said when I came to the end of my story. "Like you, I was born in Belarus, but I spent most of my adult life in Poland. I fought against the Nazis, but when the Northern Front collapsed, I fled east and was captured by the Russians. Eventually, I was released to serve in General Anders's army of Polish exiles. When we reached Israel, I deserted with most of the other Jewish soldiers. Anyway, here we are. Am I to understand from this meeting that you've decided to join us?"

"Not yet," I said. "I am here to speak to you because I have a friend, a former partisan and skilled fighter, who I know would be willing to carry out operations as a free agent, if that's of interest to you."

The commander frowned. "Look, David," he said. "We are an organization with a clear ideology, and we enlist people who identify with our ideology and share our goals. Which group do you and your friend identify with most closely?"

"I can only speak for myself, but I believe my friend feels the same. I value them all, but I feel the Irgun best fits my beliefs," I said. "You mentioned that you reached Israel as part of General Anders's army. I know that Menachem Begin, the commander of the Irgun, also arrived in Israel with General Anders, so I do believe you are a commander in the Irgun."

He hesitated before responding. "If you or your friend are not willing to join our organization and operate within its frameworks, I cannot tell you which group I'm with, and it's not relevant right now anyway. What's important is that an underground organization requires just as much discipline, if not more, than a regular army. Your partisan group couldn't have survived without you as its undisputed commander. And I can't allow individuals to act without our oversight. If you or your friend wish to play a part in the struggle, you must join one of the resistance movements. And let me say this as clearly as possible: we are opposed to lone-wolf actions, even if they serve our cause."

I realized I had reached a dead end. "I understand your position," I said. "I'll speak to my friend, and we'll decide together what to do."

ON TUESDAY, SHOSHANA AND I went to breakfast at Avrum and Hannah's apartment. Without even saying hello, Avrum nodded for me to follow him into his study. "The anti-Semitism in the British police force is getting worse by the day." He paced the room as he talked to me. "If you hadn't convinced me to gather information for the Haganah, I would have resigned a long time ago. The top brass meets constantly to discuss ways to keep the Jews in check. They've even set up a new department to root out immigrants who came here with forged papers and then throw them into internment camps or deport them back to Europe. The head detective is a radical anti-Semite who practically throws a party whenever he uncovers a Jew with forged documents."

I nodded, not sure where to steer the conversation.

"You don't seem particularly interested in the matter," Avrum complained. "I understand you're still waiting for information on Inspector Jeffries, but I don't have anything new on that front."

"That's all right, Avrum," I said. "And I am interested. I'm sure Yaakov and the Haganah will be too. Tell me everything you know."

A look of satisfaction appeared on Avrum's face. "Good. I'm happy to hear that, because in my opinion, something needs to be done to put an end to the damage that anti-Semitic bastard is causing the Jewish community here. With the immigration restrictions, there's been a lot of fraud they can go after—forged papers, authentic documents with new photographs inserted, wives and children added to passports, Jews who have remained here on visitors' permits as athletes competing in the Maccabiah, for example. And many soldiers from the Jewish Brigade have even given their papers to Jewish refugees in Europe and then reported them lost or stolen."

"So, what's this detective's name?" I asked.

"Nick Ellis. He's thirty-six years old and holds the rank of detective inspector. He lives in Talbieh with all those wealthy Arab snobs."

"Do you know where exactly?"

"Emir Abdullah Road in Tarsha House, which the British

Government Housing Department leases from an Arab family. The building has nine apartments, mostly occupied by civil servants in the British Meteorological Service and their families, but Ellis used his connections to get one for himself."

"What does he look like?" I asked.

"He's tall, with a large belly," Avrum said. "Brown eyes and thinning brown hair."

"Thanks," I said. "I'll pass the details on to Yaakov."

Hannah kept glancing at me longingly as we ate breakfast. I ignored her and focused on Avrum and Shoshana.

"Did you notice the way Hannah was looking at you?" Shoshana asked me after we had left. "How can she behave like that in front of Avrum and me? Perhaps we should stop having breakfasts with them."

"Hannah is a bit of a flirt," I agreed. "And if she makes you uncomfortable, we can certainly limit our time with them."

She nodded, and we walked the rest of the way home in silence.

AT THE RESTAURANT THAT AFTERNOON, I told Alec about Ellis and how we would target him for our next mission.

"You've given up on Jeffries?" he asked.

"We just don't have enough information to go after him now," I said. "I suggest you pay a visit to Yaakov tomorrow. Ask him to meet with us as soon as possible."

"Do you think the Haganah will help us take out Ellis?" Alec asked.

"No," I said, "but maybe we can get some more information from them. To avoid creating any dots that might later be connected, we must not tell Yaakov anything about what Ellis looks like or where he lives. More than that, we need to confuse the trail. I don't want it to go directly from Avrum to us to the corpse in the morgue."

Alec grinned. "You are something. You think of everything."

Alec and I met up with Yaakov the following morning. Once again, we sat on the ledge across the street from the Tnuva dairy. I told Yaakov about Nick Ellis and his department but didn't share any of the details about what he looked like or where he lived.

"I haven't heard anything about this," Yaakov said. "Thanks for the information. I'll pass it on to the right people, but I don't expect they'll do anything to him directly—we don't work like that, as you know, though I wish we would."

Yaakov lit a cigarette, snapping his metal lighter shut with an angry clank. "The British have stopped nine of our ships in the past six months. That's ten thousand immigrants, all of them rotting in the Atlit internment camp near Haifa. After all our people have been through, another camp? Makes my blood boil! Maybe the Irgun and Lehi are right; maybe we should wage an all-out war against the British."

Alec started to agree with Yaakov, but I signaled him to remain quiet. A short time later, we parted and Yaakov returned to the dairy.

"I'm going to do some reconnaissance around Ellis's building," I told Alec. "Then we'll meet to make a plan." Alec nodded. We agreed to meet later and parted.

I walked to Talbieh to scout around Ellis's apartment. A British soldier guarded the entrance to the building, and it didn't look like he was going anywhere. I waited two days and then returned early in the morning, in the hope of catching a glimpse of Ellis on his way to work. I wasn't disappointed.

He was exactly as Avrum had described—a tall, balding man with a paunch. When I saw him, he was standing by the soldiers at the entrance to the building, glancing at his watch. After a few minutes, a car pulled up, and Ellis climbed inside and was driven away.

If Alec and I tried to hit him as he left or came home from work, we'd have to contend with the guard and possibly the driver as well. Even if we managed to kill them, it likely would take us too long to escape. If we had a team, we could try to block his car somewhere and gun him down in the street, but I didn't want to expose my work to the underground organizations yet—or cede control over the operation.

I gave up on the idea of carrying out the hit on the street and came to the conclusion that I had to find a way to get into his building. I remembered meeting a man at the YMCA boxing club who worked for the Meteorological Service. I couldn't remember his name, but he had been talkative, boasting about knowing what the weather would be like days ahead of time. He'd seemed boring and shallow, and I had not paid attention to him.

THE NEXT DAY, I SHOWED up at the YMCA and visited my boxing coach, Yousef.

"David!" he exclaimed. "It's so good to see you! You haven't been here in ages."

"I know, I'm sorry," I said. "I've been busy, but I've missed our boxing sessions."

The meteorologist wasn't at the club that day or the next few days that followed. Luckily, he showed up at the beginning of the next week. I recognized him immediately—tall, with glasses, and neatly combed hair parted in the middle. I pointed him out to Yousef. He told me the man's name was Colin Swift. I approached him, extended my hand, and introduced myself.

"Hello, I'm David. Do you remember me from our training sessions a while back?"

"Yes, I do," he said. He seemed surprised that I had approached him.

I went out of my way to be nice to him during our training session. When it was over, I suggested we share a cup of tea with Yousef at the club café. He hesitated for a moment and then consented.

Colin ordered a large cup of tea with milk, English style. I ordered plain tea, and Yousef asked for a small cup of Turkish coffee, Arabic style. I laughed at Colin's jokes, even though I didn't really get them—perhaps I didn't entirely understand English idioms or appreciate his dry British humor—but he seemed to enjoy his own wit immensely.

After I got tired of pretending to laugh, I steered the conversation to the subject of the weather, marveling at his ability to offer an accurate forecast for the coming days. When I asked him to explain how he made his forecasts, Yousef gave me a confused and curious look.

But Colin was thrilled to have an attentive audience, telling me all about the weather station's offices, which were located in the former Palace Hotel near the Mamilla cemetery.

"The British government leased the building, and it serves as the headquarters of the Land Registry, the Agricultural Department, and other official bodies," he said. "The people in charge of the building are paranoid. They think the underground will blow up the building at any moment." He snorted. "They've even wrapped barbed wire around the drains and gutters."

"And where do you live?" I asked.

"I actually live in a very nice place," he said. "The government leased a small apartment building in Talbieh, where I live with my wife and two children. Do you play rummy, by chance?"

As if Baruch wasn't enough, now I had run into a British version. But meeting Baruch had helped me with Sergeant Perry, and I was hopeful Colin would prove equally useful.

"How did you guess?" I responded. "I love it but can never find anyone to play with me."

"It's not a very popular game in England. Back home people prefer bridge, whist, even canasta, and I don't have anyone to play rummy with. If you have some free time right now, perhaps you'd like to come over for a game?"

"Gladly," I replied. Yousef politely declined Colin's offer to join us, and after bidding him goodbye, my new friend and I went down to the locker room on the ground floor. We showered, dressed, and walked to his apartment, which was just down the street from the YMCA.

"He's my guest," Colin said to the guard at the entrance to the building. The guard nodded hello and held the door open for us.

Colin quickly introduced me to his wife, Jenny, who had her hands full with their two small children, a son and daughter. After introductions, we immediately sat down to a game of rummy. He turned out to be a good player, but the many hours I had spent playing with Baruch had improved my game, and I held my own against him.

After a few rounds, Jenny offered us tea and cake. I readily accepted, and she sat down to join us.

"Does everyone in the building work for the Meteorological Service?" I asked, after asking Jenny a few polite questions about her children.

"Yes, everyone does," she said, "except for that rude policeman who lives next door to us. He's always complaining that our children are too noisy. You've seen how good they are, but if they get even a little loud when they're playing, he comes banging on the door to complain. Horrible man."

Colin didn't say anything, but I could tell from the look on his face that he shared his wife's sentiments.

"It was very nice to meet you both," I said when we had finished our tea and cake. "Thanks for your hospitality."

"We enjoyed your company very much," Colin said. "Can you come by again sometime for another game?"

"I'd love to," I said, and we arranged to meet up again in four days.

I checked out the building on my way out, looking for a way to get in without being spotted by the guard. I found nothing and resolved to take a closer look on my next visit.

When I returned four days later, the guard at the entrance didn't remember me and called Colin on the intercom before he would let me in. We played for about an hour before Jenny appeared with tea and cookies. At that moment, the children playing in the next room shrieked loudly. Someone pounded on the wall to hush them.

Ellis, I thought.

"Have you done anything yet about that damn policeman?" she snapped at her husband as she sat the tray down with a clatter.

"Yes, we're taking care of it," Colin said. He looked at me and frowned. "The past few days have been awful," he said, a look of disgust on his face. "His wife just went back to England on holiday, and he's turned their apartment into a brothel. Every evening around seven, a prostitute, caked in makeup, goes up to his apartment and then leaves around midnight. It's unacceptable. The building is home to families with young children. I've spoken to the other tenants, and we've decided to lodge a complaint with the Housing Department and ask that he be removed from the building."

Jenny began to clear the cups and plates from the table, and I couldn't help but admire her delicate facial features. In a way, she reminded me of Alec. She could have been his twin—except for the makeup of course. A light dawned suddenly within my mind. Nelka was a beautician. With her help, Alec, with his own delicate facial features, could dress up as a prostitute and simply walk in through the front door. I wanted to leave at once to tell Alec about my plan but didn't want to offend Colin, so I stayed for a few more games.

Alec wasn't thrilled about dressing up as a woman, but he was fired up by the opportunity to assassinate Ellis. We went to see Nelka, and I told her that we were going to play a prank on one of our friends. When she heard our idea for Alec to dress as a sexy woman and pretend to proposition one of our friends, she laughed and agreed to help.

"But you can't tell anyone," I added. "Especially not Max. He doesn't approve of our foolishness."

Nelka smiled. "My lips are sealed. I'll take Alec's measurements now, and then you can come back tomorrow at four o'clock. Alec, you must shave thoroughly or this won't work, despite those sultry eyes of yours."

"I will," he said, and I saw a sudden gleam in those "sultry" eyes. "But I'm not going to do this alone." He glanced over at me and grinned. "Although you'll likely be the ugliest woman on the street, you're coming with me, friend."

"I can't see how anyone would believe that I'm a woman," I protested. "I'm too manly!"

Nelka laughed. "You underestimate my abilities, David. I can make you quite presentable, I promise."

Alec's grin widened, and I gave in. I was concerned about letting my friend go into the apartment building without backup anyway. It hadn't occurred to me that I could pass as a woman too. I still wasn't sure, but I decided to trust Nelka's talents.

WE CAME BACK THE NEXT day, and Nelka showed us the costumes she had put together for us. First, we put on large padded bras. Alec got a low-cut red dress that hugged his body so tightly he had to do some strategic tucking so the bulge in his crotch wouldn't give us away. The dress came above his knees, and I frowned.

"You shaved your legs?" I asked.

He raised one brow. "And my chest. Didn't you?"

I smiled slightly. "Not going to happen, friend."

"The guards will never believe you're a woman if you don't," he complained. "You look like a wolfman."

Nelka intervened with a solution. "I have a floor-length evening gown," she said. "It will cover your legs, and the blue will go wonderfully with your dark skin, David."

I rolled my eyes. "Lovely."

The blue dress was as low cut as Alec's, but Nelka provided a stylish matching cape that covered my chest. I felt so silly.

Next, she opened two large round boxes and took out two wigs: a long blond, itchy one for me and a dark one, pulled back into a chignon, for Alec.

"You both look ridiculous," Nelka said, "but some makeup will fix that!"

She applied long false eyelashes to our eyelids, and although we had shaved before coming, we still needed a thick layer of face makeup to make our skin look more even. She used eye shadow and eyeliner to highlight our eyes and painted our lips with a bold shade of red lipstick. We refused the false nails, knowing how much we'd have to use our hands, but we allowed her to paint our nails dark red. Nelka laughed frequently through the whole procedure.

I kept reminding myself this was all necessary. I looked at Alec and blinked. He really did look like a sexy woman. I couldn't help myself. "You look great, honey," I said.

"If you were a man, I'd say maybe we should go straight to bed," he responded in a womanly voice. We all burst out laughing.

"This is the most I've laughed in years," Nelka said. She looked at us appraisingly. "You're tall, David, so you should wear flat shoes."

She handed me a pair of fancy flats. I was relieved. I'd had visions of tripping over my own feet as I tried to walk down the street in heels.

"Alec, you're shorter, so you can wear these." She reached into a box and pulled out a pair of high heels. She handed them to him with a teasing smile.

Alec waved his hands in front of him in protest. "Oh no—no, no, no! There's no way I can walk all the way from Geula to Talbieh in those shoes! I'll break my neck!"

We came to a compromise: Alec would wear his regular shoes until we neared Ellis's building, and then he'd change into the heels, carrying his regular shoes in the handbag Nelka had provided.

Once dressed, we headed out, knowing we had to get to Ellis's apartment building before his nightly prostitute arrived at seven o'clock. On our way to Talbieh, we encountered curious and interested looks from men we passed by. To be honest, it was Alec who got most of the stares and propositions—which was perfectly fine with me. Fortunately, none of the men were very persistent, and we quickly made our way undisturbed down the street.

Thirty minutes later, we stopped around the corner from Ellis's building to let Alec put on the high heels. He stashed his regular shoes in the handbag.

"You talk to the guard," I said. "Talk in a feminine voice. And don't forget, you can always use one of your shoes as a weapon." I grinned. "The heels are like spikes."

"True," he said, "but I have something a little deadlier in mind."

I stopped smiling and glanced at my watch. It was 6:40 p.m. Getting ready for the mission had been amusing, but now it was time to get down to business. I peered around the corner and saw that the guard, as usual, was sitting at the entrance to the building.

"Let's go," I said.

Alec walked around the corner of the building with a convincing swing of his hips. I followed.

"We're here to see Mr. Ellis," Alec said in his high-pitched voice. The guard gave us a dirty look and told us Ellis's floor and apartment number. As we climbed the stairs, Alec opened his handbag and took out a short, thin knife. He stuck it through the bun at the nape of the wig he wore.

"Clever," I said.

When Ellis opened the door, he only saw Alec at first. "Good, you're early, my darling," he said. Then he saw me, and his beady eyes lit up. "What a nice surprise—I asked for one girl, and they sent me two. Don't worry, I can handle both of you, and I will pay you generously."

He ushered us in, locked the door, and immediately grabbed Alec, fondling his breasts through the padded bra. The look of surprise on his face when he felt Alec's muscular chest under the padding was priceless. I wanted to laugh, but things quickly turned serious.

Alec pulled the knife from his wig and shoved Ellis against the wall, holding the weapon to his throat. "Inspector Ellis," he said in his pseudo woman's voice, "I entered Palestine on a forged passport, and I want to turn myself in to your corpse." Ellis panicked and pushed Alec with both hands, making a break for the door. I tripped him on the way, and he sprawled across the floor. Alec was on him in seconds, his blade making short work of our enemy. As soon as we confirmed he was dead, we headed back down the stairs.

The guard was surprised to see us leaving so soon. "Mr. Ellis doesn't like us; he wants another woman," Alec explained in his feminine voice. The guard rolled his eyes and waved us on.

We walked around the corner, and Alec changed back into his regular shoes. Then we hurried back to Nelka's apartment. We stopped in the shadows near her place, waiting until the street was empty before walking quickly to her apartment.

"That was quick," Nelka said after opening the door and welcoming us back in. "How did your prank go?"

"Perfectly," I said. I pulled the wig off, glad to be free of it. "We couldn't have done it without you."

"I was glad to help," she said. As she smiled at me, I suddenly realized that it would be better to get rid of the costumes and the wigs in order to avoid any connection to Ellis's murder.

"Would you mind if we held on to these?" I asked. "We might want to pull another prank in a few days."

She raised her eyebrows in surprise but nodded. "Of course. If you need help with the makeup again, just let me know."

"Speaking of makeup . . ." Alec said, pointing to his pretty face. "It comes off, I hope?"

Nelka smiled and helped us remove our makeup. We changed back into our regular clothes and put the costumes in a bag. I hoped Nelka wasn't too attached to the clothes or wigs, because she would never see them again.

THE FOLLOWING DAY, I WENT to work my shift at Café Pinsk. As the dinner rush was dying down, Avrum appeared in the window and waved me outside.

"Nick Ellis!" he said in an excited whisper.

"Yeah, what about him?" I asked.

"He was murdered yesterday," Avrum said. "At first, they thought it was the underground, but it turns out he was ordering prostitutes to the house while his wife is back home in England. Two women were there last night, and the police think maybe they got into a fight over money or something. One of them stabbed him—can you believe that?"

"Based on what you told me, it doesn't sound like there's much reason to mourn the man," I said.

"On the contrary," Avrum responded. "I'm starting to believe that maybe there's someone up there, watching over the Jewish people after all their terrible suffering."

"Maybe you're right," I said. "I sure hope so." *And maybe there's someone down here too*, I thought.

Ellis's assassination had been a satisfying and well-executed operation, but it did nothing to soothe my frustration about Inspector Jeffries. I was more determined than ever to get rid of him too.

14

"READY AS ONE TO
FACE THE FIRE"

(FROM "ON GUARD WE STAND," A POEM BY
AVRAHAM SHLONSKY, 1941)

A week later, when I was working my evening shift at the restaurant, a British soldier came in and notified me that I had an appointment with General Barker for the following Monday morning at ten. He said I should be at the Schneller Barracks thirty minutes early with my ID.

Max heard the conversation, and he approached me after the soldier left. "What's going on? Are you collaborating with the British now?"

Pulling him aside, I explained how I had fooled Inspector Jeffries with the newspaper clippings about General Barker and the liberation of Bergen-Belsen. When I told Max that Jeffries had arranged a meeting with the general to allow me to thank him for saving my aunt and uncle, he actually smiled.

"I have to admire your resourcefulness," Max said. "I think you should update our man from the underground as soon as possible." I agreed, and he wasted no time contacting the unnamed commander.

My familiar muscular chaperone appeared at the café just before closing time. Some fifteen minutes later, I walked into the house in Talpiot.

"I understand you've become someone of importance," the commander said. "General Barker, no less, wants to meet with you. Can you tell me why?"

I repeated my explanation, and the commander took a moment to think. "Barker is a cruel and harsh opponent of Jewish immigration to Israel," he said. "He is our top target for assassination, as you must remember, and an anti-Semite of the worst kind."

"Any plan based on my meeting with Barker is doomed to failure," I said. "I've visited the Schneller Barracks before, and it's impossible to smuggle in a weapon. There will be other people at the meeting too—aides and bodyguards. Even if I were willing to undertake a suicide mission, there's no way I'd be able to kill him inside the barracks. You'll have to think of another way."

"Unfortunately, I have to agree with you. We'll try to think of another plan, and I'd like you to reconsider my offer to join our organization. You can let me know through Max if and when you are ready."

I reported to the gate of the Schneller Barracks on Monday morning, and after a thorough search, a soldier escorted me to Inspector Jeffries's office. I thanked him for arranging the meeting with General Barker.

"You deserve it," Jeffries said. "You're the only person who has given me any useful information about Sergeant Perry's murder, although we still have no suspects. Come, I'll escort you to the bureau of the base commander. You'll meet the general there."

I was patted down again before entering the commander's

bureau, and General Barker walked in at precisely ten o'clock. He was a relatively small man, with a thin mustache and a severe look on his face. In spite of his size, his presence filled the room. The officers and soldiers snapped to attention and saluted him, and he returned the gesture.

"Sir, this is David, whose aunt and uncle you saved when you liberated Bergen-Belsen," Jeffries said.

The general extended his hand, and I thanked him with all the groveling I could muster.

"To begin with," Barker said, "I must point out that I was not single-handedly responsible for the liberation of Bergen-Belsen. The brave men I had the honor of leading into battle also deserve your gratitude. Secondly, I appreciate your loyalty to your benefactors, which is far too rare among your people. We rescued them from the bloody Germans and provide peace and order to this—" Barker stopped and composed himself. "Your aunt and uncle, where are they now?"

His question threw me for a moment, and I inwardly cursed myself for not having prepared a story. "The Jewish people owe the British nation and its courageous armed forces a huge debt of gratitude for their efforts to defeat the Nazi enemy," I said, buying myself a moment. "My aunt and uncle are currently in a displaced persons camp in Italy. Due to the restrictions on Jewish immigration, they haven't been able to obtain the official permits that would allow them to come here."

Barker scowled at me. "I'm a soldier," he said, "and I don't intervene in politics. The British government made its decision concerning immigration as part of its efforts to maintain peace and coexistence between the Jews and Arabs in Palestine. We're allowing fifteen hundred Jews into Palestine every month. The Jewish Agency decides who gets in, not us. Your aunt and uncle should talk to them."

"Of course, sir."

And with that, our conversation ended.

Jeffries accompanied me to the gate of the barracks. "Do you have any contacts in the Jewish Agency?" he asked. "Perhaps you could grease the wheels a bit. And if you're short of cash, you should know you could earn good money working for us. We pay handsomely for information that leads to the arrest of a wanted underground member. Even more if it's a senior level member. How much do you earn as a waiter at the restaurant?"

"Two pounds a month and perhaps another pound in tips," I replied.

Jeffries smiled. "For information leading to the capture of Lehi leader Yitzhak Shamir, we'd pay you fifteen hundred pounds—your total wages for fifty years! What do you say, David?"

"Fifteen hundred pounds is a lot of money indeed," I said. "I'm not helping you for the money, but that's certainly an attractive offer to consider."

THE FOLLOWING MONTH, JUNE 1946, was a painful one for the British, for the underground fighting the British, and for the entire Jewish community. On June 10, the Irgun launched a coordinated attack on the rail lines from Lod to Jaffa, Haifa, and Jerusalem. On June 12, the British government reneged on its agreement to permit one hundred thousand Jews from displaced persons camps in Europe to immigrate to Israel. The following day, a British military court sentenced Irgun fighters Yosef Simhon and Michael Eshbal to death by hanging. The two had been injured and captured in the Irgun's assault on the Sarafand base.

On the night of June 16, the Haganah carried out an operation known as Night of the Bridges, blowing up nine major bridges, from Metula in the north to the Gaza region in the south. On June 18, Lehi fighters attacked a railroad maintenance facility in Haifa, causing extensive damage to engines, cars, and other rail equipment. On their way back from the operation, the Lehi fighters ran into a British ambush. Nine Lehi members were killed and twenty-three others, men and women, were captured. That same day, Irgun fighters stormed the Yarkon Hotel in Tel Aviv, kidnapped five British officers, and announced that they would be released only if the British authorities retracted the death sentence handed down against Yosef Simhon and Michael Eshbal five days earlier.

On June 29, the British responded with Operation Broadside, a large-scale military offensive that became known among the Jewish community as Black Sabbath. A general curfew was imposed in all cities throughout the country. Seventeen thousand British soldiers conducted raids on Jewish settlements and institutions in an effort to seize weapons held by the Jewish underground. Some five thousand individuals were apprehended, several of the Jewish community's senior leaders among them. On the same day, British soldiers opened fire and killed three people during their raids on the Ein Harod and Tel Yosef kibbutzim.

Mr. Glickstein, whose home we'd used for the meetings of our Jerusalem group, was one of those arrested on Black Sabbath. Yaakov escaped the purge, and he announced that the upcoming meeting would take place at the home of the Cohen family, the owners of the grocery store. I was surprised to discover that the Cohens were active in the Haganah. I had learned in Belarus, and also here in Israel, that looks could be deceiving during times of war.

"What brings you here, Mr. Don Juan?" Mrs. Cohen asked when Alec and I walked into their apartment. "If you're here to look for pretty girls, I'm afraid there aren't any today."

"Don't be so modest!" I exclaimed. "If it weren't for Mr. Cohen, I would have tried to seduce you a long time ago." My attempt to kid around was met with her usual look of displeasure and suspicion.

Yaakov began with a review of what had happened on Black Sabbath. He said that despite the concerted British efforts, the underground organizations hadn't been dealt a lethal blow and the Jewish Resistance Movement remained active.

"I'm expecting a stormy July," he said. "The British have violated the rules of the game. They aren't allowing Jews to immigrate to Israel, they've banned the establishment of new communities and settlements, and many of our leaders have been arrested. The Haganah's political arm won't allow us to strike at the British, but the Irgun and Lehi will hit the British hard. I hope it teaches them that they can't ignore our demands."

When the meeting was over, Alec and I told Yaakov that he had our support and we would think of ways to help him.

I received indirect confirmation of Yaakov's report a few evenings later, when Max asked me and Shoshana to join him for a brandy after the restaurant closed.

"I had a talk with our mutual friend, the commander," Max said. "Because the Haganah is under constraints from its political leadership, the Irgun and Lehi will lead the retaliation against the British for their brutal actions on Black Sabbath. And he asked me to see if you were ready to join up now. This month is going to be a critical one, and if you want to take part in the struggle, you should join now."

"Stop pressuring him," Shoshana said. "He's already done so much for the Jewish people, and he's put himself at enough risk. He'll let you know when he's ready."

Max didn't say a word as we sat in the restaurant drinking our brandy, the silence between us like a heavy blanket.

"Let me think about it," I finally said. Max gave me a disdainful look, rose, and left the room.

A FEW DAYS LATER, I was at work when a familiar-looking British policeman walked into Café Pinsk and ordered a drink at the bar. He downed it quickly and immediately ordered a second. When he noticed me looking at him, he winked, and I walked over. "Your service has improved greatly," he said.

"Thank you," I said. "We're always trying to improve."

I returned the following morning to the Schneller Barracks, and after the routine security check, I was escorted to Jeffries's office, where I found him sitting at his desk with a pensive look on his face.

"I'd like to have a serious talk with you," he said. "But first a drink—a good one." He stood up and poured us each a glass of Glenfiddich whiskey.

"The mass arrests we carried out were very successful," he began, "and our political leadership is conducting talks with their counterpart in the Jewish community. We feel the pressure has paid off, and the Jewish Agency wants, for the time being, to keep things quiet. Their influence, however, is restricted to the Haganah, not the Irgun or Lehi. We don't expect them to end the campaign of violence against us, though of course we will respond with even harsher actions of our own."

I listened quietly, wondering why he was telling me this, but I didn't have to wait long for the answer.

"I want you to work as my agent in one of these organizations," Jeffries said. "You're an intelligent young man, who would be an asset to any underground movement. Especially with their recent loss of manpower, you'll be playing a part in operational activities in no time at all."

There was something alarming about his tone, a warning that this wasn't merely a friendly request.

"My solidarity with the British is sincere," I said with caution, "but it's hard for me to see myself joining the underground just to betray them. I endured a great deal of suffering before I came here, and all I want right now is some peace and quiet."

Jeffries glanced at me. "I thought you'd say that, and that's why I'm not giving you a choice. A few months ago, we set up a new department to examine the papers of all the new arrivals in Palestine. I ran a check on your papers and those of your girlfriend. The check took some time, because the head of the department was murdered. But two days ago, I received the results. You were cleared, but Shoshana wasn't."

His words startled me, but I kept a straight face. Apparently, Nelka and I had managed to obtain exceptionally good forgeries, while Shoshana had not.

"In keeping with regulations," Jeffries continued, "I should have issued an arrest warrant against Miss Shoshana Bukstein, in which case she would already be at the Atlit detention camp, awaiting deportation. But because of your cooperation, I haven't yet, and I assume you'll continue to cooperate in the future."

My eyes were fixed on his neck while he was speaking, and I clenched my fists at my side as I fought the urge to strangle him.

"Come now," he said, apparently picking up on my agitation and trying to calm me down. "It's not so bad. We'll brief you thoroughly on how to join the underground organization you're sent to, and I'll make sure you are handsomely rewarded for your troubles."

"And Shoshana?" I asked.

He raised one brow and smiled. "Now, if you'll excuse me for a moment . . ." Jeffries stepped out of the office. He obviously wanted to make me sweat over Shoshana's fate, but I wouldn't allow him to shake me. Soon he returned with one of his men.

"This is Sergeant Richards," Jefferies said. "He'll guide you in how to join the underground."

Richards gave me a stiff nod, his thick British accent grating on my nerves as he gave me instructions. "Go see Reuven Haimovich. He owns a furniture store on the corner of Geula Street and Yonah. Tell him you want to join the underground to fight the British."

"And what if he asks me how I found him?" I asked.

Jeffries and Richards looked at each other. Richards shrugged. "Tell him that someone you met at the restaurant sent you," he said. "Someone who wants to remain anonymous."

"In the meantime," Jeffries said, "you and I will stop meeting for a while. We'll get together again only after you have information to pass on. If you're ever captured by our men, wait until someone from the CID shows up, and tell him to call me."

For the first time since I'd become a partisan commander, I found myself taking orders rather than giving them, and I didn't like it. But Jeffries had the upper hand . . . at least for now.

"Don't forget," Jeffries said after the sergeant had left the room, "I'm the only reason your girlfriend isn't in a detention camp right now. But I promise that if you prove yourself to be a good source of information, I will personally make sure she obtains legal status here."

As soon as I got to Café Pinsk that afternoon, I asked Max to contact his superior and tell him I needed to meet urgently.

When I arrived at the house in Talpiot that night, I told the commander about my meeting with Jeffries.

"British efforts to plant moles in the underground are nothing new," he said with a stern look on his face. "On a number of occasions, they've managed to cause serious damage with the help of those traitors, but we pick ourselves up and press on with the struggle. Do exactly as Jeffries instructed and remain in touch with me via Max. We'll take the necessary measures to protect ourselves."

"If you have any intention of killing Haimovich," I said, "I ask that you hold off for a while. The British would suspect me of ratting on him."

The commander's face darkened. "You think we don't know what we're doing?" he snapped. "Don't worry, we won't put you at risk, and we'll feed you information to help you maintain your cover."

When the driver dropped me off at home, my burly chaperone surprised me by getting out of the car and offering me his hand. "I'm Shimon," he said, and I realized that he now considered me a member of the underground.

15

"THE ENEMY CREEPING
EVER CLOSER"

(FROM "ON GUARD WE STAND," A POEM BY
AVRAHAM SHLONSKY, 1941)

The next morning, I followed Sergeant Richards's instructions and went to see Reuven Haimovich. He looked like he was in his forties, full figured, with piercing eyes. He motioned for me to follow him into the small office near the entrance to his store. "What can I do for you, young man?" he asked in a distinctly Polish accent.

"I came to Israel from Belarus about a year ago," I replied. "I needed some time to recover from everything I went through during the war. Now that I'm back on my feet, I want to play a part in the struggle against the British."

"Who sent you to me?" Haimovich asked.

"I work as a waiter at Café Pinsk," I said. "A customer and I were talking about the restrictions the British have put on immigration, and I told him how angry it made me. He asked if I was interested in doing something about it. I said I was, and he wrote down your name and address. I haven't seen him since."

Haimovich looked me straight in the eyes. "Are you willing to sacrifice yourself for the sake of your homeland?" he asked.

I could have simply said yes, but I thought that might seem suspicious. "Let's not go too far," I said. "I'm willing to enlist and help the underground, and I know it's dangerous. I think that's enough at this stage."

"Okay," Haimovich said. "Come back in an hour."

"Wait," I said. "Which group are we talking about?"

"You'll find out if you're accepted. Now leave."

I was getting tired of being ordered around, but I did as he said. I spent the hour walking, my mind on the past. When I returned to the store at the given hour, a car, a driver, and an escort were waiting for me. We hadn't traveled farther than a block when my escort—a short, thin man with a mustache and curly hair—pulled out a blindfold and tied it around my head, covering my eyes, sending me into darkness.

We reached our destination about twenty minutes later. I was helped out of the car, and we walked for several minutes. We stopped. I heard a door open, and I was pushed forward. I took a few steps and stumbled over what seemed to be a threshold or entrance. A door clanged shut behind me.

"You can remove the blindfold now," the escort said.

I pulled the cloth from my eyes and looked around. We were in a small room. There were several chairs and a desk, and from their industrial look, my impression was that we were in the office of a small factory. A few seconds later, a door on the other side of the office opened, and a tall, thin man, with a hooked nose and thin lips, walked in. He looked at me quizzically and began questioning me about my past in Belarus, my time in Israel, and my political viewpoints. He wanted precise details, and I lost my patience a few minutes into the interrogation.

"Would you like to know my shoe size too?" I blurted out.

"A few months ago," he growled, "a man just like you sat in that same chair. We accepted him into the organization, and he turned out to be an informant working for the British. We caught him, and he was punished, but he caused significant harm to our organization. Stop joking and answer my questions, or you can go back to where you came from."

The interrogation went on for another hour or so. "It'll take me a few days to verify what you've told me," the man said when he was done. "If we approve your request, we'll send someone to Café Pinsk. If not, you won't hear from us again."

A few days later I was chopping carrots before my shift when a young man entered the restaurant, exchanged a few words with Max, and then approached me.

"You've been accepted into the organization," he said in a low voice. "Your first task is to post leaflets around the city. Go to Reuven's furniture store tomorrow night after work."

Posting leaflets wasn't exactly what I had in mind for my first task, and I felt somewhat offended. I also disliked the idea of having to work with a man I knew to be an informant. But this was the situation I found myself in.

"I've decided to join the underground," I told Shoshana on our way home from work the following night. "I'm going to post leaflets tonight."

"Post leaflets?" she stared at me in disbelief. "With all your experience, that's what they've given you to do?"

I had no intention of telling her about Jeffries's coercion, but I didn't want to lie to her either. "Well, I am still very new to the organization. I assume I'll get more important tasks in time."

Shoshana stopped walking and looked up at me. "I'm fine with your decision to join the resistance." She gave me a small smile. "Who knows? You may even end up posting leaflets I helped prepare at the printing house."

We parted with a quick kiss, and Shoshana went into our apartment. I headed for Geula Street. The office at Haimovich's store was filled with stacks of leaflets that read:

break the shackles of slavery.
be a proud and free man.
volunteer for the fighting liberation underground!

Underneath the words was the emblem of the Irgun—an arm holding a rifle against the backdrop of the Holy Land. So now I at least knew which group I had joined.

I picked up a large stack of leaflets, a bucket, and a brush and headed out with Haimovich. Following his directions, we turned right from Geula Street onto Chancellor, pasting leaflets on walls and fences all the way up the street. I cursed Jeffries as I worked—and myself and the forger of Shoshana's documents.

When I saw the policemen, it was too late to run.

One of them raised his club with the intention of bringing it down on my head, and I instinctively blocked his arm and kicked him hard between his legs. As he bent over, I heard the click of a revolver and raised my hands in surrender. Haimovich's hands were already raised. The policeman I'd kicked, slammed his club against the side of my head. Blinding pain laced through my head as I fell to the ground and blacked out.

I woke to find myself in a detention cell. My head ached, and when I touched it, I could feel a large lump. I called out to Haimovich, but he wasn't in the cell with me. I assumed he had already identified himself to the police and been released. I lay back and slept a little despite the pain and woke later to the sound of someone opening the hatch in the upper part of the cell door. A British face appeared at the opening.

"Where am I?" I asked.

"You're in a CID holding cell," the man said. "I'm taking you for questioning now—and for your own good, I suggest that you don't try anything like you did last night."

"Before you do anything," I said, "call extension 8611 at the Schneller Barracks and speak to Inspector Jeffries. Tell him you have David Gabinsky in custody."

The investigator looked at me and then closed the hatch without saying a word. I could just imagine what he was thinking—*another despicable informant.*

When the door to the cell opened some two hours later, the CID officer had returned with a British policeman.

"He's all yours," the officer said. I was escorted to Jeffries's office in the Schneller Barracks. The inspector ushered me into a chair, forgoing the whiskey this time. He looked angry.

"I thought we agreed that you wouldn't resist if you got arrested," he said, his voice terse. "And yet you assaulted a British policeman. You're lucky you weren't shot. I didn't take you for such a fool."

"You're right," I replied, "but when the policeman raised his club with the intention of hitting me in the head, my instincts took over."

"It was foolish," Jeffries said, "and a mistake that you mustn't make again."

"I'm sorry, sir."

"I understand you've been recruited by the Irgun."

"Yes, sir. I guess I'm on probation for now. It's safe to assume that I'll be doing trivial missions for a while. I'm sure they'll be cautious and keep an eye on me before I hear any significant information."

He nodded. "That's fine. The upcoming month is a critical one, but I see you as a long-term investment. Contrary to the foolish hopes of the underground, we will be here in Palestine for many years to come. With the help of people like you, we will eliminate the terrorists down to the very last one."

I kept my curses to myself, left his office, and hurried home.

I found Shoshana lying in bed when I walked in. I quietly crossed to the bed and put my hand on her shoulder to wake her. She sat up, blinked, and then threw her arms around me. "I thought they arrested you!" she cried. "I was so worried!" I sat down on the bed and held her tightly.

Shoshana caressed my head, and I gave a little hiss when she touched the large lump left by the policeman's club. "Oh, no, what have they done to you? Let me help you!"

She jumped up and ran out of the room. In a few minutes, she came back with a small chunk of ice chipped from the block we kept in our icebox, wrapped in a piece of cloth. She sat down beside me and gently pressed it against the lump on my head.

"It's almost time to go to work," she said. She brushed her hair back from her eyes with her free hand and sighed. "Let's stay home. I didn't get any sleep at all, and I know you didn't either. Max will understand."

"I'm all right," I said. "My head hurts a little, but I'll be fine. Honestly, I couldn't sleep even if I stayed. You rest up, and I'll ask Alec to take your shift. I need to talk to him anyway."

"You're the one who risked his life last night, not me," she said. "I wish I had been there with you."

I cupped her face between my hands and saw the weariness in her eyes. "I'm so glad you weren't. I'm fine. Go back to bed, please."

She leaned against my shoulder for a moment, then sniffed my shirt and looked up, her eyes widening. "Uh, why don't you take a shower?" she said with a laugh. "I'll make you something to eat."

I grinned and went into the bathroom to have myself a nice

cleansing shower. When I came out, I had on clean clothes, and Shoshana gave me a hug. I ate a slice of bread topped with margarine and cheese that she had prepared for me.

Shoshana walked me to the door as I left for work. "Please tell Max I'll be there tomorrow," she said. "And tonight, I want you to tell me how you got that lump on your head."

"Clumsiness," I told her.

She kissed me lightly on the lips. "I want to hear all about the 'wall' you ran into."

I made no promises but gave her another kiss and left to find Alec in the Bukharan Quarter. On our way to work, I told him what I had been through.

"You won't be able to rest until we kill this Jeffries scum," Alec said.

"You're right," I said, "but I need a solid plan, and I've yet to come up with one."

"David," Alec said, trying to suppress his frustration, "I don't think you've been very focused lately. That bastard has got you dancing on the end of a string, and you're not doing anything about it."

I didn't respond, but I knew he was right.

When we entered the restaurant, Max was bursting with excitement. "I have wonderful news!" he exclaimed. "Nelka and I are getting married. We want you and Shoshana to be with us under the chuppah. The wedding is next week at my apartment."

"Congratulations," I said sincerely. "Shoshana and I are happy for you both."

"Thank you." He frowned. "Speaking of Shoshana, where is she?"

I explained why Shoshana was not coming to work and then told him briefly about my arrest. He said he would inform his commander.

When I got home from work, Shoshana was overjoyed to hear the news about Max and Nelka.

"That's wonderful!" she said, clasping her hands together, her eyes shining. She poured me a glass of wine. "Shall we toast to them?"

I picked up the glass and clinked it against hers. I took a drink and then shook my head. "Who would have thought that Max was such a romantic?"

Shoshana gave me a worried look as she sipped from her glass. "How is your head?" she asked. "I saw Brigita today and told her you had been injured."

"You didn't tell her that I've joined the resistance, did you?"

"No, no," she assured me, "of course not. I told her that you were reading a leaflet when a policeman struck you."

"Shoshana!" I raised both brows in surprise. "I didn't think you capable of telling a lie."

"It isn't a lie," she said, a little defensively. "I assume you were reading the leaflets as you posted them." She smiled then, and I couldn't help but smile back. "She asked me to say she would like you to visit her tomorrow before work."

"Very well, but please, don't tell Brigita anything about me that isn't necessary."

Shoshana put her glass down and slipped her arms around my neck. "I can think of something right now that is very necessary."

When I arrived for my appointment the next morning, Brigita welcomed me with her customary cup of tea. She kicked off the conversation as I settled into the armchair.

"I've been thinking about you a lot since our last meeting," she said. "I think I have a better understanding of you now, and

I can identify with your feelings. On the other hand, we have Shoshana, whom I feel very close to and responsible for. When you were single, you had every right to do as you pleased, but you are Shoshana's only emotional support, and you have to take that into serious consideration. She was devastated when you were injured last night."

I raised one brow. "Did she say she was devastated? I thought she seemed to take it in stride."

"Did she now?" Brigita nodded. "Well, perhaps she'd had time to conceal her concern before you got home."

"Or maybe she's tougher than you think," I shook my head. "It was just a misunderstanding with the police."

"Yes, so she said." She gazed at me for a long moment. "Are you willing to sacrifice her peace of mind to fight your war?"

"It's not that simple," I responded after some thought. "Clearly, we all need to consider those around us, particularly those who are very dear to us, but there are bigger things at stake. After all, if we think only of our loved ones, we will remain without a homeland. If there's one lesson to be learned from the Nazis, it's that the Jewish people need a national home in Israel."

Brigita frowned, then sighed. "I can't argue with you," she said. "Things are tough whichever way I look, and I'm worried. I think I understand how parents feel, because I feel that kind of affinity toward you and Shoshana. Look after yourself, David—for the sake of you both."

"I'll do my best, and I hope things work out well for all of us," I said.

Our conversation turned then to one of my missions during the war, but her words echoed in my mind long after I left her apartment.

MAX AND NELKA'S WEDDING TOOK place at Max's large corner apartment in the affluent neighborhood of Rehavia, near the center of Jerusalem. It was a joyous event attended by Max's surprisingly large number of friends, many of whom I had seen before at Café Pinsk. I spotted the commander in the crowd.

I introduced him to Shoshana, and he bowed and kissed her hand in true Polish style. He and Nelka chatted in Polish, which I struggled to follow, but she mentioned my name several times, so I assumed she was telling him about our time in Poland. He glanced at me now and then as she spoke, and his expression seemed to be one of approval.

The ceremony under the chuppah took place on the roof, under the evening sky. While the rabbi prayed, Shoshana and I stood next to Max and Nelka. They looked like a pair of beaming young lovers, and it thrilled me to see Nelka so happy.

I recalled the woeful look in her eyes when I'd met her for the first time in Krakow—an Auschwitz survivor stripped of everything. And here she was, in Israel, with a wealthy partner who loved her. I was happy too, but for the pain of remembering the loss of my family. That pain, I knew, would never go away.

After the chuppah ceremony had concluded, we went back down to the apartment, and it was time for the bride and groom's speeches. Max spoke first, saying that Nelka was a unique woman who had changed his life for the better.

"Nelka, you make me happy and add flavor to my life," he concluded, sealing his words with a kiss.

"Darling Max," she responded, "you bring joy and sweetness to me every day."

Then we sat down to a sumptuous meal the likes of which I had never seen before—chopped herring, mushrooms in heavy sour cream, and cauliflower latkes to start, then leg of lamb with rice and stuffed peppers, followed by an assortment of cakes and cookies for dessert. Amazingly, Max, with the help of a small staff, had prepared the entire feast. He had acquired admirable culinary skills during his many years as a restaurateur.

When the feast was over, Max brought out his phonograph and put on a Frank Sinatra record. I watched Alec dance with Eva. My friend seemed to have a sweet, soft look in his eyes. He came over to talk to me when the dance ended.

"You know," he said, "Eva is amazing. I don't know why I didn't see it earlier. I think I'll give it a go with her."

"Good for you," I said, slapping him on the shoulder.

Shoshana finally persuaded me to dance, and we moved with my arms wrapped around her to the sound of Sinatra's voice. At that moment, my heart and mind were free of the dark clouds that too often cast their shadows over me, and I danced in the light of joy.

IN THE DAYS FOLLOWING THE wedding, we started to hear rumors that the underground organizations were planning reprisals against the British. For the time being, though, the uneasy stillness was holding.

On July 8, Shimon, my burly chaperone, showed up at the restaurant at the end of my shift and said the commander wanted to see me. When we reached the house in Talpiot, the commander, along with two men who didn't introduce themselves, was waiting for me.

"David," the commander said after greeting me, "there are plans to carry out a large-scale operation against the British in the coming days. Your job will be to provide Inspector Jeffries with some information about the operation ahead of time, to boost your credibility. I'll give you the intel in a few days."

I nodded. "Very well."

"But before that," he went on, "I want you to arrange a meeting with Jeffries to pass on a piece of political information I believe he will find most interesting. I'm referring to the relationship between the Irgun and the Haganah. The British are generally aware of the situation, but you're going to give them more specific details. I want you to tell Jeffries that the information came from a meeting with Irgun members whose names you don't yet know. Also, tell him that the meeting included a discussion about a large-scale operation scheduled for the near future but that you weren't able to learn anything more about it."

"Of course," I said.

The commander turned to one of the other two men in the room. "Tell him," he said in a tone that clearly indicated the man was one of his subordinates, perhaps a close aide. Something about the aide's appearance made me think his background was in politics or intelligence rather than actual combat.

"Chaim Weizmann," the aide said, "president of the Zionist Organization, is adamantly opposed to any action against the British and has threatened to resign if the Haganah gets involved. Ben-Gurion has gotten cold feet as well. So Moshe Sneh, head of the Haganah national staff, cannot conduct any operations through the Haganah. But he has been in direct contact with Menachem Begin, pushing for a large-scale operation by the Irgun as payback for Black Sabbath. He believes the British need to be taught a lesson."

Moshe Sneh had the right idea. For a moment, I wished I could join him and play a larger part in the revenge he had planned. But my place was here, at least for now.

"You need to relay these details to Inspector Jeffries as soon as possible," the commander told me.

I reported the following morning to the Schneller Barracks

and was admitted after the usual thorough body search. The two soldiers escorted me to Jeffries's office, flanking me closely, as if I were a prisoner. The security measures at the barracks had clearly been significantly tightened.

"What news do you have for me?" Jeffries asked as he poured our customary glasses of whiskey.

"I think the Irgun is starting to trust me a little more after the night I spent in detention," I said. "I was invited to one of their meetings, and I think you'll be interested in what I heard."

"I'm listening," Jeffries said, taking a generous sip from his glass.

I told him about the dispute within the Jewish Authority and the Haganah. Jeffries appeared particularly interested when I said that Sneh had been in direct contact with the Irgun.

"So Sneh met with Begin," Jeffries said. "Do you know where?"

"No," I replied.

"We've been making a huge effort in recent months to get our hands on Begin. I give you my word, if you bring me information that helps us capture him, I will make sure you get not only a significant reward but also all the necessary papers for your girlfriend to stay here legally."

"Thank you," I said. "Of course, I will do everything I can, but I have more to tell you. I heard during the meeting that there's going to be a large-scale operation against the British this month. I don't know any more right now, but I'll try to find out."

Jeffries smiled, and his British accent broadened. "I think you've definitely earned yourself another glass." He poured another round. I wanted to throw the whiskey in his face, but drinking it somewhat eased my sense of disgust.

When I got back to our apartment, Shoshana was waiting

for me so we could walk to the restaurant together. I kissed her and went to the kitchen for a glass of water. She followed me. As I drained the glass and refilled it, she stopped beside me and laid her hand on my arm.

"I know you well enough to sense you're plotting something," she said. "You've been lucky until now, but you know from experience that the more risks you take, the greater chance you have of ending up hurt."

I remembered my conversation with Brigita, and I felt for Shoshana, but I had to deal with Jeffries.

"I have one more mission to carry out, and I must go through with it," I said, putting my arm around her. My gaze went from her gentle face to the window. "You know, I often think about why no one else in my family survived and why I lived when so many of the brave men and women I fought alongside were killed. I know I have skill in combat, and I'm very careful about not making mistakes. But I also believe there's an element of luck or divine intervention." I smiled down at her. "Sometimes I get the sense an angel is watching over me."

"I hope there is an army of angels watching over you," she said softly.

"Yes," I agreed. "I need all the help I can get with my next operation." My smile faded. "It's the most important one so far."

Shoshana looked up at me, her eyes large and intense. "David, lately I've been thinking that it isn't right you're willing to risk your life for our nation, while all I do is design leaflets." She lifted her chin in a gesture I was beginning to recognize. This was important to her. "I want to be more involved in the operations against the British. I'm going to talk to Max and to the commander about it."

I could barely believe what I was hearing. This was certainly not the fragile woman I had met not too long ago. Shoshana was becoming stronger, more daring. The look in her eyes reminded me of Leah, but unlike Leah, she had no training. And even with training . . . My mind flashed back to the woods, Leah in my arms, bloody and lifeless. I took a deep breath.

"Shoshana," I said, "before you talk to Max, first listen to me. This is a very dangerous business. I've been a fighter for years and have only survived by the skin of my teeth." I brushed a lock of hair back from her face. "Your desire to contribute is admirable, but I suggest we look into this very carefully and see how you can get involved without too much risk."

"But I know I could do this," she said. "I could help in the fight."

"Yes," I agreed, "but your lack of experience could cost you your life, and that, my love, is an unbearable thought." I kissed her briefly, but I could see she wasn't convinced.

We left for work, both of us deep in thought, hardly exchanging a word. Max seemed to sense our heavy mood and tried to tell a few jokes, but when we didn't respond, he left us in peace.

"The commander wants to see you on Sunday," Max told me when the shift was over. "He also asked me not to put you on the roster for Monday, because you'll be busy."

"Okay," I said, concealing my excitement. The operation was about to kick off.

16

"AND WHERE A SPURT OF OUR BLOOD FELL ON THE EARTH"

(FROM "SONG OF THE PARTISANS" BY HIRSH GLICK, 1943)

Shimon came to collect me two nights later. There were several other people at the house in Talpiot when we got there. The commander led me into an empty room, sat down, and gestured to a chair across from his desk.

"There's going to be an assault tomorrow on a building that houses British government offices," he said. "You don't need to know exactly which building, but I do want to stress that the plan is to hit the building itself and not the people who work there. You need to go to the Schneller Barracks tomorrow morning at eleven thirty and tell Jeffries that you've learned of a plan to blow up one of the British government buildings."

"Is this true or a bluff?" I asked.

He frowned. "It is very true. All you need to know is that the building is in Jerusalem and that the explosion will occur between 12:15 and 1:15 p.m. If they evacuate all their buildings in the city, they won't suffer any casualties. We are planning to corroborate this to the Brits through a second channel, but the information should certainly earn you points with Jeffries."

We shook hands, and I was driven back home with much to think about.

The next morning, I arrived at the gate of the Schneller Barracks at eleven thirty sharp. I asked to see Inspector Jeffries and was told I would have to wait at least an hour.

"I'm here on a very urgent matter," I said. "Ask the inspector's deputy to come to the gate." Some thirty minutes went by before a police sergeant came to see me.

"I need to see your superior right away," I told him. "There's going to be an attack within the hour!"

His gaze swept over me in disdain, and then he shrugged. "I'll see what I can do," he said before turning away.

I waited, pacing back and forth for another twenty minutes, and still nobody came. "I must speak with the man who was here earlier," I said to the guard through the gate.

"He knows what he's doing," the guard replied. "If he told you he was dealing with it, that's all you need to know."

"But it's a matter of life and death! I must speak to him immediately!" I insisted.

The guard, who had been somewhat courteous until that point, reached the limit of his patience. "I suggest you keep your mouth shut or get the hell out of here, or I'll call the MPs, and you'll—"

His threat was cut off by a thunderous explosion. I looked up to see a huge cloud of smoke rising over Jerusalem. A glance at my watch told me it was 12:37. Furious, I threw up my hands and walked away from the gate. I found a bench nearby and sat down, leaning my head in my hands. There was no way to know if the people in the building had been evacuated or not. I decided to wait for Jeffries.

It was nearly two o'clock when a car stopped at the curb and Jeffries got out. I stood and approached him.

"What are you doing here?" he asked with a frown.

"I came here to warn you about the bomb," I replied tersely, "but your sergeant ignored me. I've been waiting here for hours."

"Come with me to my office," Jeffries said. He led the way, and once inside, he called in his sergeant, who had no choice but to confirm what I had said.

"You bloody fool," Jeffries hissed at him. "You'll be court-martialed for this. Now piss off!" The man left, and Jeffries sank into his chair behind his desk. He stared out the window, and I waited impatiently until he finally turned to me, his tone uncharacteristically gloomy.

"This is a dark day for Great Britain. The Irgun blew up the south wing of the King David Hotel. We lost government offices and our military HQ. No final death toll yet, but it's going to be high. I heard estimates of close to a hundred."

One hundred people. Had they gotten my warning ahead of time, the outcome would have been different.

Jeffries poured himself a large glass of whiskey with a shaking hand. "Two minutes later and I would have been dead. I was right outside the hotel when it happened. Two of my men and I go swimming every Monday at noon at the YMCA pool across from the hotel, and then we have lunch at the hotel restaurant. My men and I ran over right away, pulled people from the rubble, and carried them to the ambulances."

He gestured to the blood on his uniform. "I saw people with their arms and legs blown off, crying out in pain." He paused for a moment, sat up straight, and fixed me with a piercing stare. "Those accursed Jews who committed this crime won't know any rest until we get our hands on them."

I barely heard his final sentence. I was stunned to learn that Jeffries was in the habit of spending every Monday afternoon at the YMCA swimming pool—right under my nose. The YMCA was like a second home to me, yet I had never seen him there. Assuming he showed up for his swim the following Monday, he now had less than a week left on this earth.

Jeffries's phone rang, signaling the end of our meeting. A policeman standing outside the door ushered me to the front gate. As I looked at the guard who had ignored me, I couldn't help myself.

"One hundred people are dead because of you," I said. He didn't respond.

THE BOMBING DOMINATED THE NEWS reports for the next two days. It turned out that the operation had begun with Irgun fighters overpowering the guards at the hotel's service entrance. They had made their way into the restaurant's kitchen on the ground floor of the hotel's south wing.

The leader of the operation had dressed as a Sudanese waiter, and his commandos had been disguised as Arabs. They had brought seven large milk cans, each filled with 110 pounds of explosives. The Irgun fighters had assembled the workers in the kitchen, then fixed the cans to the building's foundation, with timers set to detonate thirty minutes later. When the fighters exited the hotel, they'd come under fire from the Arab Legion, and two of the Irgun members had been injured.

I learned from the reports that even if my warning had been received on time, the casualties from the blast likely wouldn't have been avoided. It turned out that at 12:10 p.m. the Irgun had placed calls warning the editorial desk of the *Palestine Post,* the King David Hotel management, and the adjacent French consulate. And indeed, the employees at the French consulate had opened their windows to prevent them from shattering in the explosion.

The hotel's management had evacuated all its guests, but the south wing, which housed the offices of the Mandate authorities, wasn't evacuated. It was reported that Mandate Chief Secretary Sir John Shaw had prevented all British personnel from leaving the building.

"I am here to give orders to the Jews, not to take orders from them," Shaw was said to have responded.

Initially, the British government denied receiving a warning about the operation but was forced to retract its denial after a switchboard operator at the *Palestine Post* testified under oath that immediately after receiving the warning, she had called the duty officer at the police station and conveyed the message word for word.

For my part, now that I had learned where I could kill Jeffries, the countdown to my real operation had begun, and I had just a few days to prepare.

MY RABBI IN MINSK OFTEN began his lessons by quoting Rabbi Tarfon from *Ethics of the Fathers.* "The day is short, the labor vast." I remembered these words as Alec and I began to plan Jeffries's assassination.

I decided we would use the weapons I had hidden in the stone wall at the back of my apartment. With that in mind, I knew we'd need some practice to brush up on the weapons skills we had acquired during our time as partisans. Late that night, Alec and I met by the stone wall in the backyard. I removed the rock and retrieved the four firearms and all the ammunition from the box I had hidden there. I gave two of the revolvers to Alec, along with a spare key to the box. We agreed to meet up the next morning for weapons practice.

"What were you and Alec doing in the backyard?" Shoshana asked when I returned to our apartment.

I didn't want to lie to her. "I gave him two guns that were hidden in a box behind a loose stone in the wall, by the apricot tree," I said. "We have to train for an operation I hope to carry out this Monday."

The color drained from Shoshana's face, and she got into bed without saying anything. I slid under the covers next to her and wrapped her in my arms.

"Don't worry," I said. "We won't take any unnecessary risks."

She didn't say a word but laid her soft hands over mine and squeezed them tight.

Alec showed up at eight the next morning, and we walked through the Tel Arza neighborhood to the Nabi Samuel Ridge. According to Jewish faith, this land held the grave of the Prophet Samuel.

The slope below the ridge was completely deserted. We began our shooting drills and soon learned we had lost a good deal of our accuracy and reaction speed. After training for two hours, we ran out of ammunition. It was clear we were going to need another drill session.

I thought about asking Max's commander for ammunition, but I wasn't ready to tell him about our plan. I knew he'd probably want to get involved, even have his own people join us, and I wasn't ready to accept that.

When I arrived at work that afternoon, I signaled to Max that I wished to speak to him in private. He sent his cook out and gestured me into his small office.

"I need 150 rounds for a .38 caliber revolver," I said. "Don't ask me why, and don't tell anyone about it. And Alec and I need a three-day vacation, Saturday through Monday."

Max frowned. "Maybe you should involve the commander in whatever you're doing."

"I thought about it but decided not to," I said.

He hesitated for a moment and then nodded. "Just be careful. If something were to happen to you, Shoshana would be devastated."

"I think Shoshana is stronger than any of you realize," I said.

After the restaurant closed, Max gestured me into his office again, handing me a large bag as I entered. Inside were four boxes of fifty rounds each. I thanked him.

"Just be careful, you and Alec," he said. "That's the main thing."

I planned to kill Jeffries and his bodyguards in the locker room of the YMCA's swimming pool. The room had two entrances: one from the main building, where a guard was on duty, and the other a service door in the side of the building. The service door afforded access to the swimming pool from the running track next to the soccer field. The advantage of that entrance was that there would be no security check. The disadvantage—the service door wasn't always open. We had to get a key to the door.

Alec and I went to the boxing gym, which wasn't far from the entrance to the pool. There, I introduced Alec to Yousef, explaining that Alec had done some boxing before coming to Israel and wanted to start training again.

"Do you mind checking out his form?" I asked.

"Of course," Yousef said. "I would be happy to do so."

"While you do that, Alec, I'm going to run on the track," I told my partner.

"Fine," he said. I started to walk away and then turned back. "Oh!" I snapped my fingers. "May I borrow your key to the service door?" I asked Yousef. "It's faster to the track that way."

"No problem," Yousef said. "Just don't stay too long. I have a student coming for training soon."

He retrieved a ring of keys from his pocket and pointed out the right one. I went to the service door, opened it, and then sprinted to the main road to a hardware store. I asked the clerk to make two copies of the key. When he was done, I raced back to the service door, made sure both keys worked, and returned to the boxing gym out of breath.

"Your friend is in good physical shape," Yousef told me, then turned to Alec. "However, I'm surprised your previous trainer didn't correct your footwork. You hold your hands too low as well. If you want to make any progress, you should train with me twice a week for a few months."

"This is a good idea. I'll check when I can be free from work, and I'll let you know," Alec said. "In the meantime, thank you very much. What do I owe you?"

Yousef smiled and shook his head. "This was just an audition, for both of us. If you come back, we can talk about rates."

When we left the gym, we both burst out laughing over Yousef's critique of Alec's previous trainer—Alec had never taken a single boxing lesson in his life.

From there, we went to the pool's locker room. On our way, I gave Alec one of the spare keys to the service door. The men's lockers were in a room that contained five rows of steel cabinets. Each cabinet had two lockers, one on top of the other. The doors to the lockers were fitted with rings for padlocks. We decided that on the day of the assault, we'd use the two lockers against the wall at the far end of the room in the first row. From there we could make our move and escape quickly.

After the scouting mission, we developed a plan. On Sunday evening, I'd go to the Y with two padlocks and lock the two lockers we'd selected so no one else would take them. The next morning, Alec and I would enter through the gate to the soccer field. There was no security guard at the gate, and no one would notice us.

We'd wear white tennis gear, sunglasses, and visors, which would help conceal our faces as much as possible. Instead of heading to the tennis courts, we'd enter the locker room via the service door, go to our lockers, and wait there for Jeffries and his men to enter.

The locker room was in an isolated area, far from the guard at the entrance. The plan was to kill them as they walked in, after they'd finished swimming and showering. Then we would make a quick escape the same way we'd come in.

We left the Y and went shopping for our outfits. The next day, we returned to Tel Arza for more shooting practice. After firing off about a hundred rounds, we were satisfied that we had regained our lost accuracy and speed.

We each had two revolvers—two Webleys for me and a Webley and an Enfield No. 2 for Alec. Both types had a major drawback: They were top-break revolvers, and reloading required tilting the weapon to the side, releasing the spent rounds, and then loading the cartridges one by one.

Each revolver held just six bullets, so we'd have only twenty-four shots to complete our mission, since it would take too much time to reload. I missed the magazine-loaded Walther P38 that had served me so well during my time as a partisan, but we were forced to make do with what we had.

Alec and I went our separate ways, and on my way home, I decided I needed to speak to Shoshana about all the contents of the concealed metal box. I wasn't particularly concerned about the upcoming operation, but I knew that in war, death could come at any time.

I suggested we go to Café Wien before work. My invitation pleased her, and she hugged and kissed me.

"You're so romantic!" she said cheerfully.

I returned her hug silently. We locked up and walked down the street, holding hands. She talked about what a beautiful day it was, but I was lost in my own thoughts.

We reached the café, and once we were sitting at a table, I reached over and took her hand. "Shoshana," I said, "there's something you need to know."

"Is something wrong?" she asked, a worried look on her face.

"No, not at all," I said quickly. "There's just something important I've been meaning to tell you."

"All right," she said, "I'm listening."

I glanced around and then lowered my voice. "You know the metal box that I told you about, the one in the wall by the apricot tree?"

She nodded. "Yes."

"Well, inside that box is some jewelry. Whenever I need money, I take a piece out and exchange the jewelry for cash at Zargary's jewelry store on Jaffa Street."

Her face went pale. "I understand that your operation is going to be dangerous," she said with a tremble in her voice.

"No," I replied. "It won't be particularly dangerous, but I'll feel better if I explain everything to you. I probably should have done it a while ago."

"Where did the jewelry come from?" she asked.

"The war," I said. "Believe me when I tell you that I liberated it from men who had stolen it or committed crimes they needed to pay for."

"I do believe you," she said.

"When we get home from work tonight, I'll show you exactly where the box is and give you a key. If you ever have to sell a piece, realize that the owner of Zargary's will offer you about a quarter of what he's actually prepared to pay. Don't give in until you've haggled him back up. He might yell and shout a little, but don't take it personally. I think he enjoys the haggling more than the profit he stands to make."

After we ate, we walked together to the restaurant. As we started our usual duties, I could tell Shoshana was preoccupied.

When our shift was over and we returned home, I showed her how to remove the rock in the wall and reach the box. Back inside the apartment, I gave her the key and wrote down the jeweler's address. She carefully placed the key and piece of paper in her jewelry box on our dresser. As we lay in bed that night, Shoshana hugged me tightly.

SATURDAY MORNING ARRIVED. ALEC AND I went on another scouting mission at the Y. The gate to the soccer field was open, but this time there was a guard there. He told us the gate would be closing in an hour, because the field was hosting a Beitar Jerusalem soccer match. I said we were going to play tennis for an hour and that I was a big fan of the team, especially striker Simon Alfassi. That was enough for the guard to let us in, but he made us promise to be out before the match started in an hour and a half.

I doubted the gate would be closed for another professional match on Monday, but even if it was, we could just climb over the fence. We made our way to the locker room, going through the motions for the operation to come, timing our movements down to the second. We left about forty minutes later, thanking the guard as we walked out.

We went back to Tel Arza on Sunday for a final round of shooting practice, and our accuracy and reaction speed were excellent. That evening, I went to the Y and padlocked the two lockers.

I met Alec at his apartment on Monday morning. We both wore sneakers. The revolvers and our white tennis clothes were in the backpacks that we slung over our shoulders, and we changed into our tennis gear in a secluded spot west of the Mammilla pool in the nearby Muslim cemetery.

Thinking back to the day of the attack on the King David Hotel, I remembered that when I had arrived at the Schneller Barracks at half past eleven, Jeffries had already left the base. When the bomb had gone off at 12:37, he had already been out of the locker room and on his way to the hotel.

There was no way to know how long he usually swam or how long it took him to shower and change, but Jeffries didn't seem to be in the best shape; I doubted he could last for more than half an hour in the pool. Certainly, he wouldn't leave the locker room any earlier than a quarter past noon. I thought it would make sense to carry out the assassination around noon, because most of the swimmers used the pool either early in the morning or after work in the evenings.

We followed the narrow alley that led directly to the soccer field. Pleased to find the gate open, we made our way along the track toward the service entrance. After making sure no one was around, I opened the door with the spare key. We were in the locker room shortly before noon.

I undressed, walked over to the showers, and peeked through the opening into the pool area. There I saw Jeffries swimming a slow breaststroke. I had never been so happy to see him. "Enjoy the last swim of your life, you bastard," I said to myself.

About twenty minutes later, Jeffries got out of the pool and started walking toward the exit. I expected that he and his men would shower before heading to the locker room, but I wasn't sure. I hurried to my locker, dried myself off, and got dressed.

I stuffed one of the revolvers into my pocket and then pulled back the hammer of the other pistol so it was ready to fire. I gripped it in my right hand and covered it with a towel. Alec did the same.

Some thirty seconds later, we heard Jeffries and his men talking in the row of lockers just beyond ours. I nodded to Alec. Things moved quickly. Alec shot the first man in the head before he could even look up. The second man, dressed only in his underwear, lunged for his locker, but Alec was quicker and killed him too.

Jeffries looked at me in shock. I shot him once point-blank and then again as he fell to the floor.

I heard a gunshot from behind and felt a red-hot pain in my thigh, as if someone had stabbed me. Alec got off two rounds and killed the shooter. My leg instantly went numb, and blood poured from the wound, soaking into my trousers.

Alec quickly went from one Brit to the next, putting another bullet in all four of them to make sure they were dead, then rushed over to me.

"We have to stop the bleeding," he said. He removed his shirt and tied it tightly around the upper part of my thigh to stem the flow of blood. Next, he wrapped a towel around my leg to help absorb the blood and prevent it from leaving a trail behind us.

As soon as he had me secured, he collected the weapons and ammunition from the corpses and packed everything into his backpack. We made our way toward the service door and from there to the gate of the field, with Alec supporting me all the way.

My leg just wasn't working, and I was slowing Alec down. I tried to pull away from him. "Leave me," I said. "I'll say the shooter shot me too." Alec shook his head and dragged me along.

As I hobbled down the running track, the nerves in my leg began to recover from the shock, and every step sent waves of agony through me. Once we'd made it through the gate to the soccer field, I knew I couldn't go any farther. Alec grabbed me and turned me to the left, toward the road heading west instead of the alley we had walked through earlier.

Max leaped out of a parked car and ran to us. Together he and Alec picked me up and pushed me into the back seat. Max got into the driver's seat, and the car surged forward. We could hear the sirens of the police headed to the scene.

Alec knelt on the floorboard of the back seat and removed the shirt he had tied around my leg. It was completely saturated now, red and dripping with my blood. He cut away the bottom of my tennis shorts and started to disinfect the wound with iodine from a first aid kit emblazoned with a red Star of David.

I grimaced as the liquid hit the hole in my leg, and I tried to breathe slowly while Alec dressed the wound with a large bandage. The pain was almost unbearable. Finally, he turned and yelled to Max.

"He's lost a lot of blood and needs to get to a doctor fast!"

"We're on our way to my apartment," Max said. "I have a neighbor who is a doctor. He's also an underground member and has treated several of our wounded. He'll take care of David and won't breathe a word about it."

"Where did Max come from?" I managed to gasp through gritted teeth as Alec finished dressing my wound, binding it tightly.

"From me," my friend said. "I didn't tell you about Max,

because I knew you wouldn't approve, since secrecy is your paramount concern. I decided we needed backup."

"You did the right thing, Alec," I murmured, just before the darkness took me. "We're still a good team, and you're a darn good friend."

17

"THE BITTERSWEET OF DAYS THAT WERE"

(FROM *THE HOUSE OF THE WOLFINGS* BY
WILLIAM MORRIS, 1889)

The pain jolted me back to consciousness as Alec pulled me out of the car. We were outside Max's building. I held on to Alec's shoulder for support as we slowly made our way inside and up the stairs to Max's apartment.

Nelka looked pale and worried as she ushered us through the door. "Take David to the bed in the study," she said.

As I lay in bed, staring at the ceiling, exhausted and in pain, Max walked in with a short, balding man at his side. The man wore glasses over determined dark eyes, and his immediate interest in my wound gave away his identity. He pulled a chair up to the bed and removed the dressing Alec had hastily applied to my leg.

"Not a pleasant injury but not terrible either," he said, peering at it closely. "No damage to the bone or any major blood vessels. I'll dress it properly and give you sulfonamide to help with infection, along with something for the pain. Most importantly, you need to stay off your feet for a while and wait for it to heal."

"How long will that take?" I asked.

"You're a strong and healthy young man," the doctor said. "If it doesn't get infected, you should be all right within a few weeks. You're very lucky. The tiniest deviation to the left or right and you could have been crippled—or bled to death."

"What's your name?"

"Elisha Kaminitz."

"Thank you, Dr. Kaminitz, for helping me," I said.

After he'd finished treating me, I fell asleep. It was dark outside when I woke. Shoshana was sitting by the bed, looking at me sadly.

"I'm glad you're here, Shoshana," I said. "I'm feeling fine, and the doctor said I'd be well in no time."

"Thank God you're alive and not seriously hurt," she said, caressing my hand. "I was so worried. Maybe it's time for you to let someone else take the risks for a while?"

"*Inshallah*," I said, recalling the Arabic word I had learned from Yousef, which translated to "with God's help" but more commonly meant "hopefully."

Max and Alec returned from the restaurant just before midnight. "I spoke to the doctor and was pleased to hear your wound isn't life-threatening," Max said. "But your absence from the restaurant, your apartment, etcetera needs to be explained."

"I've thought about that too and have come up with an idea," I replied. "If anyone asks, tell them I received word that my aunt and uncle, survivors of the Bergen-Belsen concentration camp, are here in Israel and that I've gone to look for them."

"Excellent idea." Max smiled. "I see that your mind still functions well despite your injury. The commander told me he wants to speak to you. I said I would ask if you're up to it. Shall I tell him he can visit tomorrow morning?"

"Perhaps this can wait until David recovers," Shoshana said.

"Let's see how I'm doing tomorrow." I squeezed her hand, and she nodded.

"Of course," Max said. "We should let you get some sleep. Alec, would you walk Shoshana home?"

"Already? I'd like to stay a bit longer," Shoshana said, giving me a hesitant look.

"I'm sure David would love for you to spend the night with him," Max said, "but you must keep up appearances and be prepared to explain David's absence. If you disappear too, it might arouse suspicion."

Shoshana agreed, kissed me on the cheek, and left with Alec. Grateful to be able to simply rest, I took two painkillers and a sleeping pill and fell into a fitful sleep.

I slipped into a dream about Leah that felt familiar and hauntingly real. It came to me in flashes—I saw us leaving Belarus and wandering through Europe together, happy and in love—then on a ship, full of hundreds of refugees, carrying us from Italy to Israel—lying in bed together, in the very same apartment where I lived with Shoshana—me looking at Leah, and Leah gazing back with her beautiful blue eyes.

"You promised that when we got to Jerusalem, we'd get married and have two children," she whispered. "Don't you remember?"

I woke drenched in sweat and burning with fever. I managed to turn on the bedside lamp and then just lay there, feeling weak and helpless. After a few minutes, Nelka stepped into the room, dressed in a nightgown and robe.

"I saw the light on," she said. "Do you need anything?"

"Water." My throat was dry and hot.

She brought me a glass, and I sipped the water thankfully.

"I had a terrible dream," I told her.

She sat down and rested her hand on my forehead, her eyes widening. "Oh dear. You have a high fever. I'll wake Max and tell him to get the doctor." She hurried out of the room.

I drifted in and out of sleep, dreaming of Leah. I didn't know how much time had passed before I opened my eyes again and saw Max and Dr. Kaminitz staring down at me. The doctor frowned as he took my temperature.

"You have a fever of 103.6 degrees," he said, reading the thermometer. "The wound must be infected. Fortunately for you, we have penicillin in Israel now. I'll give you three shots today. Nelka, starting tomorrow, you'll give him two shots a day. I'll show you how to do it."

As the doctor filled a syringe with liquid from a small bottle, Max helped me turn on my side. I lay there, shaking and dripping with sweat, so ill I barely felt it when the doctor jabbed the needle into my hip.

"We're fortunate," I heard him say to Max and Nelka afterward. "During the war, penicillin was worth more than gold. Even today, it's not readily available in the private sector, but I have my connections. Now let's clear the room. David needs to rest. No visitors and no lengthy conversations."

"But we have an important meeting scheduled for the morning," Max protested.

"Don't even think about it," Kaminitz growled.

Nelka brought me a cup of tea, and I swallowed two more painkillers. I continued to shake and sweat for some time before falling into another fitful sleep, disturbed by more strange dreams. I woke some time later to find Shoshana sitting at my bedside with a worried look on her face.

"You must have been having a bad dream," she said. "You were calling out 'No, no' in your sleep."

"Yes . . ." I tried to remember but couldn't. ". . . I was having bad dreams, but now that you're here, everything is fine."

Shoshana smiled and took my hand. "Rest quietly. I'll sit here with you until I need to leave for work. And I'll come see you again later tonight with Alec."

Max stopped in the doorway, looking weary, and shook his head. "Shoshana, my dear, David has an infection. The doctor says he'll get better, but he needs to rest."

Shoshana caressed my forehead and promised to come again the next morning. A few minutes after she'd left, Dr. Kaminitz came back into the room, along with Nelka, and administered a second shot, explaining the procedure to her in the process.

I spent the day in and out of sleep, with the pain in my leg still searing. I had a lot of time to think, although I found it hard to focus. We had pulled off a very difficult mission, and I was pleased with the success of our operation. Despite my injury, Alec and I had been extremely lucky.

By that afternoon, my sweating had subsided, and my body wasn't shaking as much either. Nelka gave me the third shot of penicillin later that night, with the doctor's supervision. He left her with syringes and several vials of penicillin, which he instructed her to keep in the refrigerator. After changing the dressing on my wound, he told me to take a sleeping pill and get a good night's rest.

I did manage to sleep for a while. When I woke in the early hours of the morning, I could feel that my fever had dropped, and I was no longer sweating or shaking. My mind was more focused too. Relieved the medicine was working, I lay back and thought about all that had happened.

Had I made a mistake in failing to consider that Jeffries might come to the Y with more than two guards? I didn't think so. After all, Jeffries had trusted me completely, up until the final seconds of his life, and had told me himself that he usually went to the pool with two of his men.

In any case, the incident had proved that any further operations against the British meant more chances for something to go wrong. Maybe the bullet hole in my thigh was a warning that I shouldn't take such risks in the future.

"You're looking better today, David," Nelka said. She stood in the doorway, holding a tray filled with tea and cookies. I was sipping my tea when Max stepped in a minute later and asked how I was feeling.

"Better," I said, "and if the commander wants to come and have a talk with me, I'm up to it."

"Great," he said. "I'll let him know right away."

Shoshana came by again, and she and I chatted until I heard someone enter the apartment. Max brought his commander into the room and asked Shoshana if she would mind waiting outside. She stood up to leave, but I intervened.

"I would like her to stay. Shoshana is a part of my life," I said to the men. "She knows what I've done, and she's a member of your organization. You can trust her."

The commander and Max were visibly displeased, but neither chose to object. Instead, they pulled up two chairs and sat down at my bedside. Shoshana sat on the edge of the bed.

"I didn't know you were such an accomplished fighter, David," the commander said. "That was a well-executed operation. You caught them with their pants down, as they say, in a place they considered safe, and you took them out perfectly. There is chaos in the city. The British don't know where to begin. Their informants haven't been able to provide a single lead that could point to the organization responsible for the assassination."

"I'm glad to hear it."

The man's face became stern, and he leaned forward as he continued. "I realize this wasn't your first operation since you arrived in Jerusalem. Perhaps you thought your silence pro-tected you, but"—he gestured to my wounded body—"we now know you'd certainly be hanged for this if you were ever caught. There's no reason not to be open with me and tell me about your previous activities and see how we can work together in the future."

With a sense of regret, I accepted that he was right. I began with the night I had attacked the British soldier and taken his gun and then quickly moved on to relate how I had fired into the Schneller Barracks from the rooftop on Geula Street. I left out how I had gotten my hands on Avrum's rifle, mainly because Shoshana was in the room. Max's eyes became moist as I told them about Greene, the British officer I'd killed on Ben Yehuda Street. I finished with the stories of Sergeant Perry and Inspector Ellis.

I was done, and after a moment, the commander said, "If anyone but you had told me such tales, I'd think I was listening to a liar. I don't know anyone here in Israel who has carried out such daring and dangerous operations without a single fail-ure. I can only admire your planning and execution skills, and you appear to have luck on your side too—very important for someone who is willing to take such risks. Now, since you've been open with me, I will be open with you too." He paused, gave me a considering look, and then continued.

"My name is Zvi. Contrary to what you might have been thinking, I do not belong to the Irgun. I lead the Wolves. Have you ever heard of us?"

I shook my head.

"Good," he said approvingly. "That proves our ability to act in absolute secrecy. Some of our members are affiliated with other resistance movements, and we have a network of informants in the British army and the police force. With their help, we stay up to speed on everything that happens. I'll fill you in on our past operations another time."

I was tempted to ask more about the organization but stayed silent.

"As I've already told you, I was born in Belarus and spent most of my adult life in Poland. I fled Poland with my wife and kids—a son and daughter—immediately after the Nazi occupation. The border guards opened fire on us, killing my wife and children. If my son were alive today, he'd be about your age. I was wounded but managed to escape into Russian territory. I joined General Anders's army, and when we reached Israel, I deserted, along with most of the other Jewish soldiers."

I could hear the edges of emotion he held at bay. This man had been through as much as, or more than, I had, and I felt a sudden kinship with him.

"Despite my heartfelt appreciation for the British and their determined struggle against the Nazis, I can't forgive them for their injustice toward the Jewish survivors in Europe, for not allowing them to immigrate to Israel. The Brits violated the commitment they had made in the Balfour Declaration to endorse the establishment of a Jewish home in Palestine." He nodded in my direction. "Like you, I have experienced the dangers of betrayal that lie in wait for members of a resistance movement. As a result, I, and a close group of friends who also deserted General Anders's army, set up a small underground organization that requires absolute loyalty and secrecy from its members. Just as you have trusted no one here in Israel but your partisan comrade, I have trusted only a handful of my Jewish friends from Anders's army.

"We've gradually increased our numbers, very selectively, and we've become highly effective. In the meantime, I've also established a successful business that partially funds our organization. Losing my wife and two children was very difficult for me. At this stage of my life, I'm not cut out for starting a new family, and I'm devoted entirely to the struggle against the British."

Zvi went quiet for a moment. Again, I felt a great deal of empathy with the man, and I shared his sorrow over losing his family. "I think I understand," I told him.

He nodded and then continued. "You've been stalking the British in Jerusalem as a lone wolf, and we wolves are deadlier in packs. Together we can tear out the throat of the British occupation in Israel. If you'd like to learn more about the philosophy behind our organization, I suggest you read *The House of the Wolfings* by William Morris. He wrote it in England at the end of the nineteenth century. The book tells of a tribe that lived an idyllic life in nature until it was attacked by legions of Roman soldiers, who killed or enslaved everyone in their path. Max has a copy, I believe."

"I'd like to read it," I said.

Zvi stood up and extended his hand. "I'm an observant man, and I think I can safely say I know the Bible. The Book of Judges tells us that before Gideon embarked on his decisive battle against the Midianites, an angel appeared before him and said, 'Go in this thy might, and save Israel from the hand of Midian.' And now, David, I say to you, go in this thy might, and save Israel from the hand of the British."

"Thank you, sir," I said, shaking his hand. "I will do my best."

Max accompanied Zvi to the front door and then returned to my room, beaming. "I feel so lucky to have hired you," he said. "God only knows how I would have wormed my way out of trouble with Greene had you not killed him. I foolishly continued to insult you . . ." His eyes glistened with tears. "I hope you can forgive me."

"Forget it, Max," I assured him. "You gave me a job. And when I really needed it, you were there to help me. That's all that matters."

Max blushed and cleared his throat several times. "Well then, I'm going to the restaurant. See you later."

I fell asleep with Shoshana's hand caressing mine and slept for most of the day. The pain in my leg woke me twice, and Nelka gave me painkillers. Sometime that night, the pain subsided, and my fever dropped to normal.

Shoshana and Alec came to visit after their shift at the restaurant. I asked Shoshana to tell Avrum and Hannah that I was out of the city, focused on finding my aunt and uncle, and for Alec to tell Yousef the same thing.

I woke the next morning feeling much better, and for the first time since being shot, I devoured the breakfast Nelka made for me—an omelet, a salad, and a glass of hot chocolate.

When Max came into the room, I asked if he could bring me his copy of *The House of the Wolfings*. Max owned a first edition, printed in London in 1889. It was a mixture of prose and poetry, and I struggled to understand many of the words.

The book was interesting, telling the story of an extended family, a tribe of sorts, known as the House of the Wolfings. They lived in harmony with nature in a clearing in a forest enveloped by mist. They were idealists who wished to live in peace but knew how to defend themselves and fiercely guarded their independence. The book was steeped in mystery and myths about gods and magic.

When I got to the part that told of an attack by the Roman legions, I understood why Zvi had suggested I read the book. The Romans, just like the Nazis, were evil, imperialistic aggressors. They had no qualms about "burning old men and women and children in their dwellings," as one of the warriors from the House of the Wolfings said. I also saw a certain similarity between the Romans and the British imperialists, who may not have been burning people in their homes but who were, like the Romans, seeking to rule over other nations and willing to kill those who opposed them.

I decided to join the Wolves. I was excited at the thought of meeting with Zvi again and couldn't wait to start working with him. The risks that were sure to be a part of such an association faded when I realized how much we could accomplish together.

When I'd first arrived in Israel, I had truly been a lone wolf. My family had been murdered, my beloved Leah had been killed, and aside from Nelka, I didn't have a single friend in the country. Things were very different now. I had Shoshana. Alec was here. I had friends who were like family to me. And I had just joined a wolf pack that was fighting to create a national home for the Jewish people in their ancient homeland.

Zvi reminded me of Zusha, who had taken me under his wing after my escape from the ghetto. And as I thought of Zusha, I remembered the promise we had made to one another in that forest in Belarus years ago—that if one of us was killed and the other survived, the survivor would find the other's family members and tell them about our resistance efforts.

Zusha had told me he had a son, Izak, whose whereabouts were unknown. It occurred to me now that I had failed to uphold my promise. I swore to myself that as soon as I recovered, I would look for Izak. If he was still alive, I wouldn't rest until I told him of his father's heroism fighting the Nazis.

18

"ONLY DEATH WILL DISCHARGE US FROM OUR RANKS"

(FROM "UNKNOWN SOLDIERS," A POEM BY
AVRAHAM STERN, 1932)

Six days after my injury, I felt hardly any discomfort in my leg when I was lying down, but I still couldn't walk around Max's apartment for very long before the injured muscles in my thigh started to seize up. Nevertheless, I tried to walk as much as possible and got back in bed only when I couldn't bear the pain anymore. Dr. Kaminitz checked on me every other day and said the wound was healing well.

Shoshana visited me every day and kept me company for hours. She told me Avrum had come to the restaurant looking for me, and she'd satisfied him with the story that I was looking for my aunt and uncle. Avrum had told her the CID was in an uproar in the wake of the assassination—they had no leads, he'd said, but suspected that Jeffries and his men had been killed by the same people who had strangled Sergeant

Perry. The British believed there might have been a traitor in Jeffries's division, and they were considering dismantling it and reassigning everyone to other departments.

"Avrum also said there is a personal matter that he wants to discuss with you as soon as possible," Shoshana added. I felt a bit alarmed at this news and hoped the "personal matter" didn't have anything to do with Hannah and me.

Max had placed a radio in my room, and I spent most of my time listening to the news and other programs, often impatiently turning the dial from one station to the next. I was restless and ready to move on to helping the Wolves. He also brought me a copy of the *Yedioth Ahronoth* evening newspaper every day, and since I had so much time on my hands, I'd read it from cover to cover. I learned a lot about what was happening in the Jewish community and its relationship with the British, which had deteriorated markedly in the wake of the King David Hotel bombing.

A month had passed since Black Sabbath—or Operation Broadside, as the British called it—when the British had launched a second operation, code-named Operation Shark, which had been carried out mostly by red beret soldiers from the Sixth Airborne Division. They had imposed a general curfew on Tel Aviv, conducted widespread searches, and arrested 730 underground activists and Jewish community leaders, including Yitzhak Shamir, one of the three leaders of the Lehi. I also learned that the relationships between the Haganah, Irgun, and Lehi had fallen apart after the attack on the King David Hotel.

Coincidentally, Operation Shark had taken place on July 29, the same day I had assassinated Jeffries. We were lucky Shark had been in Tel Aviv and not Jerusalem, else our plans would have been jeopardized or even prevented entirely.

The lack of unity among the Jewish community was a

source of much frustration to me, and I discussed the matter with Max when he came in to check on me. I lay resting in my borrowed bed as he paced back and forth, talking.

"It's even worse than you hear on the radio or read in the paper," Max said, clearly upset. "Ben-Gurion has declared that the British government and its policies are the enemy but not the British soldiers, policemen, or government officials. Even worse, the Jewish Agency has decided that the struggle against the British could threaten the establishment of a Jewish national home." He twisted his hands together.

"As far as Ben-Gurion and the Haganah are concerned, the prime objective is the establishment of a Jewish state and a strong defensive military force that will be able to stand up to the Arabs. So now the Haganah focuses only on bringing in immigrants and increasing settlements. Ben-Gurion and his followers don't understand that if the British remain in control here, we will never be able to establish a Jewish national home."

"I see the logic in establishing a strong defense force, bringing in immigrants, and settling the land," I said. "But the British are doing everything in their power to stop it. I heard on the radio that the British navy intercepted several immigrant ships off the coast and deported the Jews on board to Cyprus." I frowned and swung my feet to the floor, feeling suddenly restless. "I've had enough of lying around doing nothing. These people have suffered enough, and we need to help them. Let's have Zvi come over to discuss what we can do next."

Zvi stopped by the next day.

"Max told me that you're recovering," Zvi said. "I'm glad to hear it." The three of us were sitting in the living room of Max's apartment. "He also said you're looking for ways to fight the British and help Jews get into Israel. Let's see what we can do."

"Zvi," Max interjected, "before we talk about David, I

would like to bring up another issue. A short time after David was wounded, Shoshana approached me and said she'd like to be involved in future underground operations. She also insisted David has risked his life enough, and we should give him a break for a while. I told her I hoped David would have no objection and that I'd discuss it with you, Zvi."

Zvi looked thoughtful for a moment and then nodded. "I have no objection to her being involved in future operations, and I hope that you, David, don't have any objection either. In any case, Shoshana needs to go through intensive training first."

I didn't feel comfortable talking with them about Shoshana, but I decided to be open about my thoughts. "Honestly, I don't want Shoshana risking her life. She needs to stay behind the scenes."

Zvi gazed at me, arms folded over his chest. "We have many women fighters, David. You know this."

"Yes. It isn't because she's a woman."

"It's because she's your woman." Zvi smiled.

I refused to make this about me. The fact was that she could get killed.

"Look, if it's a matter of needing more people to work the operations, put me in. I'd rather take the risk myself than have Shoshana risk her life."

"But that's not what she wants."

I stared at the ground, trying to find the right words. Finally, I nodded. "You're right. And she's a free and independent woman. I know I don't have the right to tell her what she can or can't do. But please—let me talk to her first. I have to make sure she understands what she's getting herself into."

"All right," Zvi said. "Talk to her. And speaking of operations, I think it would be a good idea for you to start helping bring refugees to Israel. Are you ready for it?"

"Of course," I said.

"The Irgun and Lehi have a number of offensive operations against the British planned," Zvi said, "but when it comes to immigration, we aren't doing well at all. The British navy is intercepting almost every refugee ship that approaches Israel lately. The best solution we've found is to smuggle Jews in through Lebanon. The Haganah has brought in several groups this way in the past, but they've stopped those efforts, and I don't know why. In any event, we've looked into it, and it does seem feasible. We'd have to get the people to the Lebanese border, help them to cross it, and then transport them to a Jewish settlement in the Galilee. Your thoughts, David?"

"I'll be happy to play a part in an operation like that," I said.

"You won't simply play a part," Zvi said. "You're going to lead it. Of course, it will be a complex operation requiring meticulous planning and preparation. Shimon was born in Rosh Pina, not far from the Lebanese border, and he knows the area like you apparently know the Scriptures. I've instructed him to help you. Max will let me know when you are fully recovered, which should be soon, by the looks of it, and then we'll get to work." He started to stand up, but I motioned for him to remain where he was.

"Wait, please. There's a personal matter that troubles me a great deal," I said. "Jeffries, damn his soul, tried to force me to cooperate by threatening to deport Shoshana. I know that his division has been shut down, but I'd feel a lot more comfortable if you could use your connections in the Jewish Agency to secure an official permit for her."

"I can't promise anything, but I assure you that I'll do my best," Zvi said. He shook my hand and left the room with Max, who saw him to the door.

"You're welcome to stay here with us for as long as you

like," Max said as he came back into the room, "although I'm sure you'd like to return to your apartment. But with Shoshana at work until late, we thought perhaps it would be better for you to stay a while longer. Nelka is here all the time and can continue to take care of you. When you do go home, don't rush into this operation. The doctor said you'll need to rest for another couple of weeks at least."

"You're right," I said, touched by his concern. "I'd like to say that I'm back in shape, but that wouldn't be true."

"Shoshana told me that your landlords asked about you. When you get home, I suggest you tell them you learned your aunt and uncle are definitely in the country but that you didn't find them yet and will keep looking. That should help explain your absence when you're busy with the operation in the north."

FIVE DAYS LATER, MAX DROVE me back to my apartment. I invited him in, but he politely declined. "I think you need some time alone with Shoshana," he said with a wink.

A vase with red roses stood on the table by the front door, along with a note that read: *My beloved hero has returned.* Shoshana was waiting for me by the bed, dressed in nothing but a satin robe that hung half open. She hugged me and pulled me into bed. My leg still hurt, but I soon forgot the pain.

Max had given Shoshana the day off, and we spent all morning and afternoon in bed before I fell asleep. When I woke up, dinner was ready. Shoshana opened a bottle of wine, and we sat down at the table and raised our glasses in a toast to life, which seemed more wonderful than ever in that moment.

After we finished our drinks, we shared a few kisses before Shoshana began serving our plates from the steaming bowls of food on the table.

"I spoke to Max about helping with the underground in a more important capacity," she began. "He said he would discuss it with Zvi."

"Every role in the underground is important," I muttered around the food in my mouth. She gave me a pointed look.

"You don't want me to fight, do you?"

"It isn't that I don't want you to be part of it," I said, staring down at my plate.

"Then what is it?"

I lifted my gaze to hers, my voice calm. "I don't want you to die."

She reached across the table to take my hand. "Oh, David," she whispered, "I don't want to die either."

"Being a fighter—an actual fighter in the underground—is extremely dangerous," I told her. "It takes special training, but more than that, it takes a special mindset. There is no room for hesitation or weakness."

"I know." She waited.

I sighed. "What you do now, behind the scenes, is just as vital in its own way. Couldn't you continue as you've been doing?"

"I could," she said, "but you see, my dear love, you've ruined me for such things."

I jerked my head up. "Me? I haven't done anything."

"But you have," she went on, her eyes shining, filled with an earnestness I'd never seen before. "You've risked your life for our people, both in the war with the Nazis and now in Jerusalem." She squeezed my hand tightly. "You let me go when I needed to find myself again, and you took me back when I was ready. You've shown me how to be brave, and you've shown me compassion. With you, David, I've grown stronger, and I want to keep growing. More than anything, I want to fight at your side against the enemy." She hesitated. "Unless you don't think I can."

"It isn't that," I said. "You're a strong, capable woman, and you amaze me more and more every day. I just simply and honestly fear that if you join the physical fight against the British, I'll lose you. And if that happens . . ." I shook my head. "I don't know if I can go on." I looked down at our hands intertwined, remembering Leah.

"And yet, dear David," she said softly, leaning forward, "we have both gone on in spite of all we have lost, haven't we?"

Her words jarred me, and I glanced back up at her. "Yes," I admitted, "we have."

Shoshana lifted my hand and kissed my rough, bruised knuckles. Then she spread my palm against hers and met my gaze. "You have taught me what it is to be brave, to sacrifice, and yes, to be brutal—but also to be merciful. And together or alone, we will continue to go on, no matter what may come. No matter if one of us dies. Because the future of our people, and our country, is bigger than us." Her lips trembled slightly. "It has to be."

I took a deep breath and released it, then brought her hand to my face and held it there for a moment. "You are a very wise woman," I said. "Very well, but you must promise me one thing."

"Anything," she said.

I gave her a wicked smile. "I get to train you."

She returned my grin. "I can't wait," she said, obviously delighted. She began cutting the meat on her plate and then stopped. "Oh! I forgot—Avrum came looking for you again. He wanted to meet with you the moment you returned. Unfortunately for him, I wanted to meet with you the moment you returned also."

"Lucky me," I said with a wink.

"I told him I thought you'd be back today. He said if you did come back, we should stop by for breakfast tomorrow morning. Do you feel like going to see them?"

"Sure," I said, now curious. Why did Avrum want to see me so urgently?

"All right. After we're done eating, I'll walk over and tell them we'll have breakfast with them tomorrow. You stay here and get some rest."

When she left later to deliver the message, I tried to imagine what Avrum wanted. All of my ideas left me feeling edgy and uneasy.

The moment we walked through their door the next morning, Hannah threw her arms around me and gave me a more-than-just-friendly hug. "We're so glad to see the two of you!" she cried, clinging to me far longer than necessary for a greeting. "It's been too long!"

I pulled away from her and put my arm around Shoshana. From the look on my girlfriend's face, it was safe to say she wasn't thrilled about the other woman's enthusiastic welcome.

Avrum apparently wasn't paying attention to his wife's behavior or simply didn't care. Without a word, he gripped my shoulder and led me to his study.

"They fired me," he said at last, clearly agitated as he shut the door behind us. "I expected it. They're all anti-Semites there, except for my boss. I got into a confrontation with one of the other officers a month ago. He said something about arresting all the dirty Jews, and I said he was the dirty one. If my boss hadn't intervened, we would have come to blows!" He began to pace around the room. "And last week, during a briefing about an investigation into a major robbery at a jewelry store on Jaffa Street, I pointed out we had intelligence reports indicating that British soldiers had committed the crime. The senior commander just snorted and told me to focus on the Jews. Thieves and money-grabbers, he called us!"

"This upset you," I stated. It was hard not to smile at Avrum's newly discovered outrage.

"Upset me! I couldn't stop myself! I said that my experience in the police force had taught me that if a competition was held to find the biggest thieves, the Jews wouldn't have the upper hand over the British. The superintendent didn't say anything, but my boss called me in the next day and said that because of 'cutbacks,' I was being let go!"

"I'm sorry to hear that," I said, and I meant it.

Avrum shook his head. "Don't be. The only thing I'm sorry about is that I didn't quit first and deny them the pleasure of firing me. I can hardly believe how much my opinions have changed these last few months. If someone offered me the chance to join the Irgun or Lehi, I wouldn't hesitate! I'd be willing to give them all the weapons I have—and if I had the courage, I'd use them myself on a few of those Jew-haters in the police force!"

I was astounded to hear Avrum ranting against the British when he had always so fervently defended them.

"Keep what I've told you to yourself for now," he added. "Hannah doesn't know. I told her I'm on vacation."

"Don't worry, things will work out," I said, putting my hand on his shoulder. "We're friends, and you have my support no matter what."

Avrum clasped my hand. "The day I first met you at the cobbler's, I could tell you were a good man. I'm happy to have a friend like you."

I felt relief that I had long ago ended my relationship with Hannah. I had never expected Avrum to become a good friend and a supporter of the Irgun and the Lehi underground.

On our way home, I told Shoshana what Avrum had said to me. "Would you ask Max to hire him, for the time being at least?"

"Of course," she promised.

The next day, I went to the Cohens' store to reintroduce my presence in the neighborhood. "How are you, Mr. Don Juan?" Mrs. Cohen greeted me in her familiar mocking tone. "I haven't seen you around here for a while. Have you been out hunting for new young women?"

I suppressed the urge to say something sarcastic and took a serious tone. "I've been looking for my aunt and uncle, who survived one of the concentration camps and apparently managed to make their way here. I tracked them to the Sdot Yam kibbutz, but I don't know where they've gone since."

"Well, I'm pleased to hear you don't spend all your time flirting with young girls," Mrs. Cohen said.

"Please don't be offended by my wife," interjected her husband, who was busy stocking the shelves with fresh loaves of bread. "That's just what passes for her sense of humor."

Shoshana had yet to leave for work when I got home. "There's something I'd like you to do for me," I told her. "On your way to work, please go to the office of the Jewish Agency on King George Street and ask to place an ad with the Bureau for Missing Relatives that reads: *David Gabinsky from Minsk is looking for Izak Levkowitz, the son of Zusha from Minsk.*"

After explaining that situation to her, I added, "And when you get to the restaurant, tell Max that I'm ready to meet Commander Zvi in Talpiot. If that's possible, they should send Shimon to collect me."

"Another dangerous mission."

"Hopefully not," I said, pulling her close. "I'll just be helping a group of refugees into the country through Lebanon."

She wrapped her arms tightly around my neck and looked up at me. "Somehow every mission you're involved in becomes dangerous," she said.

"Every mission has the potential to be dangerous," I told her. "That's what you're signing up for if you become a fighter." I cocked my head. "Still in?"

"Yes." She lifted her chin. "But that doesn't mean I'm not going to harass you about being careful."

I kissed the tip of her nose. "Same here."

When she came home that night, Shoshana told me the meeting had been arranged for the following afternoon.

THE NEXT DAY, SHIMON PICKED me up and took me to the house in Talpiot. As he escorted me inside, I was happy to see a black ribbon draped over Inspector Jeffries's photograph where it hung on the wall. Zvi came into the room to greet me and chuckled as I gazed up at the picture.

"Generals Cassels and Barker mourn their friend—as do we," he said with a smile and a wink. "And we should do our best to reunite them."

"I heartily agree."

"I promised Max and Shoshana that I wouldn't include you in dangerous operations until the end of the year, but with your help, I hope we can drape their photographs in black ribbons in the year to come."

I waved away his words. "I suppose you'll be glad to know that Shoshana and I had quite a talk, and she will be joining the underground as a fighter."

"Excellent," he said, beaming.

"But I want to train her."

He nodded. "Of course. You want to make sure she has the

very best instruction. Well done. I think she will be a very good addition to the team. Now, about the refugees . . ." Zvi laid a map on the table in the room. As he spread it out, I could see the outline of southern Lebanon and the north of Israel.

"In early September," he said, "a ship carrying a group of about ninety survivors from the displaced persons camps in Europe will set out from the port of Piraeus in Greece." He stabbed one finger down at the map. "The ship will dock in Beirut. From there, the refugees will be transported in trucks to the Lebanese village of Al-Adisa, near the border with Israel. With the help of one of our guides, they'll make their way on foot to the border and then to Kfar Giladi, where they'll be driven to Rosh Pina. Arrangements have been made to scatter them among various communities."

"But how will they get past the border guards?" I asked.

"That's where you and Shimon come in," Zvi said. "The crossing is manned by four Arab guards and two British policemen who oversee them. It's your job to find a way to get them through."

"I imagine that will take some convincing," I replied. "Can we just pay them off?"

"That should work only with the Arab guards," Zvi explained. "Shimon grew up in the area and has lived among Arabs since he was a child. He speaks fluent Arabic, so he'll deal with them. As for the British policemen, you may need to neutralize them. But let me stress that when I say *neutralize*, I don't mean *kill* them. We need to keep this route open in the future."

I could tell Zvi noticed the confused expression on my face. "Neutralizing may be a complicated matter," I said. "But I'll think of something."

Zvi continued. "You'll have to devise your plan based on

facts on the ground. That's why we've come up with a way for you to scout the area without arousing suspicion. You and Shimon will pass yourselves off as ornithologists, which will allow you to conduct tours in the area without arousing suspicion." He walked over and opened a door, leaning out for a moment. "Come in," he said to someone outside the room.

A pompous-looking man wearing horn-rimmed glasses and a shabby suit came inside. Zvi gestured toward him. "This is Dr. Yaakov Mermelstein, a leading ornithologist. I've asked him to help by giving you a brief overview on the subject of ornithology."

Without any acknowledgment of my presence, the man began to speak. "The Land of Israel," Dr. Mermelstein began, with an overwhelming attitude of self-importance, "is a major flyway for birds migrating from Europe to Africa in the fall and then back to Europe in the spring. When you are in the north this fall, you'll have the chance to observe flocks of birds from northern Europe and Asia as they migrate south." He took a piece of paper out of his pocket and adjusted his glasses as he peered at it.

"I've made a list of the birds you can expect to encounter, along with photographs," he went on. "To look like professional ornithologists, you should observe the birds through binoculars, photograph them enthusiastically, and talk excitedly to one another when you see them, especially when other people are watching you." He raised both bushy brows. "Do you think you can handle it?"

"I don't think it will be a problem," I said, trying not to sound sarcastic.

"When we have precise details about the ship's schedule," Zvi explained, "we'll decide when to send you north on your first scouting mission."

After talking a few more minutes, Shimon and I thanked Zvi and Dr. Mermelstein and collected our binoculars, cameras, and field guides.

"There is one more thing," Zvi said. He handed me a brown envelope. "Open it."

It was a certificate—an official immigration permit issued by the Jewish Agency in the name of Shoshana Rosa Bukstein. Forgetting myself, I embraced Zvi, who seemed a bit embarrassed.

"Thank you," I said, stepping back. "I'm very grateful to you."

When Shimon and I got outside, I asked him if he could stop at the YMCA for a few minutes on our way back. I wanted to pay a visit to Yousef, whom I hadn't seen in almost a month. When we pulled up outside the building, I was surprised that Shimon got out of the car and joined me.

Yousef was in the middle of a training session when we walked into the boxing gym. "I'll be done in fifteen minutes," he said when he saw us, and I noticed that he nodded and winked at Shimon.

"I used to be Yousef's trainer," Shimon told me. "He was an excellent student." I was amazed for a moment by the strange coincidence—and the fact that Shimon could be so friendly.

"Are you still boxing?" I asked.

"I quit," he replied. "It's a long story, but I'll tell you one day, if you like."

When the session was over, Yousef embraced Shimon, then turned to me.

"Where did you disappear to?" he asked me.

I told him about my aunt and uncle, and he didn't seem to suspect anything.

"Are you ever going to come visit my family in Ramallah?"

Yousef asked Shimon. "My mother's mosakhan chicken will change your life."

"I'm pretty busy these days," Shimon said, "but I promise to come as soon as I get the time."

After Shimon dropped me off at my apartment, I took a nap until Shoshana returned from work. She told me that Avrum was taking well to his new job.

"He made more tips from his two tables than I made from eight!" she said, laughing. "Not that he could have handled any more than that. He spent so much time chatting with the customers, he might as well have sat down with them."

"I know." I chuckled. "He's a friendly fellow."

"And Alec too. You should spend some time with him. I think he's feeling a little neglected."

"I'll go see him tomorrow morning," I replied.

Shoshana took a shower, and when she was drying her hair, she noticed the envelope I had placed on her side of the bed. "What's that?" she asked.

"Open it and have a look," I said.

When she saw the certificate, her eyes filled with tears. "How did you get this?" she asked, clasping the paper to her heart.

"Zvi gave it to me this afternoon."

Shoshana leaped into my arms and kissed me. "No one but you could have gotten this for me," she said. "Have I told you lately that you are the dearest man in the world?"

"Yes," I said with a smile, "but I'm willing to hear it again."

19

"WELCOME BACK TO MY WINDOW, YOU LOVELY BIRD"

(FROM "TO THE BIRD," A POEM BY HAYIM NAHMAN BIALIK, 1891)

While I waited for word from Zvi, I focused on getting back into shape, with plenty of calisthenics and walking. I held off on running for the time being, even though I felt my wounded leg regaining its strength.

Just like the previous months, September was politically stormy and tense. In Haifa, Lehi fighters killed the British CID officer who had picked out underground commander Yitzhak Shamir in a police lineup. In another operation on the same day, the Lehi blew up the headquarters of British Intelligence in Jaffa, killing several people. The Irgun played its part too, sabotaging railroad tracks, communication lines, and bridges throughout the month.

Shimon turned up at my apartment one day to inform me

that Zvi wanted us to go up north to Rosh Pina. "He's already been in touch with the people in the Kfar Giladi kibbutz," Shimon said. "We have six days to scout the area and make our plan; then it's time to put it into action."

I packed my things, deciding after some thought to take along two of the Webley revolvers and ammunition. I said nothing to Zvi about it. If he knew, he might order me to leave them behind. The preparation stage of the operation wasn't supposed to be "wet"—the term used to describe activities involving firearms—but I wanted to be prepared regardless.

Shoshana hugged me tightly before I left. "Please promise me you'll look after yourself and not take any avoidable risks," she said, looking me straight in the eyes.

"I promise," I said and kissed her goodbye.

She waved from the door and said, "I wish I could go with you. I hate when you leave."

"I'll be back soon. I love you," I said, and with that, I left without looking back.

Shimon and I drove off in the same car he used for my meetings with Zvi. Soon we had left Jerusalem and were heading north through the Arab cities of Nablus and Jenin. As we drove through another Jewish area, the Jezreel Valley kibbutzim, I told Shimon about the two revolvers hidden in my bag, one of which was for him.

"Why didn't you tell Zvi?" he asked angrily. "This is not how we work. Honesty is a cornerstone of our organization."

"I didn't think I needed to," I said. "They're only a last resort."

Clearly not appeased, Shimon sunk back into silence. He wasn't much of a talker.

It was my first trip to the north, and I enjoyed the scenery we passed along the way. The plowed fields of the Jezreel Valley and the shimmering water of the Galilee looked so different from Jerusalem. It took about five hours to reach Rosh Pina, including a stop for fuel and food in Afula.

"We'll be staying with my aunt and uncle," Shimon told me as we drove into Rosh Pina. When we arrived at their home, they were very welcoming. After warmly embracing Shimon and joyfully shaking my hand, they showed us to the room they had prepared for us.

Shimon's Aunt Bracha was a large, cheerful woman. "You'll soon learn that she's an accomplished cook," Shimon promised, and he was right. She prepared a wonderful dinner for us, and we both ate twice as much as usual. As we ate, his Uncle Chaim enthusiastically told me all about the history of Rosh Pina. I was surprised to learn it had been settled in 1882 by a group of thirty Hasidic families from Romania.

When we retired to our room later, I took one of the revolvers out of my bag and handed it to Shimon, along with a handful of cartridges. "Just in case," I said.

He gave me a dirty look but didn't say a word as he slipped the gun into his bag.

We woke to a beautiful sunny morning. I advised Shimon to load the weapon and hide it in his camera case, under the camera. He wouldn't be able to close the case with the camera inside, but at least the gun would be hidden. We drove north toward the checkpoint on the border with Lebanon to do some scouting. We parked the car about two hundred yards from the border and walked the rest of the way, getting off the road from time to time to peer through our binoculars and take photographs.

We were about thirty yards from the checkpoint when we heard someone shout "Halt!" in English. "Who are you, and what are you doing here?"

We approached slowly to find a plump, red-faced British policeman standing with two Arab guards.

"We're ornithologists." I pointed out a hoopoe, which I recognized from Dr. Mermelstein's photos, perched on a branch overlooking their small nest. "Look at its beautiful orange-and-black crown!" I said as I quickly snapped photographs. "You're so lucky to work in an area that attracts such a broad range of species."

The policeman looked at me as if I had lost my mind. "You can have them. All they do is chirp. Drives me crazy."

"I think the same thing of people!" I said. "All their yelling and clanging. It's too bad I have to live in the city instead of a beautiful place like this."

The policeman snorted. "This has to be the most boring place in the world. You can't even get a beer up here. The Arabs don't drink, and the Jews only rarely do—not that I blame them, with that sickeningly sweet kosher wine of theirs."

"That's not entirely true," I said. "I love beer too. What kind do you like?"

"I haven't had a proper stout since I left Sussex," the man sighed, "but in this infernal heat, what I'm really craving is something cooler. I spent a few months in the Netherlands and developed a taste for their Heineken. Do you know it?"

"I don't just know it," I said. "It's one of my favorites too."

The door to their building opened, and a second British policeman stepped out. "Someone mentioned beer?" he asked. "Do you have some?"

"No, we're just talking," the plump one said with another sigh.

"Don't look so sad, my friend," I said. "In a couple of days, I think I'll have a surprise for you."

"God bless you," he said, and we shook hands.

We continued to scout the area, taking photographs and— just to be on the safe side—calling out excitedly whenever we came across a new bird. Some two hours later, we left for Rosh Pina.

"Those British policemen will be our best friends if we get them a few bottles of Heineken," I said to Shimon. "We have to get our hands on some."

"That may be tough," Shimon muttered. "We'll have to check with Zvi."

When we got back to Rosh Pina, we went to the community's secretariat and asked to place a call to Jerusalem. Shimon got hold of Zvi and explained our request.

"Zvi thinks you're right," Shimon said after hanging up the phone. "He suggests we go to Haifa tomorrow. There's a liquor store there, and the owner is sympathetic to us. He'll speak to him tomorrow morning. He also gave me an update—the border crossing by the refugees will occur in three days at eight in the evening."

WE LEFT FOR HAIFA EARLY the next morning, and when we arrived at the liquor store, we found that Zvi had already called the owner and asked him to give us a good price on three cases of Heineken beer. That seemed like a lot, but Zvi must have assumed we'd be better off having too many bottles rather than too few.

After loading the cases into the car, I suggested we get some laxatives and sleeping pills to mix into the beer, should the need arise. We went to the drug store, but the pharmacist said he couldn't sell the sleeping pills we wanted without a doctor's prescription.

"Sir," I began, "I'm suffering from chronic constipation, and my wife has insomnia—"

"Then go see a doctor," the pharmacist snapped.

"Sir," I said, looking around and lowering my voice. "My wife and I don't have papers. If we went to a doctor, he could report us to the authorities."

The pharmacist nodded, then started rummaging through his drug cabinet for the pills we needed. He instructed me on how to take the medicines and warned me not to exceed the recommended dosages.

From Haifa, we drove to Kfar Giladi, arriving late in the afternoon. Shimon sought out Sonia, our contact there, and she told us that she planned to hide the ninety immigrants in the kibbutz's cowshed and chicken coop for a night. The next day, four trucks would arrive to start shuttling the people to Rosh Pina, where cars would drive them to their final destinations. I was disappointed that after all these people had been through, they would have to spend their first night in Israel with cows and chickens, but I realized it was the only option.

THE FOLLOWING MORNING, SHIMON AND I packed our ornithological equipment into the car, along with an icebox and ten bottles of Heineken. As we drove to the border, we agreed that I would invite the British policeman to join us for a beer. Shimon would decline, staying behind to chat with the Arab guards.

We parked the car near the crossing and made our way on foot toward the guard station. The British policemen waved to us, and we struck up a conversation.

"It's so boring here," the plump one complained. "Aziz and Faisal should be able to handle the work themselves, but they have no sense of duty. If we weren't here, the hashish smugglers would simply bribe them and go about their business."

"That must be frustrating," I said. "How about a cold Heineken to get your mind off your troubles?"

He looked at me incredulously. "Are you serious?"

"Yes," I said. "Come with us to the car. It's easier than carrying the icebox all the way here."

"Of course," the policeman responded happily.

Shimon, as planned, demurred, saying that he had found a great spot near the crossing where he could observe and photograph a particular bird that he was excited about. The policeman and I walked to the car. "George," he introduced himself on the way, and we shook hands.

"David," I replied.

"You seem like a good chap, David. Maybe a bit dotty for birds but not obsessed with them like your friend."

I smiled but didn't respond. When we got to the car, I retrieved two bottles of Heineken from the icebox, opened them, and handed one to George. His eyes lit up.

"God bless you, David. Cheerio!" He took a big swig of the beer, licked his lips, and then raised the bottle to his mouth again. He polished off the first and then a second bottle in no time. I retrieved four more bottles from the icebox. "Two for you and two for your friend," I said. He thanked me profusely and asked, a bit hopefully, if I would be returning to go birding on the next day.

"I believe so," I replied. "This is migration season, and the birds here are wonderful."

We returned to the border checkpoint, where Shimon was waiting for me. I said farewell to George, and we walked back to our car.

"How did it go?" I asked.

"The guards can definitely be paid off," Shimon said. "But

the local guards at the border like to haggle, so I had to take that into consideration. We finally agreed that each of them will get six pounds—that's got to be at least twice what they make a month."

We left the border and drove a few miles before stopping and hiking to a hilltop that Shimon said offered a clear view of the route the refugees would be following. We figured we'd have to find a spot about one hundred yards inside Lebanese territory where we could signal the guide and direct the group to the border crossing.

As we were walking down the hill to our car, two Arabs rounded a bend in the valley and galloped toward us on horseback, rifles in their hands. They signaled us to stop, and one of them shouted at us in Arabic.

"They're robbing us," Shimon muttered. "He says they'll let us go if we give them our money and equipment."

"On my signal, I'll take the one on the right, you take the left," I said.

Our private conversation seemed to enrage our would-be robber, whose yelling grew louder. I reached into my pocket for my wallet and placed it on the ground in front of me. Then I removed the binoculars from around my neck and placed them on the ground too. The robber gestured toward the camera bag, playing right into my hands. I pulled the camera out and tossed it toward him, and his gaze followed after it.

"Now!" I shouted. I jerked the revolver from the camera case and fired at the rider on the right. He toppled from his horse as Shimon took out the man on the left. They both dropped to the ground. We ran over and checked to make sure they were dead.

"Good job," I said. "You know they would've killed us either way."

Shimon nodded. "If you understood Arabic, you would have known that right after they stopped us, one said to the other, 'As soon as these Jews give us their stuff, we'll kill them.' I apologize for getting angry with you about the guns. You saved our lives."

We dragged the bodies to a suitable spot off the beaten path and covered them with stones. We released their horses and placed their rifles and ammunition in the trunk of our car before starting our drive back to Rosh Pina.

As Shimon drove, we planned the last details of our operation. The refugees would be arriving in two nights. We'd go to the border crossing in the evening and generously share our beers with the British policemen, doctoring one man's drinks with sleeping pills and the other's with laxatives. Both would soon be out of commission, with no suspicion thrown our way, since each man would have different symptoms. The Arab guards would then be free to help us bring the refugees across the border. We decided to go back to the crossing the next day with more beer to nourish our blossoming friendship with the Brits.

At dinner that night, Shimon's uncle recounted how the famous Jewish hero Joseph Trumpeldor had visited Rosh Pina when he'd first arrived in Israel in 1911 and how he had been killed in the nearby Tel Hai community in 1920. Several hundred armed Arabs had swarmed into the village and searched for French soldiers, who had occupied the area during World War I. Trumpeldor had been mortally wounded in the ensuing battle and died several hours later.

"In the final moments of his life," Chaim continued with great pathos in his voice, "Trumpeldor said, 'It's good to die for our country'—words that will be forever etched into the history of the Jewish nation. Joseph Trumpeldor and many others

sacrificed their lives without hesitation for our homeland, and I
thank God there are some who are willing to do so today as well."

I lifted my glass in a silent toast.

IN THE MORNING, WE FILLED our icebox with bottles of
beer, placed it in the trunk of the car, and drove back to the
border. The two British policemen greeted us with cries of joy
as we approached the checkpoint. I invited them to join me at
the car, while Shimon stayed behind with the Arab guards to
make the final arrangements for the refugees' crossing.

Standing behind our car and leaning into the trunk, I
opened the beers while they were still in the icebox. I wanted
to establish this as a habit so that doing the same thing the next
time would not arouse suspicion, and I'd have those private
few moments to slip the powder from the laxatives and sleeping pills into two of the bottles.

After we'd each finished off a bottle, I handed each of them
a second one. "We're leaving the day after tomorrow," I said,
"but we'll come by tomorrow evening to say goodbye—and
bring some more beer, of course."

"Thank you," George said.

"I have a small request," I added. "It's silly, but could you
let me walk a few dozen yards beyond the border crossing so I
can tell my wife that I was in Lebanon?"

"No problem," George said, and his friend nodded in
agreement. I walked through the crossing and entered Lebanese territory with a single purpose—to find a vantage point
where I could signal the refugees' guide. After I'd found a
good spot alongside a large rock that would be easily visible at
night, I returned to the crossing, and we said farewell to the
British policemen.

When we got back to Rosh Pina, I asked Shimon to go to the secretariat and call Zvi to make sure the refugees would arrive at the crossing by eight o'clock the next evening and also to let the guide know he should be on the lookout for our signal.

The next morning, I crushed the pills I'd bought into powder and pushed the two small heaps into separate paper bags, marking the laxative with a pen. We bid farewell to Shimon's aunt and uncle, and Shimon made another call to Zvi to confirm that nothing had changed before we left.

When we arrived at the crossing, George was pleased to see us. "Our sergeant paid us a surprise visit yesterday, and he found the beers you gave us. He insisted on joining us for a drink today."

"No problem, George," I said. "We have enough beer for your sergeant too."

The three Brits, excited at the thought of the cold beers waiting for them, walked with me to our car. I opened the bottles as I had done the day before and, blocking what I was doing, tapped the powders from the bags resting in the icebox into the drinks. George, the friendliest of the three, got the bottle with the sleeping pills, while his friend and the sergeant got the laxative. When they'd finished their beers, I gathered up the empty bottles and gave them each an untainted bottle, and we parted on friendly terms.

Meanwhile, Shimon spoke with the Arab guards and informed them that we'd be back in an hour and a half to get the people coming across the border.

When we returned to the crossing, we saw only the Arab guards. They told Shimon that shortly after we left, George started yawning and then fell asleep, while the sergeant and the other policeman were struck with severe diarrhea. They had called a nearby base, about six miles from the crossing, and a car had been sent to take them to a clinic.

At a quarter to eight, I crossed the border and found my spot at the large rock. At 7:55, I started signaling with my flashlight. About seven minutes later, I spotted a return signal deep inside Lebanese territory. I continued signaling for another forty minutes until I saw the line of people headed toward me, with a guide leading the way. I thanked the guide in English, and he turned to make his way back to Beirut.

Shimon stayed back to pay the Arab guards and then joined the group of immigrants to lead them on foot toward Kfar Giladi. My leg ached, so I got in the car and drove to the kibbutz, wondering what George would think when he finally woke up. When I arrived in Kfar Giladi, I went straight to Sonia's house to tell her the operation had succeeded. She rewarded me with a good supper while I waited for the rest. Shimon showed up with the group about an hour and a half later.

They looked on the verge of collapse as we led them into the kibbutz dining room. I thought about the atrocities these men and women had endured in Europe and how they had been forced to suffer more hardship to reach their homeland. Once again, I felt anger and resentment toward the British.

I was making my way around the dining room, pushing a cart laden with pots of tea and coffee and plates of bread, butter, and olives, when I stopped dead in my tracks. Was I hallucinating? There in front of me were the big blue eyes of my beloved Leah. I blinked and looked again. The eyes were just like hers, but the face was her brother's.

"Misha," I said softly.

He blinked, and then his blue eyes registered who I was and widened in disbelief. "David?"

"Yes!" I hadn't seen my old friend since our partisan group had disbanded. His shoulders were still impressively broad, but he was very thin. I hugged him warmly and introduced him to Shimon.

"This is Misha, a very brave warrior who fought alongside me as a partisan. Leah, his sister . . ." I swallowed hard. ". . . She was a big love of mine. Misha, if you like, I would be honored if you joined us on our drive back to Jerusalem."

"That—that would be wonderful," he said, his voice hoarse with emotion.

I clasped my arm around his shoulder, even though the joy I felt was bittersweet. Misha was here, and that was good. But Leah was gone. Still, I was so grateful to have found him.

"Welcome home, old friend," I said. "Welcome home.

20

"IN TOWNS AND VILLAGES SHALL WE RAISE OUR BANNER"

(FROM "UNKNOWN SOLDIERS," A POEM BY AVRAHAM STERN, 1932)

Four empty trucks arrived at Kfar Giladi early the next morning to transfer the exhausted refugees to Rosh Pina. As someone who had escaped that accursed abattoir of Europe not too long ago, I hoped with all my heart that their Jewish brethren, born and raised in Israel, would have sympathy for the suffering they had endured. Much to my dismay, I had often encountered indifference to that suffering. Many of the native Jews weren't particularly accepting of us newcomers, who often looked different and barely spoke Hebrew.

After all the new arrivals had been sent on their way, Shimon and I returned to his aunt and uncle's house with Misha. Shimon now felt free to tell Bracha and Chaim what we'd been doing over the past few days.

"I wasn't fooled for a minute by your bird-watching non-sense," Chaim said after his nephew had explained. "I suspected it was a cover story for something, and I said so to Bracha. My suspicions were confirmed on your second day here when I spotted two beautiful western yellow wagtails flitting about in our garden, and the two of you didn't even notice. But why didn't you tell us? Don't you trust us?"

The man looked stricken, and Misha and I exchanged glances as Shimon looked uncomfortable.

"Of course, Uncle," he began, "but you see, that is, you have to understand—"

"We couldn't place the two of you in that kind of danger," I interrupted. "The whole thing could have blown up in our faces, and we wanted you to be able to honestly deny knowing anything, if the situation arose."

"Humph," Aunt Bracha puffed. "Well, I suppose we will forgive you this time," she said sternly and then laughed. "Since you helped save over ninety of our people!" She hugged Shimon tightly, patting him on the back, while Chaim shook his head and smiled.

We left for Jerusalem the next morning, and Misha and I caught up on the way. "Do you still have any of the spoils from our operation against that bastard Nikolai?" I asked.

"Hardly anything, unfortunately," Misha said. "The group of refugees I joined was robbed in the Taurus Mountains on our way to Lebanon."

"Don't worry," I told him. "I'll help you find a room in Jerusalem, and I'll try to find you a job too."

We spoke in Belarusian, of course, and I kept our conversation short so as not to offend Shimon, who didn't understand a word. "Shimon," I said in Hebrew, trying to include him in the conversation, "perhaps now you'd be willing to tell me why you quit boxing?"

He kept driving for a few minutes, as if he hadn't heard me, but then broke his silence. "All right, I'll tell you. I used to be one of the best boxers in the north. No one could beat me—except for Yiftah Zaid, who never lost a fight. I was offered a job as a boxing coach at the YMCA, so I took it and moved to Jerusalem. That's how I met Yousef. Shortly thereafter, I met Zvi." He paused, as if gathering his thoughts, then went on.

"I was competing in the ring, and at one tournament, I went up against a well-known British boxer visiting from England. The fight between us was fierce, and we were both taking a beating. Throughout the fight, he was cursing me and making crude remarks about my mother and my sister. I ignored him, but at the start of the ninth round, he called me a filthy Jew. 'Too bad the Nazis didn't exterminate you along with the rest of your bloody race, but I'll take care of you now,' he said."

Shimon fell silent. Misha and I waited several minutes for him to continue. He didn't.

"So—what happened?" I finally asked.

When he spoke again, his voice was flat. "I beat him so badly that he died before they could get him to the hospital. The British referee accused me of killing him intentionally, said I kept punching him after he had stopped the fight. The police promised to make my life a living hell unless I quit boxing. I told Zvi about it, and he said I should quit and devote my abilities to fighting with the Wolves."

After Shimon's speech, we all fell silent for a time, and then Misha and I began to talk about our days as partisans. Shimon seemed drained and didn't say another word for the rest of the drive. We reached Jerusalem in the afternoon, and Shimon dropped me and Misha off outside my apartment. Before we left, I leaned in the car window.

"We all have our memories, my friend," I said to Shimon. "Some are more easily lived with than others."

He gave me what might have been a slight nod before driving away.

"Well," I said, turning to Misha, "it's time for you to meet Shoshana."

I led him into our apartment, then forgot him as I walked straight into Shoshana's arms. After she and I hugged and kissed, I introduced her to Misha. She hugged him warmly too, without saying a word.

"I thought we would visit Alec," I said, after showing Misha where to stow his knapsack. "Introduce Misha to him."

"Yes," Shoshana agreed, "let's do that." The three of us walked to Alec's apartment, and when he opened the door, Eva was at his side. After another round of hugs and handshakes, Alec poured shots of vodka for everyone, and Eva offered her apartment to Misha for the next few days.

"I'm staying here with Alec anyway," she said. "I do have a new roommate, but I'm sure Magda won't mind sharing the apartment for a few days with such a handsome man."

Misha blushed. "You are too kind," he said.

It was still early, so we took Misha shopping for new clothes and toiletries before we went to Eva's apartment. Magda opened the door for us. She was a young, pretty woman with brown eyes and shoulder-length curly brown hair. She was surprised to see such a crowd in front of her.

"Magda, darling, this is Misha," Eva said. "He just got here two days ago. He's a close friend of David's and Alec's and needs a place to stay. Would you mind?"

When Magda looked at Misha, her gaze locked on his big blue eyes. "No, I don't mind," she said, her cheeks turning quite rosy.

We left Misha there and then parted ways with Alec and Eva in the street. Shoshana and I walked home, arm in arm. Coming home to Shoshana after being absent for days reminded me that I had a new life now, one that she had filled with joy.

The next morning, I woke up to the smell of fresh rolls. Shoshana had gone out early to fetch them. At breakfast, while enjoying them, I got an idea.

"Since Alec used to work at the Berman Bakery, he should try to get Misha a job there," I suggested as I bit into one of the delicious pieces of bread.

"That's a great idea," she said. "You should ask Misha if he would like that."

Misha was already awake when I got to Magda's apartment. She was taking good care of him—had even made him breakfast. When I asked if he would be interested in working at a bakery, he responded with an enthusiastic yes and rushed to his room to grab his knapsack.

We stopped to pick up Alec at his apartment, and the three of us walked to Berman Bakery in Mea She'arim. One of the managers agreed to speak with Misha, who timidly responded to the man's questions in halting Hebrew. "I'm happy to help a new immigrant," the manager said. "You're hired."

We left the bakery in good spirits, and Alec offered to take us all for coffee, so we stopped at Café Europa and asked for Eva.

"That's wonderful!" Eva said when Misha told her he had already found a job. "Now that you're working, maybe I could ask Magda if you could move in with her permanently? She already knows I'm planning to move in with Alec soon. What do you think, Misha?"

Misha blushed and smiled. "What can I say?" he said. "It's hard to believe that I just arrived and already have a place to live, a job, and wonderful friends. I couldn't be any luckier."

We ordered coffee and a cheesecake, which Eva brought to the table. "Have you told David?" she asked Alec.

"I haven't had a chance yet," Alec replied.

"Told me what?"

"We're getting married!" Eva exclaimed. I stood and kissed her on the cheek, embracing her and then Alec.

"Shoshana will be delighted," I told them.

"Shoshana will be wondering why you haven't asked *her* yet," Eva said, giving me a knowing smile.

I cleared my throat and sat back down. "This is delicious cake," I said and began eating it like a starving man. They all laughed. We finished our cake, and Alec left for work. Eva attended to other tables, and I sat alone with Misha, drinking coffee.

"Did I ever tell you about Zusha, my friend when I first joined the partisans?" I asked him.

"Zusha Levkowitz?" Misha asked.

"Yes, that's right." I was somewhat surprised, because Misha and Leah had joined us after Zusha had been killed.

"I was friends with his son," Misha told me. "We used to play together in the days before the war."

"Izak? Do you know what happened to him?" Perhaps I could at last keep the promise I had made to my friend—to find him or his family.

"He's dead," Misha shook his head. "He was one of the first young people to flee the ghetto. He joined a group of partisans and came back with a friend to help others escape. The Germans caught and executed them. His family is all gone as well."

I felt a pang of sorrow and remained silent for a minute before I could talk. Then I told him about Zusha and the promise I had made.

"It's a sad story," Misha said. "A whole family dead and no one to remember them. Those of us who survived have to go on with our lives, but we'll never be whole again."

"We can be whole here," I said, "in Israel. But first we have to get rid of the damn British."

"I suspect you're already working on that." Misha leaned

toward me, his hands laced together in front of him. "I'd love to join you in the struggle, if you'll have me."

"I may be able to point you in the right direction. Give yourself a few days to get organized, and we'll discuss the matter again."

Misha nodded, and we fell silent as Eva came back to refill our cups.

"I've never told anyone in detail how Leah died and I survived," I said when we were alone again. "But I'll tell you now."

"I would like to hear."

I took a deep breath and closed my eyes.

"It was a beautiful day, and Leah and I went for a walk in the forest. I loved your sister, you know. We had a blanket . . . We lay down on it, we made love, and then we dozed off. All at once I was jarred awake by a faint noise. I opened my eyes and saw two men standing twenty feet from us with rifles at their sides. I rolled over and reached for my submachine gun as they opened fire. When the magazine in my gun was empty, there was no one left to fire at—I dropped the gun and turned to Leah . . ."

I paused at that moment, opened my eyes, and immediately regretted it when I saw the tears rolling down Misha's cheeks. I couldn't go on.

"Tell me," he urged. I nodded, swallowing hard.

"Oh, my God, Misha," I said hoarsely, "our sweet girl was lying motionless on the ground, blood pouring out of her chest. Her beautiful eyes were open, and she was alive but couldn't speak. There were only a few moments of life left in her. She died in my arms."

I closed my eyes again to let the pain of the memory have its way with me—it seemed only fitting. When I opened them again, Misha's stricken gaze made my heart clench. I couldn't tell if he was judging me harshly or not. I stumbled forward with more words.

"I feel so guilty that Leah was killed and I survived. I guess I've always felt I should be punished for what happened. And I think the truth is that I expected, and even wanted, you to hate me. When you said you never wanted to see me again, I knew I deserved your hatred, and truly? I hated myself." I released a breath I hadn't known I'd been holding. "I am sorry, my friend. I would give my life to bring her back."

Misha wiped the moisture from his face and kept on gazing straight ahead. It took another moment or so, and then his eyes met mine.

"What I feel now," he said, "is a mixture of sadness and relief. I wish I had known earlier. We were partisans, and our lives were in danger every minute of every day. It's terrible that Leah was killed, but I don't blame you any longer. We will both remember Leah with love. I consider you family. You are my brother, as she would have wanted."

"I feel the same," I said, relief flooding over me and a huge weight lifting off of my shoulders. "I am so happy to have your friendship once again, brother."

We stood and embraced. After all of this time, to have Misha as my friend again, well, it was more than I could have ever hoped for. We headed over to Café Pinsk, where I introduced Misha to Max. He greeted him graciously.

"It's wonderful that your small group is forming again here in Jerusalem," Max said and then frowned. "By the way, your friend Avrum isn't happy here, and I think he wants to leave. Maybe you'd like to come back to work in his place? Or perhaps Misha would like to work here. He looks like a strong young man."

"Thank you for the offer, but David and Alec have helped me find a job at the bakery," Misha said.

"Pah! The bakery!" Max said, waving one hand. "When you grow tired of that, you come back here, and I'll put you to work."

"I might be able to pick up a few shifts," I said. "Let me think about it."

"Let me know as soon as possible," Max said. "I also have a message for you from Zvi. He wants to meet tomorrow afternoon. If that works for you, Shimon will pick you up."

"All right," I said, then looked up in surprise as Avrum stopped beside our table.

He shot Max a nervous look. Max ignored him and began talking to Misha. Avrum lowered his voice. "I need to talk to you," he said. "Can you stop by tomorrow for breakfast?"

Breakfast at Avrum's? No, I couldn't endure Hannah's hugs and alluring looks any longer. I stood. "Max, I need a word with Avrum. Do you mind?"

Max frowned. "Don't keep him long. He's slow enough as it is at keeping up with his tables."

I told Avrum to follow me out to the street. Once outside, Avrum started ranting in his usual overly dramatic way.

"Max is driving me crazy," he said, waving his hands. "He's always picking at me about one thing or another, and nothing I do pleases him! I actually like the job, especially the customers, but Max is unbearable!"

"I had the same problem at first," I reassured him. "It's a good job—decent work, and Max pays well. I suggest you give yourself a few more days, and I'll see if I can get Max to ease up on you."

"Thank you." Avrum shook my hand profusely and then began pacing back and forth, exuding nervous energy. "If you can't, I don't know what I'll do." He came to a stop. "There's something else I'd like to discuss with you. I'm seriously considering joining the Irgun or Lehi. I'm an excellent marksman, and I have a sniper rifle with ammunition. What do you think?"

Keeping secrets wasn't his strong suit—or Hannah's—so I responded cautiously. "Let me ask around, and don't say a word to anyone else about this, not even your wife."

"My lips are sealed."

"Good. Now, get back to work, and don't worry about Max."

He nodded and rushed back into the restaurant.

SHIMON SHOWED UP THAT AFTERNOON to take me to Talpiot. Commander Zvi greeted me with a warm embrace and slapped me on the shoulder.

"You showed a good deal of creativity by tampering with those beers. Shimon also told me about the incident with the two Arab bandits. I have to admit that I would have told you not to take the weapons. But your resourcefulness saved your lives and allowed the operation to go ahead successfully." Zvi smiled. "It seems like every operation you're involved in ends with someone dead, but the important thing is that you achieve your objectives."

I smiled back, and we all sat down together to discuss the reason for our meeting.

"The British public and press," Zvi began, "are beginning to express doubts about their government's policies in Israel. Churchill himself has said that the faltering British economy can't afford the cost of maintaining a military presence here, particularly since it doesn't serve their interests. In light of this change in mood, we think there's a good chance the British will leave Israel in the foreseeable future."

"How long do you think it could be?" I asked.

"Maybe anywhere between one year and three," Zvi said. "I think the best-case scenario would be the second half of 1947, while the worst-case would be around the end of 1949. Either way, we're going to have serious problems with the Arabs soon. They're opposed not only to a Jewish state but also to our presence here at all. If we can bring in enough immigrants, I think we can handle the local Arab population, but if the Arab states decide to send in their armies, we could be in big trouble.

"Some say this is unlikely, since the Arab states haven't been able to agree on much of anything lately. Ben-Gurion is convinced that a British withdrawal will prompt the Arab states to join forces to forcibly prevent the establishment of the Jewish state, and I am inclined to agree with him. With this in mind, we urgently need to prepare a Jewish fighting force that can stand up to the Arab armies. This force will have to include the newcomers, and most of them have no military experience whatsoever. David, this issue must be addressed, and I want you to start training these folks how to fight. We'll find a place where you can do the work."

"Excellent," I said.

"I also want you and Shimon to carry out an operation against a major British command post. I want it to be big, but I want the British casualties kept to a minimum."

I was surprised. "Why?" I asked. "Usually casualties aren't much of a consideration on either side of the battle."

"The Jewish Agency and World Zionist Organization believe they can convince the British to leave through diplomacy and international propaganda, but the only thing that had a real effect on public and political opinions in Britain was the bombing of the King David Hotel. Still, the large number of casualties sparked intense anger and a desire for revenge among the British, and they responded with mass arrests, lengthy curfews, and an intensified police presence that has caused major problems for the underground organizations. As a result, my fellow fighters and I have come to the conclusion that our operations against the British should be high-profile and hard-hitting in terms of morale but low in casualties in order to minimize their retaliation."

"I'd be proud to participate," I said.

Zvi clapped me on the back. "You're not merely a participant—you'll be the commander. What will you need to get started?"

"I need time to think, though I can say that I'd like Shimon and my friend Alec to work with me on the preparations—and also my friend Misha, whom you'll meet soon. He's a young Jew from Belarus who fought with me as a partisan."

"If he is that close to you and you trust him, then we will welcome him."

"I trust him completely," I responded. "There's one other man I'd like to include. His name is Avrum, and he used to serve in the British police"—Zvi frowned—"but he was fired following a confrontation with an anti-Semitic officer. I can vouch that he's a Jewish patriot. He's also an excellent sniper and has intimate knowledge of British police and military command posts. The only drawback is he is a talker, so I won't include him in the planning stage, only in the execution."

"Okay," Zvi said. "Anything else?"

"Yes. I'm going to need an experienced demolitions expert."

"That, you already have," Zvi said with a smile. "Our Shimon is a modest man, but he's actually the Wolves's best saboteur."

It was the first time I had ever seen Shimon blush.

"One more thing," I went on. "After Avrum was fired from

the police, he started working as a waiter at Café Pinsk. Max is a good man but difficult at times. He's been giving Avrum a hard time. I'd appreciate it if you could speak to Max and let him know that Avrum will be helping in an upcoming operation. If Max gains a little respect for Avrum, I'm sure it will help."

"I will talk to Max," Zvi said. "Anything else?"

"Yes, I'd like to have a general idea of our schedule."

"I suggest you select a target and have a detailed plan in place by the end of the year."

That didn't give me much time, but I'd worked under shorter time constraints. I nodded. "I think I can do that."

"I've already come up with a name for the operation. Barrels Raised," Zvi said. "It's from the poem 'Manning the Barricades' by Michael Eshbal. Are you familiar with it?"

"No," I said. "But I know Eshbal. He was wounded and captured during the assault on Sarafand. The British were going to hang him, but the Irgun put a stop to that when they abducted those British officers in Tel Aviv. By the way, have there been any new developments in the plan to assassinate General Barker?"

"I haven't dropped the idea entirely," Zvi said. "But I've heard from reliable sources that both the Irgun and the Lehi have him in their sights, and I'm worried that too much activity around him could ruin the chances for all of us. We'll let them worry about Barker for now."

With that, our meeting ended, and Shimon drove me home. As I was getting out of the car, I told him I was happy that we would be working together again. I wasn't surprised that he neither smiled nor said a word. He just nodded and waited for me to close the door before driving off.

I went inside to start planning my next mission.

21

"RIFLE TO RIFLE, BARRELS RAISED IN SALUTE"

(FROM "MANNING THE BARRICADES," A POEM BY MICHAEL ESHBAL, 1946)

Before we could start planning Operation Barrels Raised, we had to pick a target. I knew we had to hit a command post that would constitute a severe blow to British pride and hamper their ability to function in Israel. It had to be similar to the attack on the King David Hotel but with far fewer casualties.

A few days after my meeting with Zvi, I realized Avrum might be the best person to help me decide which base we should attack to provide the most significant message to the Brits. I asked Shoshana to set up a meeting the next morning for me with Avrum outside the barbershop.

"Does that mean you don't want to go to their home anymore?" Shoshana asked. "You don't want to feel Hannah's ample breasts pressing against you when she hugs you?" Frankly, I was relieved to see she was smiling when she said that.

"The only breasts I want pressed against me are yours," I said.

When I met up with Avrum the next morning, he seemed excited and happy. "Max has made a complete turnaround," he said. "He's polite and friendly. He even compliments me on my work. Did you say something to him?"

"No," I said. "I haven't spoken to him yet. I guess he realized you're a good man. I told you that he treated me the same when I first started there, but his attitude changed over time."

As Avrum beamed, I moved the conversation to the matter at hand—selecting a target for Operation Barrels Raised. "I know some people planning an operation, and I think you could be very helpful."

"I'd be glad to help," he said. "What can I do?"

"If they were to attack a British command post in Jerusalem, which one would cause the most damage to their national pride?"

Avrum thought for a moment. "Schneller Barracks would be the obvious choice—or the British police and CID headquarters in the Russian compound, if they prefer a police target. But the CID building has been attacked twice in the past two years, so I'd assume that security there has been beefed up considerably."

"I tend to prefer the Schneller Barracks," I said. "Can you get me information about the base—anything and everything? Every little detail counts."

"Absolutely," Avrum responded enthusiastically.

"Keep this to yourself. Not even Hannah."

Avrum frowned but nodded. "I understand."

We decided to talk again in a week.

Fall was advancing, and the days were growing colder. As natives of Belarus, Shoshana and I enjoyed the chilly weather, especially after the stifling heat of July and August. I went back to my job at the restaurant, and it felt good to be close to Shoshana again. Avrum kept me amused as well—there were a few older patrons who doted on him, which he loved, but he was oblivious to the polite impatience of the customers who just wanted to be left alone with their meal.

Max clearly wasn't impressed with Avrum, but every time he walked by, he'd force a smile and say, "Well done, Avrum. Good job." Avrum would glow in the light of the praise, while Max would go about his business with a look of disgust on his face.

ONE EVENING, I NOTICED A tall, well-built British soldier with sergeant stripes on his sleeves sitting at the bar, glancing frequently in my direction. His blond hair was short and spiky, and he had a fierce look in his eyes. His face was familiar, but I couldn't place him. I approached him and asked politely if there was anything he needed.

"David," he responded with a smile, "you obviously don't recognize me. I used to work for Inspector Jeffries, may he rest in peace."

"Ah, yes, as a matter of fact, I do remember you," I replied in a friendly tone. Jeffries's department had been closed after his murder, so what—or who—had sent one of his old staff to me?

"It was a good team," he was saying, "but very unlucky too. First, John Perry was murdered and then the inspector himself and three other members of the team. As a result, the HQ decided something was rotten in our department and shut it down. The three of us who were left had to hand over all our intelligence to the CID headquarters."

"That's terrible," I said. "I never met Perry, but Jeffries was a real bulldog."

The soldier smiled and extended his hand. "Bill. Bill Stanley. Thank you for trying to warn us about the King David bombing. What a mess. I can tell you that Jeffries and I were as frustrated as you were with how that played out. I want to find his killers, and I'm hoping you can help me. You were the only one who provided us with any useful information about Perry's murder. I've come to the restaurant several times this month looking for you. Where did you disappear to?"

"I quit," I said. "The owner used to treat me like dirt. No one was more pleased than me to see Inspector Jeffries hit him over the head with his club. But this place was falling apart without me, so he apologized and asked me to come back to work. He even gave me a raise. Anyway, I'd be happy to help you however I can. Just tell me how I can get in touch with you."

"You still have the number of our office that Inspector Jeffries gave you, right? The three of us who are left will be there for the next seven months."

Stanley stood up, paid his bill, and added a generous tip. "I'm an ex-commando. Our fighting style is based on innovation and creativity. I'm looking for creative ways to tackle the underground, and I hope you'll work with me." We shook hands, and he left.

"Interesting," I said to myself and then got back to work.

MAX SUGGESTED THAT ALEC AND Eva hold their wedding at Café Pinsk on a Sunday, the restaurant's quietest day of the week. Shimon, Misha, Hannah, and Avrum were among the guests. Shoshana asked that Brigita be invited as well.

"She's so lonely," she explained to Eva and Alec.

On the day of the wedding, Misha came with Magda, and I was happy to see that they were growing closer. It was nice to see Magda speaking slowly and clearly to Misha in an effort to improve his Hebrew.

Misha, Max, Avrum, and I held the chuppah poles, and after the ceremony, we all sat together around a large table while Alec and Eva made speeches thanking everyone for their love and support. Eva said that the moment she'd first laid eyes on Alec, she'd known he would be the love of her life.

As we all toasted the happy couple and drank Carmel Mizrachi wine, which came from a vinery located in the city Rishon Lezion, Brigita, sitting next to Shoshana, asked me if I would pay her a visit.

"We haven't spoken together in a long time," Brigita said with a smile.

I had no idea why she wanted to see me, but I didn't want to talk about it there, so I told her that I'd drop by soon.

On the walk home, Shoshana and I walked arm in arm, both a little tipsy. "Don't you think it's time for us to get married too?" she asked, leaning against me.

"It has crossed my mind more than once, my love," I replied. "Of course we'll get married—but only after the British have left Israel and we can live here in peace in our Jewish homeland."

It was the truth but not the whole truth. I hadn't asked Shoshana to marry me because I wanted to wait until my dangerous missions were complete, and I knew I wouldn't be finished until the British occupation had come to an end. Since I always tried to satisfy Shoshana's wishes, and to make her happy, I came up with a plan.

I would buy two rings in the Zagury's jewelry store on Jaffa Street, which had the nicest jewelry in Jerusalem: one ring for Shoshana and one for me. I'd surprise her with these two rings during a romantic evening and tell her that when the fighting was over, we would get married traditionally.

The following night, I met with Alec and Shimon after the restaurant had closed. We went for a walk through the streets as I briefed them on the upcoming operation.

"We have to start combat training for the newcomers," I

said. "I think we can find a quiet spot in Tel Arza for that. I already have a nice collection of firearms, and Zvi should be able to help us with anything we need."

"Have you chosen a target?" Alec asked. I nodded.

"I've decided that Schneller Barracks is our best bet. I have Avrum gathering information, which I'll use to formulate a plan of action, including an escape path and a rescue strategy in case something goes wrong. We also need to make sure our attack gets attention and doesn't get lost amid the fallout from some attack by one of the other organizations."

"You're so right," Shimon said unexpectedly. "If we had taken action right after the King David, the response in Britain would have been nil."

"Put some feelers out," I told them. "Let's make sure there aren't any other operations lined up against the barracks."

A few days later, I met again with Avrum outside the barbershop. I had decided to keep him out of the loop on Operation Barrels Raised for as long as possible, but I saw no reason not to involve him in weapons training for our new fighters.

"In Britain, calls for withdrawal from Israel are getting louder," I said. "But the general assumption, which I share, is that when the British pull out, the Arabs will almost certainly attack us. We must establish a Jewish fighting force that will be able to face them. I want to put together a group of instructors who can provide combat training to the newcomers. Would you like to be one of those instructors?"

"That would be perfect," Avrum exclaimed. "And I agree that al-Husseini will see the British withdrawal as an opportunity to fulfill his despicable dream. When do we begin training?"

"First, we have to find a suitable location. I was thinking we could find a place in Tel Arza, and I'd like you to join me for a look around."

"How about right now?"

"That sounds good to me." We headed toward Tel Arza on foot, as it was only a short distance away. "Have you made any progress on the Schneller Barracks?" I asked as we walked.

"Yes," Avrum said. "It was originally built by German Templers—devout Christians who came to live in Israel. They built it as an orphanage in 1860 for Christian children who had survived the massacres by Druze and Muslim forces in Lebanon and Syria. The kids got a German upbringing, and in the years leading up to the war, the German staff absorbed the Nazi ideology, even staging a choir performance on Hitler's birthday. From 1936 to 1939, the orphanage staff tried to smuggle in weapons and ammunition from Germany to prepare the kids for war against the Jews. At the outbreak of World War II, the British expelled all German residents of Israel, including the staff of the orphanage, and they seized the compound, turning it into a British military base."

"Did you find anything about its current layout?" I asked. "Potential breach points, which military units it serves, each unit's location within the base?"

Avrum scowled. "I've only just started looking into it," he said. "It takes time to find everything you want. Just be patient."

I remembered Avrum had failed to come up with anything on Inspector Jeffries as well, and I suspected I'd have to find another way to get the information I needed.

Meanwhile, we had reached the undeveloped section of Tel Arza, the same slope beneath the Nabi Samuel ridge where Alec and I had practiced our shooting before the operation against Inspector Jeffries. We wandered around for a while and then came across an abandoned warehouse near the neighborhood's industrial area. We discussed the possibility of secretly refurbishing it and using it for combat training. Avrum agreed the site was suitable.

"When do we start?" he asked.

"Within a month, I think," I replied. "There's a lot of work to do. There's one more thing . . ." I paused and stared at the ground for a moment, not liking what I was about to say.

"Yes?"

I looked up. "I want you to train Shoshana on the sniper rifle. She wants to join the fight, but I'm hoping to keep her behind the lines somewhat by teaching her how to pick off the enemy from a distance. Are you willing to help me with that?"

Avrum's brows darted up. "Of course! However, I must say I'm surprised that such a sweet girl—"

"She's a brave woman," I corrected. Of course, Shoshana was a sweet girl, but I knew now that she was so much more. "She wants to take part in some operations, and I'm going to give her the chance. I plan to train her myself to handle a pistol for short-range fighting, in order to protect herself. I've already started teaching her self-defense techniques and hand-to-hand combat in our backyard, when our landlords are at work."

"Are you sure you want to bring her into this, my friend?" Avrum asked quietly.

No, I'm not sure at all, I wanted to say. All I really wanted was to keep Shoshana safe, but she had a right to her vengeance. She had a right to fight for her people. How could I deny her that? All I could do was protect her the best that I could.

"I'll send her to you once we're ready," I told Avrum.

WHEN I GOT TO CAFÉ Pinsk at noon, I took Max aside and told him about the spot I had selected for the training sessions. I asked him to arrange our schedules to allow Alec, Avrum, and me the time we needed to be on-site for training. I also told him I wanted to meet with Zvi and Shimon at the earliest opportunity so we could all go together to Tel Arza.

Two days later, Max informed me that Zvi and Shimon would meet me at three o'clock on Thursday, October 30, outside the barbershop on Zephaniah Street.

On Thursday, on my way to meet them, I noticed an unusually large number of military and police vehicles in the streets. Zvi and Shimon arrived late and signaled me to get into the car.

"Sorry we were late," Zvi said. "I was waiting for an update about an Irgun operation—a bombing at the Jerusalem train station this afternoon. Unfortunately, three of the fighters were captured by a British ambush and another three were wounded."

"Do you think someone on the inside betrayed them?" I asked.

"I do. The Irgun suspects a man who goes by the name Yanai but whose real name is Heinrich Reinhold. He was a soldier in the British army until about six months ago. He had advanced demolitions training and was supposed to oversee the operation, but he didn't show up at the rendezvous."

"Then they should have aborted the operation and not taken the risk," I said.

"It's easy to pass judgment after the fact," Zvi retorted. He was clearly distressed by the capture of the Irgun fighters. I decided to drop it.

I showed Zvi the warehouse I had chosen. He estimated the renovation would take about a month and training could begin in early December. I suggested that the trainees should dress as though they were heading for a hike or picnic. They could take the No. 3 bus to its last stop in Tel Arza, where a guide would lead them to the training site.

"In addition to the weapons I have," I said, "we'll need at

least another ten rifles and four submachine guns. I suggest we also include a concealed weapons cache in our renovations so we can store them on-site."

"Sounds good," Zvi said. "We'll arrange everything. Shimon will keep you up to date on the preparations, and he can relay any other requests you may have. Before we go, have you made any progress on Operation Barrels Raised?"

"Certainly. We've selected the target—the Schneller Barracks. I'm busy gathering intelligence, and when I have the entire plan worked out, I'll present it to you so we can decide the timing of the operation."

"Excellent choice," Zvi said. "Remember, we must ensure the attack does maximum damage to British national pride with minimum casualties."

On my way home, I thought about what kind of information I'd need for the operation and how I could get it. I didn't have much faith in Avrum, but perhaps someone serving at the base could play the role—someone like Stanley, the sergeant who had come looking for me at the restaurant. On second thought, Stanley was an experienced ex-commando, not some naïve bureaucrat. The smallest mistake on my part could arouse his suspicions and jeopardize everything.

I had one last option—reconnaissance from a building on Geula Street. The building from which I had fired into the base would be an ideal spot. I decided to have a talk with Regina Federbusch, the woman who had come onto her balcony to hang laundry that day right before I shot the British soldiers with Avrum's sniper rifle.

I figured a couple would be less suspicious than a single young male, so I asked Shoshana if she would like to join me in a reconnaissance mission. She looked at me with disbelief for a second and then realized I was serious.

"Yes, of course I would!"

I explained that we would be visiting Mrs. Federbusch in the next couple of days. I explained the plan I had in mind, and we rehearsed our parts.

ON THE VERY NEXT FRIDAY before work, we knocked on Mrs. Federbusch's door. She opened the door wearing a faded robe, her hair disheveled, and the moment she saw us, she tried to close the door. I stuck my foot in the door and said, "I apologize for disturbing you. We just have a quick question, and then we'll be on our way."

Mrs. Federbusch relaxed. "Sorry, I'm not cleaned up," she said. "I only opened the door because I thought it was my son. He always brings me a loaf of challah for Shabbat. What can I do for you?"

"I heard there's an apartment for rent in this building," I said. "A friend of mine just separated from his wife and urgently needs to find a place to stay."

"I haven't heard anything about that, and I would know if there was one. Does your friend want an entire apartment, or would he make do with a comfortable room?"

"Actually, I think he'd prefer a room, to save on expenses," I said.

"Well, then, if he's as nice as the two of you, I might be willing to rent out a room in my apartment," Mrs. Federbusch said. "I'm a widow and have very little income. My son supports me, but I'd love to tell him that I no longer need his help."

"That sounds like an interesting idea," I said. "May we see the room?"

"Certainly," she replied. "By the way, my name is Regina."

Shoshana and I introduced ourselves, and Regina, eager to

close the deal, led us to a room with a balcony overlooking Geula Street.

"That's a lovely balcony," I said. "Can I go out and have a look?"

"Sure," Regina said. I walked onto the balcony and saw the Schneller Barracks stretched out below me, practically in the palm of my hand. I also noticed the washing lines Regina had used when I'd been on the roof above her with my rifle.

Two of the hooks that attached the laundry line to the wall were loose. "Our friend is a stickler for cleanliness," I said to Regina. "He does laundry almost every day. Will he be able to use these washing lines?"

"Of course," she replied.

"I see that some of the hooks have come loose," I said. "I'll tell him to repair them so the lines don't fall off."

"That would be nice," Regina said. "My son never seems to have time to fix anything. When will your friend come to see the room? I would like to meet him."

"He doesn't need to see it. I'm like a brother to him, and he trusts me. He'll stop by next Sunday. Don't worry, you'll like him."

The rent that Regina proposed was low, but I figured she'd get suspicious if I didn't haggle. So I did, and she gave me a small reduction. We agreed on a three-month trial period, and I paid her a month's rent in advance. She looked very happy as she put the money into her wallet.

"Who are you going to get as a tenant?" Shoshana asked after we'd left the building.

"Alec," I said.

"Alec?' Shoshana exclaimed. "He just got married. What makes you think he'll agree to be away from Eva?"

"He doesn't have to be away from Eva. He doesn't even

have to sleep there. He'll tell Regina that he and his wife are trying to work things out and that when she asks him to stay over there, he does. I'd do it myself, but we have to stick to our story. Let's go see him and talk this out."

We headed for Alec's apartment in the Bukharan Quarter. Eva opened the door for us and embraced Shoshana. "Who's the kind angel who brought you here to visit us so unexpectedly?" she asked.

Shoshana kissed her on the cheek. "We always enjoy getting together with you, but David wants to discuss something with Alec. You and I can stay here and chat while the men go out for a walk."

"Here in this country," Alec said with a smile, "the women call the shots, and if they tell us to go out, we do as they say."

"I'll have to keep that in mind." I winked at Shoshana and followed Alec outside.

"In preparation for Operation Barrels Raised," I said as we walked down the street, "I've arranged for you to live temporarily in a room in an apartment on Geula Street that overlooks the Schneller Barracks. I need you to study the layout of the base and the movements of the British, then come up with a suitable spot for our assault."

"David," Alec said, "you've been both a commander and a brother to me, but you're asking too much."

"I'd do it myself, but I already told the owner, Mrs. Federbusch, that a friend will be renting the room. And you can do the work better than anyone else. You were the one who chose to attack the German ambush force near the Minsk ghetto, and you gathered all the information we needed for the operation. You were the one who located the German supply base, and our mission was a success, thanks to you. Without your help, we wouldn't have been able to kill that bastard Nikolai. In this case, you can gather the information we need without spending much time away from Eva at all."

Alec didn't answer, but the look on his face told me he would do it.

Later, when Shoshana and I arrived at the café for our shift, Max informed me that the renovation of the warehouse in Tel Arza was taking longer than expected and would not be completed until mid-December at the earliest.

On Sunday morning, Alec and I went to Mrs. Federbusch's apartment. "He'll be an easy tenant," I said to her before giving Alec a brief tour of the place and showing him the washing lines that needed fixing. He told Regina he was happy with the arrangement and would move in the next day.

December dragged on, and the renovation work on the warehouse in Tel Arza had yet to be completed. According to Max, Zvi hadn't pushed things along any quicker, because he was negotiating the purchase of the building. Max said the contract would be signed soon, and the training sessions were scheduled to begin in January.

Alec's reconnaissance mission was taking longer than expected too. I knew the delay stemmed partly from his desire to spend most of his time with Eva, but there was another reason. He had aroused the suspicions of Regina's son, who had noticed Alec spent a lot of time on the balcony.

"I told him I enjoy the crisp winter air," Alec said, "but I've had to cut back on the time I spend surveilling the base."

Three days before the new year, Irgun member Binyamin Kimchi received eighteen lashes for his part in a bank robbery aimed at securing funds for the Irgun's activities. Along with the lashes, he was given an eighteen-year prison sentence. In response, the Irgun abducted a British major in Netanya, two sergeants on HaYarkon Street in Tel Aviv, two sergeants in north Tel Aviv, and another sergeant from the Sixth Airborne Division in Rishon Lezion. Each of the abducted British soldiers received eighteen lashes as well. The incident shocked the British people. Britain was derided worldwide, with a cartoon that appeared in a Parisian newspaper showing a British soldier using a steel helmet to protect his exposed rear end.

SHOSHANA AND I DECIDED TO celebrate the new year, 1947, in the same way we had welcomed 1946—with a dinner on New Year's Eve at Café Wien.

I realized that this would be the perfect opportunity to surprise Shoshana with a ring and a proposal. By giving the manager extra money when I made the reservations, I made sure that we would have a nice table with two candles and a violinist to come to our table and play for us.

On New Year's Eve, as the waiter led us to our table, Shoshana, who knew nothing about my plans for the evening, slapped my behind and warned me, with a smile, that if I didn't kiss her promptly at midnight, she'd give me seventeen more.

After we'd toasted with a drink of vodka, Shoshana blew me a kiss in the air. The violinist made his way to our table and started playing beautiful romantic melodies. By the time he finished, Shoshana seemed overwhelmed by the exceptional evening. She leaned back in her seat, beaming with joy.

At that moment, I took two boxes out of my pocket. I opened Shoshana's box, took out her ring, and said, "Shoshana, you are the love of my life, and I'll be yours from now to eternity. You are my woman forever, and when I am done with all my missions, if you will have me, I want to marry you in a traditional way."

I put the ring on Shoshana's finger, handed her my ring, and held out my hand. Shoshana looked stunned and, with tears in her eyes, slid the ring she held onto my finger.

"This is the happiest moment of my life," she said. "I'll be yours forever, and I'll do my best to make our union wonderful."

I gestured to the violinist to come back and asked him to play *The Wedding March* for us. Excited over our "nuptials," we continued with dinner and with more vodka.

At midnight, we kissed passionately. Shoshana smiled up at me, her arms around my neck. "You've been spared. That was a good kiss. I won't be spanking you tonight."

Later at home, after this incredible evening, as I lay by Shoshana in our bed, I hoped that only good things would await us in the new year. Then, just as quickly, I remembered that there are no guarantees in life for anyone—especially during this unrestful time in Jerusalem.

22

"THOUGH LEADEN SKIES MAY COVER OVER DAYS OF BLUE"

(FROM "SONG OF THE PARTISANS" BY HIRSH GLICK, 1943)

In the first two weeks of 1947, the Irgun carried out coordinated assaults on military and police targets in Jerusalem, Jaffa, Haifa, and Tiberias. They used mines to take out British military vehicles in Jerusalem, Haifa, and Petah Tikva. The Hadera train station was hit, and a train carrying British treasury money was attacked and robbed a few days later. In an attack on the Ramat Gan police station, Irgun fighter Dov Gruner was wounded and captured.

The renovation of the newly purchased Tel Arza property finally came to an end in mid-January. We hung a large sign—**Lumber Warehouse**—on the outside and used lumber to block off the front section of the facility, leaving only a narrow passageway that led to the back, where the weapons training would take place. Above the passageway, we stacked lumber on a platform tied to the ceiling with ropes. In the event of a raid, we could cut the ropes and block access to the back of the facility. In the floor at the rear of the facility, the renovators had installed an escape hatch leading into a narrow tunnel some thirty yards long. Our arms and ammunition were hidden in a cache under the floor, covered with another layer of lumber.

Our first training session for the newcomers—led by Zvi, Shimon, Avrum, Misha, and me—was devoted to instruction on using a handgun. All twenty of our trainees were from Eastern Europe, mostly from Poland and a few from Hungary. They had all been in displaced persons camps in Germany or elsewhere in Europe before making the journey to Israel. The majority spoke only a little Hebrew. Most of them understood Yiddish, but Zvi also translated some of our instructions into Polish. I made a mental note to bring Eva or Magda along to the next session to translate for those who spoke Hungarian.

As the session progressed, I quickly realized that some of the trainees would never be proficient fighters. When the session was over, Zvi and I decided which men would be dropped from the course. We agreed to have only three instructors for each session.

"I think we should have Shoshana start her training in one of the next sessions," Zvi suggested as we were closing up the facility. "If you still support her decision to play a role in future operations if we need her?"

I nodded. "I've made my peace with it. Now I want her to have the best training possible. Hopefully, that will help keep her safe."

On my way back to our apartment, I stopped at Alec's home and asked if he had anything new to report about the Schneller Barracks.

"I have a plan in mind," he told me. "I'll have the details finalized later in the week."

"Good. Let's get together as soon as possible and discuss it. I'll see you tomorrow." I clapped him on the back and headed home to Shoshana.

However, Alec didn't show up at work the following day. "He could have at least sent word that he's sick," Max grumbled. When he failed to appear the next day too, I went to his apartment. I knew we were in trouble the moment Eva opened the door with tears in her eyes.

"I haven't seen Alec for two days," she sobbed. "I'm very worried."

I immediately rushed over to Regina's apartment on Geula Street. I had to knock on her door several times before she finally opened it. A look of fear contorted her face when she saw me.

"Where's your tenant?" I demanded.

She hesitated before answering. "British police burst in and arrested him. They said he's been scouting their base from here."

"The police took him because your son went to speak to them," I said, clenching my fists at my side.

"That's not entirely true," she stammered. I realized there was nothing more I could do there, so I left, thinking of my next move.

Four British soldiers approached me with their weapons drawn the moment I stepped out of the building. They ordered me to put my hands behind my back and then handcuffed me. A military vehicle pulled up alongside us a few minutes later, and I was pushed inside. They drove to Jerusalem's main detention facility at the Russian compound, where the soldiers ordered me out of the vehicle and escorted me to the gate. A sentry recorded my name and address and asked me why I had been arrested.

"I have no idea," I said.

A derisive smile appeared on the sentry's face. "That's what everyone says," he sneered.

I was taken inside and searched. A soldier shaved my head, and then a doctor examined me. My clothes, wallet, and watch were taken from me, and I was ordered to put on prison clothes—underpants, an undershirt, a ragged pair of pants, and a tattered shirt made from coarse fabric. I also received two blankets, a worn jacket, and a mat to sleep on.

I was ushered into one of the cells, where I found myself with nine other prisoners. Their mats were spread out on the floor of the miserable-looking space, and I laid my mat out too. I wasn't too bothered by the accommodations—as a partisan in Koidanov Forest, my comrades and I had spent most nights sleeping on the ground. At least I didn't have to worry about rain or snow here.

I sat on my mat on the floor and waited. An hour or so later, a guard showed up to take me to the warden's office. The warden was dressed in civilian clothes, and I assumed he was CID.

"Your friend, Alec, has told us everything about your plans to attack the Schneller Barracks," the man began, fixing me with a stern look, his British accent crisp. "I know your job was simply to carry out reconnaissance and collect information. A military tribunal will send you away for at least ten years, but if you tell me who sent you, I'll make sure your sentence isn't that harsh."

"Attack the Schneller Barracks?" I exclaimed, bursting into laughter. "Do you think we're insane? Alec is my friend and like a brother to me. He would never harm anyone, much less the British people who keep us safe from the Arabs. His marriage, unfortunately, isn't working out too well. He rented a room in the apartment where you arrested him. I know this because I was the one who found the room for him, and you can easily verify that."

The momentary look of hesitation on his face gave me some hope, and I went on. "This misunderstanding saddens me, because I am a supporter of the British presence here. I personally met with General Barker to thank him for freeing my aunt and uncle from the Bergen-Belsen concentration camp. And I've gone far beyond just words of praise—at much personal risk, I was an informant for Inspector Jeffries. The terrorists who killed him would kill me too if they knew who I was. There's a note in my wallet with the number of one of his aides, Sergeant William Stanley. Call him and ask him about me. After he confirms what I've just told you, I expect you to let me out of here right away."

The warden noted everything I said with the same look of uncertainty on his face. "I'll check," he grumbled. "For your own good, I hope you haven't just fed me the same kind of imaginary tale that your terrorist friends try to sell me."

A policeman escorted me back to the cell. I doubted he would bother calling Sergeant Stanley any time soon, and I had no idea if Stanley would want to help me, but it was worth a try.

I asked my fellow detainees if any of them had seen Alec. Apparently, my friend had thrown a punch at one of the guards and had been sent to solitary confinement for a week.

I lay on my mat, feeling anxious, knowing that Shoshana must be out of her mind with worry. My feeling of helplessness, together with the loss of my freedom, weighed heavily on me. I had never felt this restricted, not even in the Minsk ghetto. After I'd fled that terrible place and joined the partisans, my life had been in constant danger, but I'd been a free man and chosen my own path. Now I was subject to the whims of the prison guards.

Left with no choice, I fell into the routine of prison life. A loud bell would wake us up every morning at five thirty. We were lined up and counted before breakfast and taken for a walk in the courtyard. Then we were sent off to the workshops. I was assigned to the carpentry shop, where we made furniture and coffins. At four o'clock, we were led back to our cells. We were counted again after dinner. Lights were turned off at nine.

The majority of the prisoners were Arabs, mainly petty criminals. There were also about eighty Jewish detainees in the facility, and most of them were suspected of being members of the underground or collaborating with them in some way. I mingled with the underground detainees, and they helped lift my spirits. I wasn't a member of their organizations, but I was proud to be in allegiance with them. I viewed them all as heroes, but a few in particular stood out.

One was Dov Gruner, who had immigrated illegally to Israel from Hungary via Romania. He was one of the first Jewish residents of Israel who had volunteered to serve in the British army, and he had seen action in Italy. After the war, he'd spent some time as an aid worker in displaced persons camps before returning to Israel and joining the Irgun. During the attack on the British Ramat Gan police station, Gruner had been seriously wounded and then captured.

The injuries he sustained, including a shattered jawbone, left him barely able to speak or eat. A military tribunal had sentenced him to death earlier in the month, and in keeping with British practice, he wore a scarlet prison uniform. My heart broke every time I saw him.

Michael Eshbal, the poet, and Yosef Simhon, a brave fighter who joined the Irgun five years earlier when he was only fifteen, had both been captured following the assault on the Sarafand British military base. We had some famous inmates, and I'd have given anything for them to be able to leave.

Eshbal's poem "Manning the Barricades" contained the line "Rifle to rifle, barrels raised in salute," which had inspired the name of our operation, Barrels Raised. I felt honored to be in this man's company, even more so after conversing with him. I learned he had been born in Poland and had arrived in Israel following an arduous journey through Iraq in the early 1940s. Yosef Simhon had been born in Tel Aviv. When he was three years old, his mother had been visiting her family in the city of Hebron just when the 1929 massacre occurred. Sixty-seven Jews were killed by Arabs. Yosef and his mother were saved by an Arabic friend, who hid them in his house.

Meir Feinstein, an Irgun fighter wounded during the attack on the Jerusalem train station two months earlier, was also one of my fellow detainees, along with Irgun fighters Yehiel Dresner, Mordechai Alkahi, Eliezer Kashani, and Chaim Golovsky. On December 29, 1946, the four had been involved in the retaliatory lashing of the British officers responsible for the lashes given to Binyamin Kimchi. That same day, the four Irgun fighters stumbled upon a British vehicle checkpoint at the Beit Dagan junction near Tel Aviv, and the police opened fire on them.

The driver, Avraham Mizrahi, was shot and later died. The remaining four were captured, beaten senseless, transferred to a nearby military base, and put on display for the British soldiers to abuse. Their clothes were ripped off, and they were made to run naked through the base while suffering beatings from everyone they passed. After they were taken back inside, their hair was torn out, and they were ordered to clean the floor with toothbrushes. When they refused, the Brits beat them senseless again and doused them in wastewater.

After five days of torture, they were moved to the detention facility in Jerusalem. I was told that when they arrived, they looked as though they had just been released from a Nazi death camp. Their clothes were bloody and torn, their faces bruised and swollen, and two of them had broken bones.

I regretted not having the opportunity to meet their torturers and give them the same treatment in return. I wondered for a moment about Brigita and what she would have said about revenge if someone close to her had been the victim of such abuse. It was easy to be detached when sitting down to a cup of hot tea and discussing such things, but when you actually saw the atrocities, it was quite different. Mercy is a wonderful thing, but the rules on the battlefield are different, and failing to uphold the principle of "an eye for an eye" could cost you both your dignity and your life.

The Brits released Alec from solitary confinement four days after my arrest. He had lost weight and looked terrible. We weren't in the same cell, but we met up in the courtyard. I finally got to hear his version of what had happened to land him in prison.

"I was on the balcony one night, with my binoculars trained on the Schneller Barracks, when four British policemen burst into Regina's apartment." Alec said. "I managed to get back into my room before they reached it, but after finding my binoculars, they started beating me with their clubs. I denied everything, but they took me into custody and continued to beat me on the way."

"Taneli says you punched a guard."

Alec rubbed his forehead. "That was unfortunate. But he spat on me! I knocked him out, and then a second guard hit me with his club. When I came to my senses again, I was in handcuffs." I frowned and he waved away my concern. "Never mind, I've endured worse. After they let me out of solitary confinement, they told me you had admitted we were planning an attack on the Schneller Barracks. I smiled at the investigator and asked him why he was telling me ridiculous stories."

"They told me the same about you," I said.

"They have nothing on us. As soon as we're released, I'll settle the score with Regina's son. I have no doubt he was the one who informed on me to the British."

"Don't do anything foolish," I warned. "If you kill him, the British will hang you. Do you want to turn Eva into a widow?"

"So, what do you suggest?" Alec snapped. "That we simply leave the bastard alone?"

"I didn't say that. I suggest that we strip him naked and each treat him to eighteen lashes."

Alec thought for a moment and then nodded. "I'll take your advice, even though I don't like it. When we fought together in the forests, we showed no mercy to informants. But we both seem to have gone a little soft since we got here."

"There is no difference between the two, but the circumstances have changed," I said. "We have women we love and would like to enjoy a future with them, right?"

Alec sighed. "I was just starting to enjoy my married bliss."

A GUARD CAME TO MY cell the next morning and ordered me to follow him to the warden's office. Sergeant Stanley stood when I came into the room.

"I'm sorry you had to wait," he said, shaking my hand. "It took me a while to speak with a senior detective. I'm hoping to secure your release shortly."

"Thank you," I said. "I've been thinking a lot about the murder of Inspector Jeffries, and I've come up with a few ideas that may help move the investigation forward after I'm released. I'd appreciate it if you could also arrange the release of my friend Alec Rozonovsky. I can vouch for him as a loyal supporter of the British authorities. He's an intelligent young man, and I believe we can make some real inroads into the investigation together."

"I'll see what I can do," Stanley said, jotting down Alec's name on a piece of paper. "In the meantime, is there anything else I can help you with?"

"There certainly is. I'm sure you can get me and Alec transferred to a cell for privileged inmates so we can sleep on beds rather than mats on the floor."

He nodded. "Yes, I believe I can arrange that for you today. Anything else?"

"Yes. Please go to Café Pinsk and tell the waitress Shoshana that Alec and I were falsely arrested and you're working to secure our release."

The following day, Alec and I were moved to a special cell for so-called privileged inmates. Those prisoners got to sleep on beds, wear regular clothes, and stroll around the courtyard twice a day instead of only once.

Two days later, Haganah member Gideon Wonders approached me in the courtyard.

"The Arabs are planning a riot," he said in a low voice.

"Do you know when?"

He shook his head and left me. I hurried back to Alec and told him. We sat up that night, trying to plan some way to protect ourselves if the riot did, indeed, happen.

The next few days were filled with anxiety and anticipation, and on January 27, an Arab prisoner attacked a Jewish detainee. When some of the other Jewish detainees tried to help him, a wave of Arab prisoners came at them with clubs, shouting "*Itbah al Yahud*," which means "slaughter the Jews."

An Arab pulled a knife, but Wonders, who was a martial arts expert, broke the blade, along with the arms of two of the Arab attackers. Alec and I got involved, and after several hours of fighting, during which both sides managed to take hostages, the British restored order with smoke grenades.

The prison's Jewish medic had been beaten to death and the prison warden seriously injured. When the dust settled, the British did what they should have done beforehand—separated the Jewish and Arab inmates into different wings of the facility.

The day before the riot, the Irgun had abducted a British major in Jerusalem and announced the officer would be held hostage to prevent the execution of Dov Gruner, scheduled for January 28. On the day of the riot, Irgun fighters in Tel Aviv kidnapped a British judge. As a result, Gruner's execution was delayed, and the Irgun released the two hostages.

I devoured newspapers smuggled into the prison by members of the underground, and the reports seemed to indicate the British were growing weary of the fighting in Israel. Despite their great victory in World War II, public morale was low in Britain. Immediately after the war, Britain had been hit by an economic crisis so severe even discharged soldiers weren't able to find work. The country was experiencing a particularly bad winter, power supplies had been cut, rail services had been disrupted, and the British government had been forced to ask the United States for coal so people could heat their homes.

With this as the backdrop, the attacks on British forces in Israel caused many people in Britain, both among the leadership and the general public alike, to think it was time to renounce the mandate over the Land of Israel issued to Great Britain in 1922. And indeed, the British foreign secretary, Ernest Bevin, announced that the issue would be decided by the UN General Assembly, scheduled to convene in September.

The first sign of a pending British withdrawal came on January 31, when the British embarked on Operation Polly, in which some nineteen hundred British women, children, and "nonessential" government officials were sent back to Britain.

THREE DAYS LATER, ALEC AND I were called to the warden's office at eight thirty in the morning. Sergeant Stanley, a big smile on his face, sat waiting for us. He rose as we came into the room, as did the warden.

"You two must have done something good in your lives," the warden said, "because we've received orders to release you. Pack up your belongings. Sergeant Stanley will be waiting for you at the prison gate."

We rushed back to the cell to collect our things, and while I was thrilled to be released, it was with a heavy heart I said my goodbyes to a wonderful group of idealistic heroes, willing to sacrifice their lives for the establishment of an independent Jewish state in our ancient homeland. As partisans, we had fought for our lives against the Germans—we'd had no choice. Here in Israel, every man in detention could have made the choice to live in peace and quiet but had chosen instead to risk everything for their people and their homeland.

Stanley was waiting for us outside the gate in a military jeep. "Where do you want me to take you?" he asked.

I didn't want to be seen in a British military vehicle near our homes and asked him to drop us off on the corner of Yehezkel and Zephaniah. On the way, he turned to me and said, "David, we'll meet tomorrow morning at ten at Café Wien." His words sounded like an order, and I knew there was no point in refusing.

When I got home, it was such a joy to see Shoshana and hold her tight. We talked for hours, and I shared the details of my extraordinary experience and the incredible men I had spent time with in jail. When night came, I couldn't sleep. She stayed up with me until I finally drifted off just before dawn.

After only three hours of rest, I had to get up to meet with Stanley. He wore civilian clothing to maintain my cover as his "informant." Despite that, his face bore the typical tough expression of a British Special Forces soldier. After some tea and chocolate cake, Stanley started talking.

"You realize that without my intervention, you and your friend would still be in prison. Both of you most likely would've been convicted and gotten lengthy prison sentences. You promised to help me, and I expect you to keep that promise in two ways: First, you will help me apprehend Inspector Jeffries's killers. Second, I want you to assist in carrying out a reprisal operation that will teach these Jewish terrorists a lesson. Are you willing to take on an offensive operation?"

His question surprised me, and for a moment I thought he could be setting a trap. "I'm going to be perfectly frank with you—even more so than I ever was with Inspector Jeffries," I said. "The foolish and pointless actions of these terrorists will doom us all to another genocide, this time at the hands of the Arabs. So my answer is that I'd be honored to help with an operation against the underground, and I hope the operation teaches them that it doesn't pay to take on Great Britain."

My response appeared to satisfy Stanley. "As a soldier who was in a commando unit during the war," he said softly, as if sharing a secret with me, "the incompetence of the British army when it comes to Jewish terrorism truly sickens me. I learned during the war that when faced with an enemy, you eliminate him. Here, the terrorists are arrested and brought to trial, and the entire process lasts months. Very few of these criminals get what they deserve—a noose around their necks."

His words made me clench my fists under the table, and it was with effort I didn't slam one of them into his face. He took another bite of cake, and as he chewed, his eyes narrowed.

"I have friends," he finally said, "all members of the army, who are very unhappy with the situation here, and we plan to exact revenge. We're going to teach those bloody terrorists and their organizations a lesson they will never forget." He narrowed his eyes, and a cruel smile curved his lips. "The group we are putting together should be operational next month," he went on. "Spend the next few weeks with your beautiful girlfriend. When we're ready, I'll come to see you at Café Pinsk to tell you what role you'll have in our operation."

"All right," I said. "I'll be waiting."

"And in the meantime, try to make some progress on finding Inspector Jeffries's killers," Stanley added.

"Of course," I nodded. "He was a good friend, and it's always on my mind."

Stanley called the waiter, then paid the bill and left. My next move was clear—I needed to have a talk with Zvi.

23

"TWO ROADS TO SALVATION—THE BLOOD AND THE SWORD"

(FROM "THE MESSIAH," A POEM BY AVRAHAM STERN, 1941)

I left my meeting with Stanley, feeling uneasy. He had me at his mercy, and I knew he could put me right back in prison if I didn't cooperate. I'd have to take care of him in much the same way I had taken care of Jeffries when he'd threatened to arrest Shoshana.

I made my way from Café Wien to Café Pinsk, where Max embraced me warmly. "It's great to have you back," he said. "I hope you didn't suffer too much."

Avrum greeted me with a friendly hug as well. "By the way," he told me, "you should know that Shoshana is the best trainee in the Tel Arza training facility. She is talented, dedicated, and very observant. I gave her a few private lessons. I expect she'll soon be a competent sniper."

I thanked him, aware of how much time I had missed being

able to train her myself in other combat procedures. I would have to make up for lost time, but first I had to see Zvi. I asked Max to set up a meeting with the commander as soon as possible, and he solemnly agreed.

Feeling at loose ends, I helped Shoshana and Avrum during the restaurant's lunch rush, which gave me a sense of comfort. Nothing had changed at all. Avrum's habit of chatting endlessly with the patrons, and the look of self-satisfaction on his face whenever he persuaded a customer to order a specific dish, still amused me.

Alec also gave me a joyful welcome when he showed up for the evening shift. "Would you like to take a walk with me in the courtyard?" he asked with a smile.

"I'd rather go with you to Europe," I replied, and it took him a second or two to realize I meant Café Europa. Luckily, the café wasn't busy, and Max agreed to let Alec leave with me.

We walked there, and over tea I told Alec about my conversation with Stanley. "When I learn more about what they're planning, I'll update you," I said.

"Of course, I want to help," Alec replied, "but we have a more pressing matter to deal with right now." I raised one brow in question. "Meir Federbusch, that informant scum. The best time to get him is Friday when he brings his mother her challah for Shabbat. He lives in Zichron Moshe, which borders on Geula. He once showed me a shortcut he takes through an empty field to visit her. We can hit him there."

Before we parted, I asked about Misha and learned, much to my joy, that he and Magda were getting serious.

That evening, Shimon showed up at my apartment to drive me to Talpiot. "I'm glad you're out of jail. It's good to see you," he said—a rather long and emotional statement for Shimon.

Zvi was alone in the house when we arrived. "I regret to

tell you that I've decided to cancel Operation Barrels Raised," he said. "A reliable source tells me the Irgun already plans to attack the Schneller Barracks. They're a much larger group, with more resources. We need to focus on our own activities and not compete with them. We'll continue with weapons training for the newcomers."

"I have something important to tell you," I said, then recounted my meeting with Stanley.

Zvi's expression grew serious. "An attack by British soldiers and police could result in dozens of Jewish casualties," he said. "We have to prevent it. Plant yourself in their organization; do and say anything that helps you get close to him. From now on, this is your sole mission. I don't even want you involved in training the recruits. If you're arrested again, we won't be able to prevent this attack."

"I understand," I said.

Zvi paced across the room, looking fiercely thoughtful, and then stopped and turned back to me. "The name of your new mission will be Blood and Sword, from Avraham Stern's poem 'The Messiah.' He was a uniquely brave man and a fierce soldier but also a talented and sensitive poet. According to the poem, 'the Messiah will be born in prison, and the road to salvation will be paved with blood and the sword.'"

On the drive home, I was lost in thought. Shimon glanced over at me. "I hope I can help with Operation Blood and Sword."

"You will," I said. "We're going to need all the help we can get. Stanley and the rest of his group are skilled fighters, and we'll have to be at our best if we're going to thwart their plans."

THE FOLLOWING DAY, I WENT to see Misha. I thought he'd be at home when I got there, but Magda said he had yet to return from the bakery. "He should be here any minute," she said. "Sit down. We'll have some tea while you wait."

Over a cup of tea and biscuits, Magda told me how happy she was with Misha and thanked me for helping him enter the country. Then her demeanor grew sad. "He told me about Leah. Knowing Misha, I can imagine just how dear his sister was to you."

Hearing Leah's name always made me melancholy, and I was still staring into my teacup when Misha walked in. He kissed Magda and then hugged me.

"It's good to see you, Misha," I said in Belarusian.

"You too, David," he answered in Hebrew. "Magda insists I speak only Hebrew. She says it's the only way I'll learn the language."

"She's right," I said in Belarusian, "but there's something I want to say that's for your ears only." Magda frowned, but before she had a chance to get a word in, I said, "I'm sorry, Magda, I have to use Belarusian to explain the matter at hand."

Magda seemed offended, but I ignored her and continued in Belarusian. "Alec and I are taking on an important operation against the British. I hope you'll join us."

"Of course, I'm in," Misha said. "What's the target?"

"I'll give you the details another time," I said, "when we're alone."

He nodded and went back to Hebrew, and Magda was happy to resume control over the conversation. Misha took her hand and stroked it. Though her overbearing attitude wasn't really to my liking, he was in love with her, and she took good care of him.

ALEC WASTED NO TIME IN preparing for his revenge against Meir Federbusch. He purchased two leather whips in the Old

City, and on Friday morning, we waited for the informant behind one of the bushes in the open field.

About an hour later, we saw him approach, with a bagged challah in his hand. We jumped out from behind the bush to confront him. He turned pale and started to tremble.

"Remember me, Meir?" Alec asked.

"S-sure, I do," Meir stammered. "You disappeared. We didn't know where you were."

In response, Alec slammed his fist into Meir's face, and blood began to stream from his nose. I remembered the words of Yousef, who had said Alec wasn't much of a boxer. Meir's sobs indicated that Yousef was wrong.

"Drop your trousers and underpants," Alec instructed. When Meir hesitated, Alec punched him in the face again. "I'm going to break your bones one by one until you get undressed."

Meir quickly removed his shoes and his trousers. He hesitated slightly before taking off his underpants, but one look from Alec was enough to prompt him into action. Alec pushed him to the ground and started lashing his exposed rear with one of the whips, counting out loud—"One lash for the rat, two lashes for the rat"—until he reached eighteen.

Our plan had been to each take a turn, but when I saw Meir's mangled and bleeding behind, I decided that he'd had enough. "I want you to know we have our eyes on you," I said. "If we find out that you've told anyone what happened here, or if you rat out one more Jew, we will find you again. And it won't be just a beating next time—you and your mother will be dead."

Meir could barely manage to dress or put his shoes on. "You're going to tell your mother that you tripped coming through the field and fell into a ditch," I added. "If you try to get clever with us, your fate will be a bitter one."

"You have nothing to worry about," he said, and with tears running down his bloody face, he slowly limped away.

ON SATURDAY, MARCH 1, A loud explosion rocked Jerusalem. The Irgun had attacked the British officers' club in the Goldsmith House on King George Street, not far from the offices of the Jewish Agency. The Goldsmith House was very close to the Yeshurun synagogue, and the news claimed the bombs had been set to go off an hour after the Shabbat morning prayers ended to prevent any Jewish casualties.

The operation had apparently come on the heels of the British interception of the *Arlosoroff* off the coast of Haifa. The ship had been carrying some thirteen hundred refugees, including nearly five hundred women who had survived the Nazi death camps. The British authorities had boarded the ship, severely mistreated the refugees, and then taken them to an internment camp in Cyprus.

The British responded to the attack on the officers' club by imposing martial law in Jerusalem and other cities around the country. All civilian courts of justice were afforded military powers, and soldiers were given the same powers as the police. The British hoped that martial law would paralyze the underground operations and undermine the Jewish economy, but we could tell they were losing control. This was the beginning of the end of Britain's rule over Israel.

Stanley contacted me at the beginning of the second week of March, a few days after the Purim holiday. I was at work, and when he came into Café Pinsk, dressed in civilian clothes, he asked me to join him for half an hour at Café Wien.

Stanley seemed angry and didn't say a word to me on the

walk to Café Wien. He didn't start talking until after our coffee had been served.

"Those bastards who blew up the officers' club didn't merely make us bleed," he said. "They dealt a big blow to morale. London seems ready to capitulate. It makes me sick that Churchill—such a hero in the war—submitted a no-confidence motion against the government, saying we should leave Palestine. Thousands of parents with children serving here called on members of parliament to work toward a pullout. And our supposed allies, the Americans, are also trying to suck up to the Zionists. They want to give immigration permits to a hundred thousand Jews!" He shook his head. "Since the war, Britain is hurting economically, and we're financially dependent on the Americans. Even here, in the British civil service and the military, there are cowards who are shitting in their pants because of Jewish terror. But my group and I have no intention of simply giving up." His hands clenched around his coffee cup.

"I'm glad to hear that," I said. "If the Zionists get their way, the Arab states will butcher us all within months."

"Our group," he continued, as if I hadn't spoken, "is about to embark on a series of actions that will completely alter the situation. We know the location of several apartments and buildings that the Irgun uses to hold its meetings. Blowing up these terrorists will be fitting payback for the assault on the officers' club. I suggested to my group that we include you in the operation, seeing as you're a Jew who speaks Hebrew."

"I'm honored that you thought of me," I said.

"My idea didn't go over so well at first, but I won them over. I reminded my fellow soldiers that the Irgun's assault on the Jerusalem train station failed only because we had a Jewish collaborator on the inside. And when they still weren't convinced,

I retrieved your dossier in which Inspector Jeffries himself, God rest his soul, wrote about your cooperation."

"What do you want me to do?"

"Nothing just yet," Stanley said. "Wait for my instructions. We'll meet here again in two weeks—same day and time."

"All right," I said and stood up to leave.

"Just a moment," he said, stopping me. "I have some good news. We've made contact with Abd al-Qader al-Husseini, the cousin of Haj Amin al-Husseini and the leader of the Arab guerillas in Jerusalem. He's helping us in various ways, including financially, and I've already received a substantial advance from him." He reached into his pocket and retrieved a bundle of cash, which he placed in my hand. "This is for you," he said, "for personal expenses."

Surprised, I thanked him and slipped the money into my pocket. I would hand it over to Zvi as a donation to the Wolves from Mr. Al-Husseini. I smiled, wondering what the Arab guerilla leader would have thought if he'd known his money was going to a Jewish underground organization.

In March, the Irgun attacked military bases near Beit Lid, Kfar Yona, and Hadera. Sabotage operations were carried out against military vehicle depots in Haifa and Rishon Lezion and on police stations in Rehovot and Sarafand. On March 12, the Irgun carried out its daring assault on the Schneller Barracks. After breaching the base's perimeter wall, Irgun fighters planted and detonated explosives that caused extensive damage to the barracks. As expected, the Irgun's operations led to increased demands for a withdrawal from Israel by the British public.

Stanley showed up to our next meeting in an even worse mood. "My ears were ringing for two days after the Irgun's attack on the Schneller Barracks," he said. "The nerve of these terrorists is reaching new heights. Even our top brass sees we have to take action. I've shared our plans with my commanding officer, a chief inspector. He'll give some support but will lay low."

"So this isn't an official operation?" I asked.

"It can't be. The higher-ups have to maintain the façade that we won't do anything that puts civilians in harm's way—and normally I would agree. But we must strike back against these vermin."

"I understand. Have you selected a target and date for our attack?" If I could find out enough details ahead of time, it would help me prepare the best way to thwart them.

"You want to get moving, I know," he replied, "but it will be a while longer, unfortunately. We've decided to go for a big operation that requires a large amount of explosives. Our man can steal only small amounts of explosives from the storage facility each time. And the Irgun are constantly changing their meeting places, as well as the locations of their training facilities. We want to be one hundred percent ready. Can't jump the gun. But I think we'll be ready by the third week in April."

From a purely professional perspective, I agreed with him. More so than operations carried out by regular army units, commando missions took meticulous planning because of the small number of soldiers involved. As partisans, we had witnessed both the Russian and German armies sustain heavy losses and keep fighting. But the men and women who had fought with me had been irreplaceable.

Stanley reached into his pocket, pulled out another wad of cash, and handed it to me. "We received more money from al-Husseini, who asked us to kill as many Jews as possible," he said. "Since you're helping us, we might as well make it worth your while, eh? Then you won't change your mind and turn on us." He chuckled, but the sound was hollow. Did he suspect me?

"I won't turn on you," I said. "I'm in this because I believe the Jewish people will be slaughtered by the Arabs if the British pull out. However," I raised one brow and smiled, "the money is appreciated." I tucked the roll of bills into my pocket.

Stanley stared at me for a moment and then laughed, a real laugh this time. "Doesn't hurt to oil the gears, does it now, lad?" I released my pent-up breath as he continued.

"The most important thing from our perspective is to crush their morale," Stanley said. "Although the more casualties we inflict, the more painful and damaging the blow—so perhaps al-Husseini has a point."

"Perhaps," I murmured.

He tossed some money on the table to cover the bill and stood. "If I need you, I'll come find you at the restaurant." I waited until he had walked away and rounded the corner, then I headed straight to the restaurant and asked Max to set up a meeting with Zvi.

SHIMON PICKED ME UP FROM my apartment the next morning, and we drove to Talpiot. "Have you come to give me news about Operation Blood and Sword?" Zvi asked the moment I walked in. He was sitting at a table and gestured to a chair beside him.

"The plans those bastards are making aren't moving at the pace they'd like," I replied, taking my seat. "They're looking to carry out a big attack that requires a truck carrying explosives. Stanley believes they'll be ready by the second half of April, but there are always delays, so they probably won't be ready before May, especially since they have yet to even decide on a

target. Oh, and we've received a donation from an admirer—
Abd al-Qader al-Husseini himself." I handed over the two large
wads of cash that Stanley had given me.

"Is this some kind of joke?" Zvi asked.

"Al-Husseini is supporting Stanley's group financially, and
Stanley's paying me out of that money."

Zvi didn't smile. On the contrary, my words made him
even more somber.

"This is of grave significance," he said. "As you know, last
month, Bevin, the British foreign minister, decided to put the
fate of Israel into the hands of the United Nations. The British public sees this as the first step to an exit. But achieving
the two-thirds majority in the General Assembly to divide the
country won't be easy, because all the Arab states and their allies
will oppose it. Bevin is a rabid Jew-hater and doesn't think the
partition plan will secure that two-thirds majority. If it doesn't,
the UN will be forced to place Israel under British trusteeship,
only now with UN financial obligations for the occupation."

"What about the backing from the Americans?" I asked.

He nodded. "We believe that in light of President Truman's
support for dividing the Land of Israel between the Jews and
the Arabs, we will secure the required majority, albeit with
some difficulty. But what will the British do then?"

"A very good question."

Zvi drummed his fingers on the table for a moment, then
glanced up at me. "I have a personal friend who served in
the OSS, the Americans' primary intelligence service during
the war, and he's set to fill a senior position in the new intelligence agency the Americans are currently creating. He was
among the Americans who went into the death camps at the
end of the war, and he supports our struggle and our right to
independence in our homeland. A few days ago, I received a

very worrying report from him. Even if our diplomatic activity is successful and the UN passes a resolution to partition the land, if the Jewish community comes under immediate attack by the standing armies of the surrounding Arab states, US intelligence is convinced we cannot emerge victorious. That would spell the end of the Zionist dream. I don't necessarily agree, but—"

"—but it's clear that the Arabs' chances of winning such a war would increase if they were to secure the support of the British," I interjected. Zvi nodded again.

"That's why al-Husseini's efforts to strengthen ties with the British are so troubling," he said. "I'm worried about a scenario in which the British supply arms, maybe even personnel, to the Arabs to be used against us."

I didn't respond, and after a brief silence, he went on. "I realize you don't have any details yet about the plan Stanley and his people have in mind, as they don't really have a fixed plan themselves, but can you give me a general idea of what they are plotting?"

"Not really, but I've given the matter a lot of thought," I replied. "If I can learn the location of their attack in advance, I can post Avrum as a sniper, and Shimon, Alec, and Misha will serve as my assault squad. Obviously, I can't work out the details until I know exactly what Stanley has in mind, but I'll let you know as soon as I do. In the meantime, it would be a shame for me to sit around doing nothing until then. Perhaps I could help with something else?"

"Don't even think about it," Zvi said. "The threat posed by Stanley is significant, and you're the only person who can stop him. Under no circumstances will I allow you to put yourself at risk. Go home and devote yourself to your wonderful girlfriend. Take her out to the movies or go dancing. You both deserve it."

I left, knowing Shoshana would appreciate Zvi's suggestion. I, however, felt restless, itching to do something that would push the British over the brink and right out of Israel.

ON APRIL 16, FOUR IRGUN patriots I'd met during my detention in Jerusalem were executed at the Acre Prison. A deep sadness filled me when I heard about the killings. The Irgun, for its part, carried out reprisals against the British all across the country.

A few days later, the British were preparing to execute Irgun fighter Meir Feinstein and the Lehi's Moshe Barazani. Feinstein had participated in the assault on the Jerusalem train station, and Barazani had been arrested for plotting to kill a British general. But a few hours before the executions were to take place at Jerusalem's central prison, Barazani and Feinstein took their own lives with a grenade that had been smuggled into the prison inside an orange.

They had intended to blow up their executioners along with themselves, but they had changed their plans after learning that a rabbi would be present at the hanging. Instead, after the rabbi had visited them in their cell, they embraced one another, placed the grenade against their chests, and pulled the pin.

24

"WE ARE THE SILVER PLATTER ON WHICH THE JEWISH STATE WAS DELIVERED"

(FROM "THE SILVER PLATTER," A POEM BY
NATAN ALTERMAN, 1947)

One evening toward the end of April, Stanley came into Café Pinsk and asked me to join him outside. When we were on the street, he said, "We will be ready for our operation in about three weeks. I'll contact you again soon."

"I look forward to it," I said.

On Sunday, May 4, the Irgun carried out its most complex and impressive operation to date—an assault on the Acre Prison to free the underground fighters imprisoned there. Max turned up at the restaurant later than usual that day and seemed highly agitated as he came over to me.

"Zvi wants to see you tomorrow," he whispered. "Shimon will pick you up here at seven o'clock."

When I got to the house in Talpiot, I was surprised to find twenty other people there, including five women, all members of the Wolves. Shimon and Zvi were the only ones I knew. It occurred to me that Zvi hadn't actually told me about a single operation carried out by his organization, unless I had been personally involved. The man certainly knew how to maintain secrecy—and to his credit.

Zvi kicked things off once everyone was seated. "Yesterday afternoon," he said, "the Irgun mounted an assault on the Acre Prison with the purpose of freeing forty-one underground members—thirty from the Irgun and eleven from the Lehi. The fighters were dressed as British soldiers and arrived at the prison in a convoy that included a British military truck, two vans painted in British camouflage, and two civilian vans. The assault force included twenty-three Irgun fighters, who were up against the prison's hundred and fifty guards. The raid was carried out by Dov Cohen—or Shimshon, as he's known in the underground—dressed in a British captain's uniform, complete with British decorations on his chest."

Zvi paused for a moment and cast his eyes over the room. "One of my favorite sayings of the sages is 'From all my teachers I have grown wise.' Although we are a much smaller organization than the Irgun, and we don't have the ability to carry out operations on such a scale, we have to learn all we can from them to attain the highest proficiency in our planning and execution.

"The prison break went well, but problems occurred during the retreat. The escapees encountered a British force that opened fire on them and caused casualties. Furthermore, the Irgun's blocking force, which was supposed to withdraw at the end of the operation, failed to hear the signal to retreat. They remained in place and were captured by the British. Ultimately, twenty Irgun and seven Lehi made it out of the prison. Three members of the Irgun's assault force and six of the escapees were killed, and five Irgun fighters and eight escapees were caught and imprisoned. I don't have all of the names of the dead yet, but I do know that Michael Eshbal and Shimshon were among them."

I was overcome with sadness at the thought of Eshbal's death. We hadn't spoken much when we had been in prison together, but I knew he was a patriot, a skilled fighter, and a man of words who had given us the gift of his moving and inspirational poetry.

"The operation dealt a severe blow to British pride," Zvi continued. "Although the Irgun sustained casualties, the bottom line is that the operation was a success—and showed an impressive level of planning and execution. Even the *New York Herald Tribune* dedicated its top headline to the operation, writing that the Irgun carried out 'an ambitious mission, its most challenging thus far, in perfect fashion.' Let's just hope the operation will add to the pressure on Britain to withdraw from Israel."

On our way home after the meeting, Shimon broke his usual silence. "What's happening with Stanley and his crew?" he asked. "I'm tired of sitting around twiddling my thumbs, waiting for them to make a move."

"Don't worry," I replied. "Stanley told me they'd be carrying out their operation this month."

Ten days after the Acre Prison break, the UN General Assembly convened to discuss the question of Israel and decided to establish UNSCOP, the United Nations Special Committee on Palestine, tasked with submitting recommendations on the matter.

Stanley showed up at Café Pinsk during the fourth week of May and motioned for me to join him outside again. "I'll meet you at Café Wien tomorrow morning at ten o'clock," he said.

"Fine," I said. "Is the operation ready to move forward?"

"You'll find out tomorrow," he said.

The next morning, I found Stanley in civilian clothes at Café Wien, and he didn't waste any time with niceties. "We've managed to collect the explosives, and we have a plan in place," he said.

"What's the target?" I asked.

"I understand your curiosity," Stanley responded, flashing me a wry smile, "but I'm not going to divulge that just now. If you had my experience with commando operations, you'd know that secrecy is critical. You may have proven your loyalty in the past, but you won't learn the target until we're on our way there."

I was disappointed, but I knew there was no way he was going to change his mind.

"The attack will take place in two days, at 11:30 a.m. Make sure you have the day off work. I'll pick you up outside your apartment at a quarter to eleven."

He retrieved another wad of bills from his pocket and handed it to me. "Here's another cut of the money from al-Husseini. I mentioned to him that we have a Jew in our group, and he said I was making a mistake, even suggested that I kill you. I told him how you warned us about the King David bombing. He simply said, 'The only good Jew is a dead Jew.' But don't worry, just as Inspector Jeffries trusted you, so do I." With that, he called the waiter, paid the bill, and left.

I hurried to Café Pinsk and asked Max to arrange an urgent meeting with Zvi and Shimon at the restaurant that same evening. Then I notified Alec, Avrum, and Misha.

"I met with Stanley today," I began when we were all seated at one of the tables after closing time. "He told me the truck bomb is scheduled for the day after tomorrow. Operation Blood and Sword is now in motion. Stanley refused to divulge their target, which is a problem. Nevertheless, I've given it a lot of thought, and I think I have a plan."

"Tell me, David," Alec interjected, "wouldn't it be easier to simply kill this Stanley bastard and stop his operation?"

"I considered that," I replied. "But Stanley is only one man out of a group, and killing him won't stop the operation. Furthermore, it's safe to assume that some of the members of his team are aware of my existence, and if Stanley is killed, I'll be the first person they point a finger at."

"David is right. Let's hear him out," Zvi said.

"Before I get in the car with Stanley, I'll tell him I need to know the target before I risk my life. If he tells me, I'll say it out loud, acting surprised. Alec, you'll be hiding behind the pine tree in the yard. Meanwhile, Shimon, Avrum, and Misha will be waiting in a car nearby, out of sight. When Stanley and I leave, Alec will join you three, and you'll all drive to the target."

"What if Stanley refuses to tell you?" Avrum asked.

"If Stanley refuses to tell me or if Alec doesn't overhear, you will all follow us at a safe distance. Once we arrive, Avrum will quickly get into position with his sniper rifle. When I raise both my arms, that will be the signal for Shimon, Alec, and Misha to storm the British commandos. That's the best I can come up with. Does anyone have any thoughts?"

Zvi was the only one who commented. "In general, the plan sounds good. But I'd like to suggest some changes. Instead of one car, we should use two—one for Shimon and Alec, the other for Avrum, Misha, and Shoshana. That way, if one car runs into trouble, the second can continue on to the target. Let Shoshana hide behind the tree and listen for the location."

"Shoshana?" I said, startled.

He nodded. "I would like her to be involved in this operation. I hear she is good with guns and has become a competent sniper. She can take cover behind the pine tree in the yard and, later, be there to back up Avrum."

I was both surprised and unsettled upon hearing about such a role for Shoshana. My hope had been to keep her out of harm's way. Still, I had promised to support her desire to be part of an operation, so I didn't offer any objection.

"You're right," I said. "Shoshana will be a strong addition to our unit. I have a personal request. My Webley revolver isn't ideal. The reloading mechanism is clumsy. Can you get me a German-made Walther P38 with three fully loaded magazines? I used one as a partisan, and it's an excellent weapon. If something goes wrong and I end up having to take them all on myself, the extra firepower might give me a chance."

"I'll do my best," Zvi said.

The others were silent, but Avrum suddenly came to life. "I'm going to show those bastards what a good sniper I am," he said. Everyone laughed, and the tension was broken for a few seconds. Then I spoke up.

"Let's meet tomorrow morning in Tel Arza for some last-minute training exercises." I thought it was important to practice and to brush up on our weapons skills before the operation, especially for Misha and Shoshana. My time with Shoshana's training had been limited, but she was truly a natural at self-defense. I was more concerned about her proficiency with a pistol in close quarters, and I wanted to work with her one more time on that.

When I got home, Shoshana greeted me with a kiss but no welcoming smile. She seemed agitated. I asked her what was wrong.

"Max told me there was going to be a meeting tonight."

"Yes," I said.

"But I wasn't included. I thought since I had begun my training, I was considered part of your team now? I know a new operation is being planned."

I smiled and cupped her face between my hands. "I have a surprise for you, my love. You are going to be part of this operation." Her face lit up, and I kissed her lightly. "And tomorrow morning, we will all be meeting for extra training, including you."

Almost bouncing up and down, she led me to the couch, and we sat together, discussing what was to come. I briefed her about the operation, and she asked many questions, some of which I couldn't answer.

"Are you nervous, love?" I asked.

"A little nervous," she admitted, "but mostly excited!"

The next morning in Tel Arza, Shimon showed up with the Walther P38 I had requested. Having this desirable pistol helped boost my confidence in our ability to thwart Stanley's evil scheme. Avrum arrived with two human-shaped targets and found a suitable area where he and Shoshana could practice with sniper rifles from a distance of about three hundred yards. When he was done, he proudly showed us a tight cluster of bullet holes in his target's head, as well as the impressive results from Shoshana's rounds.

"Shoshana is a great sniper, almost as good as I am," he said.

Dressed in her gray khakis, her blond hair a mess, glowing with pride, Shoshana had never looked so beautiful to me.

"My turn," I told her, grinning. "And I won't be as easy as Avrum."

She gave me a challenging smile in return. "Last time you were way too easy," she said, scoffing.

For the next hour, I instructed Shoshana on how to shoot with a Webley that I provided. In the last few weeks, I had taught her how to take the Webley apart, assemble it, and also how to aim and handle it. Now it was time to train her on how to actually shoot, using real bullets. Watching Shoshana practice assured me that she could hold her own.

Alec, as usual, showed himself to be highly proficient with his weapons. Shimon was a little rusty but improved measurably during our training session. Only Misha still seemed slow when we finished. Shoshana's face was flushed with her accomplishments, and we walked home hand in hand.

ON THURSDAY MORNING, THE TEAM arrived at our home in two cars. Shoshana hid behind the pine tree in the courtyard while Shimon kept the car running nearby. Avrum and Misha parked down the street.

As arranged, Stanley showed up in a military jeep at a quarter to eleven, along with two of his men. I recognized one as a member of Inspector Jeffries's team.

Dressed in baggy trousers with large pockets, in which the P38 and magazines were hidden, I approached their vehicle and ducked my head to look into the open window.

"You don't have to worry about me telling anyone now," I said to Stanley, "so I think it's only fair you tell me the target before I get in."

After a slight hesitation, Stanley uttered just four words, but they were enough to send chills down my spine. "The Jewish Agency building."

"The Jewish Agency building?" I said in practically a shout. "You said we were hitting the Irgun." A noisy motorcycle was speeding by at that moment, and I prayed that Shoshana had managed to hear me.

"Get into the jeep, and I'll explain on the way," Stanley growled.

"Why the Jewish Agency and not the Irgun as originally planned?" I asked as I climbed in. "The Jewish Agency works with the British."

"You're right," Stanley said with a shrug. "But the Irgun is always changing locations, so we couldn't find a reliable target. Anyway, the Jewish Agency is the government of the Jews of Palestine, and they have always been an option, so far as I was concerned. It will be fitting retribution for the attack on the King David, our HQ. When we get there, you will convince the agency officials that everything is fine, or I'll put a bullet between your eyes. Understood?"

"Yes," I said. "I'll do it."

Stanley seemed satisfied and continued with his explanation. "The truck with the explosives is coming from the Arab village of Bir Zeit, near Ramallah. We'll rendezvous at the intersection of King George and Mamilla, and from there we'll head to the agency and park outside the entrance. The cover story is that we've come to collect documents—just like during Operation Broadside. Your job is to explain that we're only there to collect documents and no harm will come to them if they cooperate.

"Once the truck is in place, we'll tell them we're leaving to get a second truck, because we're collecting a ton of documents. The truck's five hundred pounds of explosives will be hidden under a tarpaulin. One of our people will wait there until five minutes before the blast to make sure no one looks inside. The timer is set to detonate thirty minutes after we arrive. Our demolitions expert has also booby-trapped the timer, so if anyone tries to disarm it, the bomb will go off."

"Sounds like you've thought of everything," I said. In truth, I had already noticed a few weaknesses, but the driver—one of Stanley's commando friends—wasn't one of them. I was alarmed to notice that he kept a loaded machine gun at his side. *This guy could really hurt us badly*, I thought.

For the next few minutes, we drove through the streets of

Jerusalem in silence, and when we reached the King George–Mamilla intersection, Stanley pulled over to the side of the road and waited. About twenty minutes later, we saw the truck approaching. Stanley signaled to the driver to follow us, and we made our way up King George Street to the gate at the entrance of the Jewish Agency building. The guard on duty looked us over and inquired suspiciously as to our business there.

"We're British soldiers, and we've been ordered to collect documents," Stanley said, drawing his revolver and pointing it at the guard.

He signaled me to play my part, and I repeated the sentence he had instructed me to say. "We're only here to collect documents, and no harm will come to you if you cooperate."

"I need to check with my supervisor," the guard replied.

Stanley jumped out of the jeep and slammed the butt of his revolver against the side of the guard's head. The man collapsed to the ground, unconscious. The Brit dragged him into the guard hut and opened the gate, and the jeep and truck drove through. Stanley stayed with the truck and jeep, sending me and two of his men into the building to tell the workers about our supposed task.

"If anyone resists, don't hesitate to kill them," he instructed his men.

As we were making our way along the corridor, a guard approached and ordered us to stop.

"Who gave you permission to come in here?" he shouted.

One of the commandos drew his weapon and shot him in the head. I realized it was time to act before they killed anyone else. I pulled the cocked and loaded Walther P38 out and shot both of Stanley's men. They fell to the floor.

Returning the gun to my pocket, I turned around and ran

outside. Just as I was approaching Stanley, I heard a weak cry from behind me, "The Jewish bastard's a traitor! He shot us!" I glanced over to see one of Stanley's men standing at the doorway, his face covered in blood. He immediately fell to the ground.

Stanley drew his weapon and turned on me. "You Jewish son of a bitch," he hissed. "Rot in hell."

I raised my hands in surrender—coincidentally, it was also the signal to my comrades to move into action. Thinking these were likely my last seconds on earth, my breathing quickened as I thought about Shoshana and what would happen to her. My life flashed before my eyes—Minsk, fighting the Nazis, Shoshana. I had failed to keep my promise to take care of myself, but I hoped she'd stay strong.

I heard two shots but didn't feel a thing. Confused, I looked at Stanley and saw blood trickling from a hole in his forehead. The gun in his hand dropped to the ground, and a second later his body collapsed. A blood stain quickly spread across his chest.

Shimon, Alec, Shoshana, and Misha raced forward, and Stanley's driver managed to fire a burst from his machine gun in their direction before Alec killed him. Misha cried out, and I couldn't believe what I was seeing—my friend was doubled over, clutching his stomach, his shirt turning red. Alec ripped off his own shirt and pressed it against the wound to stem the flow of blood.

Shoshana rushed to his side, and she and Alec dragged him behind Stanley's jeep. Kneeling beside him, she pulled a first aid kit out of the knapsack she carried and went to work. It was then that I noticed Shimon lying on the ground, clutching his right arm.

I ran to Shimon. Blood stained his right sleeve, and I ripped the cloth away to examine his injury. "It's a flesh wound," I told him. "You'll be all right."

"Something is wrong," he said through clenched teeth. "I can't move my hand."

"Let's get out of the open." I put my arm around his waist and hauled him to his feet. We stumbled behind the jeep as well, and I leaned him against the back tire. Shoshana was giving Alec instructions on keeping pressure on a large square of gauze across Misha's abdomen.

"Is he all right?" I asked.

She bit her lip and shook her head. "We need to get him to a doctor."

"Can you take a look at Shimon? His arm has been hit. It looks to be minor, but he can't move his hand."

She moved to Shimon's side, bringing the first aid kit, and quickly sterilized the wound and bandaged it. She gave him a pill and a cup of water to wash it down. Shimon took both gratefully. "It's more than a flesh wound," she said. "The bullet is still inside and may be pressing on a nerve. It needs to come out. I gave him a strong painkiller."

Shimon was shivering in his own sweat, obviously suffering.

My mind raced. Shimon was our only hope to deactivate the explosive material. Only he had the skills. I tried not to think about what would happen if we failed to do so.

I looked at my watch. "Shimon, I know that you're in pain and you feel terrible, but the truck has five hundred pounds of explosives set to go off in fourteen minutes. The timer is rigged. Zvi says you're the best sapper in the business. I know nothing about it. Can you make it to the back cargo area in the truck if I help you?"

"I can't move my hand, David," he said and then groaned.

"Can you use your left hand?"

He shook his head and grimaced. "It's a delicate procedure. You'll have to do it. I'll tell you how."

LONE WOLF IN JERUSALEM

I swallowed hard. "All right. What have we got to lose?"

Shoshana jerked her head toward me, her eyes widening in alarm.

"Get my backpack and bring it," he said. "Then help me to my feet."

Shoshana ran to get his pack while I put my arm around his waist and got him upright. It was quiet around us now, but I was concerned someone had informed the British police about the shooting and a patrol would come to check.

Shimon made it to the window of the truck's front cabin and peered inside. "See the two black electrical wires going from the truck's battery to the back cargo area? This is the power source of the activating system of the bomb. I am sure that there is a backup power system in the cargo area. If we just disconnect these two wires, the explosion will occur." He nodded toward his backpack slung over my shoulder. "Get out the big knife I have in there, the pliers, the wire cutter, the utility knife, and the small flashlight. Hurry up and cut the tarpaulin cover, and then we can analyze what kind of a situation we are in."

Shimon swayed, and I put a hand on his back to steady him, then helped him walk back to the cargo bay covered with the thick tarpaulin. He leaned against the truck while I took the needed tools out of his backpack and put them in my pockets, except for the huge knife. I used it to split open the tarpaulin cover. I helped him as we climbed into the vehicle's cargo bay.

Ten round metal containers, about fifteen inches wide and thirty inches high, sat in the front of the cargo bay, attached with metal wire to the trunk frame. No doubt these contained the explosive material. We moved closer, and Shimon pointed at a small black box with wires sticking out of it, some leading into the metal containers.

"Cut the tarpaulin over the box," Shimon said, "so I can see better." I did as he asked, and sunlight poured in through the ragged hole. He sank to his knees. "Good, now we don't need to use the flashlight. I can see already that the people who put together the explosive material and the activating system are very professional. They used state-of-the-art technology, unlike our poor underground members." He pointed to the wires. "There are booby-trap wires. If they are cut, it will trigger the activated system. Then it's goodbye to all of us."

"If we cut the wires from the truck battery, we explode. If we cut these wires, we explode. Are you saying you can't deactivate it?" I asked.

Shimon sighed. "I estimate that our chances of deactivating the system are fifty-fifty. I suggest you give me two minutes to learn what's going where while you make sure that everyone leaves the area. This is a large explosive, and if we mess up, it's enough that both of us will die without taking everyone else with us."

I looked at my watch—eleven minutes before the bomb went off. I jumped from the truck, and when I hit the ground, Avrum came running up, holding his rifle, a smug grin on his face.

"I saw that bastard draw his weapon, and I saw you give the signal. I shot him in the head, and Shoshana shot him in the chest. We made a good team!"

I was thankful to him, but I had no time to give praise now. I gave him a big thumbs-up and clapped him on the back as I rushed past. "Well done!" I said and ran toward the jeep where Alec and Shoshana were still hiding with Misha.

"We've got to evacuate the area!" I told Alec. "I've got to help Shimon, and we only have a fifty-fifty chance of stopping the explosion. It's up to you and Shoshana to get everyone out of here immediately, including the Jewish Agency people!"

Alec turned and ran toward the Jewish Agency building, shouting, "Bomb! Bomb! Everyone out!"

Shoshana stood and grabbed both my hands. "I can't leave Misha," she said, looking up at me. Her face was ashen, and there were traces of tears on her face. "He's barely hanging on."

I glanced down at my friend. He was lying very still on the ground, his eyes closed. He had bled through the gauze beneath Shoshana's hands, which were bright red. I checked his pulse, which felt faint. I thought about Leah, and I knew I couldn't allow her brother to die too.

"I can help Alec," Avrum said solemnly, all trace of his gleeful excitement now gone.

I looked at my watch. I had one minute left before I needed to go back to Shimon.

"No, help Shoshana," I told Avrum. "Help her get Misha to Max's house. Take the car you came in. Ask for Dr. Kaminitz, and tell him it's an emergency. Alec will have to take care of alerting the rest of the people in the area."

I glanced at my watch—it was time. "Shoshana . . ." I began, but I had no words. "Be safe," I whispered, and then I ran back to Shimon.

He was still examining the wires, looking frustrated. When he saw me, he shook his head. "The sons of bitches did such a good job that it is a mission impossible to find out which wires we should disconnect. First, we have to disconnect the wires of the booby trap. I have two options to do it, but I have to decide which one is better, and when I say 'which one is better,' I mean that cutting the wrong wire will cause an explosion."

He closed his eyes, either in order to concentrate or because of the pain. When he opened them, he pointed with his left hand at a green wire. "Let's cut this green one, and to be on the safe side, let's say a short prayer."

I took the wire cutter out of my pocket and took a deep

breath. I prayed and said, "*Shma Israel!*" Shimon closed his eyes again. I took a deep breath and cut the green wire.

Nothing.

Shimon opened his eyes and gave me a huge smile. I grinned back and looked at my watch. It was seven minutes before the explosives were due to go off. We were ready for the next step.

Shimon began examining the wires again. I didn't say a word. He touched the wires coming out of the activated system, talking to himself and frowning. Apparently, he couldn't come to any conclusions. I looked at my watch. Three minutes left.

With a sigh, I gave him the news. "Time to decide."

Shimon looked up at me and then pointed to a white wire. "It is either this wire we must cut"—he shifted his hand and pointed to a blue wire—"or this one."

"So, there's no way to know for certain which is right?" My thoughts flew to Shoshana. At least she was safe.

He shook his head and then shrugged. "Maybe the blue wire is a better choice. I don't know. And even with more time, I don't think I could arrive at a better solution. David, cut the blue wire—but first say your *Shma Israel.*"

I looked at my watch. Two minutes. "*Shma Israel!*" I cried and cut the blue wire, closing my eyes as I did.

We didn't blow up.

I opened my eyes and saw Shimon's smiling face.

We both began laughing, and I grabbed him by the shoulders, making him cry out. "I'm sorry," I said. "But we did it!"

Shimon went suddenly still.

"What?" I asked. "What's wrong?"

"I just remembered that sometimes these things are double rigged. It might still blow."

"You just remembered?" I cried. My watch showed one minute left. "Let's get the hell out of here!"

This time Shimon didn't need my help getting out of the truck. His adrenalin must have been pumping through his veins as hard as mine. We ran to King George Street. When we arrived there, it was one minute past the time the truck was supposed to have exploded.

I threw my arms around my friend. "You saved us and prevented a disaster. You are a hero, my friend!"

"It figures I had to miss out on all of the hero stuff," a familiar voice said from behind. I turned around to see Alec standing a few feet away.

"Alec!" I ran to his side. "Why did you stay? I told all of you to evacuate."

"Well, if I had, who do you think would help you get rid of the truck and the dead British soldiers?" he asked with a grin.

"Good thinking," I said, clapping him on the back. We had done it.

25

"As the hour that we longed for is so near"

(from "Song of the Partisans" by
Hirsh Glick, 1943)

Alec and I loaded the bodies of the British soldiers onto the truck. I instructed Alec to drive the vehicle full of explosives to Geula Street and to park it by the Schneller Barracks. Even after the truck was discovered, it would take some time for the Brits to figure out exactly what had happened. I asked Alec to come to Max's apartment afterward.

By the time we finished, Shimon looked pale. I put Shimon in the car that he and Alec had come in and drove to Max's apartment.

Nelka greeted me at the door with a hug.

"Thank God, you made it!" she exclaimed. "Come in!"

I helped Shimon over to the couch in the small living room. He groaned as he sat down heavily, cradling his arm to his chest.

"He's been hurt?" Nelka asked anxiously.

"A flesh wound, but it seems to have done some damage to his hand," I told her. "He needs to see the doctor."

"Yes, of course." Nelka clung to my arm, her eyes filled with worry. "Misha's bleeding has stopped," she said. "Max told me that Avrum and Shoshana saved your life."

"Yes, I was lucky to have them with me," I said. "Where is Misha?"

"Dr. Kaminitz is treating him now." Nelka gestured to a closed door. "He ordered everyone out and said we weren't to come in until he was done."

"And where are Shoshana and Avrum?" I asked. I felt eager to put my arms around the woman I loved. There had been several moments at the agency when I thought I would never see her again.

"They went to work," Nelka said with a laugh. "Thanks to all of these heroic people on his staff, Max is shorthanded! Shoshana said she was bursting with energy, and Avrum agreed."

I sank down beside Shimon to wait. He was asleep, or unconscious. I wasn't sure which. After fifteen more minutes, I was tapping one foot in nervous impatience. What if Misha didn't make it? What if I had failed to protect Leah's brother?

When the doctor finally opened the door, I jumped up and blocked his way. "How is he?" I asked. Dr. Kaminitz blinked at me and then smiled slightly.

"You aren't the only one who seems to have a guardian angel," Kaminitz replied. "This time it was a close call. His injuries are worse than yours were, but luckily no major organs were hit. The bullet passed through, and I was able to repair the internal damage and stop the bleeding. I think—I hope— that he'll be fine."

I sighed in relief. "Thank you," I said, my voice hoarse. "May I see him?"

"It's best to wait until tomorrow. He needs rest."

"Very well," I said reluctantly. "In the meantime, would

you please take care of Shimon?" I gestured toward my friend. He was struck in his right arm and has lost the use of his hand."

Dr. Kaminitz looked straight into my eyes for a long moment before speaking. "I see that you have all been very active today." I remained silent. He sighed. "Don't worry, I'll take care of him. Did the bullet pass through his arm?"

"Shoshana said it did not," I told him.

He nodded. "Probably pressing on a nerve. Well, I'll get washed up. Nelka, can you assist?" The two helped Shimon into the other room, and I began to pace. I wanted to see Shoshana. I needed to see her.

At that moment, there came a knock at the door, and I froze. I cautiously opened it a few inches and then smiled in relief.

"Alec!" I pulled him inside and shut the door. "You're just in time. Misha is doing better, and Dr. Kaminitz is looking at Shimon. Can you stay here until the doctor makes sure he's all right? I need to go and see Shoshana."

"I was just envying Shimon for taking a bullet," he said with a wry smile, "thinking if I'd been shot, I could skip waiting tables for a while. I'll stay. Just tell Max it was under your orders."

I left Max's apartment and went to the restaurant, impatient to see Shoshana. This time I forced myself to walk at a regular pace. I breathed deeply as I walked, trying to get my heart rate down to a normal level.

Avrum met me at the entrance of the restaurant, still gloating. "Did you see how I got him right between the eyes?" he said in a hushed voice. "I asked Shoshana to back me up and shoot him in the chest, and she did it. Our rookie came through like a pro."

I pressed a kiss to his forehead. "Avrum, I owe you my life. If you weren't such a crack shot, they'd be preparing my funeral."

Shoshana was standing at the far end of the restaurant when

she saw me. She ran across the room and hugged me tightly, then rested her head against my chest.

I bent my head and kissed her for a long, wonderful moment, then hugged her to me tightly. "You are really something, my guardian angel," I whispered. "Who would have thought? I love you so much, Shoshana."

THE NEXT DAY, I WENT to visit Misha.

On my way up the stairs to Max's apartment, I bumped into Magda on her way down. "It's good to see you, Magda," I said, smiling at her. She didn't smile back. She lifted her chin and gave me a cold look.

"Misha has been here for only a few months, and you put him in such a dangerous situation?" she demanded. "Misha is not going to fight anymore!"

There was no point in responding, so I simply said, "I hope Misha gets well soon." She waved her hand dismissively and stomped down the steps.

I knocked on Max's door, and Nelka opened it with a smile. She chatted briefly as she led me to the bedroom where Misha was recovering. He looked pale and tired. I sat down beside him. "I'll get you both some tea," Nelka said softly and closed the door behind her.

"Thank you for your help," I said. "I want you to know that I won't be asking you to do this again. Your sister died by my side. I won't put your life at risk again."

A hint of a smile appeared on his face. "Did you speak to Magda just now?" he asked. "How many times did we almost get killed as partisans? We're fighters, and as long as I can help, I'll fight alongside you."

I kissed him on his forehead. "You're a good man, and I

love you," I said. It occurred to me that I was becoming rather sentimental, going around kissing men on their foreheads. What would Brigita have made of that?

Remembering how all the visits had worn me out when I'd been recovering from my wounds, I didn't stay long at Misha's side. When I got home, Shoshana was waiting for me, and I kissed her on the forehead too and then on the lips.

"You did well yesterday, my love," I said.

"I had a good teacher." She smiled. "Two good teachers."

SHIMON ARRIVED AT THE RESTAURANT a day later with his arm in a sling and told Max that Zvi wanted to see me.

"How is your hand?" I asked. "Can you move it yet?"

"Only a little," he said. "The doctor told me I likely have some nerve damage, but it will hopefully heal over time."

I nodded and got into the car. On the way, I was lost in my own thoughts over what had taken place in the last few days. Shimon was a good friend and a good fighter. I was glad that he hadn't suffered a worse injury, like Misha. And Misha—I was so thankful he was going to be all right.

At the house in Talpiot, Zvi greeted me with a warm handshake and invited me in.

"You and your friends prevented a horrible disaster," he said, gesturing for me to take a chair at his table. As I took my seat, Zvi moved to a sideboard, where a bottle of wine and two glasses sat. He poured the glasses both half full and handed me one before continuing. I took a sip. It was excellent.

"You thought of everything," he went on. "You had a backup plan in the event of any mishaps, and you improvised and showed initiative during the operation itself. I don't know anyone who could have done a better job. You weren't spared a bullet from Stanley's gun merely by chance. You made sure in advance that Avrum and Shoshana would be in place in case of trouble—and trouble there was."

"Thank you, Zvi," I said. "But the success wasn't mine alone. We did it as a team."

"An excellent team! The British, the Jews, and the Arabs are all trying to figure out who foiled Stanley's plans, but no one has a clue," Zvi continued. "The Jewish Agency checked with all the underground organizations, even ours. But we've survived this long through absolute secrecy, and I have no intention of changing that now—certainly not before we have an independent Jewish state. And that day isn't far off!"

"Do you know something the others don't?" I asked. Zvi was privy to all sorts of information. Had he heard something?

"Not at all," Zvi said. "But this is the consensus these days, from the Jewish Agency and the Haganah to the Irgun and the Lehi. The fate of the British Mandate is now in the hands of the United Nations, and there's a real chance the member states will divide the Land of Israel between the Jews and the Arabs. The Arabs will attack us with all their might—not just the Arabs living in the Land of Israel but also the armies of the surrounding Arab states. Abd al-Qader al-Husseini is gathering thousands of armed fighters while also funding anti-Semitic mercenaries like Stanley."

"And what will the Wolves do?" I asked.

"Up until now, our main task has been to wear down the British and convince them to withdraw from the country. But we will soon be faced with a new task—to battle against the Arab enemy." Zvi took a long draught from his glass and set it down heavily. "The Irgun and Lehi don't share my assessment of the situation, and I expect they'll continue to strike at the British over the coming months. They don't need our help, so for now at least, we won't carry out any more operations against the British."

"I intend to take a break myself," I said.

He smiled. "Good, get some rest. Because you, David, will make a talented and distinguished commander in the regular army we will create at the end of the British Mandate, which will be formed by the Haganah. I'll pull a few strings and get you into a Haganah officers' course."

The thought of being in a unified army sent a rush of anticipation through me. "That sounds exciting, Zvi," I said.

"Are you satisfied with your work as a waiter?" he asked.

I blinked, a little surprised by the abrupt change in topic. "It certainly isn't very challenging," I replied. "I don't love waiting on people, but I've worked at Café Pinsk almost since I first came to Israel, and the place has been like a home to me."

He nodded. "Ah, yes, what we all have longed for."

I leaned back in the chair and took another sip of wine. How different my life—and the lives of my friends—might have been if the British had allowed Israel to become an independent state right after the war with Germany. Reflecting on the arc of my life and how it had led to my current situation, I went on to tell Zvi more than he'd probably expected to hear in response to his simple question.

"I was a schoolboy when the Germans invaded Belarus," I said, "and the war denied me the opportunity for an education. I had no time to think about my future. I wasn't sure I had a future. For the past six years, almost every single thought has been devoted to planning the elimination of my enemies in the most efficient way."

"Tell me, David," Zvi interjected. "Did killing your enemies in Israel give you a sense of personal satisfaction?"

I paused, thinking about his question for a long moment.

Finally I answered, "Certainly not. Although it did please me to know that the people of Israel were rid of some enemies thanks to me and the people who fought at my side." I took a drink of the wine, and Zvi nodded.

"Go on," he said. "So you felt no personal satisfaction?" He arched one brow, as if in disbelief.

I shrugged. "I'm not sure if those are the right words. Personal satisfaction? What satisfaction can there really be in taking a life when it won't bring back the ones who are lost?" I shook my head. "I must admit that sometimes during the war I would think of the terrible things the Nazis did to my family and friends, and it would fill me with a tremendous anger—a righteous rage. This staggering hate would spur me on, giving me the power to usurp whatever conscience I had left and pull the trigger on my enemy or choke the life from him!"

I realized I was standing, my fists clenched at my side. Regaining control, I sat back down.

"I made those choices," I said and looked up at Zvi. "I do not regret them."

I fell silent, and Zvi spoke up again. "And now, tell me, do you see different choices ahead?" His tone was surprisingly gentle.

I shrugged. "Someday, perhaps? If I get the chance one day, I'd like to live a quiet life with Shoshana, to study, and to find a career that doesn't involve fighting and killing. I hope that comes true one day."

Zvi nodded and gave me a small salute with his glass of wine. "Education and career are important for a young man," he said. "In my civilian life, I'm a furniture manufacturer—not a big one, but successful. After the British leave and we defeat the Arabs, I would like you to consider joining me. Perhaps we could even be partners."

His offer touched me. "I appreciate the faith you have in me," I said. "And when we have no more enemies to fight, I will gladly take you up on your offer."

We finished our wine and then shook hands. I had much to think about as Shimon drove me back to Café Pinsk.

THE MONTHS THAT FOLLOWED PROGRESSED just as Zvi had foreseen. With attacks on military vehicles, command posts, various British buildings, and the oil refineries in Haifa, the Irgun and Lehi continued to make the lives of the Mandate authorities miserable.

And then came November 19, 1947. Max closed the restaurant early, and Shoshana and I went with him to his apartment, where we listened anxiously to the live radio broadcast of the vote of the General Assembly of the United Nations on the Partition Plan for Palestine. It called for an end to the British Mandate and the establishment of two independent states— one Jewish and one Arab.

When the resolution was adopted by the required two-thirds majority—albeit just barely—the center of Jerusalem filled with people dancing in the streets. I had never before seen such massive crowds of happy people.

Max beamed at us. "Tomorrow night, my friends, I will close the restaurant to outside guests at ten o'clock—and all of our close friends will be invited to come and celebrate! But tonight—tonight let us all go to Ben Yehuda Street to dance!"

Shoshana and I walked with our friends, her hand tucked in mine, all the way to the intersection of Ben Yehuda Street and King George Street. At first, we all simply watched the celebration but then, two by two, joined the dancing.

"Are you happy, my love?" Shoshana whispered.

I smiled. "Whenever I'm with you," I said, "I am beyond content."

The next night we all gathered at Café Pinsk—Max and Nelka; Avrum and Hannah; Alec and Eva; Shimon; Zvi; Brigita; Misha and Magda; my landlords, Varda and Binyamin; and Shoshana and me. We pushed several tables together while Max set out bottles of wine, vodka, brandy, and champagne and many small plates filled with assorted delicacies.

When everyone was finally seated at the table with a full glass, Max asked all of us to raise our glasses for a toast. "I'm moved to tears," he said. "Let's drink to our new state and to all of our futures!"

After the toast, it was time to eat, but before we could, Shoshana clinked her glass against mine. "With your permission," she said, rising from her seat, "I'd like to say a few words."

Shoshana was normally quiet and reserved in a group, and it was not like her to make a speech. I gazed up at her, as did the others around me, curious to hear what she would say.

"My dear friends, this is a very happy day for all of us," she began. "It's a wonderful day for all Jewish people, but for those of us whose families were murdered in Europe during the war, this day heralds something extraordinary. After the Germans occupied Belarus and murdered my entire family, I gave up all hope." She fell silent a moment, her gaze on the glass in her hand. Then she looked up with a smile.

"But not only have I survived, I am also witnessing the realization of an age-old dream: the dream of renewed Jewish sovereignty in our homeland. And this dream has come true thanks to people like Max, Zvi, Alec, Shimon, Avrum, Misha, and"—her voice softened—"David." She gave me a warm smile and then turned back to our friends. "Our nation is rich in people who are willing to sacrifice themselves for the sake of our homeland." She glanced over at me again. "At first, it was terrifying for me to watch David risk his life. I knew that if he were killed, my life wouldn't be worth living. At the same time, I always deeply admired what he was doing."

Out of the corner of my eye, I could see Brigita watching Shoshana with a big smile. I smiled myself, guessing that we were both thinking how Shoshana was stronger than either of us had ever known.

"I'm not the only one here who has lost family," Shoshana continued, "but when I look around, I feel like I've gained a new family in all of you. David and I are not alone, and I know you feel the same way I do." She lifted her glass to everyone.

Max, Nelka, and I blew her kisses, and all the others applauded. I was proud of her. I had always known Shoshana was smart and sensitive, even though she wasn't much of a talker—though she had proved me wrong on that score tonight—and I was happy everyone else could now see how amazing she was too. She took her seat, and I leaned over to kiss her cheek.

"Who knew?" I whispered, and she blushed.

Max asked Zvi to say a few words as well, and he obliged.

"Today is truly a great day for all of us," he said. "We got here thanks to the Jewish nation's soldiers, fighters like Shimon, David, Alec, Misha, Avrum, and Shoshana. Today, we are celebrating our huge political achievement, but we'll soon be facing a war with the Arabs." He frowned. "They are determined to strangle our nation in the crib. It won't be an easy war, and we'll suffer losses, but I can assure you now that we will triumph!" We all cheered and lifted our glasses high!

The eating and drinking went on for another two hours. Later, when Shoshana and I were lying in bed, wrapped in each other's arms, I turned to her and said, "I can't stop thinking about the words from 'Song of the Partisans'—'As the hour that we longed for is so near, our step beats out the message: We are here!'"

"We are here," she echoed and then kissed my neck. My soul soared.

"You and I will never forget our parents and siblings who were murdered," I said, holding her close, "and we will always remember that we are the lucky ones. We are among the first Jews in two thousand years to be free in our ancient homeland. But as Zvi said, the battle hasn't ended with the British, and we are going to face a war with the Arabs."

"I have faith that you'll triumph, my hero, and I'll do my best to play my part," Shoshana said. "Just promise that you'll come back to me when the battle is over."

"I promise," I said, "if you'll do the same."

She smiled and kissed my cheek softly. "I will."

We made love, and afterward, Shoshana fell asleep the moment her head hit the pillow. I struggled to quiet my wandering mind and turned to gaze at the woman lying in my arms.

We have overcome thus far, I thought. *We have survived hell. We have come to the end of a perilous journey, down a long and treacherous road. Now we need to ready ourselves for a new chapter and a new challenge. After all we have been through, with Shoshana at my side, I have no doubt we will prevail.*

BIBLIOGRAPHY

1. Banai, Yaakov (underground name: Mazal). *Hayalim Almonim* [Unknown Soldiers]. Yair Publications, 1989.

2. Begin, Menachem. *HaMered* [The Revolt]. Ahiassaf Publications, 1978.

3. Ben-Tor, Nehamia. *Sefer Toldot Lehi* [The History of the Lehi], volumes 1–4. Yair Publications, 2010.

4. Bermatz, Zeev. *HaPartizanim Shel Belarus* [The Partisans of Belarus]. Private publication, 2012.

5. Evron, Joseph. *Gidi Ve-HaMa'aracha LePinui HaBritim MeEretz Yisrael* [Gidi and the Battle to Drive the British Out of the Land of Israel]. Israel Ministry of Defense, 2001.

6. Gilad, Zerubbabel and Mati Meged. *Sefer HaPalmach* [The Book of the Palmach]. United Kibbutz Movement and Organization of Palmach Members, 1957.

7. Golan, Zeev. *Mahtarot BeMa'asar* [Undergrounds in Detention]. Yair Publications, 2014.

8. Greenstein, Yaakov. *Ud MeKikar HaYovel* [A Cinder from HaYovel Square]. United Kibbutz Movement, 1968.

9. Hananel, Moshe. *Hayerushalmim* [The Jerusalemites]. Eretz HaZvi Publications, 2007.

10. Haruvi, Eldad. *Haboleshet HaHokeret* [The CID in the Land of Israel]. Porat Publications, 2011.

11. Herman, Judith L. *Trauma and Recovery*. New York: Basic Books, 1992.

12. Kister, Yosef. *HaEtzel* [The Irgun]. Israel Ministry of Defense, 2005.

13. Lapidot, Yehuda. *BeLahav HaMered: Ma'arachot HaEtzel BeYerushalayim* [In the Blade of the Revolt: The Irgun Campaigns in Jerusalem]. Israel Ministry of Defense, 1996.

14. Lapidot, Yehuda. *HaEtzel BeHaifa HaAduma* [The Irgun in Red Haifa]. HaMehaber Publications, 2006.

15. Livni, Eitan. *HaMa'amad: Mivtsa'im VeMahteret* [Status: Operations and Underground]. Idanim Yosef Publications, 1987.

16. Meltzky, Menachem. *Emet Ahat VeLo Shtayim* [One Truth and Not Two]. Yedioth Ahronoth Publications, 1995.

17. Mor, Yelin Natan. *Lohamei Herut Yisrael* [Israel Freedom Fighters—Lehi]. Shakmona Publications, 1974.

18. Morris, William. *The House of the Wolfings*. London: Reeves and Turner, 1889.

19. Naor, Mordechai. *Aliya Bet* [Second Immigration]. Yad Yitzhak Ben-Zvi, 1982.

20. Naor, Mordechai. *BaYam, BaYabasha, U-BaAvir* [On Land, On Sea and in the Skies]. Yehuda Dekel Library and Council for the Preservation of Heritage Sites in Israel, 2015.

21. Naor, Mordechai. *HaHaganah* [The Haganah]. Israel Ministry of Defense, 1992.

22. Naor, Mordechai. *HaHa'apala* [The Illegal Immigration]. Israel Ministry of Defense and IDF Museum, 2007.

23. Nedava, Yosef. *Mi Giresh Et HaBritim MeEretz Yisrael* [Who Drove the British Out of the Land of Israel]. Association for the Dissemination of National Consciousness, 1988.

24. Niv, David. *Alei Barikadot* [Manning the Barricades]. Israel Ministry of Defense, 1984.

25. Niv, David. *Ma'arachot HaIrgun HaTzva'i HaLeumi* [Campaigns of the Irgun], volumes 1–5. Klausner Institute and Hadar Publications, 1976.

26. Ramon, Amnon, Aviel Yelinik, and Assaf Vitman. *Yordim HaIra* [Going into Town]. Jerusalem Institute, 2011.

27. Segev, Tom. *Yemei HaKalaniot* [The Days of the Anemones]. Keter Publications, 1999.

28. Shalit, Shmuel. *Shimshon, HaLohem HaNoaz BeDoro* [Samson, the Bravest Warrior of His Generation]. Zion Publications, 2000.

29. Slotzky, Yehuda. *Kitzur Toldot HaHaganah* [A Brief History of the Haganah]. Israel Ministry of Defense, 1986.

30. Tal, Zvi. *Ne'arim BaMahteret* [Youths in the Underground]. Yair Publications, 1989.

31. Zipori, Mordechai. "Pritzat Keleh Akko" [The Acre Prison Break]. *Ma'arachot*, volume 55, booklet 201A. 1969.

External References

32. Ahavat Yerushalayim [Love of Jerusalem] website and Rafi Kfir tours

33. The Etzel [Irgun] website

34. The Haganah website

35. Wikipedia